To Cheryl,

Hope you have a wonderful birthday.

Best wishes,
Katherine
Blakeman

X

CONTENTS

PROLOGUE – VE DAY, 1945

They were both as different as different could be, Patrick mused. He'd never really thought about how their lives had come together in the first place. Of course, it was all down to the war, but really, what were the chances of him turning up in her town, a mental and physical mess, a product of his past?

After all, their upbringings were so different. Hers was one of love, a warm little terraced house in Manchester, with a mother who worked in a fishmonger's and a father who flitted from job to job when his unfortunate criminal past caught up with him. It had been a financially unstable childhood, and having to leave school at ten for being too daring hadn't helped. She'd spent all day at home, with the same furniture and the same wallpaper and the same little dog, and yet she'd loved it regardless, and carried this attitude forward. Accepting her lot, with a smile on her face and an undying love for whoever was kind to her. She'd had to do that all her life, and maybe that was why she'd always been loved in return.

His upbringing was less rosy. Surrounded by silver, maybe, but it hadn't all been as bright. His mother had tried, bless her soul, but she'd been filtered, censored, beaten down by his father. Patrick shuddered at the thought, especially now he knew the whole story. He'd been barely allowed to leave the house as a child, and despite having a kindly nanny and a top-level tutor, he'd been bored. Maybe that was why that first war had appealed to him – some excitement at last! Sometimes he wished he'd never gone, for it had dictated his entire life – although ultimately for the better, he reminded himself.

They'd been pushed together by nothing but a taxi, really. The driver had simply deposited him in Monthill, Manchester and driven off. Somehow, he'd made his way to the nearest building – a posh restaurant – and the manager there had sorted him with accommodation and a job. That was where he had met her, although what had really secured a connection was her kind heart.

Whether he'd have gone ahead with it, he wasn't sure. But she'd rescued him, dragged him away, and from there they'd just carried on bonding. Twenty-seven years later, here they were. Older, wiser, far more so than they'd ever expected. They'd never really had any plans beyond marriage, let alone being such a major part of other people's lives (and not just those of their children).

But it hadn't been all plain sailing. Their story wasn't like the ones he had read so often in books, which generally spanned a few days, weeks or months and had a clear beginning, middle and end. Real life wasn't like that. If it was, surely he'd be on the easy stretch by now?

They'd had their ups and downs, but things would be different now. He'd said that before, he was painfully aware of that, but tonight was a night to lay the ghosts to rest. It was VE Day, a turning point for all those affected by the war, and he especially wanted it to be one for himself and his wife, who was currently resting her head on his shoulder. He'd done all he could – for that moment, they were just enjoying being together. Once her eyes were dry, they'd go back into the party, apologise for their brief absence, join in with the dancing again.

But for now, it was just them. Just Patrick and Dorothy. The way it would always be. He exhaled slowly, a breath he'd been holding lest it disturb her, and opened his eyes.

Ahead of them, in the neatly mowed grass at the bottom of the steps, he was aware of a growing light. Ah, there they were. He'd always known that they'd be back.

CHAPTER 1 – 1900-1910

Whip!

Slash!

Crack!

"There you go, young man!" said Father-Sir, in such an abrasive voice that it quite pained the listener. "And make sure I never hear of you pulling your big sister's hair again!" He opened the door and let the five-year-old leave, nursing his bruised backside. No sooner had he vanished, six-year-old Gertrude ambled up, tears running down her little face.

"What now, Gertrude?" her father snapped. "I've dealt with Patrick – now what?"

"He hit me, Father-Sir!" she burst out, with a certain wariness. Ordinarily she would go to Mother, but the new baby was due any time soon and Father-Sir had explicitly told her not to interfere in case she upset anything.

"Which *he*?" Father-Sir replied, before answering his own question – "Well, Andrew, of course. He certainly has form for doing this. Never mind, Gertrude, go and find your eldest brother and send him straight to me."

"Very good, Father-Sir," Gertrude mumbled, before repeating it in a clearer voice as she knew that she would be pulled up on it.

A few minutes later, the seven-year-old, Bruce's eldest, appeared, with a tiny smile on his face. It had been good fun to tease his sister, despite what came after it. He was promptly laid on his front, and received a few good smacks with his father's belt. The pain did not bother him any more – he was used to it.

Meanwhile, Father-Sir was wondering what the world was coming to. When he was a boy, seven-year-olds would certainly have known better, he thought as he went upstairs to check on his wife. She was ready to deliver – but apparently, the baby wasn't. He couldn't wait to meet it and start training it.

Edna was quietly dozing, not causing any trouble at all. This pleased him enormously. He'd heard of women being unfaithful during their pregnancies, but Edna was on her fourth now, and so far, so good.

"No signs yet?" he asked, opening the window to let in some air.

"Well, there have been some twinges. I think something is beginning to happen. I wish it would hurry up, though – I can't wait to get back on my feet."

"All in good time, all in good time, Edna." Bruce replied cheerily.

"I do hope this baby is going to be worth it, Bruce..." Edna said, momentarily faltering. She'd tried so hard to be upbeat lately (as she knew her husband detested "moping around") but it hadn't paid off yet.

"As long as you give birth to a boy, it will be fine. The way Andrew and Patrick are going, I'll eat my hat if they turn out capable of carrying on the family name. I mean, Gertrude is fine, wonderful even, but it doesn't hide the fact that she is a girl."

"That's a bit harsh!" Edna said, shocked and caught off-guard. Bruce picked up on the tone immediately, and shot her a warning look before leaving. His authority normally went un-challenged, and this change raised his hackles significantly. To calm himself, he went to look out of the landing window.

From there, he could see little Gertrude skipping in the gar-den, unscathed after being targeted by her brothers. He smiled at her resilience – it would stand her in good stead, to become a decent little wife when the right man came along (vetted and approved by himself, of course). For now, he had to carry on training her to have the characteristics that all men desired: meekness, deference, acceptance of her place, to name a few.

Once he'd trained his wife, it would be a lot easier to im-plement the same traits onto his daughter (and, God forbid it, any future ones). Edna had been a lot more challenging lately. There was a thin line between being too melancholy and being too loud and disrespectful, and she was inching ever closer to-wards crossing it. He decided to up the restrictions that he had been placing on her recently.

At this point, the doorbell rang, and Bruce rushed to answer.

"I say, is Edna awake? She'll never guess what I've just seen! Old Colonel, staggering about, half-delusional!" chirped Mrs Downe, the gossip of the street. Father-Sir pursed his lips. Maude Downe was the very definition of what nobody wanted in a woman: forthright, confident and far too chatty. And, judging by this comment, some sort of spy.

"Shocking!" Bruce remarked, bristling. "She's upstairs, so go on up – just see that she doesn't go off in some aromatic faint!"

"Coo-ee! It's Maude!" Mrs Downe called, sailing up the stairs. She had barely been up there thirty seconds before she tottered back down again.

"What's the matter? Is Edna all right?"

"Ah, Bruce, she says it's happening now. Should I fetch the doctor?"

"No, I'll get the cook to go. Please would you sit in the parlour with the children for a little while? I don't want them unsupervised."

Maude agreed and Bruce ran up the stairs. Edna was sitting up in the bed, grimacing.

"Everything all right?" Bruce said, noticing her expression.

"Well, there's my waters gone!" she said triumphantly, before wincing as another contraction kicked in.

"The doctor is on his way," Bruce soothed her, "so just take your time, and do not rush. We want this baby in as healthy a state as possible. It's up to you now."

It was on the tip of Edna's tongue to ask, "What about my state?" but she knew that that ship had sailed. He didn't care about her at all any more, and she had come to terms with that years ago. But every once in a while, it still stung.

. . .

Pure joy in her gait, Dorothy toddled at (for her) a breakneck speed towards her mother. Wilhelmina often grew impatient with how slow her three-year-old daughter moved, but she adored her all the same.

"Come on, Dotty!" she called, aware of the time. "I'm runnin' late!"

"Wait, pleeeease!" Dorothy wailed. She was scared of being alone in the poky back yard, mainly because of next door's ferocious Alsatian that routinely terrorised their Yorkshire Terrier. She lived in fear that the dogs would decide to involve her in their bickering. Wilhelmina held open the back door as the little girl came in, closely followed by Monty the dog.

"Now, Daddy will be in his office while I'm at me meetin'. Yer not to disturb him, so just ye sit quietly an' sleep while I'm out.

Yes?"

Dorothy nodded, her eyes filling with awe as her mother arranged a cream shawl over her green dress and perched a white hat on her cropped brown hair in preparation to meet up with her fellow suffragists. Wilhelmina Fox was thought terribly modern by the rest of the street, but to Dorothy she was the best being in England. Charlie, Dorothy's father, was equally wonderful, but he spent most of his time working in his study, and therefore he was never really available to play games like Wilhelmina was.

As Wilhelmina departed, Dorothy promised to be "really, really good and not disturb Daddy". Satisfied, Wilhelmina kissed her goodbye and left. But Dorothy certainly wasn't going to sleep, oh no! No sooner had Wilhelmina shut the front door, she trailed down the corridor of their tiny house and beat with her fists at Daddy's study door.

"'Allo, my little Dotty," Charlie greeted her, opening the door. "I suppose you want to watch me work. Come on, then!"

He picked her up and gazed lovingly into her brown eyes. "Proper bit of frock, you are, ya know that?" he murmured. Dorothy patted at his stubbly beard and then squirmed, wanting to be let go to explore the study from her great height of three feet and an inch. There was nothing much to see, aside from a clotheshorse (there was no room for it under the stairs) where Dorothy's tartan dress was drying. Charlie placed her on the chair on the other side of his desk, and she got the great treat of watching his fingers dart about all over the place on the keys of his typewriter. The light tapping sound, and the rhythmic ting at the end of each line, served as white noise to lull her to sleep after all. She awoke with a start as the front door closed and Wilhelmina announced her return.

"Dot's in 'ere!" Charlie shouted. Seconds later, Wilhelmina was in the study and scooping Dorothy up.

"Yer a bad girl, ye know that? I told ye not to disturb

yer daddy!" Wilhelmina scolded her daughter. Dorothy looked downcast, so Charlie assured his wife that she was fine as she was. Tutting, Wilhelmina placed her back down on the seat and went to peel the potatoes. Nonetheless, her heart was full of love for their perfect little daughter, and she knew Charlie felt the same way. How anybody could beat their child, she didn't know.

CHAPTER 2 – 1910-1915

"Now, Patrick," Father-Sir said solemnly, sitting opposite his son at his desk. Patrick looked around nervously, although he thought he knew what was coming.

"As you may know, I have had this conversation with Andrew, and when Michael turns twelve years old he will have this talk too. I need you to listen hard, Patrick. Have you seen what a good young man Andrew has become in the last few years? I need you to understand this like a man and a Hammond."

Patrick felt rather concerned. Was there some big family secret that he had to know? The gothic fiction that he recently adopted had widened his imagination. His mind had skipped ahead to a big announcement, and Father-Sir transforming into Edward Hyde in front of his very eyes. He waited.

"One day, you will have a wife of your own. I know it seems hard to believe – don't grimace! – but every respectable man gets married to a subservient woman, and has children as a way of carrying on the family name. You are a little young for it yet, but it is essential that you know, understand and agree to this to be regarded as my son. Do you understand, Patrick?"

The son in question felt – and looked – rather disappointed. He'd been expecting a dramatic denouement, one that would turn his life one-hundred-and-eighty degrees, so to simply have this lecture on protecting the family name was rather an anti-climax!

"Now that you are twelve, you are well on the way to becoming a proper man. And this is why I'm telling you now: I need you to start helping the family, and acting like a good, responsible elder child. You will have noticed that the staff have taken up most of the formal duties recently, and your mother's job has solely been to nurture. You should expect your wife, when you find one, to nurture you and the children, as has always been the way.

"However, you must do your bit too, in protecting the Hammond name – not just in the future, but starting right now. Behave well, protect your family and your religion, and defend them too. *'So we, though many, are one body in Christ, and individually members one of another.'* – that's Romans 12:5. Live your life by the Bible, Patrick. It's the key to happiness and the key to Heaven.

"Now," Father-Sir said, leaning forward and intensifying his authoritative tone, "I need you to promise me that you will amend your ways. Recently, you have been behaving in a decidedly insubordinate way, which you have picked up from your younger brother. I do not like it. If you do not change your ways, and your general attitude… well, you can say goodbye to your inheritance!"

Patrick was stunned. His father was impassioned, to say the least! His nostrils were flaring, and he was gripping his cane very tightly with white knuckles, lest he need to demonstrate his point further. Since Mike had been born, soon after their move to Highmore Park, he had upped the restrictiveness of his family policies.

He knew that his mother in particular had been shocked by how things had changed. Female members of the family – and in this he included the staff – were not to step outside of the house unaccompanied. They all had to be careful what they said, because anything that could be viewed as "disrespect" was severely punished. The children had to eat every scrap on their plates, even if it was something that disagreed with them, which happened often to Bessie, the second youngest. All correspondence with the outside world was controlled by Father-Sir, and him alone.

Patrick didn't like it. None of the children did. They hadn't discussed it with each other, just in case one of them went and told tales to Father-Sir. But they had noticed, and they were beginning to feel stifled.

So apart from the odd letter from Mother to their ex-neighbour, Maude Downe, Father-Sir had cracked down on everything that he deemed unacceptable of his wife and children. He'd heard of the suffragists and was almost apoplectic at their behaviour – it was a frequent topic of his lectures. Women had no business in politics, he said, and they should leave it to the men who knew best. Patrick had never been allowed to consider having any other opinion, and therefore he agreed, just as he had to agree to everything that Father-Sir said.

"Do you promise, Patrick, to be a good, scholarly boy and a credit to the Hammond family?" Father-Sir said, staring right into his son's eyes. Patrick had never been the best at maintaining eye contact, and so it was almost painful trying to do this now, under such scrutiny. "Do you promise to give over your entire being, if necessary, to protecting our family and its esteemed name? Do you promise never to be led astray into the world of sin?"

Patrick dropped his gaze momentarily, then looked back up again. In his clearest voice – as much like his father's as was possible – he spoke.

"Yes, Father-Sir. I shall be an asset to the family, and to you." he agreed. Father-Sir nodded and smiled, satisfied.

"Very good. You are dismissed."

. . .

"How I wish I could join ye, Mam..." Dorothy said plaintively, her hands rummaging through the glory hole in search of her mother's shoes.

"Yer too young, and ye know that," Wilhelmina replied firmly, pulling on her gloves. "Ye can join us when yer thirteen, and not a moment before."

Dorothy knew that there was no point in arguing further, and so she sighed and went in search of her mother's best hat. She'd been longing to join the suffragists ever since the Mud March, three years previously. Wilhelmina had predictably said no. Dorothy understood – she had been seven back then, and far too young for anything like that! But she was ten now, much more grown-up, and she didn't know why her mother was being so obstinate about it!

She'd been trying to impress Wilhelmina with her dedication to the cause. So deep was her passion, her wardrobe barely stretched beyond purple, white and green (the colours of the movement). She'd even copied out a quotation from her heroine, Millicent Fawcett, and practised the letters in her diary until she got it looking just right. She then wrote it on a piece of pale purple card, using Charlie's fountain pen, and hung it up on her bedroom wall in a little frame. She had caused conflict at school by objecting to the inequality of education between the sexes, and had even dared to tell her headmaster that "*a large part of the present anxiety to improve the education of girls and women is also due to the conviction that the political disabilities of women will not be maintained.*"

She'd been expelled in the end, which had only incensed her further. She vowed that one day, after women had been given the vote, she would write a book about the inequality. She wrote rant after rant in her diary, in chaotic ten-year-old scrawls, about how she would show the world that they had been right all along, and that one day men and women would be equal in everything, including education. These were the saving of her those days, those diary entries – they stopped her exploding with rage. It was strange how a few pieces of paper and some ink could have the ability to change lives.

Wilhelmina was partially impressed, and partially worried about how seriously her daughter was taking it. Over the past three years, she'd become obsessed. Aside from her age, of course, there was one major reason why she was forbidding her daughter to attend the meetings: she did not understand the crucial difference between the peaceful suffragists and the more dynamic suffragettes.

"Now, be good, and don't disturb Da!" Wilhelmina said as she departed. It had become a tradition for her to say this every Saturday as she exited the house. Dorothy was long past the age where she was liable to run rampant around Charlie's study and distract him, of course, but Wilhelmina was worried that she'd end up bursting into his study at some point to share her latest suffragist musings. It had happened before!

When Wilhelmina came back, she was absolutely shaken. She had been approached by a very intimidating man on the streets. She was so upset at what he'd said, she'd had to sit down and drink a cup of soothing tea. His words echoed around her head, destroying all the lovely feelings of unity and strength that had been conjured up during the meeting.

"What's this?" he'd snarled in an unusually clipped accent, stepping into her path and blocking the way for her to escape. "Out on the streets unaccompanied? Good grief, when will you foolish women learn? You must stay in your house with your husband, at all times! And I suppose you are one of those harridans that call themselves suffragettes, aren't you? If you were a daughter of mine, you'd be whipped from here to next week – and I have never used the belt on a girl. And I bet your husband is dead set against your lot, as well. After all, what does the Bible say?"

At this point, Wilhelmina had tried to push her way past, hardly believing that she was hearing this diatribe, but the man had stepped forward and taken her wrist in a vice-grip to stop her walking away. He could hardly believe that he was seeing one of those 'harridans' in the flesh. He was clearly keen to impart this message to his wife and five children, as well as her, and he was giving it to her with both barrels.

"I'll tell you what the Bible says. *'Wives, submit to your own husbands, as to the Lord'*. Oh, I can tell you are not a Christian, lady. Christians follow the Bible. Christians do not subject the nation to your shocking displays of indignity. Christians know that men come above women – how hard is it for you to accept that? You'll be going to hell – you and your family!"

At this point, Wilhelmina had neatly elbowed him in the stomach, freeing herself in the process. She'd run away, tears forming in her eyes. At one point on that long walk back home, she'd even considered refraining from being a suffragist altogether! But as the tears turned to pure rage, she was shocked at herself for even considering it. No, she was a suffragist, and she was one to stay.

She waved away Dorothy's concern, and said only this: "What was said to me just now is a prime example of why I'm a suffragist. It's people like that who need to be shown! In three years' time, we'll show 'em together, Dotty. Are ye with me?"

"I'm with ye, Mam!" Dorothy said joyfully. She could not have been more devoted at that moment, although this was primarily youthful fervour, and immaturity too. She was prepared to march straight into Parliament and take down every member, one by one, and she fantasised about it in her head whilst she brought in the washing, and vowed never to give in.

Meanwhile, Wilhelmina was making vows of her own. She promised herself that a man like that would never get anywhere near her Dotty. She almost wished that she could pick her daughter's husband for her – but that was silly, she knew. Only controlling, domineering parents would do that. Nonetheless, the following morning, when she had recovered enough to talk to her daughter in more detail about it, she told Dotty about the ideal type of man. The one who would treat her like a human being, rather than an inferior one. The one who would listen to and respect her opinion at all times, instead of dismissing it. These were not unrealistic expectations, she said, as much as society tried to tell her so.

Dorothy felt inspired, and she felt more confident than ever that life would be good. She was mature enough to be aware that the best years of her life were stretching out ahead of her, ready to fill with whatever she chose. And succumbing to oppression was not on the list.

. . .

Patrick was in utter turmoil, as was Andrew. Ever since war had been declared the day before, they had been debating fiercely within their own heads, whether to stay or go. Father-Sir had automatically presumed that they would be Hammonds and stay with their family in this time of national instability, but the boys weren't so sure. A leaf through a newspaper had planted little seeds of patriotism in both of their minds. They had turned to each other – quite unusually, as they'd never been the closest of brothers. They sat on Andrew's bed, lost within their own thoughts.

"I don't know why we're deliberating!" Patrick cried out eventually, slapping his hands on his thighs and standing up. Andrew looked at him quizzically.

"Don't you? I can tell you a few good reasons!"

"Oh, come on, Andrew! Our country needs us! We must go! The King needs as many people as he can to fight for his country!"

"But Father-Sir will have us banished! And then who knows what he'll do to Mother and the girls?"

"Oh, Mike is there to protect them! What's the worst he can do to them?"

They had no idea what Father-Sir was doing to Mother these days. They both stopped, and Patrick shrugged at Andrew as if to say – "I'm going, are you going to join me?"

A little part of Andrew still objected, and so he said, "Shall we consult the Bible?"

"Oh, of course! Naturally!" Patrick exclaimed with sixteen-year-old enthusiasm.

Andrew grabbed the shiny black book and opened it at a random page. He skimmed down, until his eyes rested on some words that he had had no need to read until now.

"Here – *'Then Jesus said to him, "Put your sword back into its place. For all who take the sword shall perish by the sword."'* he read aloud. The pair of them sat in silence for a few seconds, and Andrew closed the Bible softly.

"Well, that seems pretty clear to me." Andrew said conclusively. Patrick nodded, mute. His hopes had been dashed. He'd had visions of himself moving forward onto a battlefield, surrounded by jovial copies of himself, and beating their evil opponents to a pulp.

"I just…" Patrick murmured, searching desperately in his mind for a loophole.

"I know. But the Bible comes first, just as it always should. There's nothing we can do about it, so we'll just have to lump it." Andrew snapped. Wounded, Patrick trotted back to his room. He picked up his own Bible and leafed through it, desperate to find any quotations that contradicted the aforementioned one. But no, none were as clear as that. Eventually, Patrick told himself that he would have to come to terms with it. There was no chance that he would ever be handling guns or digging trenches, or doing anything that those brave soldiers would do.

When they went into town later that day, though, everything changed. Father-Sir stalked his way through the crowds of patriotic young men, exuding disapproval, but Patrick became swept up in their enthusiasm. After an old man stopped him in the street and called "Good luck, young man! You'll show those ruddy Germans!" his mind was made up.

"I'm going to sign up, Andrew!" he whispered to his older brother. Andrew's eyes nearly popped out of his head and he set his mouth determinedly.

"Are you out of your mind?" he whispered back fiercely.

"Perhaps I am! I know that we'll be back by Christmas, so I might as well go and see what it's like in another country." Patrick said decisively. Andrew pursed his lips and looked away with a grunt, inwardly jealous at his brother's youthful decisiveness. There were barely two years between them both, but sometimes it felt like decades.

Now, Patrick thought, how do I tell Father-Sir?

Patrick knew that telling his father of this decision was not to be considered an easy feat. His father had been especially dour recently. Ever since the suffragettes had slashed his favourite piece of art, come to think of it. He remembered their trip to Manchester a few years ago, and Father-Sir's angry words to the foolish suffrage woman that they'd met there. He didn't fancy being on the receiving end of any of those words himself, and so he knew that he had to tread carefully.

Patrick decided that quiet but firm was the way to do it. If he was too confident, then he knew that Father-Sir would be angry at the lack of respect, and that would be the end of that. On the other hand, if he was too hesitant, then Father-Sir wouldn't realise how dedicated he was. He shut himself in his room and rehearsed his lines, then said them aloud two or three times until he achieved the desired tone. He went to Father-Sir's study and rapped on the door smartly.

"Enter!" called Father-Sir imperatively, if a little distractedly. His heart in his mouth – although he'd never have admitted it – Patrick entered. This was it. He was about to change his life.

"Father-Sir," he said, "I have an announcement."

"That sounds exciting." Father-Sir replied sarcastically, "Do enlighten me."

"I would like to be part of the team of boys that saves this country from the grip of evil. Please may I go to fight, Father-Sir?"

Patrick's heart rate accelerated as he said this sentence, and he waited for the response. He didn't have to wait long.

"You're too young, Patrick!" Father-Sir laughed. "The war will be over by the time you're eighteen!"

Patrick had not rehearsed for that bit, and he was momentarily knocked off his stride. Nonetheless, he continued with his patriotic clichés, before Father-Sir cut him off.

"Besides, war is a satanic montage of bloodshed, hatred and death. Why on Earth would you want to be a part of it?"

"It's the thing to do, surely, Father-Sir?"

"Not in an ideal world, no. *'You shall not murder.'* – that's Exodus. Is that not clear to you?"

"Everyone in town is going…"

"And? That just makes them all evil fools as well. Patrick, *'do not resist the one who is evil. But if anyone slaps you on the right cheek, turn to him the other also.'*"

"What does that mean, Father-Sir?"

Father-Sir smiled a little. If his son was still asking him for advice, then he couldn't be all bad. He still held some power, at least.

"It means you must accept that the evil Germans are going to plague our country – and most of God's world – with everything they can. They will do everything in their feeble power to annihilate us. We just have to accept it and go along with it, for that is God's will."

"Surely, Father-Sir, that will just let them walk all over us? Won't that just make *us* seem weak and feeble?"

Father-Sir's eyes darkened until the pupils almost disappeared into the mahogany-coloured iris. He almost spat out his next words.

"Are you arguing with the Bible? Are you disobeying God's words, with which He has commanded obedience?"

Patrick had had enough of this pious talk. He squared his shoulders and said, "Yes, Father."

The implications of this short sentence, as well as the lack of title that had always been a mandatory part of his name, as well as the sheer preposterousness of the boy, infected Father-Sir with a fury that cannot be described in fewer than one hundred pages. He looked behind him for his cane, but it had fallen over onto the floor. The nearest thing to hand was a ruler. With an inhuman roar, he stood up and raised the ruler high above Patrick's head, preparing to bring it down with a snap.

The next thing that happened was the ruler being snatched out of his hand, and instead held aloft by Patrick. The son was not quite as tall as his father, but he seemed to grow three inches in as many seconds.

"You touch me again, and I swear I will hurt you! I will hurt you like you've hurt me! You will stop!" Patrick shouted, sounding older and more commanding than anyone his age. Bruce tried to respond, but words failed him.

As fast as it had flooded in, Patrick's terror-fuelled anger died away. He looked truly shocked at what he'd just said. Bruce finally regained his voice, but used it to say only one word: "Out."

"I beg your pardon, Father-Sir?"

"Carry on begging. I told you to get out."

So Patrick got out. He got out of there, and in the process saved himself from the ever-increasing wrath of his father. He asked Edward the driver to harness a horse and take him down to town in the smaller carriage. Then he packed a few essentials and got in the carriage. When he got to town, he went and enlisted.

. . .

It had been nearly a year since Dorothy had joined the National Union of Women's Suffrage Societies, and the thrill that she felt as she entered the meeting place still hadn't left her. In fact, she wasn't sure that it ever would.

There had been a few mixed feelings about the slashing of the Rokeby Venus, which had happened a few months before. It had been the same with the death of Emily Davison the previous June. That week had been Dorothy's first week, and so she had been rather overwhelmed by how passionate the suffragists really were about the actions of their sister suffragettes.

This incident had provoked similar reactions, and a debate had been organised for that week's meeting. The first lady who spoke was named Charity Shaw, and she reminded Dorothy of Millicent Fawcett, in a way.

"I know that some of us are on decidedly frosty terms with the suffragettes, and that is understandable." she began, her voice loud and clear. "Some may argue that although it has now been eleven years since their split from us, the disappearance of many of our strongest members, who decided to take more violent action, has shaken our local community to the very foundations, and that we need to reunite. However, it is important for us all to realise that their actions could mean that the relationship that women have with Parliament could turn sourer. This is why it is imperative for us to distance ourselves from them as soon as possible so that our cause still has some hope.

"We suffragists are decidedly less... volatile than our sisters. We prefer to argue our case in calm, measured ways, which to the paranoid and uneducated people in Parliament may make us seem sly and rather underhand. These are all insults I have had thrown at me, amongst others that are too impolite to pass my lips. They fail to realise that we simply want to protect our reputation. We want to be remembered in history as influential people, for the right reasons.

"On the other hand, the suffragettes take a more violent approach to the campaign. This, I'm sure, is the subject of most speeches today. I cannot tell you the content of any of my fellow speaker's speeches, but I hope that to demonstrate the above denotations of a suffragist, we will listen to every viewpoint courteously and politely. I can assure you that I, and my sister and brother, will do so, so I ask you to listen to mine."

At this, Charity's brother stood up, said "Hear, hear!" to support his sister, and sat back down again.

"Their avoidance of peace will do to us nothing but aggravation and unnecessary bother. Despite our very different approaches to getting the vote, the final aim of the suffragists and suffragettes is one and the same. However, their foolish and dangerous actions are simply going to hinder any progress that we may make! We suffragists need to stick together to repair the damage they are doing.

"One of these days, we will get the vote. Times will move on, and we women will flourish! It is simply a matter of time. I don't know about you ladies (and gentlemen, begging your pardon), but I am getting on in years and before I die, I want to see our aim reached. My sons, although only young at ten and twelve, are prepared to carry on the cause if necessary, but the more separated we are with our – dare I say it? – daughters in the WSPU, the quicker we will show ourselves worthy. Thank you very much."

The room was filled with applause, and sounds of agreement.

Charity Shaw stepped down from the little podium and a tall, slim young woman took her place.

"I argue against your speech, Mrs. Shaw." was her opening declaration. A rumble greeted it – as a general rule, very few people argued against Mrs. Shaw. Charity stood up again and attempted to speak, contrary to what she had just said about listening to each other, but the new speaker quelled her with a raise of a hand. Miss Katharina Starkall was only nineteen and rather nervous, and it showed in her strong Swedish accent despite her authoritative posture. A couple of women sniggered at it and mimicked it under their breath, but she ignored them and waited for the buzz to die down before speaking again.

"Do not resist my point, Charity," Katharina said calmly, "because I have listened to your speech. Now, please be so courteous as to listen to mine."

"Ladies and gentlemen, I agree that something needs to be done about the suffragettes. Their performances of violence, impurity and indignity must be stopped before there are any more fatalities or injuries. But as for segregating ourselves... here I disagree.

"The suffragettes need to be persuaded to join our group once more. They need to see things from our point of view. We suffragists do not go hurling ourselves under horses to show our devotion to the cause – we are dignified! See the result of Emily Davison's attempt at martyrdom. It has not had the effect she craved: instead of being seen as devoted, she is being seen as deranged! That has reflected badly, not only on her sister suffragettes but on we suffragists as well. And to the uneducated eye of Parliament, we are one and the same. If the suffragettes are to be labelled as demented pictures of hysteria, then we will too.

"We simply cannot push them away and leave them to look after themselves, with no communication whatsoever. We are all women, at the end of the day, fighting for the same cause. If we do not trust them, how is the government supposed to? The only way to work on trusting them is to reunite, to scrap the WSPU before anyone else gets hurt. We must persuade them to merge back with the NUWSS, to make us a united front, and to achieve our goal so that we can get on with winning this war. We must contradict their slogan, ladies. We must persuade them – not with our deeds, as that will lower us to their level – but with our words (harsh if need be), as has always been the way. Thank you."

There was a smattering of timid applause, but most of the women looked stunned. Charity Shaw stood up and made for the podium, just as another woman did likewise. While they quietly argued as to who would speak first, the whole room dissolved into a heated debate. Dorothy and Wilhelmina were on Charity's side.

"It's outrageous how that Swede has the audacity to say that! She's nineteen, for goodness' sake! Especially to Charity – she is such a well-respected lady!"

"Well that's a blasted lie for a start – she's the most little-known woman in Monthill!"

"I think that's *you,* my dear."

"Excuse me? I think you'll find that she said that everyone is entitled to their own opinion!"

"How dare you twist her words? If I were a lesser woman, I would…"

"Order!"

Everyone's voices cut off as one. Dorothy was rather excited. There hadn't been such a heated debate since Emily Davison's death!

"We are all a little perturbed, aren't we? I think that everyone has spoken enough, and therefore we shall retire for today. Next week is a clean slate, where no insults will be heard."

Everyone agreed and since there were no further announcements, they all made for the tea and biscuits that were supplied by one of the elderly women every week. Dorothy and Wilhelmina adored anything sweet, so they took a cup of tea and a ginger biscuit each and stepped back to start new conversations.

For Dorothy, the ginger biscuit proved to be food for thought, and once Wilhelmina had finished her conversation, Dorothy took her aside.

"Ye know, I do see what Katharina meant, Mam," she said.

"Oh, yes?" Wilhelmina responded sceptically.

"I mean, she's far more practical, for a start! An' she makes a lot more sense, if ye look at her point properly. After all, yer no good to th' movement if ye end up in prison, or even in yer grave as a result of yer actions. Parliament ain't goin' to listen to us if we're not all in agreement with each other!"

Dorothy sounded quite passionate, and she certainly was, but she didn't realise how loud she was speaking until she looked up into the cold eyes of Charity Shaw and the rest of the women. Even Wilhelmina, who was normally quite willing to listen to all sides of the story, looked steely.

"Mrs Shaw," Wilhelmina said, bobbing a curtsey at the sophisticated, glamourous lady, "I do beg yer pardon for me daughter's opinion. Be assured that I'll show her right – you see if I don't!"

Charity's expression didn't change, and she didn't speak, instead thinking hard. Unfortunately, her far more brash brother decided to speak instead.

"I don't know why you expect us to listen to you... Dorothy, isn't it?" he said.

"Why, Sir?" Dorothy asked faintly, nodding at the question.

"Why? Why, she asks!" the man laughed. "I'll tell you why,

Dorothy. If someone can't speak with proper diction, constructing proper English-language sentences, then she quite clearly doesn't have the sufficient education to put together a logical argument!"

"I disagree entirely!" Katharina replied, pushing her way to the front of the crowd forming around the man (smirking) and Dorothy (speechless) to stand next to the latter.

"Prove your point, then." the man said defensively. "Come on, you've made your point, now back it up."

"Well, I could be rash and call you hypocrites, but I won't." Katharina began. There was a small cry of indignation, but most of the people simply wore shocked expressions at the insult, and did not vociferate.

"Back up your point, I said." the antagonist hissed, his face pinched.

"For all your talk of letting everyone have their own opinion, and respecting said opinions, your reaction to young Dorothy's has completely contradicted that! You, Sir, were mentioned in particular by your sister as respectful of the views of your peers, and you even agreed yourself. If that doesn't make you at least a little Pharisaical, then I don't know what does."

"For shame!" someone at the back shouted, despite not knowing what the word meant.

"Similarly, for all your talk of suffragists being united, you are certainly contradicting that, too. Why, your foolish sneering at Dorothy's accent – the local accent, I hope you notice – means that you are alienating a potential up-and-coming member!"

The man wore an angry expression and exhaled sharply with anger. Eventually, throwing up his hands, he said, "I don't know why we're worrying about a mere child!" and stalked out of the building, followed closely by his supporters.

In thirty seconds, the room was very quiet, consisting only

of Katharina's supporters – and Charity Shaw herself. Charity stared right at Dorothy and Wilhelmina for a few seconds, then suddenly smiled.

"That was good, Dorothy. I am impressed!" she said, shaking the girl's hand. Dorothy looked bemused, but shook the hand back. "I can see that you'll be a very good fighter for the cause when you're older. Thank you for bringing her, Mrs Fox."

"May I apologise once again for me daughter's audacity, Mrs Shaw?" Wilhelmina grovelled.

"Don't worry about it. I know that my brother is firmly in the camp that thinks that children should be seen and not heard, but I have two of my own, whereas he has none. I'll talk to him, and everyone will be all right by next week. Carry on having your own opinions, Dorothy. Don't necessarily share them as yet, but have them all the same. You are going to represent the suffragists of 1914 for the suffragists of the future, so we need you to form your own opinions early on and develop them as time goes on."

Dorothy beamed and thanked her.

"And as for you, Katharina…" Charity said, turning to the willowy nineteen-year-old, "well done for sticking up for yourself. I know my brother, and loathe as I am to admit it, his words about Dorothy's accent were very likely aimed at you as well. Again, I will speak to him, and you will have an apology next week."

"Oh, that's quite all right!" Katharina said good-naturedly. "I'm just glad that our generation-" referring to herself and to Dorothy, "-is stepping up. Women are fighting for their rights, and the men are fighting for everyone's rights. If men and women are never to be equal, I suppose that must be the way for now."

Dorothy smiled at her, and Katharina told her that she would talk to her next week. Everyone shook hands, friends again.

And at that moment, Dorothy was one hundred per cent sure that she would be a suffragist forever.

. . .

"Blow out your kite,

From morn 'til night,

On boiled beef and carrots!"

The boys' vocal ability was inversely proportional to their enthusiasm but all the same, the atmosphere was decidedly jolly. And to make a change, this time the lads were not fuelled by alcohol! Patrick beamed and sat back in his seat, looking around cheerfully at his new friends. In the time that he'd known them, he'd decided that they'd all be friends for life.

After signing up, he'd hit a bit of a wall and ended up sleeping at the house of an elderly lady who'd taken pity on him. Eventually, he'd met up with his fellow soldiers from Highmore and the rest was history. Initially, he'd been endlessly teased about his posh accent and his shyness, but their laughter was infectious (and they told the funniest tales). He was one of them now.

The night before their departure, they'd all gone out to a public house and had one or two drinks. It had been Patrick's first ever drink of alcohol, and while he didn't particularly enjoy the taste, he did enjoy the mellow feeling and the buzz in his head after two beers. The oldest boy in their little sub-group (Patrick was youngest, although he pretended he was eighteen), told the other boys that they were amateurs at the old drinking, and wait until they got to his elevated age of twenty-five!

In the clear light of day when he was sober, Patrick often marvelled at the liberty to which the other boys were accustomed. They often did the obscenest things, and said the rudest jokes, with nobody batting an eyelid. At first, Patrick had restricted himself to a vague chuckle, but after he had been given a little education on the ways of the world, he understood most of the jokes.

They'd had very little solid training – just about three months of it. The boys had found it very exciting. Of course, they had no real idea of what awaited them on the battlefields, but they reasoned that it couldn't be too bad. How powerful could a bunch of Germans be? Patrick had told them that God would be protecting them, and all the boys agreed. Whether it was out of desperation or true faith, only the individual himself knew.

In the cramped train carriage, Patrick hadn't had much opportunity to look around for fear of inadvertently staring at someone. He noticed one of the men chatting easily to the only girl in their carriage – obviously one of the nurses who couldn't fit in any of the other carriages. The nurse looked uncomfortable, but the man was entirely at ease.

Maxwell, Patrick's best friend, noticed him staring.

"Old Bill's got himself right in there," he whispered confidentially.

"What do you mean?"

"Them ladies are going to be few and far between..." Maxwell said wistfully, probably thinking of his own back home, "so you get one if you can, Pat. Once you get yourself a sweetheart... you have something to live for. You become fixated on them. Their face is constantly in your mind, and their voice in your ears, especially if they sing. Remember that, Pat. If she sings, you've got a good one."

This gave Patrick food for thought. He'd never really thought of his mother in that way, as a girl. She had always been a woman, one of those inferior beings that Father-Sir had had full control over. He'd never heard her sing. In fact, he'd never really thought of his mother as a human being, and it was likewise with his sisters.

Now he'd come to think about it, his father was not like any of the fathers that his new friends described. The other boys' fathers were, by the sounds of them, very relaxed and jolly. As for their mothers, they sounded sweet enough, but it was the fathers that the boys idolised. It was their fathers that had taught them how to be men. Patrick found that he was able to join in with this conversation in a way that he had never before. He pretended that the conflict between him and his own father did not exist, had never existed, and began to speak loudly and proudly.

"Oh, my father's wonderful!" he began fervently, clasping his hands in his lap. "Father-Sir says that… what?"

That last word was in response to snuffles of laughter from all of the other boys. Patrick looked around, bemused, until one of them finally revealed the reason for their mirth.

"Father-Sir?" he repeated amidst the hysteria, "Who on Earth calls their pa Father-*Sir*?"

"…Is that not normal? Father-Sir has told me that it's a customary expression of respect from the child to the parent."

"Well, he's wrong there, I can tell you that now!"

Patrick subsided, looking embarrassed. The laughs had stopped now as everyone noticed his expression. The subject was abruptly changed.

As the train rattled on through – well, they didn't exactly know where – the carriage quietened down as the adrenaline and conversation topics ran out. At last, the train chugged into the station and ground to a halt with a painful creaking sound. Maxwell stretched out his legs as much as he could and said, "We've arrived."

. . .

Dorothy had been decidedly bored since the local meetings had stopped. Now that Wilhelmina went out to work in the local fishmonger's every day (bar Sundays, of course) from nine until four, she was relegated, once more, to wandering aimlessly around the house. Only this time, she had nothing to think about, since it had been agreed by all that until the ghastly war was over, the suffrage movement would come to a temporary halt. As Christmas 1914 inched ever closer, the prospect of the war being over by Christmas was slowly becoming more and more unrealistic.

Since turning fourteen in October, Dorothy had been asked to do a little bit more around the house. With Wilhelmina's new job and Charlie's tiring pre-existing one, the housework was slowly getting abandoned. Dorothy jumped at the chance to be useful and so the house was looking cleaner than it had done in years.

Dorothy checked the old clock in the hall. Twenty to four. Wilhelmina would be home in the next hour. She went into the kitchen and rummaged in the pantry, emerging with a jar and half a loaf of bread. It was to be potted cheese with bread that evening – cheap, filling and easy to prepare. After setting the table, she went and sat down to write her diary entry for that day. It was the one way in which she kept her brain in shape these days. Monty, the geriatric Yorkshire terrier, settled down on the rug by the unlit fire, in vain hope that if he sat there for long enough, it would magically ignite and warm him up.

Just as she closed the cover, there came the sound of Wilhelmina's key in the door. Sometimes the fishmonger gave her some fish to take home, but not today.

"Evenin', Mam!" Dorothy called, going into the hall. She made to hug her mother but recoiled at the smell of fish. She made the same mistake every day and each time it made them both laugh.

"Evenin', Dotty! Is th' dinner ready?"

"Yes, Mam. It's all ready an' on th' table."

"Good lass. I'll just wash an' change an' we'll eat. Charles, I'm home!"

When Wilhelmina came back down, she followed her daily

routine of regaling them with stories of the awkward custom-ers in the shop. It was the same sort of story every day, but Dorothy never tired of hearing them, for she knew that she would be going out to work soon enough. Charlie, however, did tire of hearing them, and in the end he said, "Well, that's what ya get when ya work in the town with them posh people: a bunch of whining snobs."

"Oh, listen t' yerself!" Wilhelmina chuckled, "If it weren't for me reputation then I'd slap ye!"

"What reputation?" Charlie responded with a laugh.

"Well, to fit in with me employer, ye have t' know yer apples from yer pears. An' as a shop woman, I have to be all meek, bobbin' curtsies to all the fancy people. I hope ye'll end up bet-ter than that, Dotty. Don't ye be like that to anyone, especially men. A wife must be heard by her husband, ye hear? They'll try to take away yer rights, but just ye stand up for yerself, ye hear?"

Dorothy nodded, although her mother's words hadn't exactly given her a vote of confidence for the future. She didn't want a husband, anyway. She just couldn't imagine loving someone so deeply that she would do anything for them – and she certainly couldn't imagine anyone loving her in that way! She said as much to her mother, who laughed.

"Ah, just ye wait, lass. In a few years, ye'll be well on yer way to getting' married. Yer very easy to love – the lads will be fallin' at yer feet."

Dorothy scoffed in response and excused herself. She went up to her room to think about what her mother had just said. Her nose wrinkled in distaste at the thought of marrying one of the pompous gentlemen that her mother so often talked about in the shop. In fact, she felt a little ashamed at her feeling of re-vulsion. She wondered if her feelings were normal. Surely girls of fourteen should be well on their way to marriage by now, she thought. She decided that next time she was in town, she

would start making sheep's eyes at some of the lads coming to and from the boy's school.

And it was in that way that Dorothy made her first teetering step into the world of the grown-ups, and realised that life was not quite as simple as she'd first thought.

CHAPTER 3 – 1916-1918

My dearest Mother, Father-Sir, and siblings,

I am writing to you on this unseasonably chilly June night, from wherever we are now, as a peace gesture. I know full well that it may be the last chance I get.

You'll be pleased to know, Father-Sir, that your teachings about God were not all futile. The first thing I do in the morning is always the same: I pray sincerely for victory and safety. I repeat this prayer several times a day. We all do. I have converted my fellow fighters – we are putting our lives into the hands of God, and we are at His mercy.

Despite this, I believe that I am unrecognisable from the child that so foolishly defied you, Father-Sir, and the teachings of God. I have filled out at last, for one thing. My muscles have developed with all the physical work I do, and I am growing a small moustache on my upper lip to make me look a little older. After all, I am not even eighteen, not for another four months. The fact that I have filled out is nothing to do with the food here – oh, it is awful.

I do miss home cooking. The tea is the only decent thing around here: a reminder of home. Although, to be fair, the thought of home does not bring the best connotations to me. I know that if I were to come back, the doors would be closed on me, and I do not blame you for this. I would probably do exactly the same thing in your shoes – everything the Bible says about war is true.

The trench is my current home – and it's not in the best condition, if I'm honest. It's about seven feet deep, I suppose (deep enough to hide the tallest of our men, at least) but we're often up to our knees in freezing cold, murky water. We don't get much respite from the water. We sleep in poky little caves that are hollowed out – not that we get much sleep. As I write, it is almost midnight. I can't go on any longer without writing this. It's doubtful that you'll even get this, that it will survive the censoring. On the off chance that it does, I hope you'll know that I am regretting coming to war, and that I still care for you all.

They don't care about us, though. We're no more than accessories, that simply function to intimidate the enemy (some hopes!) and fire the guns. I've seen some of my fellow soldiers, once proud and strong men, simply howling with pain and the sheer hideousness of it all. I've tried to be strong, but it gets very lonely down here, especially when you see your friends dropping like flies.

But I have shed no Christian blood.

I say this with confidence, because I have come to a theory, to help me cope out here. None of us soldiers are true Christians, because we have all come out to fight in this war, which the Bible forbids. We have all murdered, therefore we cannot call ourselves Christians, and therefore, none of us are shedding Christian blood. It's the feeblest theory you will ever hear of – but it's surprising what we cling to in times of despair.

Whatever possessed me to enlist? What on Earth was I thinking? I'd rather have a hundred white feathers decorating my room than be right here, right now, writing this. I know that I wouldn't like the feathers, but if the other option is this torture, this internal decay, then I know what any sane human would choose. I like to think that, even after everything, I still have my sanity.

But I ramble. On Saturday, that's tomorrow, we're going over the top. I'm dreading it. We all are. But it's our duty; we're fighting for our country, and for our lives, but mostly for you at home. Pray for us, please. On second thoughts – when you get this, it will be too late. Goodness only knows when you'll get my letter, if at all.

I might as well tell this to you straight, my family: there's a very high chance that I will be dead before you even get this. At least, if I die, then I'll have died for a good cause: protecting God's world from the evil Germans. I know that I was rash and disrespectful when I left. But let us put it behind us now, Father-Sir. I'm probably going to die.

Please, forgive me.

I send my love and blessings to everyone at home – anyone I've met in my nearly eighteen years of life. May God bless you all. Goodbye, and thank you.

Your ever-loving son or brother,

Patrick Hammond.

. . .

Dorothy scuttled home from work, desperately trying to avoid detection by the callous lads on Green Lane, who taunted her relentlessly every single day. It didn't work. The wolf-whistles and catcalls became a cacophony of raucous noise, away from which she found herself sprinting. She caught the eye of a newspaper-seller, who promptly thrust the latest news almost up her right nostril. She furiously batted the paper away. She didn't want to hear about whatever it was the Good, Brave Men had been getting up to. As far as the war was concerned, avoidance was her coping mechanism.

But she couldn't avoid it for long. Wilhelmina was, surprisingly, ebullient.

"We're showin' them Germans!" she crowed as Dorothy walked into the living room. "We're showin' 'em once an' for all! The Battle of the Somme – the battle to end all battles! Them Germans are dyin' by th' lorryload!"

Dorothy nodded her approval and smiled.

"Anyway, how was work? Anythin' interestin' happen?"

"Nope, just the usual: people buyin' stationary, people buyin' books, people buyin' sweets. An' th' standard rude people who grab their purchase, thrust a few coins at me an' waltz straight back out again. Oh, an' then them vile lads constantly harassin' me.

"Aye, they're nasty bits o' work, some of 'em. Ye just block 'em out, ignore 'em, an' they'll soon give up th' ghost.

"What's this? What's happened?" Charlie asked, coming into the kitchen and registering Dorothy's upset expression.

"Oh, just some lads makin' comments at our Dot, is all." Wilhelmina explained, a touch of pride in her voice.

"What?"

"Of course, she gets them looks from me…"

"Mina, she's sixteen! I'll give them little ragamuffins an 'iding, see if I don't! What street, Dot?"

"Green Lane, mainly."

"Now, don't ye go doin' anythin' silly, Charles!" Wilhelmina called as, incensed, her husband picked up his coat and hat and flew out the front door, picking up his shoes on the way. Wilhelmina shook her head.

"What's Da goin' t' do?" Dorothy asked fearfully.

"Who knows, Dot? He gets downright angry on occasion, so I just hope that nothin' bad happens to ruin him. Let's hope that he controls himself, th' silly man."

But he didn't control himself. Nobody messed around with Charlie's little Dotty! He came back about an hour later, nursing his knuckles but looking very pleased with himself.

"Oh my word, Charlie! What've ye done?" Wilhelmina cried.

"I gave those kids a right good seeing-to, that's what I did!"

Charlie replied proudly.

"What on Earth did ye do to 'em?" Wilhelmina shot back, examining his knuckles.

"Well, I found the ringleader of the little gang and it's safe to say that it won't be bothering our Dotty again, and neither will its cronies."

"What did ye do to 'em? Charlie, ye've got blood on yer hands – literally! Don't lie to me, just tell me what ye did." Wilhelmina said forcefully, sitting her husband down on the sofa. Dorothy could not take her eyes off the blood on her father's hands. Was it his own, or…?

"Da, tell us!" she gasped eventually.

"A punch 'ere and a kick there, that's all."

Wilhelmina looked at him, hard.

"Anythin' else? Where's th' blood from?"

Charlie dropped his gaze.

"I may have punched a wall at one point, rather than the kid's nose."

Dorothy nearly laughed, but her father's hands looked so painful that she shook her head and went to get some water for her mother to clean up the wounds. Satisfied, Wilhelmina reached in the cabinet for a dusty bottle of solution to put with the water.

Despite the pain in her father's hands, Dorothy couldn't help but feel that his actions were justified. She found it horribly de-humanising. Wilhelmina had been telling her that she should be proud, that she was well on the way to getting a man of her own, that she was lucky to have looks that men adored, and other women coveted. But Dorothy detested people looking at her and only seeing the skin and the figure and the frock. It was horrible for them to look at her and only think of what they'd like to do with her.

It was later that evening, after a rushed dinner, that the truth came out.

A furious hammering on the front door made them all jump. Wilhelmina rushed to answer it, hoping desperately that this would not be more trouble.

"Now look here, I want a word with... Wilhelmina Fox?"

"Mrs Shaw? What brings you here?" Wilhelmina said, putting on her poshest voice in an effort to calm the angry-looking lady.

"I want a word with your husband, Mrs Fox! He can't keep his dirty little hands to himself! My son is black and blue, and he followed the perpetrator home – to this address! Bring him forth at once."

"I didn't think your son was old enough to be cat-calling girls. He's only about ten, isn't he?"

"I have two sons, Wilhelmina." Charity said pointedly. From the shadows behind her appeared a boy, who had a very close resemblance to her, aside from the nasty and fresh-looking black eye. His sleeves were rolled up to appear several more bruises.

"Charlie!" Wilhelmina almost screamed.

Charlie appeared, scowling.

"Is this him?" the visitor consulted the smug-looking boy, who nodded. Charity nodded back and turned to Charlie.

"If you want an apology, you ain't getting one." Charlie said before she could even get a word in.

"I think the opposite, Sir. I demand an apology."

"I am not at all sorry, you rude woman. That kid deserved it. He was making obscene comments towards my daughter!"

"That doesn't excuse what you did. Apologise – or else I'll be calling the police, and that will be an end to you!"

Charlie had no choice but to apologise. Dorothy barely heard the mumble from the living room, where she had been cleaning out the fire.

"Louder!" Charity Shaw commanded.

"No, you heard me. Now leave, rude woman!"

Dorothy stepped into the hallway, just in time to see Charity Shaw (who was around the same height as Charlie, but of slimmer build) step forward and deliver a sharp slap onto his right cheek. Charlie took a step back, stunned. Charity nodded and turned to Wilhelmina, a picture of fury.

"I will be having words with your employers." she said severely.

"Very well." Wilhelmina replied.

"And when this awful war is over and we suffragists get back together, I will be telling everyone about what your husband is. Common as dirt, you are, you and your little... what, Russian? ... friend. Good evening."

Dorothy stepped forward to watch Charity totter back towards the road again. Her son lingered a moment, eying Dorothy's coal-stained hands with triumph.

"Hey, sweetheart," he drawled, and Wilhelmina turned back, "it's good to see that you're putting those pretty hands to good use. I'll find them a use in my house when I get my hands on you – what else can you do with them?"

"Strangle you?" Dorothy said sweetly, and shut the door in his face.

Wilhelmina smiled for the briefest second, then turned on her husband.

"Upstairs, Dorothy." she said firmly. As Dorothy scuttled upstairs, she began furiously whispering, "Ye said that ye hit him once or twice, not turned him into a bluebottle! How could ye, Charles? I'll lose me job now, an'..."

. . .

Once she got to the end of the letter, Edna leant against the cupboard with her eyes closed. The room spun around her as mixed feelings fought for space in her head. Eyes still closed, she felt for the bed and sank down onto it. She felt numb.

Her second son was potentially dead. She might not see him again.

Like any mother, Edna was devastated.

Before reading the contents of the letter, she'd skipped to the bottom to find out the sender. Her heart had almost leapt out of her body with shock and pure joy. Her son was alive! The letter was proof – he was alive! Even better, he still had a sane thought in his head – contrary to the dark images of insanity that her husband had fed her. But after reading the second sentence – *I know full well that it may be the last chance I get* – and the paragraphs that followed, the fizzing in her heart turned to stillness. At one point, she put her hand on it to check that it was still beating.

How could she cope when a piece of her had been torn away? She'd come to terms with Patrick being at war, but to hear his first-hand thoughts, and how he'd come to terms with death, was like a bullet through her. The imagery and pain made her cry out loud.

After sitting on the bed for a minute, she dashed to the bathroom and was violently sick. Bruce heard her moan and came running.

"Edna? What's happened?" he said guardedly.

"Patrick... Patrick's dead." she gasped, the lack of oxygen from her hyperventilation turning her almost purple.

"Patrick?" Bruce replied in a steely voice. Edna handed him the letter. He read it through twice, but he felt nothing. It was like reading about a character in a book: it didn't seem real. He was brought back to Earth by Edna clutching his arm and swaying, nearly falling.

"We don't know for certain that he's dead, Edna." Bruce reminded her, although his every instinct was telling him to walk away before he said something rash.

"He is dead! I can feel it – I'm his mother, Bruce!"

"You've had a shock. Come to bed; you need a rest. Have a sleep and absorb the shock."

"Sleep?" Edna repeated hysterically, "How can I sleep when my son is in No Man's Land, dead or dying?"

"God would not allow that. Have you been praying for Patrick every night?"

"Of course I have, you know that!"

"Then God has kept him safe. Now, to bed, and enough of this hysteria."

Edna spent the rest of the day in bed, trying to process what Patrick had said. Bruce told her to sleep, but she couldn't. Every time she shut her eyes, Patrick was there, lying in a cold grave, completely unaware of how much his mother still loved him.

When Bruce came up to bed, she asked him whether he forgave Patrick.

"What?" he said distractedly.

"In his letter... he asked us to forgive him. Do you forgive him?"

Bruce paused, mulling over the thought as far as his mind would allow.

"Go to sleep, Edna," he said eventually. "You'll feel better in the morning."

Well, it was better than a no. Edna drifted off soon enough. But later that night, or early the next morning, something strange happened to her. She swore to God that it had happened. Bruce dismissed it as the hallucinations of an over-emotional mother, but Edna knew in her heart that it was real.

She heard a rapping on the window, a constant and persistent sound that cut straight through her slumber. Bleary and drained of energy, she went to the window and looked out. It was already open, so there was no reason for anyone to be knocking, and there was nobody there anyway. Just as she was about to go back to bed, she heard something.

"Mother? Let me in, please." a whisper came. It was barely audible, and she could not distinguish the manly voice. She pressed her ear to the window and listened hard, and the voice came again – "Please, Mother. I know Father-Sir hasn't forgiven me, but I need my family now."

Edna knew at once who it was. It wasn't any of her other children playing a foolish joke. They didn't know about Patrick yet, and besides, they wouldn't be so cruel. She cast a terrified glance at Bruce, debating whether to wake him up. Either way, she'd be in big trouble.

"Don't tell Father-Sir. He doesn't need to know just yet. I'm here, Mother. I'm right outside. I'm at the back door…"

"I can't let you in," Edna found herself murmuring. She felt disappointment seeping out of her son's invisible body and flowing through the opening in the window. She fought the urge to close it – she wanted to keep hearing her son's voice.

"Why not? Please, Mother…"

"I have to stay loyal to my husband. A wife must always obey her husband. He would not let me live, not if I allowed you back."

Even as she spoke, Edna loathed herself. She didn't know why she was being so direct about it. With every fibre of her body, she wanted to let him in. Her mind flew down to the back door and thrust it open, but her body stayed stubbornly at the window, her breath misting up the glass, frozen in fear of her formidable husband. He stirred suddenly, and Edna gasped – not loudly, but a quick intake of breath.

"I'll hide, Mother. I'll hide downstairs." Patrick's voice had a note of panic to it now.

"My love, I must go. But I love you with all of my heart, remember that?" Edna whispered, and she made to move back towards her bed.

"You wouldn't be doing this if you know what we're all going through out here. Let me in, Mother. I'm still waiting."

That last sentence sounded like he was slipping away. Edna ran to the back door and opened it wide, but there was nothing but a breeze.

. . .

Patrick surveyed the poor trench, and for the millionth time, wondered what on Earth he was doing there. It was dark, and he couldn't see much – but was that a good thing or a bad thing? Fear of the unknown, and happiness at being relieved of the sight, battled in his mind. It was ironic that light, which normally brought connotations of relief and joy, could in this alternative universe be the harbinger of the opposites. But then, when it came to war, nothing made sense.

He allowed his mind to drift back home. Would they have received his letter yet? And if so – how much of it? He knew that the officers read every letter and blacked out any bits they deemed able to help the enemy with black marker pen. What fell into this category, he had no idea.

He'd addressed the envelope to Mother for several reasons. For one, she never received post, and therefore she'd be more likely to open it straight away. Father-Sir often forgot about his and ended up opening it a few days later (much to the frustration of the sender). And for another reason, Father-Sir would take one look at the name of the sender and throw it straight in the fire. Mother was much more likely to actually read it, to hear what he had to say. It was strange how a few pieces of paper and some ink could have the ability to change lives.

He wondered if Mother would be upset. After all, he'd never actually said goodbye to her – he'd been in too much of a hurry to leave. His last memory of her was at the breakfast table, eating a poached egg, listening to Father-Sir rant about whatever the world was coming to, when war and hatred prevailed and killed the children of God.

The memories of home brought a sudden pain to his stomach and he groaned quietly, waiting for it to go away. He would have given anything to be there, in the uncomfortably hot lounge with the fire burning, reading in silence, safe in the knowledge that death was far, far away.

But no. Here, he could almost taste death.

He shut his eyes and, in his mind, flew across the ocean to his house. He forgot everything else as he channelled it, letting himself hear the chiming of the huge grandfather clock, the high voices of his two sisters, the noises of the horses down in the stables. He smelt Mother's perfume, the musty smell of the back stairs, the fragrance of freshly baked pie down in the kitchens. He travelled up to his room, and pressed the door open. His bed was made, with a note on it – 'I miss you'. It was from Mother.

He tried to go to her room, then stopped short, remembering that Father-Sir would be in there. He was temporarily stuck, until he remembered that the window to their bedroom would be open. He could talk to her through that.

So he did. He begged her to let him in, but she wouldn't. Patrick pleaded with her, but for all her talk of loving him, she could not or would not let him in. She said it was because of Father-Sir – but what was the worst he could do to her? Patrick woke up with a start and set his mouth.

"What's up with you?" Maxwell said, awakening at the same time and instantly picking up on Patrick's mood.

"I've just realised something." Patrick said.

"What? What have you realised?"

"That family is just a word. Nothing more. If it was, then Mother would have let me back in."

Maxwell didn't have a clue what Patrick was on about, but he was an intuitive man, and so he shuffled closer to him and patted him on the shoulder.

"What, was it a dream?" Maxwell said. Patrick nodded.

"But it reflected reality. If I make it home, I won't be let in. Family doesn't exist any more for me – what is there to fight for? I might as well just go out there and see where the war takes me."

"Now, listen to me. You are not going to die in this war, Patrick. You are going to survive, and you are going to go back to England, and one day, you are going to create yourself a new family. A family that will be what you make it. You just need to wait out this bloody war, all right?"

Patrick nodded, secretly wishing that Maxwell would just leave him to his thoughts. After a moment, Maxwell retreated, and Patrick became lost in his mind again. Despite what Maxwell had said, his resolution to just carry on, and let fate take over, reigned.

So he did. And the following evening, it became his downfall.

· · ·

"Excuse me, Sir?" Dorothy interrupted the shopkeeper's activity of reading the newspaper. He folded it and looked up stonily.

"Yes?"

"I wondered if ye had any positions suitable for myself in yer shop?"

"For you? You're the Fox daughter, aren't you? In that case, certainly not! I've heard what your father has been up to, smashing children to smithereens!"

Dorothy curtsied and left him alone. She wasn't upset. For one, she'd heard what a dreadful attitude that man had. For another, every other attempt at getting work in the two weeks since Wilhelmina had lost her job had gone the same way: tainted by association. She felt a surge of resentment towards her father (who had been given a stern warning by his employer, and his wages docked), and then a surge of shame. Her father had done it for her, she told herself. He meant well – it was his desperate attempt to protect her.

But it had backfired spectacularly. Now, people whispered in the streets when they walked past. Charity Shaw was an immensely popular lady. A couple of people had even crossed the street to avoid them. This made Wilhelmina very upset, and she took out her frustration on her husband. After all, she said, he was the reason that all of this happened!

"Ye had to, didn't ye?" she shouted on one occasion. "Ye couldn't keep yer hands to yerself! Look what it's reduced us to! I've lost me job, you've had your wages docked, we can barely manage!"

Each time, Charlie would take it for so long, then erupt. He'd shout back, saying that if lads these days would start behaving decently, then he would never have taken things into his own hands. Wilhelmina would shout back at how boys would be boys, nobody could expect them to change, it was up to women to avoid their attentions if they didn't like them.

Dorothy had to side with Charlie – although she never participated in their shouting matches. She couldn't believe that Wilhelmina, a suffragist, was deferring to men! She was rather concerned about her mother at that point, but she couldn't talk to her about it, because even mentioning their current situation made her angry.

One evening, Wilhelmina sent Dorothy and Charlie out to

pick up some groceries. They were cheaper at the end of the day, and Dorothy's special mission was to charm the greengrocer into reducing the cost a little more. But they never made it to the shop.

Dorothy got wolf-whistled halfway down Green Lane. Charlie jumped out of the shadows next to Dorothy and attacked the perpetrator. "I'll teach ya to tease my Dotty, little tyke!"

Dorothy ran home to get her mother, while Charlie scrapped with the burly boy. When they got back to Green Lane, Wilhelmina in her bathrobe and slippers, Charlie was being dragged away by policemen and arrested. Wilhelmina didn't even look at him.

. . .

"Hello? Hello? Speak if you can!" Patrick whispered, gingerly negotiating his way through the land, which was ridden with holes. The air was electric with the echoes of bullets and of cries of pain. Patrick gasped aloud as he tripped, almost falling. The boots of the brave soldiers, a pair of which he was currently wearing, had kicked up dust that had yet to settle. The shouts of men and thud of footfall still rung in his ears from earlier that day. If he shut his eyes for a split-second, he was back on the very scene, being splattered with dust and dazzled by the sun.

But now it was dusk on the battle-site. It was time to bring back the bodies.

This was the job that everyone hated. It was worse than everything else: the rats, the food, even the killing of their opposition. It was the fact that their once strong, healthy friends had been reduced to "body" status. And this time, Patrick was afraid. Maxwell hadn't come back.

"Maxwell? Anyone?" Patrick whispered, trying not to make too much noise for fear of attracting the attention of the enemy. "I've come to save you. Speak, if you can."

There was a whimper from somewhere to the right, and a whisper of something unintelligible.

"Who's there?" Patrick asked.

Again the same feeble whimper. And when Patrick found the owner of the whimper, he knew that the lack of voice was justified. Maxwell was there, but how changed! His arms were contorted and his legs didn't seem to be fully attached to the rest of his body. In the moonlight, Patrick could just make out his face: bloodied and swollen.

"Come on," Patrick said, going to his knees and trying to pick him up, "I'm taking you back to the trench."

"No, no..." muttered Maxwell, "I'm better off out here."

"Don't be silly." snapped Patrick, scooping him up.

"Go to someone who needs you... I know I'm dying."

"Don't be silly," Patrick said again, but this time without much heart. His friend's breathing was getting shallower with every inch that they moved together across the treacherous ground.

"I know you mean well, and thank you for it. You're a good person, Pat."

Patrick said nothing in response, because his emotions were running high and he knew that if he said anything equally tender, he'd be likely to drop his friend.

Instead, he thought about how he would like to be comforted if the roles were to be reversed. He pictured himself, tangled and mangled, in Maxwell's endlessly bruised but effortlessly capable arms. At the paralysing weakness that suddenly attacked his limbs, he lost his balance and, after desperately scrabbling around with his legs for a second, ended up on the floor. Maxwell let out a juddering breath.

Scrambling back up, he remembered something that Father-Sir had told him, and decided to act on it.

"Pray, Patrick." his voice echoed. "Praying is the only way to find comfort in dark times."

So Patrick prayed, loud enough for Maxwell to hear. He begged God to save his fellow soldier. He reached the end of the prayer just as they reached the trench.

"You'll be all right now, Maxwell." Patrick said comfortingly. "God's going to look after you. Just say *Amen* to seal the deal."

Nothing.

"Maxwell? Say *Amen*."

Still nothing. Patrick suddenly realised that Maxwell was an even heavier weight than he had been at the start of their trek. When he got a look at his face, he saw that the eyes were slightly open, as was the mouth. Patrick nearly dropped the body again, and was very happy to put it down and into the care of someone else once they'd slithered into the trench.

"Dead." was the response when Patrick asked after Maxwell a while later. Patrick flinched. That one word changed everything.

"Dead? But..." Patrick stammered. He couldn't believe it. "Where is he? Can I see him?"

"You want to voluntarily see a body? You posh people are odd. He hasn't gone anywhere yet – I'll take you."

Contrary to all literary depictions of the dead, Maxwell did not seem to be at peace. Patrick knew that he'd had a turbulent childhood, with his father a drunkard and his mother off the scene. Maxwell had told him that he'd hoped to reconcile with his father after some time away, and he'd never lost that hope, even though Patrick had with his own. But Maxwell's hope was all in vain now. Suddenly, Patrick felt a ball of fire surge through his upper body. It was loathing for whoever or whatever was the cause of this ghastly war.

Maxwell's troubled face brought him back to the present. Patrick stared at it for a minute, taking in every cut, scrape and bruise, hoping that it was all some big mistake and that he was just taking a nap. But it was all very real.

"Heavenly Father, please forgive my friend for his sins, as he had hoped to forgive his father. Amen." he prayed. As he half-opened his eyes, he almost saw some sort of being, purest white to represent Maxwell's beautiful soul, rising up and up to Heaven. That made a lot of sense to Patrick. Father-Sir had told him that it was in the first few hours after a body's death that God took the soul to Heaven (or to Hell, in the case of evil). Patrick knew that he was privileged to have witnessed it. At least, he reasoned with himself, Maxwell would be looked after in Heaven.

He knew that he would never forget his friend. That was for certain. The bonds of friendship were not going to be slashed by war.

"Good luck, old chap." Patrick said, taking Maxwell's freezing cold hand and shaking it for once last time.

When the time came to sleep, sleep eluded Patrick. He went over and over Maxwell's last minutes in his mind. He remembered how he'd fallen, jarring the poor man. A cold feeling came into his veins. Well, he'd killed the man, hadn't he? His clumsiness (for which he was forever being pulled up by Father-Sir) had killed his friend.

He would go to Hell. He would never forgive himself.

And had his religion not been quite so set in stone, the fact that God had not saved Maxwell would have taken away his faith as well.

. . .

Everyone seemed to be frantic with joy, in the Fox's world. There were two main reasons for this: the new-found peace due to the end of the war (which had yet to properly sink in) and the fact that it was Christmas!

Dorothy and Wilhelmina both had to work on Christmas Day. Charlie was alone at home for the whole day. The two women worked at the same place: the Memoir Restaurant at the other end of town. They started work at nine, and so they had to leave at half past seven in order to walk there in good time.

After the second incident two and a half years previously, Charlie had lost his job. He'd never gotten a permanent new one. He'd hopped from workplace to workplace, anywhere from the fishmonger (denying all relation to the disgraced Wilhelmina Fox) to the cab office (he hated horses, but a job was a job and he ended up quite enjoying it). Because he was rather a good liar – something that made Wilhelmina quite sceptical and worried – the denial trick worked wonders until the employers put two and two together, came up with four, and sacked him.

By Christmas 1918, he was jobless once more, having been sacked from the newsagent. Dorothy and Wilhelmina, on the other hand, had had much more luck in terms of job hunting. They'd filled two vacancies at the Memoir Restaurant, the poshest and most ridiculously grandiose restaurant in the whole of Manchester. Waitressing wasn't the most fulfilling job, but after being there for near enough two years, they both knew the ropes.

At first, they found it hard to adjust. Dorothy was forthright and playful by nature, and found it hard not to laugh at, or comment on, the fancy names of dishes as she wrote them down. Wilhelmina hadn't had to write so much since school, and her fingers were raw by the end of the second day. Dorothy's hands were fine – writing in her diary every evening, often for pages at a time, had given her hands of steel.

Despite this, they were happy with their jobs, and they were treasured by the team of waiters and waitresses. Invaluable, one colleague called them. Dorothy was quick and light on her feet, delivering posh food to aristocratic diners in record time.

She was also very attractive, having blossomed and gotten her growth recently, and there were several young men who were visibly charmed by her, despite the accent. (Only the cream of society dined at the Memoir.)

After hearing about the said young men, Charlie had been all for giving them a beating, and had vociferated this loudly. He'd ranted on and on about whatever the world was coming to, where stupid young men preyed on innocent young ladies, ready to have their wicked way with them. Wilhelmina had listened stonily for a while, and then snapped.

Ever since she'd lost her job at the fishmongers, she had been doing a lot more snapping. Hearing her howling at her husband after a long day was a common occurrence, berating him for his uselessness, lack of self-control and tactless comments. Eventually, Charlie had bitten back and now they were often to be heard going at it hammer and tongs of an evening. This often resulted in Wilhelmina to bed early, in tears, with a medicinal gin for company.

But on Christmas Day 1918, they tramped home from work at three o'clock after their shift, rather the worse for wear but happy all the same. Because the manager wasn't in that day, the waiting staff had helped themselves to a couple of free drinks, agreeing to share the blame. As a newly turned eighteen-year-old, Dorothy had been permitted to drink by Wilhelmina and had discovered rather a penchant for table wine. After two glasses (or two gins, in Wilhelmina's case), they both felt very giddy and very festive.

They tumbled through the door to find that Charlie had prepared a Christmas dinner for them. All the bad air was forgotten as Wilhelmina threw her arms around Charlie with a loud squeal.

"Blimey O' Reilly, how much have you had?" he laughed, staggering backwards.

"Oh, only a little, Da!" Dorothy laughed, hugging him too.

When the dinner was ready, they devoured it in some sort of animalistic feeding frenzy. It wasn't anywhere as good as Wilhelmina's roasts, Charlie himself admitted that, but Wilhelmina brushed away his self-deprecating comment, declaring the beef almost on par with manna.

Other families would have been utterly shocked by this blasphemy, their Christmases ruined, but Charlie simply laughed uproariously and carried on eating. Once they'd cleared their plates, they retired to the front room, clutching their stomachs.

"I'm afraid there's no Christmas pudding, Mina." Charlie said, "I didn't have any money left on me after buying this lot!"

"Don't be sorry – ye've just produced us a wonderful dinner with very little money! I've taught ye well, Charles." Wilhelmina replied.

"I couldn't eat another crumb, anyway!" Dorothy added, sinking onto the sofa.

It was only after their dinner had settled, at around half past five, that Charlie produced their final surprise: two wrapped parcels.

"Charles!" Wilhelmina exclaimed, "We said no presents! We only got somethin' for yer auntie, ye know that!"

"Mina, war is over, and that alone is cause for celebration. I've been saving and saving for these!"

Wilhelmina went even pinker as she tore open the parcel. Inside was a set of four crystal wine glasses. Dorothy discarded her brown paper to reveal a slab of the best chocolate. Chocolate was a rarity for them, and so she almost swooned at the sight of the confectionary in its delicate paper. From Charlie's aunt, they received a bottle of red wine between them all, which they opened immediately, pouring liberally into the new glasses. Then, placing their three full glasses on the shelf, they decided on a singsong and began to prance around the room.

They were so enthusiastic, in fact, that they all lost control a bit over their limbs. Arms and legs flew everywhere as they sung up-tempo versions of carols such as *Hark the Herald*. And at the end of *O Little Town Of Bethlehem*, the force with which the last word was shouted matched the force with which Wilhelmina exultantly thrust her arm out.

The elongated word "Emmanuel" was punctuated by an awful crash and a quieter splash. Wilhelmina turned around to find their three glasses of wine in a puddle of glass and red liquid on the floor by the fireplace. Charlie tensed, bracing himself for the furious yowl that normally greeted this sort of occurrence.

But in her drunken state, Wilhelmina simply laughed indulgently and started another carol.

. . .

"Stop talking!" Father-Sir whispered indignantly to the children next to him. They looked up and nodded guiltily, and their own father glared at them. The organist flexed his fingers and stared at them coldly. Father-Sir held up an apologetic hand, even though they were not his children. No sooner had he done so than the organist launched into *Ding Dong Merrily On High*.

Edna was fairly good at singing, because she knew how to harmonise. But for the past couple of years she had sung the normal tune, because since Patrick had sent that letter, she'd had no enthusiasm for Christmas. Christmas was a time for family, and for the past four Christmases there had been a piece of their family missing. Before the letter, she had held on to hope that Patrick was still alive, still soldiering on. But since the letter, she'd completely and utterly convinced herself that the incident in the night had been a premonition to his death. The stabbing pain that she had felt around midday the following day had emphasised that – she thought that it had coincided with his final breath. All this meant that she was convinced that her son was gone.

After a couple of readings, they came to a song that they hadn't sung for a couple of years. Edna swallowed hard. It was Patrick's favourite carol. She barely made it to the end of the first verse before she had to go outside because the memories of her son's voice were too raw. In her mind's eye, she saw him lying at the bottom of a ditch somewhere, forgotten by all except his mother.

In the carriage on the way back, Father-Sir caught her arm roughly.

"And where did you disappear to?" he whispered in her ear angrily.

"I'm sorry, Bruce," she whispered back, "I couldn't stand hearing *Adeste Fideles* without our Pat being there."

"Patrick," Father-Sir said aggressively, "is dead. It is not that hard for you to comprehend, Edna. And he was a sinner anyway – you are better off without him."

"Don't you miss him?"

"Well..." Father-Sir began, softening momentarily. Then, embarrassed at his brief display of weakness, he tightened his grip on the top of her arm.

"Bruce! Don't!" Edna exclaimed, making the children look.

"Stop speaking! Don't show such heinous disrespect, you harridan!" he spat back.

"But I..."

"Stop speaking! I won't have that child's name mentioned, especially not on Christ's birthday, when God is on the lookout for sin."

"Loving your family is a sin?" Gertrude inquired softly. Father-Sir's head whipped around and in one quick movement, he smacked her hard.

"How dare you question me?" he shouted. Stunned, Gertrude sat back in her seat. The other two wisely said nothing. Father-Sir hadn't had to use violence for the last couple of months, ever since he'd had The Talk with Mike on his twelfth birthday. Even before that, he'd seldom hit either of his daughters, nor his wife. Gertrude and Bessie knew that if they were struck by Father-Sir, they'd done something disgraceful. Questioning the authority of their father was definitely on the list.

When they got back, they sat around the fire and exchanged their presents. But before Father-Sir signalled permission to open them, he waited for silence.

"I want to hear expressions of undying gratitude, to the provider and to the Lord. Is that clear? Remember Acts 20:35... *'I have showed you all things, how that so labouring ye ought to support the weak, and to remember the words of the Lord Jesus, how he said, It is more blessed to give than to receive.'*"

Everyone nodded.

"You may open your gifts."

There were exclamations of delight as gifts were revealed. Bessie cried out with joy upon receiving a pair of silk gloves. They were the first proper pair she owned, the other being a scraggy woollen pair that she had knitted herself, years ago.

When everyone had finished, Father-Sir waited for silence once more.

"Thank you, Lord, for these gifts." he said simply.

"Amen." agreed the rest of the family. The maid began clearing up the discarded paper as quietly as she could. Edna remembered how a few Christmases ago, they had all been there together. Now, Patrick was dead, and Andrew was... well, nobody knew where. He'd argued with Father-Sir, just like Patrick had, and gone.

All the way through dinner, Edna longed to toast Patrick and Andrew, but she didn't dare. Gertrude was still a little dazed from her slap earlier, and she didn't want to rile her husband at all if that would be the consequence. So while Father-Sir was saying grace and everyone had their eyes closed, she raised her own glass of water and mouthed a toast. She shut her eyes and in her mind's eye, she saw the rest of her family lift up their glasses and return the toast. She hurriedly put her glass down, just before Bruce opened his eyes.

They stuffed themselves silly during that meal – or at least, the two men did. As usual, the girls had smaller and more lady-like portions. Edna was normally satisfied with this, as it kept her figure for her husband's approval, but for once she wished she had more, so that she could squash the feelings of grief with the more appropriate weight of food.

Maybe one day Christmas would be different, she told herself. Maybe one day she'd be allowed to eat as much as she liked, without being half-starved or blackmailed into starving herself. But for now, she'd have to put up with it.

. . .

"Everybody, we have a new waiter for our restaurant!" announced the manager of the Memoir Restaurant. Everyone turned around to see the new arrival, who was staring at the floor and shifting his weight from foot to foot nervously. "This is Patrick, and he's just returned from war."

There was a collective intake of breath amongst the assembled staff and they all peered at this new specimen.

"A war lad, aye?" Wilhelmina whispered to Dorothy, "Just yer type, Dot."

"Oh, shut up, Mam!" Dorothy replied fiercely.

"Well! Yer eighteen, an' he looks about th' same. You'd go very well together." Wilhelmina decided, just as the manager left the room. Immediately, everyone crowded around the new person.

"How long have you been back, then?" was the first question

to be fired at Patrick.

"Since Boxing Day, I think it was, two days ago, yes, Mrs."

"Was it so very bad?" another person asked.

"Well, yes, sir, it wasn't comfortable, but we coped, sir."

Patrick continued to answer questions awkwardly, eyes roaming the room without actually focusing. Eventually the questions ceased, and the women started tutting to themselves, because that war had obviously done something bad to his wits. Why else would he be choosing to work at the Memoir? A good joke indeed!

"I suppose our uniform makes a change from soldier's uniform, eh, Patrick?" the manager joked, giving him a friendly nudge. Patrick flinched away and started adjusting his collar. The manager rolled his eyes at the lack of sense of humour.

That day, Dorothy's break coincided with his and they found themselves sitting next to each other in the small but comfortable staff room. The Memoir Restaurant certainly treated their staff well (and they had been surprisingly good-natured about the pilfered drinks). Dorothy said as much to Patrick, but received no reply. When she looked up from her book curiously, she saw that he was rocking back and forth with his head in his hands.

"Be good. Be good. Don't let them see anything. Be a martyr. Be good. Serve them well." he was muttering.

"You what?" Dorothy said, clear and sharp. He jumped to attention.

"Yes, Sir?" he said automatically, then twitched with embarrassment.

"I just wondered whether yer all right, that's all."

"Quite all right! Quite all right! Thank you, Ma'am. Now, woman, can you tell me whether we're anywhere near Highmore Park, in Houghton Regis?"

"Highmore? Never heard of it. Where do ye mean, specifically?"

"Well, Houghton Regis is in Bedfordshire, woman. Near London?"

"We're in Monthill, Manchester. That's a way away from London."

Patrick's face fell. "How far?"

"Ooh, I don't know, pet. Let me-"

"Pet?"

Dorothy realised that she had been treating him like an infant. She quickly backtracked.

"I said Pat."

"My name is Patrick." he said stiffly.

"Well, I'm sorry, *Patrick*." Dorothy said sarcastically. "I'll ask me mam on her break."

At that moment, Wilhelmina entered the staff room.

"Yer break's over, both of ye. Back to work!" she informed them.

"Mam, Patrick's wonderin' how far it is to...."

"Houghton Regis?" Patrick jumped in. Wilhelmina thought for a minute.

"I'd say yer best bet is two 'undred miles, love."

"Two *hundred*?"

"Two 'undred."

"*Two* hundred?"

"Two 'undred."

"Two 'undred... hundred?"

"Two 'undred."

Dorothy rescued the situation before it became even more

paralysing. "Why d'ye ask?"

"That's where I was born, and where my family is." Patrick said. He tensed up and made for the door at high speed, nearly knocking over Wilhelmina in the process.

"Nice to meet ye too, Patrick." Dorothy said, shaking her head at his rudeness. "So much for yer match-makin', Mam."

"Now, now, none o' that. I think he's a little shy an' nervy. Well, it is his first day, bless him. You play yer cards right, because if he'd from down South then he's likely well-brought up an' with good connections. An' if ye marry into a good family, who knows where ye'll end up? Dinner parties, posh balls, th' like!"

"Mam, I'm not interested in posh parties. Me life is up 'ere, in Monthill."

"Aye, an' look what Monthill's done to me. I wish I'd have channelled them book characters yer so in love with, an' moved away years ago, before I'd ever set eyes on yer father. Now, run after that Patrick quick-sharp, an' get t' know him before he sets his sights on another woman."

Dorothy trotted away, purely to get away from her mother. She was just in time to see Patrick disappearing out of the staff door in a great hurry. Since nobody was permitted to leave in the middle of their shift, Dorothy decided to retrieve him. She was sure that he had a reasonable explanation: perhaps he'd forgotten how to tell the time while he was at war. Dorothy herself barely knew how to tell the time, but he was a well-educated man. But in the few seconds between her spotting him and her reaching the door, he had disappeared into thin air.

"Dorothy! Get back here this minute!" the manager shouted, seeing her about to step out. She spun around guiltily.

"I'm sorry, Sir..." she began, but he cut her off.

"What on Earth do you think you're doing? Walking out during work hours? We can easily dock your wages, you know."

"I'm sorry, Sir, but I was simply wonderin' where Patrick had gone!" Dorothy explained.

"Patrick? Who's Patrick? If your sweetheart has been visiting you at work, I'll have his guts for garters!"

"No, no, Sir! Th' new lad!"

"Oh, the new boy! Well, why? Where did he go?"

"That's what I was tryin' to find out."

The manager made for the door and threw it open, peering left and right.

"You say he went out here? I'll have *his* guts for garters! Preposterous boy! Carry on with your work, Dorothy, and when he deigns to show his face again, he will be dealt with, most severely."

So Dorothy went back to work, but all through the rest of the day she wondered where he had gone. Unsurprisingly, he didn't return. But she couldn't stop thinking about him, worrying about him, even while eating dinner that night. Wilhelmina was her usual frosty self towards Charlie, and he responded by offering snide remarks every now and then. Dorothy grew fed up in the end, and after taking their dog (not Monty, but a rather doddery old terrier) out for his evening walk, she stalked up to bed.

. . .

"Mother's taken to her bed again..." Gertrude sighed to Bessie.

"Is she grieving over Patrick again?" Bessie responded sadly.

"Yes. He died two and a half years ago now – is she not over it yet?"

"Gertrude! How can you get over a death? How can one get over their son? I'm shocked at you!" Edna said from behind the pair, on her way to the kitchen. The girls spun around, shocked.

"Mother, I'm sorry, I…"

"For your information, it is not possible to just *get over it*. I'm disappointed that you think it is. Now, I must get to the kitchen. Oh, but girls – don't tell your father I'm out of bed. It's a… it's a game we're playing – you know how competitive he is! Deal?"

The girls nodded, looking slightly confused. Edna smiled, then scurried off. She hated lying to her children, but she didn't want them to know what their father was doing. She didn't want them to know that their mother had been forced to stay in bed.

Bruce's exact words were "I can't trust you to roam the house, so you'll be staying in bed, where I can control your movements, for the foreseeable future."

Edna had objected, of course, but he'd just turned nasty. He'd crowded her against the bathroom wall and asked her "How much do you value your safety?". Edna had cried once he'd left. She couldn't believe that the man she had loved and married had become this. She couldn't believe that *she* had become this. She should have married someone else.

And all because of a few extra slices of meat. She'd gone down to the kitchens late on Christmas Day. Bruce had caught her at it and had to physically restrain himself from beating her. He'd howled an incomprehensible Bible verse at her (something about gluttony) and dragged her screaming up to their bedroom. Luckily, the children were all in bed, and they didn't see or hear any of it.

She hadn't voluntarily taken to her bed, of course she hadn't. She wanted, with all her heart, to be able to move freely about the house like she'd been able to before Christmas. She was hopeful that Bruce would relent soon.

That was, until he went into the kitchen and caught her at it again. She wasn't even eating this time, just getting a newspaper. He didn't say a word, but he took her hand lightly in his and led her up to the bedroom. They passed the girls on the way up, and Mike was with them, whispering. Edna somehow smiled at them and mouthed "He found me!", as if it really was all a game. Father-Sir turned to the children and smiled too.

"Children, the cook has just baked a nice treacle tart. As a post-Christmas treat, why don't you go and have some? I'm sure she won't mind baking another for dinner tonight."

The children looked at each other, then nodded and obeyed. Edna swallowed hard. The kitchen was the furthest point possible from their bedroom. And it was to the bedroom she was led. He gently helped her into bed, touching her stomach briefly and half-smiling. He turned away and locked the door.

"Bruce, how can I keep my figure for you if you've ordered me to bed?" she asked quietly, hoping that by talking, she could somehow hold off whatever he was about to do to her.

"If you hadn't gorged yourself on Christmas Day, then you wouldn't be in bed in the first place, would you?" he replied, in a light tone that worried her even more.

"But I've suffered no ill effects – I'm fit as a fiddle!"

"Hmph. Podgy, to say the least." Bruce scoffed.

"Exactly, darling. How can I get back my figure, for you, if you're keeping me in bed?"

Edna said this gently, trying to charm him into loving her like he used to, but it didn't work.

"Excuse me?"

"What?"

"Don't you disrespect me, Edna. You know what happens when you disrespect me, and you may not be "in the mood" for it!"

"I'm not, Bruce…"

"You're not "in the mood", or you're not disrespecting me?"

Edna was lost for words. Fear had taken everything from her. She backed up in the bed, holding a pillow in front of her for protection as he took a step forward.

"If you're not "in the mood", then don't provoke me. Let me remind you, Edna, that you are a mere woman! Some women may have the vote now, but you are my property and therefore you will obey me at all costs. Genesis says: 'Your desire shall be for your husband, and he shall rule over you.'"

Edna snapped, absolutely petrified.

"Well that's flaming ridiculous!" she retorted, then clapped her hand over her mouth, as if trying to shepherd the words back and down her throat.

In a split-second, everything happened. Bruce gave a roar and launched himself at her. She tried to scramble out of the bed, but it was too late – he was on top of her. He beat her hard with his fists, simply roaring with unrestrained fury.

"That was a mistake! That was a big, big mistake! You'll pay for that! You're paying for that!"

And what he did to his wife, and not for the first time, she was definitely not "in the mood" for, and is too despicable to be written in any such reading matter.

. . .

Under any other circumstances, the scene would have been idyllic. There was a fresh dusting of snow decorating the roof of every building, and the churchgoers were throwing their heart and soul into singing so that it could be heard the whole way down Round Street. Monthill was savouring the last remnants of Christmas before the year melted into 1919. Round Street was known for being one of the nice areas, so taking a little amble down it was almost certain to improve one's mood. Nine times out of ten, one would turn the corner into Manton Road (and back into the notoriously grotty Monthill) with a smile on their face.

This was not one of those times, for Dorothy's early-morning perusal had done nothing to aid her mission. She'd peered into every doorway with hope. She'd convinced herself that since he came from an aristocratic background, her moving target would have been attracted to Round Street. But alas, the thorough search down the road had proved fruitless. And, as Dorothy found when she met up at Pickney Green with the rest of the search party, so had the other searches.

"Patrick's obviously vacated the town," sighed the manager. Everyone else sighed too, none louder so than Dorothy. She was a caring girl, and she could tell that her newest colleague had not been in the best state. When he had not turned up for his shift the previous evening, the manager had been spitting pips.

"First he walks out in the middle of the day, now he doesn't turn up at all! He'll be getting the sharp side of my tongue when he deigns to drop by!" he'd raged. But then Mrs. Lloyd, a lovely Welsh lady who opened her doors to any waifs and strays, had turned up looking very worried.

"Have you seen Patrick Hammond today? He's staying with me and he didn't come home last night. He mentioned that he was working here...?"

And that had been that. Mrs. Lloyd had become almost hysterical after learning of his disappearance. The next morning, a search party had been rounded up, interrupting many hard-earned lie-ins. Wilhelmina, ever the early bird, had been half-way through a boiled egg, while Dorothy had been fast asleep. By eight o'clock, they had been wrapped up warm, outside in the darkness, armed with what little light they could muster from hand-held lamps. The clouds were threatening rain, so they knew that the frost would not last long.

Despite Round Street being so uplifting, the disappointment of the search was debilitating. The weather did nothing to lighten the mood. It was one of those days where the sky was so grey that it sapped all the jubilance from the people below it, as if it would never get light again. Mrs. Lloyd, who had been relatively calm during the search, began to become agitated again.

When they met back up at ten o'clock, they decided to call off the search. It never crossed anyone's mind to call the police, since the police force in Monthill was worse than useless. Waves of disappointment radiating off of them all, painting the air quite blue, they began to disperse.

Dorothy knew that they'd all been assigned an area to search, but even so she wracked her brains to think of any area that they might have missed. She could find none, and so she asked herself – who was the least likely to do a proper job? One boy in particular came to mind, a bumbling and gormless lad whose thoughts stretched no further than his next meal. He had hardly been listening to the instructions at all, therefore he had been assigned the smallest area, which was around the blacksmiths. The blacksmith's wife was a bit like Mrs Lloyd: Welsh, a kind-hearted soul that often took in people in distress. A tiny flame of hope ignited inside Dorothy.

"Mam, I'm goin' to take another little walk an' see if I can see him." she told Wilhelmina.

"Ye won't have any luck, love. We weren't good enough for him, so he's upped his sticks an' gone. Probably halfway t' London now. But still, do what ye like."

It took a good half-hour to walk to the blacksmith's, by the lake, and Dorothy was freezing cold by the time she got to her destination. As she crossed the bridge over the lake, she looked to her left and stopped so suddenly that she nearly fell over. There was a figure sitting by the edge, huddled up in a ball, resting his chin on his knees. He had short, brown hair (a darker shade of brown than her own) and was hunched over, arms wrapped around legs, as if physically restraining himself.

Dorothy knew, just knew, that it was Patrick. She hurried to the end of the bridge, only to be stopped from reaching him by the thick holly bushes lining the pathway. She walked along a little way, but there was no gap in them at all.

"Desperate times call for desperate measures," she told herself. With that, she got on her front and slithered through the cold mud, straight under the bush, her eyes tight shut to protect them from the prickles. It seemed like an age that she was under there, inching through the mud, but she reached the other side with only a few scratches. She stood up and smiled despite the situation. She'd always wanted to get hideously muddy like that – and now she had an excuse. Her dreary pinafore, which she'd thrown on for ease and comfort, was slathered in sludge. Ah well, silver linings.

Then she focused on the task in hand. She could see the figure more clearly now, and she could tell that it was definitely Patrick. She took a brisk step forward, but her left foot shot to the right and her body followed, landing with a bit of a splat on its side. Taking a deep breath, she scrambled to her feet and almost skated to her destination. Even as she approached, with more squelches than she would have liked, Patrick did not stir until she coughed without thinking.

He leapt to his feet and spun around, somehow managing to keep his balance on the slope. Dorothy's heart was in her mouth as she pictured him sliding straight down the slope and into the waiting lake. Or was that what he wanted?

"Stay away!" he shouted, sounding unusually young and boyish. Dorothy stayed where she was for a moment, then stepped forward as she started talking.

"Patrick, we've been looking ev-"

"You take one more step forward and..." he indicated the lake with a motion of his head.

"Ye know it's a crime to commit suicide. Please be reasonable

– come back with me. Please?"

There was a long pause, whilst Patrick turned his face to the half-frozen lake.

"Why should I? I shouldn't be allowed to live."

He sat down again, as if the effort of standing was beyond him.

"Eh?"

"It was all my fault."

"What was?"

"He died because of me," Patrick said, his voice wavering. Dorothy took a tiny step forward, although her heart was racing. She knew that she had to tread carefully – literally and figuratively. One false move, and either she or Patrick, or both, would be in that lake. She swallowed hard, then sat down beside him. He made no attempt to get up. When she spoke again, the guarded edge was gone from her voice, and it sounded caring and motherly.

"I doubt that very much. I'm very good at readin' people, and yer not th' murderin' type. Tell me exactly what happened an' I'll be the judge o' whether it's yer fault or not. If I think it is, I'll go ahead an' leave ye to it. If I don't, yer comin' back with me. Do I have a deal?"

"Fine. I know the answer, so fine."

Dorothy had no intention of leaving him to it, of course. They shook on it, and out it all came.

"I went to rescue my friend off the battlefield, I took him back, I fell over, the fall finished him off, therefore I finished him off, therefore I'll go to hell and I might as well not waste Satan's time and just get all it over with now. The end."

"Ah, not enough detail. I want to hear it all. Take me back to th' scene an' walk me through exactly what happened."

Patrick took a deep breath and pictured the dark and bloody battlefield. He stood up and turned away from Dorothy, as if he couldn't bear to look a human being in the eyes while talking about the death of one. He chose instead to look out to the water. He spoke so quietly that Dorothy had to stand up to hear him.

"I was walking, and searching for signs of life, when I heard a noise. That noise was my friend, Maxwell. He was too weak to say much, but I picked him up and started taking him back to the trench – not enough stretcher bearers, you see. Maxwell was convinced that he was dying, and I was trying to convince him otherwise. He told me I was a good person – and I thought, at that moment, that I was. I don't know what kind of game he was trying to play…"

"Yer gettin' distracted. He told ye that yer a good person… an' then what?"

"I fell. Father-Sir is always telling me off for being clumsy, and with good reason. The jarring must have killed him. I didn't even realise at first. I was trying to get him to pray – to pray when he was dead! I looked at his face and I thought "No… he's not dead. I've prayed, so God has saved him. He's just unconscious, he can't be dead." But as I found out later… he was. I thought I'd made my peace with him – he wasn't afraid to say it how he saw it, and he could be blunt. Then I remembered… I was the cause of his death, in the end. And as I said, I'll go to hell. I might as well not waste their time, and just end it now. There's nothing else to live on for."

Patrick was saying this all in a dull, expressionless voice. Beneath that voice, however, was a whole multitude of emotions, all threatening to rise to the surface and bring tears with them. Dorothy was silent for a minute while she took it all in. During the silence, she became aware of a change in his breathing. Of him gathering himself, ready to jump. Instincts kicked in and she darted in front of him and pushed him back, a hand on each of his shoulders. She was a slight woman, but she stunned him and knocked him over. Since he made no effort to get up, she sat back down beside him, shivering violently now. He noticed this and shook his head.

"See? I'm making you cold. That's hardly an end to the list of sins I've committed. Disobeying my father, shedding Christian blood…"

"Well, I've made me decision, anyway. An' I'm not strayin' from it. It wasn't yer fault, so yer comin' back with me. Come on."

Patrick laughed bitterly.

"How? How was it not my fault?"

"What if Maxwell wasn't dead until after ye got him back to th' trench? Ye tried to get him to pray, an' he didn't, am I right?"

"Got it in one."

"In that case, it's Maxwell's fault. Maxwell's refusal to pray meant that God gave up on him, an' he died. It wasn't *your* fault."

Patrick sucked in his lips. "I'll come back with you on one condition. Give me a supporting quotation from the Bible that backs up your point. You do that, and I'll come with you."

Dorothy frowned, but Patrick looked triumphant. Sinister as it may sound, there was nothing he wanted more than to cease to exist at that moment. He knew that this girl wasn't a devout Christian – why else would she be out and about on a Sunday? – and so she was not likely to answer this question.

And Dorothy was thinking the same. She desperately wracked her brains for anything vaguely Bible-sounding that she could say to make him step away. And by some sort of miracle – or indeed, God being conveniently kind – she got one! It was something that one of the suffragists had said at a meeting. She summoned every ounce of control over her brain to remember the words. And she got it.

"I believe it was '*The lions may grow weak and hungry, but those who seek the Lord lack no good thing.*'" she said clearly, enunciating each syllable in her best posh accent.

Patrick was completely still.

"Yer seekin' th' Lord, aren't ye?" Dorothy said, just to prove the point. And because Patrick couldn't exactly say no, he nodded. And the game was up. It was strange how a few pieces of paper and some ink could have the ability to change lives. Patrick staggered to his feet and, still gentlemanly despite his troubles, helped the lady to her feet. Dorothy knew that there was another way around the holly bushes, and that was the route they took. At one point, she almost fell over again and had to grab hold of Patrick's arm to stay upright. She kept her hand there.

"So... let's get to know ye." Dorothy said to fill the awkward silence that was ensuing.

"Right...?"

"Tell me about yerself?"

"I was born in 1898 to a Christian family. I have two brothers, Andrew and Mike, and two sisters, Gertrude and Bessie. Mother is the sweetest mother you could ever wish for but Father-Sir... Father-Sir exceeds everyone in all good qualities. He is the best father that anyone could possibly have... and I defied him."

"You what?"

"He didn't want me to go to war. But I insisted. I said all sorts of horrible things to him – I threatened to hurt him, in fact. What sort of a son does that make me? He's beaten me my whole life, of course, but I'd never retaliated until then. I think I was full of sin from the start. Anyway, that's enough about me – what about you? I don't even know your name!"

"How rude o' me! I'm terribly sorry. I'm Dorothy Fox, born October 1900 to Wilhelmina an' Charles Fox. I left school at ten but I'm good at writin' an' readin', so don't cast me off as un-educated! Me mam was a suffragist, an' I was a suffragist too-"

"You were a suffragist?"

"Yes, an' I'm well proud of it, too." Dorothy said sharply and a little nervously. She wondered whether the reaction would be of approval or disapproval.

"Well, my Father-Sir would not approve. You really should have left it to the men who know best. Now that you've suc-ceeded, your sort will cause all sorts of problems! Why won't you women realise-"

"Let's agree to disagree," Dorothy said smoothly, seeing that he was getting worked up again. She just wanted to get the pair of them back to Monthill in one piece, so that she could deposit him at Mrs. Lloyd's safely.

"I think not! In fact, if I had more influence-"

"Enough!" Dorothy snapped. Patrick's jaw hit the floor, but then he picked it up and tried again.

"If I-"

"No. Women aren't just playthings, you know. We have rights. We have to obey th' laws, so it's only fair that we get a say in 'em as well. An' if ye disagree with that when even blimmin' Parliament has seen sense, then you've got one more screw loose than I already thought!"

Patrick was silent and Dorothy was shocked at what she'd just said. She'd never torn into someone like that before, and it re-minded her of her mother's diatribes to Charlie. Normally, she tried to be like Katharina – cool, calm and collected – but it did feel good to just let go, just that one time. Once a suffragist, ever a suffragist, she thought.

"If I were my father, then I would have to leave you right here by yourself. But luckily for you, I am not that sort of man. In fact…" he said, taking her arm properly and pulling her gently to a stop, "I rather like that feistiness…"

And with that, he kissed her. Just like that. It lasted only a second or two, but it happened. Dorothy did not pull away until she felt the cold air hit her face again. They carried on walking, while she desperately fought the urge to kiss him again. It didn't work, but when she tried to kiss him, he looked horrified.

"The women don't kiss the men!" he protested.

"You what?"

"Women don't choose when they want to kiss. They wait for the men to choose. It's the same with all affection. That has always been the way, and that will always be the way."

"Oh… I'm sorry. Still… I'd like to be kissed."

Patrick smiled despite everything. "Then I am happy to oblige."

And so he kissed her again. When they broke apart, after a few seconds, she swayed and nearly fell down – and this time, not just because of the mud. Patrick had to catch her, and she clung to him momentarily.

"Does that make us sweethearts?" she asked, smiling up at him.

"I suppose it does. Do let me walk you home."

"Ye can meet Da while yer at it, then."

The walk home, harsh and bitter though it was, passed in a flash while they talked about everything and nothing. Patrick elaborated on a few funny tales from the trenches, and Dorothy encouraged him. She thought that getting everything out in the open would help her understand him.

When they reached Monthill, it was nearly half-past-eleven. Church services were over, and the streets were quiet. Nonchurchgoers weren't going to venture out in such miserable weather. They walked through the streets, saying absolutely nothing. Dorothy was rehearsing how she would break the news to her parents. Patrick was wondering how Mr. Fox would take it, picturing him as a barbarian man like his own father.

Soon, they came to the pleasant terraced house that was the home of the Fox family. Dorothy didn't have her key, since she had expected to come home with Wilhelmina, and so she rapped on the door. Wilhelmina opened the door and her face lit up when she saw the missing person on her doorstep with her daughter.

"Ah! We've found ye! Come on in, I'll give ye a spot of lunch, Patrick." she said.

"You really needn't, Mrs. Fox..." Patrick protested, but Wilhelmina cut him off jovially.

"Nonsense! Ye need feedin' up – yer so scrawny! I'll fix up a bit o' soup. Butter's on the turn but we've some drippin' if ye want that on some bread, too."

"That's lovely, Mam," Dorothy said.

"Now, I saw ye comin' up the road," Wilhelmina admitted, "so I put the soup on ready for ye. Ye looked very close together, I must say. Anythin' yer wantin' to tell us...?"

Dorothy looked at Patrick and Patrick looked at Dorothy. She shrugged, then smiled.

"Patrick an' I have decided to court, if that's what ye mean.

Wilhelmina squealed and would have jumped up and down if it wasn't for her corset. Nevertheless, her squeal was so loud and intense that it brought Charlie out of his study and flying towards the kitchen.

"Mina? What's going on?" he said, before noticing Patrick.

"Good morning, Mr. Fox." Patrick said nervously. He was wary of upsetting Dorothy's father, unaware that not all fathers were as volatile as his own.

"Morning. You are…?"

"Patrick Hammond, Sir."

"Dot's sweetheart! Patrick is Dot's sweetheart!" Wilhelmina declared joyfully. Charlie took a long look at Patrick, sizing him up once and for all. He didn't like what he saw: a muddy, gangly young man, shifting from foot to foot nervously and avoiding eye contact.

"I don't think so." Charlie responded. Dorothy's heart sunk. She had pictured Charlie being overjoyed and shaking Patrick's hand happily like in most of the books she had read. But in Charlie's mind, Dorothy was still sixteen, being taunted by young Master Shaw and friends. There was no chance of his Dotty being courted – not if he had anything to do with it!

"Charles, she's eighteen." Wilhelmina pointed out, looking slightly bemused. "We were suffragists. We're not like normal woman – ye should know that by now."

"I'm very sorry, young man, but I can't let you court my Dotty. It's just not right, at her age. By all means, stay for lunch, but there is to be no relationship between you." Charlie said firmly.

"Very well, Mr. Fox." Patrick replied sadly, letting go of Dorothy's hand. But to his surprise, Dorothy took it up again. She didn't look at him, expecting to be told off for initiating physical contact, but he didn't say anything, and he didn't drop it.

"Da, I'm eighteen now." she said gently, turning to Charlie. She knew that what she was about to say would look disrespectful on paper, but her tone of voice showed that she didn't mean it like that. "I don't want ye to dictate me life any more. Like Mam said, I ain't like other young women. I'm independent. I know that all yer mates are the patriarchal type, but you don't have to be. I want to court Patrick, an' so I will. I'm doin' something for meself, for once."

Charlie sighed and put his arm around her.

"I know, Dot. But after what happened a few years ago with all those lads, it's hard for me to let go of you."

"I know, Da."

"If you do choose to continue courting this boy, I'm afraid you'll have to take what comes with it. Courting's for grown-up adults, and grown-up adults do not live with their parents. I'm afraid that if you want to carry on your courtship, you'll have to find somewhere else to live. Away from Patrick, of course."

This ultimatum was a test, of sorts. How devoted was Dorothy to this man?

Dorothy barely had to think.

"That's fine," she said, "I understand."

She turned to Patrick, still holding his hand.

"Does Mrs. Lloyd have any spare room for me, d'ye think? Just for one night?" she asked.

"We can certainly ask," he responded.

"Good. After lunch, I'll pack me bags and be on me way."

"Are ye sure, Dotty?" asked Wilhelmina, sounding choked. When Dorothy looked at her, she saw that her mother had tears in her eyes.

"Mam!" Dorothy said, "Don't cry!"

"I know, I know," Wilhelmina sniffed, her voice unusually unsteady. "Please ignore me. I'm a little... 'ormonal today."

"Hormones are a myth, Mrs. Fox." Patrick put in, eager to put some of Father-Sir's teachings to good use.

"Eh?"

"Hormones are a myth. Just like the majority of science – just like Darwin's theory. Madness!" he said.

Wilhelmina didn't like to admit that she had no idea what

hormones actually were, nor who Darwin was. The hormone phrase was something that she had picked up from a girl at work. So she simply nodded and smiled. A curious noise from the pot distracted them all – the soup was almost done to death. With that, Wilhelmina was all business, decanting it into bowls and putting bread and dripping on the table. Dorothy slipped upstairs to get changed and discard her muddy pinafore.

Dorothy came downstairs, looking refreshed in a nice blue dress, and started eating straight away. No grace, Patrick noted disapprovingly, and had his first doubts. They were from such different backgrounds – would this actually work? Despite that, the soup tasted wonderful, even if it contained "everythin' under th' sun". He ate his fill, then checked his pocket watch. It was half past twelve. He gave Dorothy a look which said that it was time for her to get ready to go. She nodded and stood up, and started collecting the bowls.

"Oh, don't ye worry about them, you two." Wilhelmina said, looking up for the first time in a few minutes. She had been absently stirring the watery remains of her soup, picturing her tears dissolving within it in an effort to stop herself from crying.

"Are you sure, Mrs. Fox? I am quite prepared to help." Patrick inquired.

"Quite sure, quite sure. Ye can get on with whatever yer plannin'. Oh, an' ye can call me Mina, lad. An' ye can call that," – nodding at Charlie, who was looking surly – "Charlie."

"Thank you, ahm, Mina."

Dorothy went upstairs to her room, while Patrick stayed downstairs to help after all. There was a big bag, which had held her family's belongings on rare overnight trips to Devon in years gone by to see Wilhelmina's parents. Her mother told her that since there was no chance of them ever going again, she could have it.

Dorothy didn't have many outfits these days – she wore them on a weekly rotation after getting changed out of her work uniform. She'd grown out of a lot of them, and had had to sell a lot of her others. Downstairs, Wilhelmina was telling Patrick this, presumably in case he asked where all her clothes were.

Patrick felt quite concerned. Father-Sir had always taught him that people who had been sacked by their employers were particularly low, having to scrounge for money off others as a result of their actions. Wilhelmina noticed his concerned expression, and matched it on her own face.

"Yer not a snob, are ye?" she asked.

"What sort of a question is that?" he responded sharply. Upstairs, Dorothy cringed, especially at the tense silence that followed. She concentrated on folding garments meticulously neatly, even though they were sure to be tossed and turned beyond belief on the way to Mrs. Lloyd's. Once all of her possessions were packed away, she and Patrick lugged the bag downstairs (too heavy a job for one person) and put it by the door. For the last time, Dorothy reached onto the coat rack for her coat, then peered out of the glass pane beside the door. It was raining: a fine drizzle that drenches the pedestrian.

"It's a bit of a walk, I'm afraid," Patrick said, "but I have no money to get a taxi. Are you prepared to walk?"

This was Dorothy's first test of dedication. Dorothy looked up and smiled.

"Yes, I am."

"Good!"

"Mam? Da?"

Wilhelmina and Charlie both put their heads around the door of the living room.

"Yes, love?" Wilhelmina replied.

"I'm ready."

Wilhelmina came through the door first, and enveloped Dorothy in a tight squeeze. Dorothy squeezed her back, then it was Charlie's turn.

"Ouch, you're a strong girl these days, Dot!" Charlie said with a nervous laugh once he could breathe again. Dorothy could tell that he didn't want her to leave. She wasn't sure whether she wanted to either, but she knew that if she pulled out now, she could send the already fragile Patrick spiralling back down again. So she lifted her chin, smiled and looked towards Patrick. He solemnly shook Charlie's hand and bowed to Wilhelmina, who curtsied back awkwardly.

Wilhelmina couldn't resist one last hug.

"Don't forget that there's always room for ye back here. If things don't work out, I mean."

"They *will* work out," Dorothy and Patrick said at the same time, and everyone laughed.

"Well, ye can never be too careful," Wilhelmina pointed out.

"Thank you, Mam." Dorothy said, picking up one handle of the bag after slipping on her mittens. Patrick picked up the other handle and together they stumbled down the two steps and onto the pavement. The weather chose that moment to step up its intensity, and Dorothy's hair blew free from its knot. Wilhelmina and Charlie watched them walking up the road, and once they were out of earshot, Wilhelmina let go and cried.

As for the walkers, they were having a tough time of it. The screaming wind combined with the driving rain made every step a challenge. At least the rain masked the tears that were dripping down Dorothy's face. Leaving home is a daunting prospect for any young girl, and it was ten times worse for Dorothy because it was so sudden. But as she looked up at Patrick's good-looking face, with its high cheekbones and steely expression, she was excited about the future.

Patrick, meanwhile, was praying for the best. He intended to keep a firm grip on Dorothy, just like Father-Sir had on Mother. His heart lurched at the thought of his family, who were hundreds of miles away, oblivious to the fact that he was on British soil once more. For all they knew, he might be dead! But foolish pride was stopping him from going back and apologising to Father-Sir. What was that proverb? *'Pride goeth before destruction, and a haughty spirit before a fall.'*

"Left turn here, Dorothy," he said, steering the young woman just as she was about to go straight on.

"No, it's th' next left turn, isn't it?" she protested.

"Are you arguing with me?" he asked in a dangerously quiet voice. Dorothy would soon come to learn that when he asked such a question in such a tone, he was giving her a chance to rectify whatever it was that he deemed unacceptable. Patrick saw her drop her gaze, and he was pleased with himself from being assertive from the off.

"No, no. Carry on!" Dorothy laughed, wary of upsetting him. It turned out that he was right and she was wrong. Once they'd tramped through the rain, all down Mercury Street, across Pickney Green (quite a walk in itself) and down Manton Road, they were soaked through and very happy to be let in by Mrs. Lloyd, who was beyond delighted at seeing Patrick safe and well. She had a room free which she was very happy to rent to Dorothy until they found their feet as a couple, and said that they could stay as long as they needed.

"Now, there won't be a chaperone. I should state that from the off – I expect you to be responsible, because I will not be around to monitor you. I know that you are young, and in love, but real life does take priority. Understood?" Mrs. Lloyd said. She went on to set a few ground rules and a curfew (exceptions to be made for their work shifts) and then bade them good day and left them to it. Dorothy couldn't help grinning. She was on her way to becoming an individual!

CHAPTER 4 – 1919

Patrick had woken up the morning after and wondered what on Earth he had just done. What on Earth had he signed himself up to? He'd barely been in Monthill a few days, and yet already he had got himself a sweetheart. It was all too much, too soon, and that was why, on the second of January, after giving it a few days, he did what he did.

Dorothy, meanwhile, was infatuated. They'd barely left the house since the start of their courtship, aside from work, choosing instead to stay inside and get to know each other. They were in their own little bubble, Dorothy said poetically in her diary, hiding from the outside world. Time meant nothing as they chatted the days away, telling each other everything that they could think of about their childhoods, their own little quirks, what they liked the most. They hadn't kissed again, though – Dorothy had tried to drop some hints, but Patrick seemed determined to keep his distance. *Playing hard-to-get*, she'd heard it called.

It was working. She was head over heels in love. It was hard to believe that they had only known each other for a few days – she felt like she had known him forever. It was scary, being in love. She didn't understand it – simply being next to him made her head swim. She was out of her depth, out of control, but she liked it. It was new to her, and all she wanted at that time was for Patrick to feel the same way about her as she did about him. She just wanted to forget the world and stay in their little bubble, write their own love story, and craft a life for themselves like an intricate piece of art.

Not an ounce of her was given over to reality, and that was what made the bombshell hurt even more. Patrick had experienced that, when he was first training for war, which was why he was so cautious with Dorothy now, and maybe why he felt the way he did. Dorothy had heard nothing from Wilhelmina and Charlie – they were keeping their distance, waiting to see what became of the relationship. But Dorothy found that she didn't mind their absence – being with Patrick was enough.

But Patrick did not reciprocate these feelings, because like her, he felt out of control, but unlike her, he hated it. He'd not been in his right mind that Sunday, and he'd simply clung to her like a life raft in a storm. She'd simply been in the right place at the right time, and in his damaged state, he'd pushed it that little bit too far, and plunged them both into entirely new territory as a result. Reflecting on it in the days since, he'd felt more and more guilty, and he decided that he had to put things right before she fell any deeper.

All of this he explained to her, with as much tact as he could, over a cup of tea that Thursday morning before he went to work. She put down her cup and became quite motionless as he carried on talking.

"The truth is… I've been leading you on, Dorothy. I just can't see a way forward, can you? You're only eighteen – you should keep your options open. You're too good to waste on me, the first boy you ever meet. It would be best, for you, to simply turn over the page, dismiss this one as a mere tester, and move on to better things."

"I've been leading you on, Dorothy." That's what he'd said. Dorothy's world shifted.

"Who's to say that..." she began, but had to stop. Tears were threatening to choke her. She tried again a couple of times, but she just could not get her mouth to form words. So she reached for her diary, last year's one which had a few spare pages for extra notes at the back, and tore one out. She picked up the nearest pencil and began to write. She found it so much easier when she didn't have to look at him, and could focus on making her writing neat and legible instead.

Who's to say that I don't want you to lead me on?

She stopped, tapped her pencil on her lips for her second, and then carried on writing.

You've given me a direction to go, and something to strive for. I've been trying to please you, to convince you that I am the right person for you. I suppose it's been good to have a purpose. Before I met you, I'd been thinking quite a lot about the future, and wondering if I'd ever find someone that I wanted to spend the rest of my life with. And now I have. It's you, and that's why I've clung to you. Why would I want to go ahead on my own? Why would I want to live without you?

"Oh, dear. Do I have to get out the handkerchiefs?" Patrick chuckled nervously, trying to think of something to say after reading the note. Dorothy stared straight at him, hardly believing that he could be so jovial after reading her deepest thoughts. He looked away and sighed. "It's just too fast, Dorothy. I don't see how you think that this could work."

She knew that if she tried to speak, she would just end up making a fool of herself by weeping, and so she turned back to the page.

Because I believe in fairy-tale endings. The prince has saved the princess, and now they can live happily ever after.

"But I..." Patrick said, then almost laughed at the absurdity of what he was about to say, "But I'm like the princess, out of *The Princess and the Pea*. Something just feels wrong, so to put it right and make both the prince and princess happy, they have to do something about it."

They live happily ever after, though, in the end. And we can, too. All it takes is a little commitment from us both. I admit that I've jumped in head-first, but I don't regret it. We could be like characters in a novel, sticking together through thick and thin, never apart. But let's not let our lives be one of those frustrating books where the couple are constantly flitting between on and off, so much that the reader is close to giving up, willing them to just get together and get on with it. To avoid that, answer this: do you want to be with me, or not?

Truth be told, Dorothy didn't even know what she wanted any more. She was really out of her depth, struggling to stay afloat, trying not to let her emotions drown her. She didn't want to keep Patrick with her against his will, so she decided to let him make the ultimate decision.

And after reading her question, Patrick didn't know either. What she was saying was naïve and the ramblings of a young fledgling, but that was the appeal of it. It made even the most staunchly undemonstrative man want to keep her under his wing and hold her close forever. He had to admit that he was starting to regret starting this whole conversation. He was starting to see it how she saw it, and he didn't know what to say.

He still hadn't answered her question. Dorothy watched him open his mouth, then close it again, then gaze absentmindedly at the clock. *How hard is it to say?* she began to write, then stopped because he'd leapt out of his seat, muttering "I'm going to be late for work."

He made for the door, then turned around.

"Let me think on it, Dorothy. Stay here, and I'll have an answer for you tonight."

And with that, he was gone, leaving Dorothy speechless. At

first, she felt elated – after all, it hadn't been a straight no. He was reconsidering, at least. But then, around fifteen minutes after he'd gone, her happiness ran out. But it wasn't replaced by tears – rather, by a peculiar burning rage. She fought the urge to scream, instead choosing to stare in the mirror and make all sorts of hideous expressions in a hope that laughter would chase away the anger. But it didn't work.

Who did he think he was, messing her about like this? He'd waltzed into her life as if he owned the place, and now he had taken her heart and was trying to worm his way back out again. He had led her on, and now he was bored, and dropping her for some other poor woman. And just to get himself off the hook, he was painting himself as the long-suffering, silent martyr. He was trying to make himself seem kind and self-sac-rificing. For all Dorothy knew, he might never have even liked her in the first place – she'd just been a convenient stepping-stone, a way for him to get back into practice after the war. He was probably going to come back and beg for forgiveness, tell-ing her that he was the one in pain, that he hadn't thought it through, and that of *course* he wanted her.

The Dorothy of half an hour ago would have been over the moon, and life would have returned to the new normal. But now, Dorothy merely needed peeling off the roof. With that, she decided to be her own suffragist and demand the equal-ity that was so noticeably missing from their relationship. She stood up and swept out of the living room, rebelliously leaving the two empty cups on the tea-table. She strode up to her room, where most of her belongings were still packed. It took less than ten minutes for her to gather her things, write two quick notes (one for Mrs. Lloyd, apologising and explaining, and one for Patrick) and marched out of the front door with her bag.

It was only when she'd reached home and knocked on the door twice, to no answer, that she remembered that nobody was home. Wilhelmina was at work, and Charlie was at his first interview of the year. Dorothy had walked off all her anger, leaving just a vast empty space in her mind, and so she simply stopped. For the first time in her life, she had absolutely no idea where to go now. She couldn't stay outside for the next five hours, waiting for Wilhelmina – she'd freeze to death. Dorothy leant against the front door with her back to it, racking her brains for somewhere to go.

And then she remembered Katharina. She hadn't seen her for a good few years, but she still remembered where she lived – on Round Street. She'd visited her there a few years back, when Katharina had had influenza and been unable to go to the suffragist meeting. Dorothy knew that an arranged marriage had been on the horizon for her – she just hoped that Katharina, or her lovely Nurse, was still there. It was her only hope.

Dorothy knocked on the door, her heart in her mouth. Katharina's jaw dropped when she opened it, as she took in the young woman that she hadn't seen for a few years with a big bag.

"Don't worry, I'm not askin' to stay," Dorothy laughed, before they hugged.

"Oh my – I never thought I'd see you again. It's so good to see you!"

"Well, I've locked meself out for the first time ever, an' ye were the first person I thought of, so…"

"I must introduce you to my husband when he gets home – he's lovely." Katharina said in that affable manner that had appealed to Dorothy in the first place. "I've landed well on my feet with him. And how old are you now? It won't be long before you're on your way to marriage, Dotty!"

That was all she needed. Dorothy burst into tears, and that was the end of all small talk. While she wept and ranted on and on about Patrick, it was all Katharina could do to keep up with the handkerchief requirement.

"But did he actually say that? What did he actually *say*?" she kept asking, every time Dorothy speculated on what it meant.

"What do ye mean?" Dorothy asked eventually, wiping her sore eyes for the millionth time.

"Do you want me to be a good friend, or a bad one?" Katharina replied.

"What do ye mean?" Dorothy repeated.

"A bad friend will lick your wounds and tell you exactly what you want to hear. A good friend will read you like a book and tell you the truth, even at risk of the entire friendship. Which friend would you like me to be right now?"

"Th' second, I suppose."

"In that case, I think that you are massively over-reacting, Dotty. You've jumped to far too many conclusions, and you've spent too long pondering what he means, and not long enough on how you can keep both of you happy. At the end of the day, you can't force him to stay with you. In almost every aspect of society, men are still above women, and I'm sure he will use that to his advantage."

"So… you don't think he's an opportunistic little so-an'-so, then?" Dorothy responded, with a little laugh.

"No, I think that he's a gallant young man who has your best interests at heart – and some severe self-esteem issues. Fancy thinking that he's setting you free! Can't he see what you see?"

"But after all this… I don't know if I can forgive him."

They went around in circles like this for hours, until the clock struck four. Dorothy thanked Katharina and left, still no closer to knowing what to do. But Katharina had given her some food for thought, and Dorothy spent the entire walk home pondering it all. By the time she got home, there was still nobody there, so Dorothy sunk down on the front doorstep and wondered just how she had got herself into this mess. A week ago, life had been great. And now her heart had been shattered.

Dorothy huddled up against the door and shut her eyes, trying to calm her racing mind. But no matter how hard she tried, her mind was writhing like a kaleidoscope, trying to make sense of the huge disillusion the last few days had turned out to be. Katharina had prepared her as best she could for the crash, saying that it would hurt for a few days, then the wounds would heal, merely leaving a scar that would fade. But Dorothy knew that it wouldn't be like that for her – how could Katharina comment when she'd never even felt exactly how Dorothy felt? She hadn't even met Patrick. Dorothy regretted going to her – she was left with more questions than answers. All she wanted, at that moment, was Patrick himself.

At some point, she must have dozed, for she woke up with a start, and with Patrick's face etched onto her eyeballs. He was wearing that haunted expression that he had worn at the river-bank, and her heart twisted with a strange protective instinct that she hadn't been aware of until now.

When Wilhelmina and Charlie arrived, having met up by chance on the way home, they both knew better than to say anything. It was just like any normal evening, aside from the hug that Wilhelmina gave Dorothy when it was time to go to bed. "Let him go now, Dotty," she whispered. Dorothy nodded and went up to bed, but she knew that nothing would ever be the same again. Patrick's face was there with her whenever she was in the dark, and she couldn't stand it. She slept with a candle burning, in the end.

And what about Patrick himself? He had arrived home, exhausted after a day of trying to act normal in front of Wilhelmina. Dorothy was gone, and he didn't know what to think. He'd been prepared to agree to give it another go, but now that she was gone, he didn't know whether to be relieved or dismayed. There was a note on his bed.

If you really wanted me, you would have said so.

And in the corner of the paper was a scrawly, cartoon version of a handkerchief. Patrick had to smile.

. . .

The next morning, it was as if nothing had ever happened. Dorothy and Wilhelmina both left the house, ready for their shift at work. Luckily, this was one of the days where Dorothy did not share a shift with Patrick. She knew that she would have to face him tomorrow, but for today, she decided to let her heart heal a little.

That was, until Patrick turned up at lunchtime. He let himself in through the side door, in his work uniform, saying that he wanted to work overtime. The manager was dubious, but nodded. Dorothy had the fright of her life when she rounded a corner with a stack of empty plates to be confronted by the very man she had been trying to forget.

"Can we talk later? Please?" was all Patrick got in before Dorothy set her mouth and brushed past impatiently, muttering that she had work to do.

But he caught her on her lunch break and followed her into the staff room.

"I think it's time to explain myself," he said, sitting Dorothy down on a chair and then sitting down himself. Wilhelmina walked in and, upon seeing Patrick and Dorothy together, walked promptly back out again.

"No explainin' necessary." Dorothy said briskly. "Yer lack of reply said it all."

"Things are different now, Dorothy-"

"It's been twenty-four hours. How different can it be? An' ye can stop the clichés right now, because I'm not fallin' for it. I trusted you – an' yesterday, it was like I didn't know who you were!"

All this was said in tones of absolute fury. It was like all the emotions from yesterday all flooded back at once and solidified in a mass of pure outrage.

"Believe me, Dorothy, I'm sorry. But-"

"There are no buts. Any man who can wreak havoc on me like that isn't worth another thought."

"Can we at least talk?"

"I can't believe that I ever trusted you. Ye can forget yer pathetic apology, because that is nowhere near sufficient to compensate for what I went through yesterday. Even if I took ye back, what's to stop ye doin' it all over again? One day of that is enough, and I know that I am worth more than that."

Each word was said in an ice-cold, emphatic tone, and it knocked Patrick for six. It was the feistiness that had attracted him in the first place, only this time it was without the eggshell-treading caution with which she had negotiated before. But the inner Bruce Hammond in him swelled with rage, and Patrick heard his voice start up an aggravated chorus in his mind.

Half of him was abhorred by what this woman thought of herself. Was this what the suffrage movement had done? Was this the future of women? But then the other half knew that what she was saying was true, and starting to admire her for pushing him back into his place. And he was also admiring her for getting it all out into the open, something which he hadn't had the courage to do in the first place.

"Dorothy...?"

"I don't need to hear yer voice any more, so get out!" Dorothy erupted, shouting these words in a raw, unrestrained explosion. There was nothing left for Patrick to say, so he slunk out, hoping that the manager wouldn't see him. Dorothy's eyes were dry. Before, her tears had signalled that she was too invested, but now, their absence meant that she'd run out of ways to care. She ate, then carried on with her day as if nothing had happened. Wilhelmina kept a close eye on her, and noticed a line between her eyebrows. For this reason, she suggested that Dorothy stop off at the library on the way home, and pick out a new book to borrow. "I've heard that new book *Spinster* is good. Herbert Jenkins, is it?"

Dorothy shot her mother a look, and Wilhelmina wanted the ground to open up and swallow her as she realised what she had just said. Just as Wilhelmina was about to apologise for her thoughtlessness, Dorothy said evenly, "That's a good idea, Mam. Will you come with me?"

It had been so long since Wilhelmina and Dorothy had taken a trip to the library together – Wilhelmina realised that as the librarian greeted them cheerily with "Haven't seen you two in a while!" She waited until she and Dorothy were hidden behind a shelf before enveloping Dorothy in a tight hug, just making the most of having her there before she was off again with some other man. Dorothy reminded Wilhelmina of herself at that age, and she just knew that Dorothy would pick herself up, dust herself off, and set off again – with Patrick, or without him.

The library was different to others in that it had an entire shelf of recently published books – that was, books that had been published within the last year. The book that Wilhelmina had recommended was there, and Dorothy picked up another one – and at the very title she knew that this would be the one to bring her a new perspective. A wartime tale about shell-shock, and the effects it had on not just the soldier, but every-one surrounding him. Dorothy sat down at a table with it, and felt like her heart would fall out of her chest as she realised that she had ensured that her soldier would never return.

The librarian watched her sit down, stare at the front cover and then cover her own face with her hands. She exchanged looks with Wilhelmina, and automatically presumed that poor Dorothy, who she had known since she was a baby, had lost a soldier of her own to war. Wilhelmina sat down at a nearby table and let Dorothy sit there and open the book, close enough to keep an eye but far enough away to give her some space.

Normally, the librarian would not have let someone read the book right there and then without checking it out, but she made an exception for what she presumed was a grieving sweetheart. She let Dorothy sit there and immerse herself in the world of the characters. Even when it got dark and it went way past closing time, she didn't dare try and shut up shop for fear of spoiling the peace in that room between the three of them. Even when Katharina saw the light on and came to check that everything was all right, she pointed to Dorothy, put her finger to her lips and made them mime "Shh."

Eventually, Dorothy began to show signs of stirring – but only to wipe her eyes, as the last page of the book was very moving. At this point, Katharina, who had been sitting with Wilhelmina, got up and walked past Dorothy, brushing her shoulder unintentionally on the way past, and she looked up.

And later that night, Dorothy wondered just how Katharina had done it. After all, she'd never met Patrick. But somehow, she made the stars align so that Dorothy looked up straight into the face of Patrick, her soldier. She folded into his arms, without even saying a word, and knew straight away that here was where she belonged, with him, and that she was there to stay.

. . .

As the beautiful cherry tree outside Mrs. Lloyd's house blossomed over time, so did Dorothy and Patrick. Their unexpected split had pushed them closer together – but even so, it still wasn't all plain sailing. An alarming new symptom of Patrick's shellshock had appeared. He had lashed out at Dorothy when she had walked in on him one night in some sort of daze, with a petrified expression on his face. Startled, he had become agitated and started to shout at her. But Dorothy hadn't been deterred, only concerned, and had provided him with a glass of water while trying to calm him. He revealed, once he had calmed down, that these attacks had been increasing in frequency and intensity.

"It's as if a ball of fire is wedged in my throat – right about here," he explained, indicating the space where the neck meets the collarbone, "and no matter how hard I swallow, it doesn't budge. Then I start to panic, thinking that I'm about to choke or throw up, or that it's going to be there forever and eventually impair my breathing."

Dorothy, like a dutiful sweetheart, stayed stoically by his side as he fought his way through each episode. They did not occur every day – more like twice a week. But Patrick was constantly paranoid that every trivial thing would set him off. There was no known trigger; the smallest thing would initiate the recollection of a horrible memory, and that was the end of all rational thought for the next few hours. And they were terrifying when they happened: nausea, chest tightening, uncontrollable shaking, the lot. Patrick had what was later known as Post-Traumatic Stress Disorder.

It was known as "shellshock" to Patrick – but he could not even bear to say the word. At war, they had been taught that shellshock sufferers were merely inflicted with cowardice, and could be shot for it. At war, his condition hadn't been as noticeable – after all, they were hallucinations of scenes of war. But it was when he was back in England, and perfectly safe, that he suddenly realised that his mind had been affected by the war and was going haywire.

But one evening – specifically, Saturday the first of March 1919 – one episode led to what would be the making of his life. The nausea had been coming in waves throughout the day, but he'd just put it down to something that he'd eaten. After he got in from work at about half past three, with Dorothy having just started her shift, he decided to have a quiet evening to himself. After dinner, he sat down with a drink and a novel – a relatively new one about war.

At second glance, it probably wasn't the best literature, subject-wise, for Patrick to have picked up. But he'd just made himself comfortable, with a whisky in one hand and the book in the other, and he wasn't planning to get up any time soon.

It was at around halfway through the book that another draining wave of nausea hit. Patrick sighed – he'd thought that they'd passed. He put his book and drink down and readjusted himself. He then felt the first feelings of panic rising, that solid mass assembling in his throat, and sat bolt upright.

"Come on, Hammond." he told himself firmly, "Pull yourself together."

But he couldn't stop the twitching of his muscles, and soon, he began to hear clatters, and moans, and the roaring of flying weapons that were ready to claim lives. He shut his eyes and saw the mud and gore of Passchendaele, and felt the persistent, driving rain against his face, and smelled things that are too horrific to name. He physically could not open his eyes – it was as if God was fusing them tight shut, forcing Patrick to take responsibility for what he had signed himself up for.

By the time Dorothy got in, Patrick had managed to open his eyes, but the rest of his body was still frozen. He was vaguely aware, with a small fraction of his mind, of Dorothy's key in the door and her light footsteps cantering up the stairs, but the rest of his mind was still in France.

"Only me!" Dorothy called, opening Patrick's door. She stopped dead upon seeing him staring into space, a barely touched drink resting on top of a book on the table in front of him. She was even more alarmed to see that he'd undone his top button. Normally, he kept every button meticulously done up, and himself immaculately groomed in general, so this was shocking in itself. She took off her coat and hung it up, then went over to him. She warily touched his arm, which helped to bring him back a little.

"Do you want to talk to me, then?" she murmured softly, trying to help him adjust to the sounds of reality again. In a kitten-weak voice that, over time, became stronger, he replied.

"All right. I'll talk."

"Tell me how ye feel."

"It's different to anything I've ever felt before. I knew what was happening, before. I knew that it would pass. But right now, I don't know if or when it will pass."

He paused, trying to form words.

"It's been coming on all day, I think. I've been feeling unmoored, somehow. I can cope with the other episodes, Dot. I can now. But I couldn't before I met you. The first one I had was awful – I remember thinking that I was on my deathbed, and that nobody in my family would ever know because I was stuck in France. I suppose… I suppose I was frightened."

He said that last sentence as if it pained him to admit it.

"Anyone would have been-"

He interrupted her. His voice was louder now, clearer, more emphatic.

"And I know you've said it wasn't my fault. I know you said that Maxwell's death was down to his failure to pray, but do you know what I keep thinking? What if it had been dark?"

He spat out the last sentence as if it had been burning his lips, and maybe it had.

"What… what d'ye mean?" Dorothy said.

"If it had been dark, then I would have had an excuse for stumbling with him. I would have been able to blame it on poor visibility. But no – it was dusk, a beautiful sunset, and I could see my fellow soldiers in the distance, searching for life. I could see every ridge – I can see it right now in my mind. I don't have an excuse now – I'm a murderer!"

Dorothy put her arms around him, regardless of his affection policy. He took it for a couple of seconds, then pulled back violently, rearing back like a captured horse.

"But it is dark now!" he said, and now his words all started to run into each other, and Dorothy had trouble working out what he was saying. "There's no escape, nobody who understands, nothing to do to stop Maxwell's last moments haunting me like some ubiquitous being. I'm stuck like this forever and I really wish that I'd jumped into that lake!"

With that ending, he stamped off, presumably to the bathroom, leaving Dorothy to pour away the remains of the whisky and tidy up his room ready for him to get into bed. But just before she was about to go to bed herself, he came back in again: calm, composed and looking for all the world like he'd been peacefully reading all evening.

"Marry me." he said, taking the book out of Dorothy's hand and placing it back on the table.

"Eh?" she replied, thinking she'd misheard him.

"I've been waiting for the perfect opportunity. I know we've only been courting for three months, but I never want to lose you, not after all you've given me. That's why I'm asking you here and now: will you marry me?"

He fell to one knee.

"Say it one more time…" Dorothy said, wanting to savour this delicious moment for ever.

"Will you marry me?"

Dorothy waited until he'd got to the end of the sentence, paused for half a second, then responded with what he'd been wanting to hear ever since they'd got back together.

"Yes! Yes, yes, yes!"

As they embraced, Dorothy knew that she'd remember the evening of the first day of March 1919, for her whole life and longer, for she was finally engaged to be married. And all because of a book, Patrick mused. It was strange how a few pieces of paper and some ink could have the ability to change lives.

. . .

Edna was in a rather pensive mood, as she often was nowadays. Whether it was the fact that she was getting older, or the fact that she was fading away through hunger, she didn't know. This latter reason was to do with the fact that Bruce had been restricting her portions more than ever, in some sort of crazed control rampage. He'd tightened the noose in all respects recently. She knew that his way was the right and natural way of things, as she'd been taught, but if ever she got a glimpse of the newspaper, she became more and more aware of what women were getting up to nowadays.

At times she longed for things to be different in the world: for a world where people were not restricted or treated unfairly simply because they were not born as male. In many ways, men and women were exactly the same. Except for a few physical differences, they all functioned in the same way. They all ate. They all slept. They all breathed. It was just a couple of minute differences that defined whether they would be confined to the house, with minimal rights and barely a penny to their own names, or allowed to move freely and decide the future of their poor, battered country.

Now that women had the vote, Edna was rather sad. She had always fantasised about being a suffragette, and several of her more pleasant dreams saw her standing at a podium, gesturing wildly with her arms as she reduced grown men to tears.

Then there was the subject of Patrick, of course. For the past four and a half years, his name had barely been mentioned. She hoped against hope that he was alive. But she knew that in reality, there was hardly any chance of this. Since the war had ended, she'd half expected a letter from him. But no, all of the post went straight to Bruce, and if there had been one, it would have been ashes in the kitchen fireplace within minutes of its arrival, she speculated.

At least, that was what she'd thought until that one wonderful morning. She'd just dressed and was trying to shake herself out of her miserable mood when she heard a roar from downstairs. It was coming from the kitchen, so it must have been even louder down there. It sounded like an animal had broken loose – and in a way, it had. Bruce was sitting at one of the worktops, a piece of paper in his hand, his mouth opening and shutting like some species of fish. The cooks had disappeared to the cellar in an attempt to avoid his wrath.

"Bruce? What on Earth has happened?" she said, taking the letter from his hand. He made a protesting noise, which in his current daze was no more than a mere squeak. Edna read the letter, and soon she was in a slightly more dignified equivalent of Bruce's state.

Mr. and Mrs. Bruce Hammond are cordially invited
to the wedding of

MR. PATRICK STANLEY HAMMOND

and

MISS. DOROTHY SUSAN FOX

on

SATURDAY 21ST JUNE 1919, at ten in the morning

at

ST. MARGARET'S CHURCH, MONTHILL, MANCHESTER.

For some minutes, Edna and Bruce were unable to speak, move or do anything other than wheeze. Edna, however, found tears escaping her eyelids. Joyous as she may been, she knew that there was not a chance of Bruce permitting any members of his family to go to the wedding of the disgraced son. Unless...

"I'll ask the maid to dispose of this post-haste, Bruce." she said in as steely a voice as she could manage. He nodded.

"Excellent – do so." he replied, sounding starved of oxygen.

But Edna did no such thing! She took it up to their bedroom and, turning her pillow over, opened her pillow case and, being careful not to tear Patrick's letter from the battlefields, slid the card alongside it.

But she wondered how she would even get Bruce to the wedding. A cunning plan, she decided, something that one would only hear about in fiction. She decided to contact her only friend, Maude Downe (she of the gossiping tendencies) for help. Maude was the only friend that Bruce had permitted her to contact since their move. Since then, they hadn't seen each other, but they exchanged fortnightly letters.

So Edna went to the drawer where she kept her flowery writing paper and took out two sheets. She filled up her pen with ink and went to sit in the drawing room, which was out-of-bounds to the children apart from at mealtimes, and therefore a place where she wouldn't be disturbed.

Just as she'd finished writing Maude's name, Bruce came in and looked over her shoulder.

"Who are you writing to? Not replying to Patrick's feeble invitation, I hope?" he said as he approached.

"Of course not – why would I want to?" she replied, trying not to flutter her eyelids (an old habit of hers from her newlywed days when she'd had no reason to be deceptive).

"Well, I know how attached you were to him…"

"Not any more, Bruce. I am quite finished with that boy. He's neglected his family and left them thinking that he was dead. To send a wedding invitation after four years of silence just takes the biscuit!"

Oh, she hated herself. She loathed herself with every single one of those words. But it had to be done. Bruce smiled: a proper, satisfied smile. Finally, his wife had seen sense.

"I quite agree. I can see now that you're just writing to Maude. Carry on!"

Edna waited until he'd left the room before settling down to write.

Dearest Maude,

This letter is sent to you with the best of wishes and hope that Matilda's baby is growing well. I am aware that it is your turn to write, but alas, I have somewhat of a predicament.

We found out this morning that our Patrick is alive and well, and engaged to be married in June, somewhere in Manchester. We have received an invitation to the wedding, and we were rather stunned! Bruce does not want to attend – but on this occasion, I am going to brave it and overrule my husband.

For this, I need your assistance. Would you be so kind as to send us a letter, inviting us to yours, asking us to arrive very early in the morning on Saturday 21st June? The wedding itself is at ten, but it will take a lot longer to get to Manchester than it will to get to you! Of course, the invitation has no need to be legitimate, as although I will reply in the affirmative to confirm that we have received it, we will not be coming. My plan is to have our driver drive us up to Manchester in the carriage at a good pace so that we can make the wedding in time.

Aside from this predicament, this letter leaves us well and hopes to find you all the same.

With best wishes, your dear friend,

Edna.

She sealed and stamped the letter and gave it to the driver to post when he went to collect the vegetables. Her pensive mood was gone. She realised now that the cause of her sorrow had been the supposed death of her second son.

. . .

"Our Dot's growing up, Mina," Charlie sighed as he slid the watercolour out of its frame and replaced it with the wedding invitation. It was a strange thing to do, but they both felt it necessary, as they knew that in the future they would look back and remember the feelings associated with it.

It was unusual feeling, that one. Part of it was sadness. The days of interrogating Dorothy about her admirers were long gone. Their daughter didn't even live with them these days. Wilhelmina saw her at work, of course, and she'd been to Mrs Lloyd's to see them a few times, but their relationship wasn't quite the same. Charlie hadn't seen her since the day she got back together with Patrick, still struggling to come to terms with the fact that she wasn't his little girl any more. He knew that he'd have to come to terms with it by the time the wedding came around, but until then he was in a state of disapproval. But he was definitely going to attend – Wilhelmina would see to that!

Another part of the feeling was intense pride. Wilhelmina had only married aged twenty-seven, after years of being told that she was destined to be a spinster, so she was overjoyed that her Dot had had the courage to strike out on her own so young. It was plain that she cared for Patrick dearly, and Wilhelmina was proud that her daughter was so compassionate. She also relished being able to announce to her friends that her daughter was engaged, and also took every opportunity to nonchalantly drop it into conversation – "Well, when our Dot gets married..."

But then there was a fraction of being overwhelmed. It didn't seem five minutes since Dorothy had regularly wreaked havoc in Charlie's study, or groomed Monty clumsily with an old comb clutched in her little hand. And how, suddenly, she was this beautiful, slim young lady. Barely an adult, she had been snapped up by a man who was rather a cut above the Fox family. And indeed, a man who Wilhelmina barely knew. She intended to get to know him well after the wedding.

Dorothy herself was delirious with excitement already. The wedding, obviously, would not be a lavish affair. She and Patrick had had a long discussion about what they wanted to do after they wed: stay in Manchester, go to Houghton Regis, or go off their families' beaten tracks and go somewhere else. Dorothy was decidedly in favour of the latter, because after eighteen years of Monthill, she was tired of it. Patrick wasn't the biggest fan of Monthill, but he disliked great change.

"Well, what d'ye most want to do in yer life?" Dorothy had asked him sincerely.

Patrick had found that question quite hard to answer, because he'd never had much of a plan. He knew that Father-Sir had never worked because of a sudden inheritance. Mother had worked in a newsagent until marrying Father-Sir. Patrick had never gone to school; all five children had been tutored until the age of sixteen. Goodness only knew what the tutor had thought when Patrick had disappeared. To be fair, Patrick had never been Pupil of the Week, so the man had probably been glad to see the back of him!

"I suppose I've always been interested in the great outdoors. Father-Sir says that we must all do our bit at some point to tend to the world God made for us. Our garden felt like Eden in the summer – it even had its own pear tree!"

"I thought that th' tree in Eden grew apples?"

"That is a popular belief," agreed Patrick, "but nowhere in the Bible does it actually say as much. But I've always been interested in all botanical matters – and animals. I rode a few horses now and again at home… that was years ago, though. What about you – any aspirations that we could build on?"

"Well, I've always wanted t' be a farmer's wife," Dorothy laughed, "because I'd have no responsibilities other than cookin' an' cleanin'."

Patrick smiled and gave her a hug. It was rather spontaneous, but they both liked that.

"I suppose I can always inquire into a few little farming properties here and there," he said.

After a slightly more grinding and reality-based discussion later that week, Patrick made some inquiries and found a beautiful little farm in a village called Little Wychwood about forty-five minutes train ride from where Patrick's parents lived. It came about that the owners were in quite a hurry to get rid of the property, and wanted the deal done before they left the country in July. A date for a viewing was arranged for early April.

. . .

They decided to make a day of it. Dorothy was wildly excited, as was Patrick (although the latter did not show it, instead remaining cautious). They caught the train at six o'clock in the morning, as their viewing was at eleven and they wanted to be there in plenty of time. It was a good one hundred and fifty miles from Manchester to Bedfordshire, and around four hours in a steam train. They were there in plenty of time and met Mr. Large, the owner of the farm, at the train station in Wychwood.

"The farm hasn't been used as a farm for as long as we've had it, but the soil is exceptionally good for growing crops." he told them as they drove into Little Wychwood in a horse-drawn cab.

"Do ye live in Little Wychwood, then?" Dorothy asked, nodding and smiling at a passer-by, wanting to make a good impression.

"Oh no, of course not. Far too quiet and dull for me. I live back in Wychwood, where we've just come from. You'll always be able to tell which road leads to it – the cobbles are far neater, for one thing! Little Wychwood is rather rustic, made up of a gigantic grass square in the middle with roads going all off it."

Dorothy and Patrick listened to a little of the village's history, and asked about the church.

"Ah yes, the church! Reverend Osbourne is a very good man, and the congregation are devout, so you have nothing to fear with them! That's the church – just there, see? Now, we're just going to take this road – that's Onyx Lane – and shortly, we will drive past a big metal gate which leads out of one of our fields."

Indeed they did, and Patrick and Dorothy were very impressed by the size of the field they could see. It was pretty much sectioned off by hedges, but it was a good size.

They travelled a little further, and they came to a pretty house that could have come straight out of Hansel and Gretel. The brickwork was the colour of gingerbread, with a door that could have been made of solid chocolate. It was the gate to this house that Mr. Large opened, and the path leading to this that they all proceeded to walk down. He produced a key and put it in the lock. It turned, but stiffly.

Their first impressions of the hallway were not quite as dazzling. A thick layer of dust covered all available objects, including the banisters. Mr. Large went in and unlocked all three doors that came off the hallway. The first room that they went in was the living room, which was the door on the right at the bottom of the stairs. It was quite small, and consisted merely of a fireplace and two chairs either side of it. The curtains were rather threadbare, and the windows were dirty, but Dorothy liked the cosiness of the room. With a roaring fire and maybe a piano, and a good scrub of everything, it would be a perfect little room for a cold winter's night.

The next room they visited was the dining room, directly opposite the living room. It was one's average dining room, with a brown table and four matching chairs, two each side of it. There was a quite a lot of excess room in there – the table could have been twice its size and it still would have fit. Again, it was quite gloomy, and dark until Mr. Large wrenched the curtain back.

The kitchen, though, was perfect. It was a lot more spacious, with a very big table in the centre and a marvellously deep oven. It was right at the top of the hallway and its width was the width of the entire house. The back door was on the right, and next to it was a cupboard. Dorothy realised why the living room was so small compared to the dining room – the cupboard made up the excess room.

"If you two are thinking of a family, then that cupboard could get very full of little shoes and coats..." Mr. Large said meaningfully. Dorothy looked uneasy for she and Patrick hadn't discussed this yet.

"I can certainly see that happening," Patrick put in with a laugh, shooting Dorothy a warning look to keep her from protesting.

"Well, this kitchen really is lovely," she interrupted, changing the subject.

And it was. The only downside was the fact that when Patrick turned on the kitchen tap, out surged a stream of disgustingly murky brown water! Since the property hadn't been lived in for several years, this was understandable.

Then they went upstairs and got a very pleasant surprise! For straight at the top of the landing, above the kitchen, was a bathroom! Dorothy had never had one of these before, and she marvelled at it. It was very small, consisting of a lavatory, a sink and a chipped old bathtub, but it meant that they wouldn't have to run to the outhouse, in the rain, at ridiculous-o'clock in the morning (or lug a chamber pot for hours on the train).

"It doesn't take that long to get used to," Patrick laughed, seeing Dorothy's incredulous face. "We have two at Highmore Park, and you would be surprised at how quickly we adjusted when we moved."

"Oh, I say! Quite the aristocrat!" replied Mr. Large a little stiffly, shutting the door and walking to the other end of the landing to open another. It was the door of the master bedroom, which was comfortably furnished with a double bed and a bedside table each side of it. The tables each balanced a small candleholder, with enough room for one other thing such as a cup of tea.

The other two bedrooms were equally pleasant. There was a larger one and a smaller one, the bigger one being at the back next to the bathroom, and the smaller one in the middle of the two others. The bigger of the two could have fit in four small beds and two wardrobes, but as it was, there was only half that. The other had room for two beds – three at a push – and a wardrobe and a chest of drawers. It all felt rather cramped, but Dorothy liked that. Patrick did, too. It made a change from the spacious Highmore Park, in which there was almost too much space that nobody knew what to do with. This house gave one the feeling of being secure, like they were in their own little nest.

They went outside, out the back door, and were submerged in green (and a bit of brown). Directly out of the door was the back yard, which was paved over and consisted of a row of sheds, each painted a different colour. They were empty, but useful for extra storage. They followed the path of stones, straight on from the back door, to the gap in the hedge. Here, the path disappeared into a primarily grassy path. They were glad that they'd worn their oldest clothes, for the moment they squeezed through the gap, they sunk a little into the mud.

Mr. Large took them left first, and walked them along a good way until the hedge turned into plain white fencing with two fields either side of them. It was a bit of an uphill walk – but worth it. They could see the horizon for miles either side. They were told that further up there were the hills where livestock could graze, and back behind them were some smaller fields for planting crops. As it was, the field on one side had wheat growing, and the other had barley. Mr. Large informed them that every year, a retired farmer planted wheat and barley on the farm to do his bit for the village. There were golden crops as far as the eye could see.

At this point, Mr. Large leant on the fence post and began talking to them in great detail about the harvesting process. The wheat would be harvested in July or early August – the retired farmer had planted early this year after learning that the farm was on the market. The wheat would then be taken to the mill a few miles away and ground into flour. There would be enough of the flour – "and I suggest that you bag it up and keep it in one of those sheds" – to make bread and other baked goods for months. Dorothy's heart leapt for she loved baking and there had been a fair few recipes running through her family for generations.

They walked on and viewed the livestock fields, which were set over the rolling hills. Patrick's heart leapt this time for he could just see himself with a sheepdog, shouting out commands whilst the dog neatly rounded up sheep. He breathed in at that moment, and he could almost taste the new life that they could have. He knew that he wanted this life – and Dorothy did, too.

There was nothing beyond the fields, they were assured. That land did not belong to Rosewood Farm. The house was quaintly but ironically named Rosewood Farm Cottage. Dorothy smiled – there was nothing cottage-like about it: it was a house, fair and simple. However, she adored the rustic charm of such a name and shivered with excitement when she remembered that this life could be hers.

They turned around and started walking back down, talking about the village. It was rather an eccentric set-up, they were told. It was as if the village had been forgotten by all who lived there as it was completely cut off, leading to absolutely nowhere. It had been left to govern itself for years, and it certainly had come into its own. The vicar, Reverend Osbourne, was the leader of the village. The entire village was devoutly Christian, and they all congregated at the church on Sundays (and sometimes on a weekday too, if required) to worship and to discuss any burning issues.

"That sounds ideal," Patrick said, smiling over at Dorothy.

"Excellent. I must say, Mr. Wright has told me that the village has been rather lacklustre recently, what with the war. When word got around that the farm was on the market, he told me that the overwhelming response has been one of hope that some fresh faces will be the key to getting this village back into the swing of things. Do you feel capable of doing that?"

"Oh, absolutely." Dorothy said, smiling back. "I can tell ye now, we will endeavour to help this village thrive."

Patrick nodded his agreement and Mr. Large beamed. They walked on, passed the gap in the fence that led back to the house and carried straight on, towards Onyx Lane. At the end of that path was the field with the gate, the one that Mr. Large had pointed out as they had driven up. They went into the field and saw two enormous buildings in one corner. These two buildings were adjacent, with a partition wall in between them. The path to them divided the big field into two smaller fields, both cordoned off with a gate to each one.

When they went into the bigger of the two buildings, they were delighted to find that it contained fourteen decent-sized stalls, perfect for stabling horses. Each stall had its own half-door and what Mr. Large called a grille, which was to stop the horses from moving their heads around too much and hurting their necks.

The other building was empty, but according to Mr. Large, it had once been used to store a plough and a cart. There was plenty of room in there. Patrick was very happy about this, even though he would have to brush up on his riding and driving skills. Perhaps he could teach Dorothy to ride and drive too!

"Me Da was a cabbie once upon a time," Dorothy said with a beam, "an' I intend to ask him to teach me to drive a cart!"

"What about riding?" Patrick said, "Can you ride a horse?"

"Nay," Dorothy said, winking. Patrick got the joke and smiled back. Mr. Large remained oblivious as he led the retreat back to the path. They knew that it would take a long time to learn their way around, especially the crop fields, and yet despite not living there, Mr. Large knew it like the back of his hand. Eventually, they came full circle and ended up back at the house.

"So!" Mr. Large said conclusively, sitting them down at the dining room table, "How did you like Rosewood Farm?"

"Oh, I loved it!" gushed Dorothy. "It's so…"

"Congenial?" Patrick said.

"I don't know that word, but I trust yer input, so yes."

"It is, isn't it?" agreed Mr. Large, "And if you ask me, I can certainly see you and yours sitting around this table in a few months' time, juggling crops and livestock. I know that Mr. Wright will give you any help that you might need for the first few months. And if you like it as much as I did when I bought it, I would be very happy to sell it to you."

Patrick and Dorothy exchanged a delighted look. After a little deliberation and much uproarious laughter, an agreeable figure was deciphered. When Mr. Large found out that Patrick was the son of one of his school chums, he shaved a little more off the price. Since he had no use for any of it, he said that they could keep all of the furniture.

The only hitch was that Patrick and Dorothy wanted to move in straight away. Mr. Large looked shocked.

"Is that what you do up in Manchester? I'm afraid that I can't possibly let you move in yet. What date is your wedding, again?"

They told him, and he shook his head.

"Well, it would ruin my reputation to let an unmarried couple cohabit. I'm afraid the earliest I could let you move in would be... well, your wedding day!"

"That sounds good to me." Patrick said. Dorothy shot him a quizzical look. "Well, our celebrations won't last very long, will they? We could always bring your parents down for a few nights to help us settle in."

This was agreed, and Mr. Large told them that he would post the keys to them nearer the time. Everything worked out rather well, in the end.

On the train back home, Patrick and Dorothy could hardly sit still for excitement. They had a home, and with that home came a career. And that career, they knew, would be the foundations of their entire lives.

. . .

Maude Downe, Edna thought to herself as Bruce helped her into the carriage, was a saviour. Then she felt a twinge of guilt and found herself glancing at her husband, checking that he hadn't read her thoughts. If he had, he would have been very displeased. The Lord, he had told her many a time, was the one and only Saviour. Comparing Maude Downe to the Lord was, at best, blasphemous.

But Edna found that she didn't care. She'd been on something of a high recently. Just the thought that her Patrick was alive and happy, very soon to be wed, made her almost shiver with delight. And Maude had worked wonders to get her to the wedding.

Maude knew how much Patrick's supposed death had affected her friend. Consequently, she had been mightily relieved to find out that he was alive after all. And after hearing about Edna's problem, she had been all too happy to help. What were friends for, after all? She had concocted her own version of a plan, and Edna agreed that it would work perfectly. So far, it was doing just that, but Edna worried about how Bruce would react when he twigged. He'd already asked her why she was wearing such an elaborate dress, and why they were leaving so early. She'd bluffed, of course, but it had sent her nerves through the roof.

It wasn't nerves, she told herself. It was excitement. But it *was* nerves. There were two reasons for this. One was Patrick's reaction. Would he remember her? Or would that damned war have addled his brain so much that he wouldn't remember his own mother? It had happened. Shellshock, they called it. The other reason that she was excessively jittery was the prospect of her husband's reaction. Bruce had a very short fuse, especially where his disgraced sons were concerned. The mere mention of Patrick or Andrew sent Bruce's jaw muscles into a frenzy of clenching and unclenching as he swallowed his wrath down. He knew that any outburst of hatred upset his wife, and he still had a little compassion.

Hitherto, she had been the ideal Victorian wife: meek, subservient and strongly maternal. Despite the Hammond's connections, they had shunned all high-class idiosyncrasies and determined to be a normal Victorian family. Bruce – or Father-Sir, as he'd insisted on being called to command the utmost respect from his children – was naturally leader of the family. Edna was a lot lower on the Hammond hierarchy, as a woman. This made her blood boil because she found it so frustrating that she was constantly undermined. She was a human too, and Bruce often failed to remember that.

Bruce had never persistently hit her, or whipped her. The odd smack, that was all. He *had* been particularly violent at other times, such as late at night with the curtains pulled and the door locked, normally when she had displeased him. When she consented to it, of her own free will – well, that was all right! But to have her own husband take advantage of her body, time and time again, and simply use it like one would a toy, was utterly crushing.

There was no way out, of course. He had seen to that.

He claimed to be protecting her. But sitting in the carriage while the two bay horses trotted along, delving into the depths of her caged mind, she knew that that was not correct. He did care for her, but he'd taken Timothy 2:12 to the next level: *'I do not permit a woman to teach or to assume authority over a man; she must be quiet.'*

Their church agreed. Women were not permitted to speak in Church, aside from singing and saying "Amen". That went for their daughters, too. If any of them made the slightest undue vociferation, they would be quelled by a hiss from Bruce and a sharp glare from the whole church, even the little boys swivelling around in their seats to stare.

She just hoped that none of these behaviours had been passed from father to son in those man-to-man talks that he'd had with each son on their twelfth birthdays. She did not know the contents of those talks and she desperately hoped that her sons would not subject their own wives to what Bruce had subjected her to. *Be nice to Dorothy, Patrick.*

But she'd never deceived Bruce like this before. She should be beaten from here to next week for it, she knew. She decided, once and for all, that when Bruce started to suspect, she would confess to everything. She prayed that he wouldn't hurt her like he had done before.

She didn't have long to wait. They had been driving for only twenty minutes before Bruce read a sign and frowned.

"This isn't our usual route," he commented, leaning forward to speak to the driver.

"The horses do like a little variety now and again, Sir." the driver replied, poker-faced. Edna had filled him in on the plan, and he had dubiously agreed to go along with it. For a few minutes, Bruce was satisfied. But just when Edna had breathed a sigh of relief and settled back down again, Bruce saw another signpost and berated the driver again.

Edna took a deep breath.

And as she revealed all, she noticed Bruce's whole body go taut. If this was a novel of her life, she thought, this would be the part where the author launched into a whole lengthy description to build up tension.

But somehow, Bruce remained calm. Edna had been expecting his words to rain down on her like little bullets, and she had put up an imaginary shield to protect herself. What she hadn't been expecting was for Bruce to breathe out, swallow hard, and nod.

"I see." he said.

"Would you like me to halt the horses, Sir?" the driver said quietly.

"No." Bruce replied thoughtfully.

There was silence for a moment.

"No," he said again, "drive on."

"Are we going to the wedding, Bruce?" Edna breathed, her spirits lifting.

"Yes, Edna." he replied. Then he leaned towards her and with clenched teeth, under his breath, said, "I will deal with you later."

Edna involuntarily twitched with fright.

"But for now, Edna, we must attend this wedding. I will forgive Patrick. Luke says, *'If your brother sins, rebuke him, and if he repents, forgive him. If he sins against you seven times in one day, and each time he comes to you saying 'I repent,' you must forgive him.'* – so that is what I will do. This invitation sounds as if Patrick is trying to repent."

Scarcely believing her ears, Edna nodded and suddenly smiled. Bruce's past comment had been temporarily forgotten, and her dream had come true. She was going to see her son marry, having been forgiven for his sins. Revelling in this sudden burst of joy, she sat back once again to enjoy the scenery.

Meanwhile, Dorothy was slipping into her dress. It was nothing fancy – plain, white and shapeless – and belonged to one of the girls from work. The girl had no longer wanted it, so it was her leaving present to Dorothy. Then, the whole team had bought her an assortment of leaving gifts, as part of the silly rivalry that they had. Unbeknownst to them, she had sold every present. They needed every penny they could get to start paying for the farm.

Once she had done up the dress, she turned around and surveyed the room that had been her home for the last six months. But how changed! It had been stripped of all her belongings. Even the teaspoon, which had sat on the table for so long that it had nearly become another resident, had been safely returned to Mrs. Lloyd's kitchen.

Patrick's room looked the same: all adornments gone. They were to move out that afternoon, something that had devastated Mrs. Lloyd. She'd become almost like a second mother to them both, cooking for them every night and keeping up with the cleaning while they were at work. At first, she had reminded Patrick of one of the maids from Highmore Park, but he knew that Mrs. Lloyd had her own thoughts and opinions (which she certainly didn't mind sharing). Which posed the question: what did all the staff at Highmore think on a day-to-day basis? The nanny, drafted in when three children (and another on the way) became too much for Edna, was nice enough, and like all the staff, had kissed goodbye to her own life once she'd moved in. But did she actually have opinions? And what about the driver, and the girls from the kitchen? Did they have opinions too? Were they just like him?

So in several ways, Mrs. Lloyd had been invaluable. She was sad to see them go, but as a wedding present had told them to forget their last month's rent. In return, they had invited her to their wedding, as their only guest bar their parents. It was the very least they could do. She had been delighted to accept, and now she bustled towards the front door to let in Wilhelmina and Charlie, the latter of whom was to give Dorothy away, after finally forgiving her. Patrick, who was out and about somewhere and hadn't seen Dorothy since last night, just hoped that Father-Sir would find it in his heart somewhere to forgive him.

If Dorothy had thought she was excited when she first viewed the farm, that was nothing compared to what she felt now. She couldn't bear to sit down, as if the chairs would singe her dress. When Mrs. Lloyd showed her parents in, Wilhelmina enveloped her in a hug and, with no hesitation, Charlie did likewise. They were both neatly dressed in their best outfits. Dorothy almost suffocated them both, trying to squeeze the excitement from her body. It didn't work, for when she finally let them go it was still bubbling and fizzing in her veins.

They whiled away the time before the wedding, simply talking and talking. Dorothy relished her parent's expressions of awe as she described the farm. They would be coming to stay for a few weeks after the wedding to help them find their feet, arriving tomorrow. But before that, Dorothy and Patrick had to get themselves there! They were getting the train at one o'clock, expecting to be at the Wychwood station by five. Since it was June, it would still be light for them.

Before they knew it, they were leaving for the church. They had to walk, since there was no hope of getting a carriage. It wasn't that far away, and luckily it was dry – no puddles to negotiate. Dorothy could barely manage a sedate pace. She wanted to skitter, to hop and jump with excitement. She resisted, of course, not wanting to attract onlookers (although there were plenty – it wasn't that often that you saw a bride-to-be walking along the pavement).

Patrick got to the church ten minutes before the wedding was due to start. He was equally excited, but for him the excitement was mixed with its near-identical twin: fear. He didn't really expect Mother and Father-Sir to be there, but what if they were?

They were.

Edna jumped up as soon as he entered the church, stumbling in high heels down the aisle. Bruce leapt to his feet, abhorred at the fact that she was plainly speaking inside a church. His heart contracted upon seeing his son. He had mixed emotions, and to his surprise, one was pride. There was a very small amount of it, but it was there.

He reminded himself that he'd forgiven Patrick. If he could forgive his son, then he could forgive his wife, just this once, for breaking a rule. He was sure that she would repent later. When Edna came back in, silent once more due to the fact that Patrick was talking quietly but animatedly, he beckoned for her to sit down again. Patrick nodded shyly at Father-Sir, before taking his place beside the vicar at the front of the church.

And just in time, too. Wilhelmina soon scuttled in, after planting two kisses on Dorothy's cheeks. She quietly greeted Edna and Bruce (not noticing how Bruce cringed when she began talking in a church) and took her place in the front pew on the other side of the church.

As the big clock struck eleven, the organist started up with the familiar bridal march. And as Dorothy stepped over the threshold, she believed every word that Patrick had said about God. Entering the church, she felt enveloped in a special spirit, as if the sky had opened and a golden mist had surrounded her. She beamed through the veil as she took in her surroundings and marched, her arm linked through her father's, up the aisle.

When she reached the top, Charlie gave her a kiss and went to stand next to his wife. Dorothy exchanged a wonderful look with Patrick, that said everything from "Here we go!" to "How did we get here?" The congregation – the two families in the front rows and Mrs. Lloyd a few rows back – sat down as one. The vicar started the service with "Dearly beloved…".

That golden mist remained with Dorothy, extending to include Patrick and all their guests within the bubble, all the way through the service. As they stepped outside the church building together, the congregation of five all clapped – no confetti. Edna and Patrick embraced again while Dorothy shook Bruce's hand earnestly. It was just the way he liked it – firm, short and with eye contact. He liked her right away. He had flinched when she started talking (loudly and confidently, something he wasn't used to) but found that she had rather a sense of humour. Ordinarily, a sense of humour wasn't something he approved of in a woman, but he didn't mind it in Dorothy.

The differences between the Hammonds and the Foxes were astounding. The Fox family were far more matriarchal, for a start. Edna barely said a word, at first, to her new daughter-in-law's family. Dorothy and Wilhelmina tried hard to bring her out of her shell, when they went to the Fox house for a very quick luncheon, but she was desperately shy until Wilhelmina made a good joke and she laughed aloud.

At one point, Bruce took Patrick into the living room for a quick word. Patrick insisted that Dorothy came too, and Bruce nodded resignedly.

"So – I hear that you are moving down south, near us," he began. Patrick nodded nervously, observing how his father still held his cane.

"That's right, Father-Sir."

"I am pleased about that, because it is impossible to say how much your mother has missed you. I could berate you for putting us all through sheer horror for the last five years, but since one's wedding day is meant to be a day of joy and new beginnings, I shall take advantage of that instead. You are forgiven, my son."

"Thank you, Father-Sir," Patrick replied, shaking his hand. Dorothy could tell that they would never be the closest father and son, but for now at least, they were civil.

They timed it rather well, really. Dorothy and Patrick quickly changed out of their wedding outfits, put them in with the rest of their luggage, and went downstairs to say goodbye. They had said goodbye to Mrs. Lloyd at the church, who had given them their luggage bags (the same ones as what they had arrived with).

"We'll meet up soon – all of us. The Hammond family and the Fox family have been brought together through God's love, and we must work with the utmost dedication to maintain this bond." Bruce declared. He placed a hand on Dorothy's shoulder and the other hand on Patrick's.

There was a pause.

"God bless you, Patrick and Dorothy Hammond." he concluded.

"Amen." replied Edna without hesitation, quickly echoed by Wilhelmina and Charlie. Then the cab (paid for by Charlie as a parting gift) was there to take them to the train station and there was a flurry of goodbyes and see-you-tomorrows. Wilhelmina wasn't at all emotional for she knew that Patrick would look after her daughter for the next twenty-four hours. Edna, however, started to shudder and gulp because she didn't know this Dorothy from Eve and was worried about what those two youths would get up to.

"Now, now, Edna," Charlie said, employing all of his charm and sitting her down. Bruce bristled and promptly cut him off, putting a stiff arm around his wife.

"Edna, dear, do not fret!" he said in as loving a tone as he could manage.

"I do fret, Bruce!" she whimpered, shrinking away from his touch.

Looking up at the kind, concerned faces of Wilhelmina and Charlie, she knew that she didn't want to go back to Highmore Park. She wanted to stay in Monthill – and not just for the change of scenery. The words *"I'll deal with you later"* echoed around her head and she knew what that meant.

But what could she do? She just hoped that Patrick and Dorothy would make it to Little Wychwood safe and sound.

And they did. Almost as soon as they stepped off the train, mistakenly inhaling deeply and almost choking on the smoke, they felt themselves relax. It had been a good idea to elope.

They had no money for a cab, and so they walked (using their memories as a map) from the train station to the village. It was a long walk after sitting on the train for hours, but it felt good to stretch their muscles. Villagers waved as they went by. The whole village knew about the new farmer and his wife taking over their largely unused farm. There were a few remarks of "They look rather young!" but they were all open to giving them a chance. This new source of food could potentially revolutionise their little village, once and for all.

Patrick and Dorothy got the surprise of their lives when they opened the front door and stepped inside. There was a middle-aged man sitting at the dining table, and a slightly younger and sprightlier woman scurrying around him, dusting.

"Who on Earth are you?" Patrick said, rudely through shock. The man exchanged a glance with the woman.

"I'm Wright, young man. Ronald Wright, right?"

"Right," Patrick replied, shifting his questioning gaze to the woman.

"And this is my wife, Rita Wright. We're the Wrights."

"Right!" Patrick said again, shaking their warm hands. "Now, don't think me rude, please, but may I ask why you are in my house?"

"Why are we in his house, he wants to know!" Ronald said to Rita, rolling his eyes, "Well, we're all decent sorts in this village, so I've been spending some time over the last couple of months, going back to my farming roots. I've planted a few crops here and there, prepared the livestock fields, checked on the barley. All that's left for you to do, with that barley, is harvest it when the time comes, and then carry on the cycle. Obviously you'll get some horses and livestock, right?"

"Right..." Patrick replied, pausing to mull this over.

"I think what Patrick means is *thank you*," Dorothy said, shaking his hand earnestly. She guided Rita towards a chair, telling her to sit down as her legs must be killing her.

"I've done a little cleaning for you, love. The kitchen's nice and clean, as is the living room, and I've just started in here. The beds are all made for you too – you've had a long journey, and you must be tired too." Rita replied with a smile. Dorothy could not believe how hospitable these two complete strangers were, and she thanked them several times.

After a cup of tea (Rita had thought to bring some tea, because nobody could function without it), they all felt a lot calmer, and an easy chatter was taking place.

"You'll be able to introduce yourselves at church tomorrow, right?" Ronald said – then to himself, "Don't be silly, of course they'll do that, Wright." – then once again to them – "Reverend Osbourne is wildly excited. We all are. You are just what we need to spruce up the village!"

With that, he stood up and lay his cup down.

"Right! We must be off. Thank you for your time, and we'll see you tomorrow at church, nine sharp, right?"

"Right!" Dorothy and Patrick responded in unison, and waved them off. The moment they shut the front door – their front door – they couldn't help but laugh. Nice as Ronald Wright was, there was no hope of getting a word in edgeways once he'd started talking! Patrick couldn't help but kiss her. Simply because he wanted to. Since it was now evening, and they had eaten a sandwich on the train, they decided to leave the unpacking for tomorrow and to go for a walk around the farm instead.

Arm in arm, they meandered around until they came to the fields of growing barley and wheat that Ronald had planted, all in neat rows with gaps in between to walk down. They opened the gate and found themselves submerged in the golden fields. And then joy overtook them and they found themselves skipping through each row, laughing uproariously with every bounce, until they tumbled over and landed on the ground. The whole world seemed to be just perfect, smiling down at them. The sun beamed its warm rays upon their bare arms and legs as they ran, falling over and picking themselves back up, shedding every little piece of their old lives in Monthill. They were now Patrick and Dorothy Hammond, and they were invincible. They knew that they belonged here, at Rosewood Farm, and it was the most wonderful feeling, one that they wanted to savour and treasure forever.

Eventually they grew tired – a pleasant tired. They sat down together in the middle of the field, with one arm around each other.

"Will you always love me?" Dorothy said, and closed her eyes as he replied.

"Of course. Wherever we are, whatever life throws at us, I'll love you throughout. You saved my life on that day, Dot, and that was why I fell in love with you in the first place. I don't know where I'd be without you. Thank you for everything, Dot. Thank you for putting up with me."

"I'll always put up with ye. I'll always be waiting for ye to be all right. I'll wait until the end of time if I have to."

And even when the sun slipped over the horizon and the orangey-red sunset melted into deep, inky black, they carried on talking. Dorothy had never felt happier in her life, nor more at peace, as she sat with her husband, on their own farm, listening to him sing her praises and then reciprocating ten-fold.

When the temperature dipped, they made their way inside, hand-in-hand. Despite it being nearly ten, they weren't at all hungry.

"I can't believe we're married now, Pat." Dorothy laughed as she pulled the curtains shut.

"You'd better start believing it then, Dot." he replied with an equally large smile.

"So... what's next?"

Patrick took her hand again and looked her in the eye.

"I suggest we go upstairs. Come with me."

"What are we going to do?"

"We are going to do what all couples do on their wedding night. Come on."

Meanwhile, Edna was getting ready for bed, and steeling herself for what she knew was coming.

. . .

Well, Dorothy was pregnant.

Ever since the doctor had confirmed it, they had been reeling. The first thing they'd done was send a telegram to Wilhelmina and Charlie, and now they were wondering how to tell the Hammond side of the family. They hadn't heard from them at all since the wedding.

Oh, but Wilhelmina and Charlie had been such a help! Them and the Wrights. The past couple of months had been incredibly hectic, and they'd barely had a moment to pause for breath. Ronald and Rita had been essentially living with them for several weeks now, arriving at nine in the morning and sometimes not leaving until eight at night. Dorothy had cooked for them all, creating lots of simple dishes out of all sorts of ingredients. Fish pie was a particular favourite, as Patrick knew how to fish. He, Charlie and Ronald took great pleasure in going down to the river – which was absolutely teeming with fish – of an occasional evening and returning with a couple of decent catches that would see them through for a couple of days.

The first thing that had happened, two days after the wedding, was that Ronald arrived with four beautiful, feathery hens and one loud cockerel. They were a gift, he said, from one of the villagers, just to get them started. And as the days had gone on, lots of the villagers had taken the message that Reverend Osbourne had given at the church very seriously indeed.

"It gives me great pleasure to welcome Little Wychwood's latest spring chickens!" Reverend Osbourne had announced. "Patrick and Dorothy Hammond have been blessed with God's love and united in marriage – just yesterday! – all the way up in Manchester. They will be, in due course, a vital part in the reshaping of our village as they proceed to take over Rosewood Farm and, in time, provide us with some daily necessities. They are here with Dorothy's parents, Wilhelmina and Charlie, who are staying temporarily to help out. I do believe that Patrick would like to say a few words?"

"Oh – me?" Patrick said, stunned, "Ah… right."

Reverend Osbourne beckoned him to the front with a smile – not to the pulpit, but to the front of the church where he could be seen.

"Well… good morning, everyone!" Patrick said, hiding his shyness with jubilance. "I am very pleased to be your new farmer. Please be assured that my new wife and I shall endeavour to bring the farm back to its former glory in time – all while living a truly Christian life. All I ask of you all is that you follow Romans 15:7, and as it says, *'welcome one another as Christ has welcomed you, for the glory of God.'* Thank you all."

There was a ripple of excitement. Patrick had just reeled off that verse without even looking it up! How splendid! Not many people could do that, and they certainly hadn't expected it from this new young chap! Well, that was settled, then. It was agreed throughout the church that they would be as welcoming as possible.

Afterwards, they had been pounced on by a couple in their late forties. They introduced themselves as Norbert and Isabelle Wood, and invited them over to their house for elevenses. While they were there, sipping hot, strong tea, they found out that Norbert and Isabelle ran the shop, which worked with a farm in Wychwood. They also had a son, Neville, who was twelve, and who would inherit the shop when he was twenty-one.

"Now, when you get yourselves together and start harvesting, we would be very happy to sell your produce." Isabelle said boldly. "You mayn't be up to the standards of our existing supplier, but eating our own village's fare would be a lovely little boost for this village's morale. As a community, we're very driven, but recently we have been lacking."

"We don't mean to rush you, by any means, but when you feel able, we would be overjoyed to collaborate with you." Norbert continued.

They agreed straight away. The more allies they could get, the better. Very satisfied with their morning, Patrick and Dorothy strolled home to do what they always did on a Sunday, which was to read and discuss the Bible and have Patrick teach Dorothy about the ways of God's world.

Patrick hadn't been able to believe that Dorothy hadn't been raised a Christian. He'd had to seriously rethink their relationship, yet again. But after praying for guidance, he had concluded that he had interacted with many non-Christians in his time, and here was his opportunity to educate another.

Since women had won the vote in February the previous year,

Dorothy, Wilhelmina and the rest of the suffragists had finally relaxed. One of their colleagues had been a steadfast suffragette and after campaigning tirelessly and aggressively for her whole life, she had burnt herself out. Dorothy herself was a much less up-front person that she had been – after all, these days she had no need to be assertive.

Patrick wasn't entirely sure that her decline in confidence was completely due to the conclusion of the suffrage movement. He had been brought up in a very patriarchal family, and he wanted that tradition to carry on. Consequently, he had slowly been asserting himself, just inching his way in front of her – and she had accepted it. After eighteen years of being a suffragist, she appeared more than happy to let a man take the forefront for a while.

And then she had found out that she was pregnant.

Wilhelmina and Charlie were overjoyed, and expressed this in an ecstatic letter. But a telegram didn't seem the right way to tell the rather more distant Hammond side of the family. So they had decided to go there and tell them in person.

Dorothy pulled on her gloves and checked that her curly shoulder-length hair was neatly brushed. Her emerald-green dress was smooth and well-fitting (although she knew that it wouldn't fit for long!). She looked the picture of neatness. They were taking the train to Houghton Regis and hoping to hitch a ride from the station to Highmore Park.

Patrick had a wonderful ability to bend people to his will, and he employed these skills to get them a ride for the second half of the walk – "My wife's expecting, you see, and we really need to get there…". Dorothy simply smiled beseechingly, and their forces combined meant that the good-natured carriage driver told them to get in the back.

Bruce let them in and sat them down in comfortable chairs in the drawing room. Edna, looking a little flustered but otherwise dignified, accompanied him as they sat down with tea and shortbread. Bessie and Gertrude greeted them and then were sent away. As young ladies, they were not permitted to sit with the adults, despite Gertrude being older than Dorothy herself by a few years. Mike was absent.

It was only when the teacups had been drained and the shortbread reduced to crumbs that Dorothy broke the news. Bruce beamed. His first grandchild!

"My dear daughter-in-law, I am absolutely thrilled! And so quickly, too – you've barely been married five minutes! Nevertheless, you are serving your womanly purpose and I am immensely pleased with you. And with you too, Patrick. This family's bloodline is going strong, and I am very glad to hear it. Bless you, Patrick and Dorothy, and your child too."

Edna said nothing, but hugged Dorothy and Patrick hard. She remained very quiet until Bruce took Patrick into his study for a man's talk.

"Well! Safe to say that someone was happy with th' news!" Dorothy said jovially, dropping her posh accent because she felt more comfortable with Edna, who smiled in response.

"I just hope you know what you've let yourselves in for. The sleeplessness, the long hours awake, the crying, the tunnel vision. And you will grow very close to your doctor as time goes on. He will see every inch of you – all dignity goes out of the window, especially during labour. But the awful thing is that during labour, you won't even care! Your body will be dedicated to getting that baby out of it, and that mission becomes priority."

Dorothy involuntarily shuddered at the prospect of pushing out a real person, then she smiled. That was the most Edna had ever said to her. Edna had surprised herself, actually. Painfully shy due to limited contact with people, Edna had expected her relationship with her daughter-in-law to be restricted, at best. But she seemed nice enough, a little forthright but not outrageously so.

"But you are happy, yes? You do love my Patrick?" Edna said, just to be sure.

"Yes, yes I do, an' I'll love this child too." Dorothy said sincerely, and Edna believed her.

"I won't lie and say that having a child is easy. It's the hardest thing you will ever do, in fact. But I managed it. I managed it five times over, and it is also the best thing you will ever do. It'll complete your life, all at the age of – what, nearly nineteen? You lucky girl. You'll be sent to bed for the rest of your pregnancy soon enough, of course."

"What for? I'm fit as a flea!"

"That is what people do. My Bruce kept me almost manacled to that bed during all five of my pregnancies, so that I didn't hurt myself by doing anything rash. I'm sure Patrick is intelligent enough to do the same."

"I never knew that! I'll ask me mam when I see her next. But I don't think we can afford for me to be bedridden. We've so many animals to take care of, we just won't manage."

"You did plan this baby?"

"Well, no." Dorothy admitted. "It was a little surprise, if ye see what I mean. An' I'm not sure if I'm really ready, y'know? I thought we'd get th' farm up an' runnin' before any babies appeared."

Dorothy stopped, looking a little pensive. Then she smiled.

"But anyway, what's done is done. We must cherish what God's givin' us, isn't that right?

"Yes, yes of course," Edna said hastily.

"An' the Lord's way o' thinkin' is erratic – but beautifully so. We have to make th' most of it otherwise He could take it all away." Dorothy continued, echoing the words that Patrick had told her at their last Bible study.

"Erratic? I suppose He is. Religion is certainly complicated, but the only way to please God and enter Heaven. Make sure you set your children on the Christian path and then you'll be reunited in Heaven."

This was a reassuring thought, the essence of which was being given to Patrick too, by an effervescent Bruce. They went to his study and sat down at the desk, opposite each other, just like they had when Patrick had left. Patrick marvelled at how nothing appeared to have changed – apart from their circumstances. Before, he'd been a weedy, impulsive little tyke who'd taken his entire life and family for granted. Now, he was a strong, well-learned and measured man with a child on the way and a wife that he was incredibly lucky to have. He knew that his brother, Andrew, had had a blazing row with Father-Sir a few years ago and left, gone without trace, just like he himself had done. Who knew where he was now?

"Well, I'm very pleased with you, Patrick." Father-Sir said pleasantly, smiling at his son. "You know that Andrew has let me down massively, and I'm glad that you haven't gone the same way. But there are lots of things I need to tell you so that this baby does not go wrong. I know how to raise children, so I recommend that you listen to what I'm about to say, and follow it to the letter. Am I clear?"

"Yes, Father-Sir. Of course, Father-Sir." Patrick said clearly. He couldn't help nervously cracking his knuckles, an automatic thing, then looked around guiltily in case he was about to be caned. But the cane was lying on the floor, untouched, much to his relief.

"So – you remember the talk I gave you when you were twelve? I told you to marry a good woman, a subservient little housewife, and I think that you did. I am very pleased with that. And now that you're expecting a child, I'm going to give you the second part of that talk.

"There's something that the Proverbs say – Chapter 22, Verse 6 – '*Start children off on the way they should go, and even when they are old they will not turn from it.'* – and I want you to keep that in mind. That is going to be the one sentence that will be central to your future. You have to keep your children on a straight and narrow path, and prevent them from sinning. That is the only way to lead them to God and to happiness. And when Jesus comes back to Earth and decides who goes to Heaven or Hell, you and all your descendants will all accumulate with Him in Heaven."

"But how can I do that, Father-Sir? Surely it is impossible for me to control every movement of my children?"

"You need to make it possible, just like I've done with you and your siblings and your mother. I got you children a tutor, and I didn't let you near the town. With you, it didn't work quite as well..." and here he paused meaningfully, his mouth pursed, "...but I'm hoping that if you do what I say now, and raise good little servants of God, you will be saved from the devil's claws and go to Heaven. The way I see you now, that piece of the devil inside you means that you'll be going straight to Hell, and we have to fix that."

Patrick felt suddenly incensed. If the speaker had been anyone but his powerful father, he would have taken to his heels after a sharp retort, but he knew that he would be caned for that. Plus, what his father was saying was starting to make sense. He didn't want to transfer any of this evil inside him to his offspring. He felt an overwhelming urge to confess about Maxwell, but he knew that if he did, he'd never hear the end of his father's horror.

"If the devil is in me..." he began falteringly, trying to stay composed.

"...we have to keep it from coming out." Father-Sir replied. "It's too late to chase it out of you, so we'll just have to build some sort of mental cage to condense it and contain it. I suggest that you visit your church several times a week to pray. I have a small fragment of hope that if you pray sincerely and repent, God will take pity on you and forgive you. But it is incredibly important not to let Satan rule over and escape from within you – at times, this will require a great deal of self-restraint on your part. Hopefully living in a small village, away from the temptations of the town, will play a part in that. But if Satan does escape, you'll have a problem on your hands because you will struggle to set your child on the correct path. You'll need the help of your wife to do that, but when possible, you should take the brunt of the work."

With both of them having had their fill of advice, Patrick and Dorothy left soon after. Patrick was decidedly disturbed. He'd been far more confident in his own ability to function since moving to the farm, but now he wasn't so sure. His father's words made him wonder. Was there a him, or was he simply the devil personified? He said as much to Dorothy when they got home. While Dorothy made dinner, he stood in the back doorway scratching their new sheepdog, Lucky, and repeating his father word for word.

"Well, what a load o' rubbish!" Dorothy said at the end of it, appearing in the doorway with a ladle in one hand and a plate in the other. Their dinner was nearly ready, so she could have a brief rest. She leant against the door frame and observed her husband. He was decidedly tense, and from this she could tell that he'd really taken the scaremongering to heart.

"Dorothy! Such a tone!" he replied, surprised.

"Well, it's true! How dare he try an' pressure ye into doin' things? This child does not belong to him! He had children long ago an' if he thinks his plan didn't work on ye, then why's he tellin' ye t' do what he did?"

Dorothy was getting quite fired up, and he could tell by her accent.

"Calm down, Dot – think of the child. Is our food ready?"

"Oh gosh, the food!" she shouted, running inside to rescue

it. Patrick shook his head and smiled – she was still rather a clumsy little housewife. She was an excellent farmer's wife, though, an expert at collecting the eggs (the majority of which she gave to Norbert and Isabelle at the shop to supplement their stock). Lucky the dog had a great deal of affection for her, although the scraps that she gave him may have had something to do with it. But the thing she liked best about the farm was her horse, Delphinium. The doctor said that she could carry on riding for as long as she liked in terms of the pregnancy, but Patrick planned to stop her in a few weeks in case she did any damage.

Come to think of it, they had quite a few animals now. They were getting to be a proper farm! There were the cows, seven of them, and nine sheep (all ewes). There were the four horses: Winston, Delphinium, Colonel and Corporal. The latter two were cart horses, young and sprightly and strong. They had the chickens, of course, five including the cockerel. There were two pigs, Dinky and Donkey, who were completely inseparable. They were yet to get goats, and Patrick fancied his hand at beekeeping at some point. But for now, with Lucky the dog on top and a couple of feral cats that passed by now and then, they had enough.

They did wonder how they would adapt their schedule to the baby. Currently, their daily routine was jam-packed. Patrick would milk all of the cows, first thing after feeding. This would be at six o'clock in the morning. Meanwhile, Ronald Wright would go through all of the animals, checking them over for injuries or signs of illness, with the dog following behind. The horses would all be groomed by Dorothy and Rita, and the carthorses taken for a spin around the village. When they got back, the milking was done and it would be eight o'clock and time for breakfast. The four of them sat at the table with mugs of strong, sugary tea and slices of bread (often toasted so hard that if thrown at a window, they would have travelled straight through).

Fifteen minutes later, it was back to business. The horses were all turned out for the day in their fields, and the stables mucked out. Everybody helped with this, a few stables each, and within ten minutes they were spotlessly clean. Ronald and Rita then cleaned out the pigs while Dorothy tended to the chickens. While they were doing this, Patrick (who had been taught by Ronald how to herd) put the dog through his paces and gave their lazy sheep some exercise. After this ensued a vigorous sweeping down of any available pavements, including the back yard, where the chickens lived in their coop and the dog slept in his kennel at night. By this point, everybody ached, so they had another tea break. Dorothy and Rita then stayed inside to start their baking (always bread first, then scones, biscuits and cakes, which they shared with each other and the shop). Ronald went and cleaned any mud off the cart and checked over all the equipment, fixing where necessary. Patrick went out and sorted the cream from the milk and bottled it. The milkman collected it for distribution and they sent him on his way with a sandwich and a flask of tea.

Although summer had been and gone, and autumn offered even more bounty, they knew that winter was on its way, and with it would come harder times. As a result, Dorothy took three or four eggs every day, whatever she could spare (the chickens laid quite a few!) and put them in a bucket of isinglass, which she obtained from the town when she went there every Saturday. She also tended to her little herb garden, which consisted of some petite oblong pots with pathetic-looking, weed-like plants searching desperately for sunlight. While things were cooking, she did the housework with Rita. Monday was wash day, and Tuesday was ironing day. There were not many clothes to wash, and so neither jobs ever took more than half an hour. Dorothy couldn't wait to be washing and ironing tiny socks and baby outfits, and had already started knitting them. All of it was tiring, however, so they took another break afterwards. The kitchen was also kept spotlessly clean, the stove scrubbed to within an inch of its life and even the curtains taken down once a week and boiled.

"I'm not poisonin' this village! If it's from me, it's clean!" Dorothy would say. She loved the smell of carbolic soap, and soon Rita had to discreetly spray lavender water around the house in an effort to mask the harsh smell.

Plenty of other cooking was also done – not just baking. Dorothy had been around the penny stalls in town, and returned home with a set of ten rather chipped plates and ten matching bowls, all with a faded rose pattern. She also found some some big saucepans and casserole dishes. She and Rita made a lot of soups, which they burned through with astonishing gusto every day at midday.

At this point, Ronald and Rita often went home for a while, and Dorothy and Patrick carried on doing their jobs. Sometimes, Ronald and Rita would stay all afternoon and most of the evening if there were lots of jobs to do. But whenever they could, Patrick and Dorothy went out for a ride. Winston was Patrick's horse, while Dorothy rode the very amicable Delph, who was a true lady's ride. It would never have occurred to them to swap horses. They were now recognised around the village, although it took a good few years to be recognised as a local, and often got stopped by housewives to have a chat. Their horses were used to the absentminded pats, and even Winston had learned to stand still. He was only a young horse, just turned four, and so he found standing still rather boring!

Their rides together were absolutely blissful. Whether they were walking loosely over the cobbles, or galloping flat-out in the winding lanes that stretched beyond their farm, they would always be smiling. Even when Winston tripped and sent Patrick straight over his head into a bush, they simply howled with laughter. Those would turn out to be some of the happiest moments of Dorothy's life. She loved the buzz that it gave her, the wind making her hair whip her face red as Delph stretched her entire body to keep up with Winston, and Patrick enjoyed it equally as much. He did wonder, now, if it was entirely healthy for their unborn child.

Actually, he wondered if the whole routine was healthy. It was exhausting, but when they tumbled into their creaky bed at the end of the day, they felt pleasantly tired, not bone tired. However, he knew that Dorothy's body was catering for two, and so he had been scheming with Rita and Ronald to lighten her workload. Both of them were willing to take on extra jobs, even if it meant staying longer. They were reducing the workload gradually, so that she didn't think she was getting special treatment, which she would hate. Anything that could have been interpreted as weakness, she avoided like the plague.

But right now she looked the picture of health. She was positively glowing, both with excitement and the sweltering September heat. Patrick stood up and went inside. The glow had rather left her, however, when she came into the dining room with the plates, and when he looked at his own, he could see why.

Nothing like a bit of tripe to dampen the spirits.

. . .

Dorothy had never been more scared in her life. Her baby was trying to come out.

He wasn't meant to, not just yet. He still had four months to go. Something wasn't right – she should be doing something to keep him in, not just lying in a hospital bed. All the doctors were telling her to just lay down and stay calm, but the pain ripping periodically through her abdomen told her otherwise. And when a flood of water left her body and soaked the bed, she knew that there was no going back. And the doctors knew it too, for they became very sombre and downcast.

It wasn't fair. All of the other women on the maternity ward were so much bigger than her, with great big bumps hidden by tent-like garments, as opposed to her barely noticeable one that still fitted in her normal clothes.

"He's not right, I feel it, our little baby..." she had whimpered earlier as she clung to her husband.

"Dot, have faith. God will save him. He'll be absolutely fine." Patrick said into her tied hair. At this point, the nurse, who had introduced herself as Nurse Page, entered the room solemnly and ripped their world apart even further.

"Mrs Hammond, it is undeniable that you are in the first stage of labour. You will be giving birth to your child today. I know it's hard to accept, but he is going to die, and the only thing we can do for his benefit is to make it less traumatic. Do you understand?" she said. Dorothy nodded, tears finally escaping her eyes.

She'd never imagined her pregnancy ending like this. It had been going so well. Her body had appreciated the reduced workload, and in turn it had bloomed. There had been the constant nausea to cope with, but it had eased off somewhat in the last month. She had adjusted well to everything happening inside her body, the new person being made. However, she hadn't reckoned on this sudden torture. A human baby was kept inside its mother for nine solid months, forty weeks, until it was well-developed and able to function on its own without help from the mother's body. Five months in, the doctors knew he wouldn't survive, and now Dorothy and Patrick knew too. It was an absolute kick to the guts, and Dorothy felt it physically too with each contraction.

As the hours went by and Dorothy battled wave after wave of knifing pain inside her, neither of them complained. They knew that they had to steal every second they could with their child while he lived inside her. As soon as Dorothy had given birth to him, he would just be another body under the hospital's roof. There would be enough time for commiserating later, the doctor told them. For now, they needed to get the baby into the world safely so that Dorothy remained safe. Death during childbirth was common, in children and mothers, and Patrick couldn't lose two people.

But despite telling herself that she just had to get on with it, as Dorothy entered the second stage of labour and started pushing, her emotions began to take over. The intolerable pain didn't help. She didn't want to let her baby go. She wanted him to stay alive inside of her for the next four months, so that she could take him home and have a family.

"Dorothy! Stop being so foolish!" the doctor told her sharply when she refused to push even though her body was telling her to. She still desperately shook her head, screaming *"no, no, no"*, until she received a sharp slap across the face from Patrick.

"You'll kill yourself doing that, you stupid woman," he said harshly. Dorothy didn't care. If her child was going to die, she might as well die with it, she thought.

"I don't want him to die, I don't want to leave him..." she whimpered, before another contraction kicked in. Patrick couldn't see why she was acting up so much and jeopardising his reputation. She was just making it ten times more difficult for the doctors. She knew that the baby would die, whatever she did, but she was just making the whole experience more traumatic than need be. He shook her by the wrist in an effort to bring her to her senses, but she pulled away from him violently.

As the contractions carried on, Dorothy saw, clear as day in her mind's eye, the face of her unborn child – but grown up. Oh, he was a charming child, and blonde. The face was almost ingrained into her brain, along with the word *cacophony*.

Yes, that was the word to describe it – a cacophony. She was completely overwhelmed. The sorrow, pain and disappointment coursed through her veins as liquid angst and she was dimly aware of herself screaming. But it was like she wasn't there. Detached. She saw herself, a sweating, tormented mess, lying on the hospital bed with Patrick on one side, Nurse Page on the other and a doctor at the foot of the bed.

"Pray! Patrick, pray!" she found herself screaming. Yet although Patrick started praying, quoting from every Bible verse he could think of, she felt none of the comfort that she had imagined from God, none of the relief that Patrick had promised. Right there, Dorothy decided that if God loved her like the church said, He wouldn't be putting her through this just to kill her child. Her faith in God would never be the same again, she knew, and with every push, it diminished as if it had never been there at all.

. . .

Later, she awoke with a start. Where was her baby? She turned over, expecting to see a little Moses basket with a baby inside of it – but there was nothing. Although she desperately rummaged inside her memory, she couldn't recall her child's face – or indeed seeing him at all. He wasn't there, though, not in her body any more. The last thing she remembered was Patrick's soothing but hazy voice saying "Every word of God is flawless... take refuge in him..."

Well, who in their right mind wouldn't? It was natural to take refuge in God. So where was her baby?

She had to find him. Leaping out of bed and then gasping at the cold floor, she staggered to the door and wrenched it open. A wave of cool air hit her, as well as the sound of a weak, feeble cry. Aha! The babies were simply kept separate from the mothers, that was all. Dorothy had to go to him. He might be hungry.

The poor lighting meant that she barely made it twenty feet before her hands reached a door handle. He was in here, Dorothy told herself. She opened it and switched her torch on, shining it into the room. The light was met by matching screams, both from the baby and its mother. Dorothy howled too. Where was her baby? Was she in the wrong room? And if this baby was allowed to sleep with its mother, why wasn't hers?

"For goodness' sake, Mrs. Hammond..." grumbled someone from behind her, taking her by the wrists and pulling her backwards. She was the Sister.

"We give you a room away from the mothers, and this is how you repay us, with all this disruption? You might have lost your son, but really now..." muttered the Sister, leading Dorothy back to her room.

"I lost me son?" Dorothy laughed aloud, shaking her head at the middle-aged woman (who she promptly labelled in her head as barmy).

"Yes, you lost your son. You have a very short memory, it seems. You've been fine all day, so you just need some sleep. Now, sleep!"

Dorothy was thrust back into her little dark room, onto her hard hospital bed. She sat up on her elbows, laughing to herself at how annoyed she had made the Sister and what nonsense the woman was talking.

But if her son wasn't here, where was he?

Then she remembered. A hand that had been loosely holding her heart suddenly squeezed it hard. Was it God, doing that? Dorothy put her hand on it and when the pain eased, she took a sharp breath in, and the sharp breath out came with a sudden sob. There she was, alone, in a place that had absolutely no sympathy or condolences beyond a pat on the shoulder. And who was paying for it? They had no insurance – nothing! What were they going to do?

She fought against the tears, fighting to regain a little sanity and to make sense of what had gone on. She only remembered snippets: the tortuous pain... her husband praying... her baby shooting out of her and being snatched away the same instant.

And then she remembered how the blood had rushed to her head as the doctor took one look at the tiny, lifeless being and said in one short sound – "Dead."

When she remembered this, the blood accumulated in her head once more, making her entire body fizz. The feeling dissipated within seconds, leaving a ringing noise in her ears. She swayed on her elbows slightly and slipped, going from propped on her elbows to completely horizontal. The corresponding jolt instigated the flood of tears that had been stubbornly evasive until now. Part of it was the hormones (they did exist, despite what Patrick said) and part of it was sheer, unadulterated grief. She had spent the last five months carrying around another human, battling waves of nausea in order to give him life, all for him to be snatched away by the doctors and put all by himself in some cold little room, never to be acknowledged again.

Dorothy had so lost her senses that she had a desperate urge to find her baby, and cuddle him, and comfort him. But she remained curled up on the bed, her body shaking as she tried not to make too much noise. She didn't want anyone to see her like this, not even the nurses, and least of all her husband. Poor Patrick – he'd been through enough with his family, and then the war, and the shellshock, without having to deal with his wife's pain too. She didn't want him to have this pain – and he wouldn't understand, anyway.

Nobody would understand how she'd felt that one brief rush of maternal instinct as she'd caught a glimpse of the defenceless little baby that she'd been nurturing, before it was whisked away out of her reach. She remembered the feeling of that maternal happiness draining away, out through her feet, collecting in a puddle on the floor and running away down the corridor to bless some other woman. And now she had the feeling of being completely alone, which she wasn't used to, after five months of her baby's almost companionship.

Somehow she must have gone to sleep, for the next thing she knew, she was being shaken awake by Nurse Page. The nurse feigned a chipper mood to try and chivvy Dorothy a little.

"Come along, come along, Dorothy," she chirped, "it's time for you to go home. Get a move on! Up you get, put on your skirt, at the double!"

Dorothy got dressed in some sort of daze, then Nurse Page took her to the exit and she was discharged. Patrick took her home in the cart, and even the horses picked up on the sombre mood as they trudged through the town. As they continued their arduous trek through Little Wychwood, they were stopped by Miss Eunice, a staid Scotswoman in her sixties who lived in a big house down one of the lanes with her friend Miss Marian. There had once been whispers that they were more than just friends, but these had long since died down and they were pillars of the community. Miss Eunice was decidedly matriarchal at the best of times, and so all rumours about herself and the gentler Miss Marian had been well and truly squashed.

"Ah, Dorothy, and Mister Patrick!" she said, patting one of the horses absentmindedly. "How are you doing with your expectancy? All doing well – no problems? We're both good with the little ones, Marian and I, so if you need any advice, you know who to ask."

"Thank you, Miss Eunice," Patrick said blandly. Dorothy smiled absently, then had an overwhelming urge to tell her the awful news.

"There is no baby any more. I gave birth to him yesterday. An' he died..." she told her, no expression at all in her voice or on her deathly pale face.

"Oh, my love, I am sorry!" Eunice exclaimed, knocked off her stride a little. Then, "Well, if you need anything... you know where I am."

"Thank you, Miss Eunice." Patrick said again, making an effort to sound thankful although he just wanted to get his wife home where she belonged. Pain was radiating off her, despite her resolution not to show it. With a click, Patrick sent the horses forward without further conversation, leaving Eunice with chills up her spine.

It was only when they were home that Dorothy lost it. All thoughts of protecting her husband went out the window as she shed her layers of defensiveness and Patrick saw the bare bones of her grief. And they were ugly: raw and sharp and tortuous. Patrick lay on the bed next to her, holding her while she struggled for breath between sobs, trying to soak up the pain she was feeling. He'd never thought he'd be capable of loving someone this much, wanting to take on everything that was ailing her. He'd always been a steely child – and yet here he was, aged only twenty, whispered "It's all right, I'm here..." to his sobbing nineteen-year-old wife. It suddenly struck him how young they both were to be experiencing this level of despondency – and indeed this level of responsibility. His siblings were barely adults still – and yet here he was, married with a stillborn son, in charge of an entire farm.

At that moment, there were footsteps on the stairs, which abruptly stopped when Dorothy's crying could be heard through the closed door of the bedroom. Then Rita, whose footsteps they were, turned around and walked back down the stairs respectfully. From the audible sobs from the normally stoic farmer's wife, she could tell that they had lost someone dear. And since she had been the one to find Dorothy having contractions in the kitchen the day before, she guessed that it was the baby.

By the end of the day, Ronald and Rita were finishing up on the farm and Dorothy had finally run out of tears for one day. The news had spread like wildfire across the village and at teatime, Reverend Osbourne, who was a kindly man in his late forties, knocked on their door to let them know that the whole village was thinking of them. Dorothy and Patrick were by no means prepared, mentally or physically, to receive visitors, but they let him in all the same. He was the ultimate level of power in their village, besides God, so what he said went.

When Dorothy entered the dining room, flushed but somewhat dignified, he stood up and took her hands gently, both of hers in both of his. It was an intimate gesture, but not inappropriate.

"Dorothy, I offer to you my deepest condolences," he said simply, before sitting down next to her at the table. Patrick came in with the teapot, and the vicar said the same to him. Then Dorothy did something strange. She sat up straight, lifted her head and looked innocently at the vicar.

"What on Earth for?" she replied.

"Well, the baby. The baby that Jesus has taken to heaven to live with him. *'Jesus said, "Let the little children come to me and do not hinder them, for to such belongs the kingdom of heaven."'* Your baby is safe with Him, Dorothy, do not-"

"What baby?" Dorothy cut him off again.

"The baby that-"

"There was no baby. I gave birth, but that baby no longer exists. Is that clear? He is not to be mentioned again."

If the Reverend was offended, he did not show it, despite the fact that he'd barely ever been spoken to like that in his life. He nodded and stood up.

"By all means, Dorothy. I won't trouble you any longer – and I'll see you at church tomorrow."

With this challenge (of sorts) he left, and Dorothy was able to relax once more. If she told herself hard enough that there was no baby, maybe she would believe it. Grief gave her a warped sense of logic, and with it, she felt very lonely.

CHAPTER 5 – 1920-1925

The coping mechanism that Dorothy employed to help her through the first few raw months following their baby's death was one that nobody had expected: denial. As far as she was concerned, their baby had never existed. She'd never been pregnant at all. This mystified Patrick – he didn't understand how she had the mental strength and control to convince herself this.

Reverend Osbourne had got the message and did not say anything more to Dorothy or to Patrick about the baby. If anyone else did, Dorothy nodded politely and changed the subject lightly. Her attitude was very much a "stiff-upper-lip" attitude – and Patrick went along with it. He'd never been one to talk about his feelings, but Dorothy had been with him in his darkest hours of shellshock and he wanted to look after her in her time of need. And it was so hard because whenever he tried to bring up the subject, she changed the subject briskly or just blocked his voice out completely. The only time they had properly talked about it was when they had decided to name the baby Maxwell, in honour of Patrick's friend.

To the rest of the village, Dorothy was completely through the death of her son. The whole situation was forgotten now, they thought, and Dorothy and Patrick were moving on together.

But secretly, they were not all right. Dorothy was not through it – not in a million years would she forget it, even though she wanted to. She desperately wanted to talk to Patrick about it, but he was under so much pressure. What with the remnants of lambing season, and their packed schedule, the last thing he needed was her pathetic whining. She *should* be getting over it, she knew, but she couldn't forget that right about now, she should have had a huge bump, soon to turn into a live, screaming, wriggling baby. Her hand kept unconsciously finding its way to her stomach, and the flatness that greeted it just kept serving as a reminder of what she had lost.

Dorothy was angry. Why wouldn't the world let her forget?

The atmosphere in Rosewood Farm Cottage changed. One could have cut it with a knife. Conversations were terse and clipped. Dorothy found herself intermittently gasping aloud, as if someone had suddenly kicked her, when in fact it was just reality giving her a little pinch. Patrick found himself only grunting in response to anything that was said. Ronald and Rita picked up on this, but they didn't feel that it was their place to mention it.

If Patrick had been a more sentimental man, he would have said that even the animals were picking up on the atmosphere. His ever-expanding menagerie had been fuelled by a mixture of warmth, sweet grass and tension, and they consequently wreaked havoc at every opportunity. Scarcely a day went by without a destroyed fence, or a scratched bit of paintwork, or a hoof through a wall. The partitions in the stable block had become disappointingly rickety, which just added to Patrick's frustrations. Then there was the added pressure of lambing season to consider. Baby animals were being churned out by the litter, each bringing a new life and new responsibility to the Hammond's shoulders.

Reverend Osbourne, who was known for being extremely

sensitive to the moods of the congregation, could tell that something was not right. He could almost see the simmering resentment increasing, week by week, in the farming family. He dropped a couple of family-based Bible verses into his teachings, such as Mark 10:9: *'What God has joined together, let no-one separate.'*

The vicar operated the church very efficiently indeed, and to a strict routine. There were three readers alongside himself: Frank Dyke, the schoolmaster, Jim Applewood, who ran the post office, and retired lawyer Stewart Awning. Each of them would read a small chunk of the Bible and talk briefly about what it meant, and how the village could become just that little bit better by following it. It was very good for sharpening the brain and learning about the world that God had created, and strengthened the amity in Little Wychwood. When the Reverend Osbourne had his weekly discussion with Mr. Dyke, Mr. Applewood and Mr. Awning one Saturday, the latter (a slow-moving but sharp-witted octogenarian) mentioned the couple.

"This new decade is showing up so many problems for our village. The Hammonds, of course..." and he sighed, his gaze flickering in the vague direction of the farm and his face wearing a very sad expression, "...well, their great loss is not to be sneezed at. They're coping so well – almost too well. One feels that there's something more beneath the surface there, something uncomfortable, that needs very little provocation to rise to the fore and run amok among this village's relative peace."

"Hear, hear," Mr. Dyke had agreed.

"We must do what we can to maintain that peace." Mr. Applewood replied. "We four shall meet again at a more convenient time to avoid the separation of what God has joined together."

"Our Lord works in mysterious ways," summarised Reverend Osbourne.

Mr. Dyke's wife had come in at that point with their daughter, and the meeting had broken up. Reverend Osbourne was glad to know that it wasn't just himself who had noticed a change in the Hammonds. And he was also glad to know that if the Hammonds ever decided to share their grief, he could inform them that he could rely on the Dyke, Applewood and Awning families to rally round.

He found out the following week that Ronald and Rita Wright had also noticed something wrong. They came to see him in the vicarage looking decidedly troubled.

"How may I help you both?" the vicar said encouragingly, sitting them down in his comfortable sitting room.

"We simply wanted to voice some concerns about the Hammonds, right?" Ronald said. He inwardly sighed. He'd been trying to get rid of his nervous habit of punctuating sentences with his homophonic surname, but the one-syllable word kept cropping up when he least wanted it. It was a wonder his wife hadn't picked it up, after forty-odd years of marriage. People would always respond in the same way: a perplexed repetition.

"Right," Reverend Osbourne replied on cue, leaning back in his seat and then forwards again.

"You see, Reverend, they seem to have just shut down completely in terms of their relationship." Rita continued. "The whole arrangement is just so... abrupt. I'm afraid to even utter the words, but... they really seem to have no love for each other."

At this declaration, the Reverend's eyebrows had almost disappeared into his greying hair. If there was one Bible verse that the whole village lived by, it was John 5:12 – *'This is my commandment, that you love each other as I have loved you.'* To hear such a vivid description of this verse's anti-climax was shocking and disappointing.

"What makes you think that, Rita?" Reverend Osbourne replied.

"Well, they don't seem to *communicate*. Ronald and I are being turned into the equivalent of human telegrams with the number of messages they send each other through us. And they're purely functional messages – "Please tell Dorothy that she left the cupboard door open last night", or "Please tell Patrick that the dog needs a run tonight", that sort of thing."

"And that's another thing, too," Ronald interrupted, "they call each other by their full names. Normally they call each other *Pat* and *Dot* like we do, but no longer, it seems."

"I see," Reverend Osbourne replied thoughtfully. "And when would you say these abnormal behaviours started?"

"Oh, I don't know, Reverend," Rita said, thinking. "A few months ago, maybe?"

"I see. And how many months ago was it that Dorothy lost the baby?"

"Two or three?" Rita replied after a moment's calculation. Then it had dawned on her and she gasped.

"What?" Ronald said in alarm.

"Reverend, do you think this is all *connected*?"

"That could well be the case."

"Oh, the poor things…" Rita murmured, looking stricken.

"But why would these behaviours be appearing *now,* after all this time? It's absurd, right?" Ronald pointed out, perplexed.

"It must have been horrendously traumatic for them both." Rita replied. "It's a bit like your cousin's shellshock, Ron, which has only just surfaced now, eighteen months after the war. But we can all agree that they haven't been right for a good few months – in fact, since they lost the baby."

For a few moments all three of them were silent, deeply saddened at the thought of Dorothy and Patrick's turmoil and the horrible twist in life that God had given them.

"But what should we *do*? Should we rebel against the messages and force them to communicate?" Rita appealed to the vicar. He shook his head.

"No – such direct confrontation could be the final straw and do irreparable damage. I think I will have to take it upon myself to offer my services in a subtle way to help them get back on track."

"And ours! We want to help too!" Rita responded hastily.

"Of course."

"Should we carry on as normal, then?" Ronald said.

"I'd say so, yes. I will pay them a visit on Monday, once I've worked out how to get my tone right."

The meeting had ended on this satisfactory note. Ronald and Rita were almost overcome with sympathy for the pair. Rita had even tried to give Dorothy a hug after church the next day, and to her surprise the recently undemonstrative young woman had hugged her back – a proper tight squeeze.

Dorothy had gone off hugs recently. Any display of public affection was seen as weakness on her part, but at that moment, the arms encircling her gave her almost an anchor. It proved that Rita knew that something wasn't right, and that she was prepared to offer her affection in an effort to make her feel better.

Dorothy just wanted an ounce of that affection from her husband.

Two days after the meeting of the Wrights with Reverend Osbourne, he paid a visit to the farm. As per his expectations, he barely got a few sentences out before Dorothy rebuked his offer of help and a listening ear.

"Why would we need yer help?" she'd interrupted him, shooting a glance at Patrick, who was frowning.

"Well, because-"

"We don't need yer help. We're fine. Th' farm's fine. If we needed help, you'd be th' first person we'd turn to. But we haven't done so – an' so we don't."

"Don't what?"

"Need help."

The vicar had returned to the vicarage very much troubled. But until they turned to him, he knew, there was nothing that he could do. Loathe as he was to admit it, his powers as one of those new-fangled *psychics* were painfully limited. For now, he'd have to give up.

But it made Dorothy think. The situation was becoming paralysing. But now her internal pain was reaching new levels of crippling and she just couldn't take it any longer. So later that evening, she finished the washing up, walked into the living room and slammed the door shut behind her. Patrick jumped out of his skin and withdrew his nose from his book.

"What is it?" he said, rather grumpily.

"I can't stand it."

"What? What's the matter?"

Dorothy wanted to talk, but she couldn't bring her mouth to form the words. She just couldn't imagine her own voice saying the words. So she went back out and fetched her diary, open at that day's page. She began to write, just like she had done before when things had gotten rough, and out it all came.

For the past four months I've been swallowing the memory of that child I had. Of Maxwell, the baby, Maxwell. I know everyone thinks I've been coping, but I haven't, I HAVE NOT BEEN COPING!!! It feels like a living thing, this grief, and I can't take it any longer. I have to tell someone, and that's you because you're my husband and I love you more than anything in the world. Even Reverend Osbourne has noticed something wrong. And now I'm admitting it, there IS something wrong. I've been keeping it all inside of me, and it's been eating me up. I thought I could conquer it but

I can't. And now it's affecting us both and I can't live like this any longer. I need help to sort myself out. I need YOU.

Patrick was silent, trying to comprehend these sentences in his mind. Dorothy had just admitted everything that he had expected, but not in the way he had expected. He realised that it was so much easier to write it down – for both of them. And what a difference it was going to make. It was strange how a few pieces of paper and some ink could have the ability to change lives.

"I'll help you." he said simply, reaching for her hand and pulling her close. She sat on his knee like a child. Then he murmured "I'll help you," – again, but quieter – "I'll do whatever it takes to help you. Because I've been feeling that too. All of that. Not quite to the extent that you have, but you have put into words my thoughts. I'll help you – if you help me."

"I will."

"Good. First thing's first – do you want to try again for a child?"

"Yes, of course!"

"Come on then!"

"What, now?"

"No time like the present."

"Can we sort things out first, then do it? I just want t' get it all organised in me head before anythin' else happens."

So they stayed up until the early hours of the next morning, just talking and talking. Dorothy shared every detail of the torment that she had been going through, and Patrick reciprocated.

Dorothy found it so incredibly therapeutic to simply talk. Once her mind allowed her to relax enough to get the words out, she talked about the whole experience of giving birth with no hope or sympathy, how she hadn't been able to even see her baby's face, how he had been snatched the moment he left her body, and how the end of his life had been summed up in one dismissive word from the doctor: "Dead."

Patrick talked too. He described how he'd felt them growing apart, how he'd felt the bonds of love, with which God had tied the pair of them together, growing taut and strained, like a piece of elastic being pulled at both ends.

"But we must be *resilient*," he said to her, looking her in the tear-stained eyes. There were a lot of tears from Dorothy, but Patrick found it physically impossible to cry. By the time they proceeded upstairs, she was dry-eyed and they were both smiling like they used to. Dorothy realised that she had made an almost fatal mistake in her handling of her grief: she had underestimated the healing properties of talking.

. . .

This pregnancy would be different, Dorothy told herself as she put on her hat and walked out into the sweltering July air. The last one had not ended well, and it had had a terrible effect on her life and her marriage. This one would be different. She told herself that she would remain steadfastly loyal and loving to her husband, regardless of anything and everything. She would keep in the best condition she could for her baby – she would keep supple, take in lots of fresh air and eat healthily.

Starting tomorrow, anyway. For today, she needed all the energy she could get. Despite telling herself this, she looked rather guiltily at the plate, decorated with cake crumbs, that she had just deposited in the sink. But she deserved it, she told herself – she was about to pay a visit to her decidedly intimidating parents-in-law.

"Come on, Dot! Into the trap!" Patrick called from the driver's seat of their borrowed light trap. They would be driving down to Houghton Regis this time. A telegram from Bruce had confirmed that they were free that day to have them over for luncheon. They were leaving early so that they had plenty of time to spare.

Patrick wasn't particularly happy with his parents, as they had completely failed to reply to his letter, informing them of baby Maxwell's death. Wilhelmina and Charlie had been far more concerned and caring – but of course Dorothy had shut them out, just like she'd shut out everyone.

Those days were over now. They had successfully created their second baby, which the doctor reckoned would be due around late December, and they were determined to make it thrive. In the five days that she'd known about the baby, Dorothy had been up to her eyeballs in early carrots and eating them by the handful, convinced that the benefits of a few orange vegetables would be the key to her baby's health.

The telegram had been answered very promptly indeed. They had been otherwise engaged until today (with what, Dorothy and Patrick couldn't guess) and so arrangements had been made for luncheon on Wednesday 21st July 1920. Dorothy had brushed up on her dinner-table etiquette and had already planned how she was going to break the news. Patrick had decided to be polite but curt. He had been deeply offended at his parents' lack of acknowledgment of the loss.

Dorothy had never enjoyed a drive more. Sitting next to her husband in the trap, holding his arm at various turbulent points, watching Colonel's strong Clydesdale body pull them through various towns and villages, and knowing that there was another tiny life form developing inside her, was all true bliss. It was the most wonderful feeling in the word to love, be loved, and have another human depending solely on her. With all of this came responsibility, of course, but the end result was love and a deep happiness that increased with every beat of Colonel's footfall. Dorothy relished the feeling, every moment of it, wanting to absorb every detail into her memory.

As the journey wore on and the temperature was cranked up a great deal, the novelty wore off a little and the nerves increased. Dorothy loved her mother-in-law, of course (as she saw her as a motherly but somewhat vulnerable lady), but she constantly felt that her father-in-law was judging her every move. She could never properly relax around him, as she had a feeling that he was analysing her and storing it all in his mind to use against her at some future point.

By the time they were trotting up the drive towards the house, Dorothy was a giggling, red-faced mess. As Patrick steered the horse towards the stables, where the groom was waiting, he sternly told her to pull herself together. By the time the maid let them in and led them to the drawing room, Dorothy was fairly serious again and could keep a straight face. And it was a good job too, as Edna looked rather mournful when they came in, although she stood up and smiled once she saw them.

They broke the news after they ate. The delicate asparagus soup, followed by fish in a creamy sauce and bread-and-butter pudding, was consumed very easily and washed down with light conversation. When the pudding bowls had been removed, Dorothy wiped her mouth with her serviette and cleared her throat.

"As you can guess, Bruce, Edna, we do have a reason for this unexpected visit." Dorothy begun, then glanced over at Patrick. He was staring into space and scowling. There had been no condolences offered, and neither of his parents had even mentioned the first baby. Patrick was fuming.

"What? I wasn't listening, sorry," he muttered. Bruce matched his son's scowl – what a display of bad manners!

"I was just saying," Dorothy continued in her best posh accent, "how we have a reason for our visit." She looked at him meaningfully – this was his cue to take over.

"Ah, yes. Well, no beating about the bush, Dorothy is expecting again."

"Wonderful news!" Bruce said gruffly. Edna smiled too.

"Congratulations – our second grandchild! How *is* our first grandchild, by the way? At home with the nanny, I take it?"

Dorothy and Patrick both looked at Edna, at Bruce and then at each other.

"Did you… did you not get the telegram?" Patrick said quietly.

"Only the one about today's visit," Edna replied, equally quietly. Bruce frowned at her – she was talking far too much for his liking, and he wasn't going to stand it.

"Ah…" Dorothy sighed.

"How can I put this…? Well, we lost the baby."

"Lost… as in… stillbirth?" Edna murmured.

"Yes, that's the most concise way of putting it."

"Oh…"

"These high infant mortality rates! They prey on the most vulnerable! Patrick, to my study, if you please." Bruce commanded, unable to sit there a moment longer. He stood up and nodded to Dorothy, and he and Patrick left the room together, leaving Edna a sort of mottled puce with embarrassment.

"I am terribly sorry if I offended you, my dear," Edna said eventually. Dorothy sat up straight again and smiled.

"Oh, don't ye worry, Edna. It happened a good while ago now – an' it hasn't been easy, but we're both so happy that I'm expectant again." Dorothy said. She was glad to drop the false accent – it took too much effort.

"All the same, it must have been a fearful shock. Now tell me – how is my Patrick, as a husband? Is he… dominating, at all?"

"Well… a little, I suppose."

"Good," Edna said, "because that is how a husband should be. There is a reason men are superior to women, you know."

Dorothy, ever the suffragist, pricked up her ears at this. She wasn't keen on Patrick's patriarchal idiosyncrasies, but she had no energy left in her to rebel. The farm, and now the baby, ensured that she was almost drained at the end of each day.

"Really? What's that reason, then?"

"Let me get my Bible."

When Edna returned, her Bible was open at Genesis (2:22). She put it carefully on the table in front of Dorothy and sat down beside her.

"Now – ah, here we are. *'Then the Lord God made a woman from the rib he had taken out of the man, and he brought her to the man. The man said, "This is now bone of my bones and flesh of my flesh; she shall be called "woman", for she was taken out of man." That is why a man leaves his father and mother and is united to his wife, and they become one flesh.'"*

Dorothy said nothing and remained expressionless.

"Do you understand that, my dear? That is why man comes above woman. Because without that rib that God took from Adam, he would never have made Eve. Eve depended on Adam, and therefore the rights of women depend on men, and to earn rights, a woman must cater to her man's every whim. My daughters understand that well, and you must too. There's something else in the Proverbs – 5:18:19 – *'May your fountain be blessed, and may you rejoice in the wife of your youth. A loving doe, a graceful deer – may her breasts satisfy you always, may you ever be intoxicated with her love.'* So as long as you keep your figure, and love my Patrick, he will love you forever. If there's one thing you should always keep in the forefront of your mind it's this: a wife must always obey her husband."

At that moment, Bruce and Patrick came in, the latter looking irate but his father looking fairly relaxed. Nobody would have guessed that just a minute previously, Bruce had been working himself up into quite a frenzy, telling Patrick how the loss of their baby was part of his punishment from God, and how he had to work harder at repentance...

Later, after they'd seen Patrick and Dorothy off, Bruce turned to Edna and said, "Did you educate Dorothy sufficiently?"

"Yes, Bruce," Edna replied.

"Yes, *Bruce*?"

Edna sighed.

"Yes, Sir."

. . .

Over the last twelve months, Edna mused, her husband had taken patriarchy to a whole new level, the likes of which had never been seen before in the Hammond family. He'd implemented a good few changes in the house, most notably that she, his *wife*, was to address him as Sir, just like the children and the staff. He had deified himself to a point at which he saw himself as almost on par with God. He told them all that God was working and communicating through him, and that if they wanted to get into Heaven, whatever he said was to be obeyed in an instant.

Edna felt completely stifled, suffocated almost. He monitored her every move, her every mouthful, her every letter. She dreaded mealtimes, for if he thought she was eating too fast, or too much, he would whisk her plate away and give it to the waitress to be taken back to the kitchens. Wherever she went, either he or Mike (whom he had roped into his project) would follow – even to the bathroom. On the rare occasions she left the house, she had been struck with some sort of agoraphobia, and ended up clutching Bruce's arm, as much to stop herself collapsing as for comfort. This greatly pleased him, and he reasoned that if his wife knew to depend on him for soothing, she wasn't quite lost to the devil just yet.

All of the females of the household – including the maids, the nanny and the cooking staff – were under his control.

Previously, the servants had had their own lives below stairs, but now he made several visits during the day to make sure that there was no sin down there. The nanny, who was nearing frailty now, had begged to be able to retire and go back to her hometown of Aberystwyth, but to no avail. She had fallen under his spell after Edna had become pregnant with Bessie, and now there was no getting out. They were all trapped – the staff, the daughters, and poor Edna.

The Christmas of 1920 was one of mixed feelings for Edna. Church was filled with beautiful singing and reading, as usual, and she remembered how two years previously, she had had to leave after hearing *Adeste Fideles.* However, this year, that same carol brought a smile to her face. Dorothy's baby must be due soon, surely? Patrick and Dorothy had promised to visit, with the baby, in the new year, and she could hardly wait.

However, on the way back she was subjected to one of Bruce's verbal diatribes, which put a slight tinge of darkness on the day. He ranted on at her, not bothering to lower his voice for the children. He told her that by clearing her throat so loudly, she had put shame on the whole family. If it was up to him, he said, she would be forced to do all sorts of things for the congregation to make up for it.

As it was, all of the women sat at the back, seldom moving, and they were not allowed to speak aside from singing. The congregation took the Bible very seriously, and very literally, which meant that the women were sometimes dehumanised and sometimes cherished, depending on who was reading and from where. Bruce was much in favour of the first option and did not seem to understand the then-unfamiliar view that the wife had carried the man's children, and was a human being, and therefore deserved respect.

It was enough to drive anyone mad. The one thing keeping Edna going was the thought of her new grandchild. She just prayed that Dorothy hadn't lost the baby again and that they were all the pictures of health.

And indeed they were. Dorothy's baby had suddenly expanded over the last couple of months, and anyone who passed her took one look at her huge bump and smiled knowingly and thankfully. These days, Dorothy always beamed back, but not all of her pregnancy had been so happy.

At around the four-month mark, when Dorothy was still unaccustomed to the changes going on in her body and the restrictions that they caused, she had sunk into a bit of a dip and didn't have the energy to get back out. That was where Miss Marian and Gwendolyn Applewood had stepped in. They were both very keen singers, especially Miss Marian, and her rich, mellifluous voice was the icing on the cake of their enthusiastic congregation. They were all lovely to hear at any time, but every Christmas they surpassed themselves as they voiced their ecstasy over what had happened all those years ago.

So in August, Dorothy was persuaded to join the church choir, which a great deal of the village attended. They met in the church every Friday evening and went through their songbooks, singing to their heart's content. Gwendolyn had been a singer and an actress before she met Jim, and so she gave Dorothy a few tips on how to avoid losing her breath on the high or long notes. After she'd married Jim, she'd given it all up and spent most days spinning wool and knitting, even though she was only in her fifties. She was content, these days, to teach others. Dorothy had taken the knitting up, too, and between them they had fashioned a few outfits for the baby.

The three of them – Dorothy, Miss Marian and Gwendolyn – began meeting up at the big house that Miss Marian shared with Miss Eunice. Dorothy was still quite awestruck, and even though she called Gwendolyn by her first name, she still called Miss Marian and Miss Eunice by their seemingly universal names. (Nobody knew their surnames, and it would have seemed improper, somehow, to just call them by their Christian names, so the whole village referred to them as Miss Eunice and Miss Marian.)

Dorothy loved nothing better than standing by the ladies' old piano, on which she had been taught to bash out a few tunes, and singing along to whatever was being played. Pregnancy had lent her voice a new sweetness, and the rough edges had been smoothed out by their tutoring to make it truly beautiful.

The best part, however, came at the end of the afternoon when Miss Marian would sing for them. Miss Eunice would often join them for this, and sat next to Dorothy, gazing fondly at her friend as she hit the dizzying high notes of the soprano part of Handel's *Messiah* whilst somehow adding in the other parts on the piano. Miss Eunice would often go to help her, staying at one end of the piano, letting Miss Marian focus on the other end and on the words. Dorothy marvelled at how they never hit the same notes by mistake at the middle of the piano! It was just testament to what talented musicians they both were.

Miss Eunice surprised everyone – including herself – one day by agreeing to do a down-tempo duet of *There's a Good Time Coming* with Miss Marian, although they changed the word *boys* to *girls* to fit the present company. Dorothy had relaxed in her armchair with a mug of sweet tea and let their harmonies fill the room.

Miss Marian was a good cook, and so they took to dining together on these afternoons. She gave Dorothy some tips and tricks, and soon both of them could rustle up a substantial meal from leftovers. Dorothy took these tricks back home and reduced her food waste a great deal.

While these little meetings were going on, Patrick had joined the local hunt for a little outing every Tuesday afternoon. Winston, his sprightly horse, loved nothing more than dashing pell-mell after their prey while Patrick lightly steered him. They had returned gleefully home from the first one with two rabbits. Dorothy had been pleased, but couldn't stomach cooking them and left that to Rita.

As the months went on, however, Dorothy grew more and more used to cooking whatever Patrick brought home – and using up the leftovers. Bones made good soup, and cold meat was just as delicious as hot meat. As a result of this increased tolerance, they had a lovely Christmas meal. They had invited Rita and Ronald, in order to reciprocate the favour of last year, when Dorothy had been too grief-stricken to cook.

Dorothy slaved for hours over the stove that Christmas. She had less than two weeks to go until her predicted birth date. Rita helped her, and she noticed that everything had to be just right, otherwise Dorothy would fret.

"Your homely instinct is kicking in, Dot," she said knowingly.

"You what?"

"When your baby is due, you'll start feeling a *need* to clean up and make a nice little nest to bring your baby into. It's all part of the maternal instinct. I did it with my first, and my third."

"Ye have children? I didn't know!"

"Four, my dear. All long since buried, I regret to say."

"Rita, I'm so sorry... I had no idea!" Dorothy whispered.

"Don't be. They all died as children, far too early, but it was a long time ago. Anyway – enough of my story! Have you had any twinges, or anything?"

"No, an' hardly a movement, either!"

"What, none at all?" Rita said, alarmed.

"Oh, some, of course. But he spends most of his time sleepin', it seems!"

"Sounds like my first – rather a lazy baby, that one. Now, about these sprouts..."

Dorothy was rather shocked at hearing about Rita's loss. She didn't press the subject; she noticed how Rita avoided talking about it and always changed the subject abruptly whenever it came up. She also remembered how upset Rita had been after finding out that they had lost the baby. It all made so much sense now, and she felt rather guilty for pushing her care away. Even if it had been months since she'd first started accepting people's concerns, she did feel a little guilt for the months in which she had buried her head in the sand.

She doubted she'd ever lose the guilt. And now she'd learnt about Rita, it stabbed her once again. How could she go on churning out babies while her closest friend and mother figure looked on, knowing full well that the said mother figure would give anything for those babies to be hers? Rita had been so brave. She'd watched Dorothy cry over the loss of one, and all the time she had been inflicted with pain that was quadrupled in severity.

For the first time in a good few months, Dorothy felt herself sink into that familiar pit of sadness as she looked at her strong friend. Rita saw the tears in her eyes and smiled bravely, and the pair of them hugged (carefully). Rita, trying not to cry herself, whispered "Come on, these sprouts won't peel themselves," but Dorothy was reluctant to let go. She then gave herself a mental smack and lifted herself out of the pit of sadness. Christmas was a time for celebration – well, she'd give Rita and Ronald something to celebrate!

"You'll be godparents, won't ye?" she whispered.

At first there was silence, and Dorothy wondered whether Rita was speechless. But then she heard a shuddering gulp from Rita and realised that they were both crying now.

"Oh, Lord," Rita laughed quietly through her tears, "I'm not hesitating – what must you think of me? Yes, my dear, we'd be honoured to be godparents."

They hugged again, and then carried on with the meal preparations. Rita could not stop staring at the baby bump, dreaming of how much she would treasure and spoil the new arrival. She would be Auntie Rita – how wonderful!

At the end of grace, Dorothy did something rather unexpected, and added to it. "An' we also give thanks, not just for the food, but for such precious friends as these. Yer goin' to be great godparents, the both of ye."

"*Godparents,* you said?" Ronald spluttered, while Patrick said nothing. He had been planning on raising the subject of making them the godparents with Dorothy, but she had beaten him to it. And for once, he was proud of her for using her initiative.

"I did," Dorothy smiled.

"We'd be honoured!" Ronald replied with no hesitation, reaching for his watery-eyed wife's hand under the table.

"All I can say is…" Rita said, then paused, composing herself, "enjoy your freedom while it lasts, you two – but enjoy the children more."

. . .

Whilst the physical pain was the same this time around, there was something different about this labour: the mental pain had gone. There was no reason for the child to die; Dorothy had successfully carried him to near enough full-term. There was still around a week to go, but the doctor assured her that the baby was a decent size and kicking nice and strongly. Over the past week – since Christmas, in fact – a giant bubble of energy had enveloped the baby, and consequently, Dorothy had had very little sleep.

This labour was the complete opposite of the first one. There was not a single scream, wail or sob. Dorothy was far less stressed, for several reasons, especially because this time she was in her home environment. But one stood out: this time, she'd have a reward at the end. Last time, there had been nothing but hollow emptiness and a sense of failure waiting at the end of the labour. But this time, Dorothy knew that she would not be left empty-handed. Provided that all went well in the next few hours, they'd have a baby for them to keep and to hold forever.

There had been a few poignant moments with Rita in the six days since Christmas. She had thanked Patrick and Dorothy endlessly for letting them be godparents. "Don't go losing this one, now!" she'd joked at one point, wiping a tear from her eye, "My heart would never stand the grief!"

Although everyone laughed, they all knew that Rita had meant what she said. To lose a child is shattering enough, and to lose four even more so. Rita had thought that the wounds had healed, but seeing Dorothy's baby bloom had made her realise that no, they hadn't. If by now, aged sixty-nine and in rude health, they weren't healed, then she reckoned that they never would be.

To take her mind off it, almost, she spent the next few days going through a vigorous list to check that everything was ready. And it was. Dorothy had been given a run-down of how to keep the baby's feeding equipment spotlessly clean. The Moses basket sat on the table next to Dorothy's hospital bed, ready to carry the baby home. Ronald and Rita would be staying at the farm for the next couple of weeks, looking after the animals.

Patrick pushed them out of his mind and focused on Dorothy. He was almost hopping with excitement, and continuously badgered the midwife to check on Dorothy's progress. Always the verdict was the same.

"Mr. Hammond, you can't rush this," Miss Page informed him sternly, smiling knowingly at Dorothy. "Your wife is doing perfectly well. The baby will come when the baby will come."

This didn't stop Patrick getting antsy. He took to pacing around the room, stopping only to coach his wife through the attacks of pain that left her breathless and gritting her teeth. The pacing, combined with the leaps towards the bed every time there was a hint of a contraction, heightened the excitement in their little bubble to a dizzying level.

(Dorothy's dizziness may also have had something to do with the fact that with every contraction, she accidentally held her breath until she was blue in the face and the room began to swirl.)

Gradually, there became a noticeable increase in the frequency and ferocity of these contractions. Patrick became, if anything, more frantic.

"Surely it shouldn't be taking this long. It's been thirteen hours!" he muttered on loop, first to himself, then to the midwife.

"You should be delivering within the next few hours, Mrs. Hammond." she replied.

Eventually, Dorothy herself was in very active labour, and their child was born at fourteen minutes past nine on the last evening of 1920. Dorothy could barely speak for euphoria. Miss Page wrapped the baby – a boy, she confirmed – in a receiving blanket, and placed him in Dorothy's waiting arms, where he belonged, where he would always belong.

For one terrible second her eyes scanned him over, expecting his eyes to be shut and his body to be blue and motionless. But no, he was pink and crying loudly, announcing to the world that he was here and he was all right. Relief flooded through her, and love.

"You don't know how hard we've longed for you..." Dorothy said to him, resting her head against his, half-laughing and half-crying. Right there and then, in her head, she promised her baby that she would be a good mother to him.

The whole world seemed to be just perfect that night. Even Miss Page smiled as she left them. She had been there with Dorothy in the hospital as she gave birth to Maxwell, and there was no better scene than seeing a previously traumatised, robbed mother with a tiny, pink, very much living baby.

The doctor, who dropped by to check that all was well after last time, wanted to get Dorothy up on her feet before the end of the year, so at ten to twelve they helped her up, still cradling the sleeping baby, and Patrick walked slowly outside with her. It was a relief to leave the hot, sticky atmosphere of their smallest bedroom. Dorothy and Patrick drunk in the cold air with relief. The air in the bedroom had been rather stale. Every time either of them looked at their son, they felt a fizzing in their veins.

"Just look at what we made..." Dorothy whispered to Patrick. As the clock struck twelve to signal the old years' disappearance into the new one, there they stood together, bathed in the light from their front door, silhouettes melting together, gazing at their new-born son.

. . .

Despite her new grandson reportedly thriving and eagerly awaiting a visit to her, Edna couldn't find it in her to go on any longer. She was past caring about any consequences: any prison sentence, any unintended (yet unlikely) sorrow from her family, or the (more likely) eternal hatred. That was why she did what she did.

She loathed herself for it, but she loathed her husband more. Over the course of their marriage, he had attempted to indoctrinate her and turn her into a compliant, meek little object, to be used and moved around to his liking. He'd found more and more ways to be controlling recently, and her life had been conducted within four solid, impenetrable walls.

One evening, sitting in an armchair and staring into a book without reading it, she found her gaze veering upwards and to the right, where her husband was sitting. His faded hair was turning a pale red at that moment from the light of the roaring fire. She glanced at Bessie and Gertrude too, and her heart ached with fondness for them both, and with sadness at all their destiny was. But the aching was instantly terminated when she looked back over to her husband. For him, she felt nothing at all. It was as if she didn't know who he was.

In an effort to stir up those feelings, long since gone, of infatuation, she recalled her earliest memories of their relationship.

If she closed her eyes, she was almost in the room of the grocery shop. Herself behind the counter, writing down in a notebook the list of purchases from the previous customer. The door opening and herself saying, without looking up, "I'll be with you in a moment!" in her best business-like voice. Looking up and finding a young man, around the same age as she was, peering over the counter to see what she was writing.

"Can I help you, Sir?" she'd said sharply, going bright red. Never before had she been so close to a man of her own age, let alone at work.

He'd asked for two dozen carrots, she remembered that. He had been well-groomed and full to the brim with charisma. As she counted out the vegetables for him, he'd inspected her approvingly.

"And with whom am I having the pleasure?" he'd asked just before he left. When she'd informed him of her name – Edna Thomas – he'd simply nodded, bowed and departed.

A few days later, she had received a letter from the young gentleman, inviting her to a ball at a nice house in Highbury, owned by an old Colonel. He hosted incredibly lavish balls with all sorts of modern food and dancing. An invitation to such a gathering at Everleigh House was the most coveted and sought-after thing in her whole group of friends. Edna had almost dropped the letter. After work, she'd set out to reply in the affirmative in her best italics.

Normally, she was one of the saucier, more outgoing personalities. At work she had to be subservient, of course, but she was decidedly extroverted anywhere else. She intended to show her true colours at the ball, and dazzle them all with the beauty that she knew she had. Because she *had* been beautiful back then, with petite stature and deep blue eyes framed by beautiful black lashes. Her golden hair – and such an abundance of it – tumbled down her back and over her shoulders, not a hint of grey anywhere. When brushed, it shone. Bruce had noticed, and he was unashamed to admit that it was this – and only this – that had attracted him to Edna in the first place.

She was nineteen, so of course she obtained her father's permission. He wasn't a particularly domineering man, unlike most of her friend's fathers, but he was over the moon that she had been invited by a man to such an esteemed event.

It turned out that Bruce was very distantly related to the Colonel (second cousin three times removed, or something like that), hence the invitation for him and a 'friend'. Since there were no other ladies on the scene, and he'd admired the prettiness of the little shop girl, he decided to take a chance. He wasn't particularly hopeful that it would amount to anything – after all, she was just a shop girl – but it would avoid him being labelled as 'Billy-no-mates'.

When he'd met her in person again, on the night of the ball, he was stunned at how different she looked. With the pigtails replaced by long, loose hair and the shop uniform replaced by a fetching blue tartan dress, she looked so different and he knew he wanted her. He also knew that he had to tread carefully, and not show his true feelings, so it was as much as he could do to smile at her and bow. Edna's father shook his hand but said very little, noting to himself the greedy gleam in Bruce's eye. Bruce had his own driver, and they all made pretty conversation as the horses bumped along the roads. They arrived at the ball and were shown in by a maid.

Remembering their manners, they first went to say *how-do-you-do* to the lady of the house. The Colonel was engaged in an uproarious conversation to the lady's left, and she was standing to the side looking rather bored. To Edna, she looked majestic and regal, and she found herself lingering behind Bruce as he stepped forward to greet her.

"Dearest Auntie!" Bruce said (loudly, since she was quite deaf). She turned slowly, stiffly, and regarded him imperiously.

"Dear cousin," she replied in a sharp, silvery voice that gave no insight into whatever emotion she was feeling.

"How are you, Auntie?"

"Well, let's see," she responded, "My back is hunching, my hands are crippling and my head pounds with pain, so I'm doing splendid."

"I'm sorry to hear that, Auntie."

"You'd be sorry if you had to endure it, child!" she retorted scathingly, before the Colonel butted in with his loud braying voice.

"Ah, more guests! Annie, you haven't the manners to ask, "with who am I having the pleasure?" – really, dear!"

"Dearest husband, you chide me and yet you haven't even the grammar to ask, "with whom am I having the pleasure?""

Her tone was biting, with only the faintest note of teasing. She clearly had no time for this ball and it was just another thing she endured on behalf of her husband. She barely sent Edna a second glance until Bruce pulled her forward and introduced her.

"Edna Thomas," repeated the lady, "I see. If you are going to be good enough to court our cousin, you must be polite and well-brought up. I see that you have not yet shaken my hand. This will be noted."

"Beg pardon, my lady." Edna bobbed nervously, wondering what on Earth had become of her. Something made her afraid of being on the end of that razor-sharp tongue.

"You, beg? That is incorrect – a good lady does not go on the floor and beg. She *faces* her adversity and overcomes it, isn't that right?"

"Yes, my lady," Edna replied, beginning to warm to her. That was the end of the conversation, for the lady turned away and called out a reprimand to one of the waiters.

That was also the first time Edna had had an inkling into the uniqueness of Bruce's family. She cursed herself for not running for the hills. She'd let herself be carried away, firstly by the novelty and then because it was just easier than resisting. She'd trusted him, followed him the whole way in blind faith, and where had it led her?

Here.

It was made all the worse because she *knew* her fate could have been so, so different. Mere weeks before meeting Bruce, she'd been swept off her feet by a young man, a Mr. Montgomery, a friend of her own cousin. They'd spent an evening at Edna's house together, in the company of Mr. Thomas, whiskey and pleasant conversation. It was not done for a Victorian bachelor to drink excessively, but Mr. Montgomery had had a small amount of whiskey and the evening went with a swing. Only at the end had he shattered her heart.

He had revealed that, despite his feelings for her, he was not prepared to court her or advance any sort of friendship or relationship. He lived far away in York, and the geography meant that communication would have been halting and limited. He'd had a lovely evening, he said, and if things had been different, he'd have married her like a shot.

Edna had been stunned. She'd completely and utterly fallen for him that night. When he'd announced this, just after Mr. Thomas had left the room, she'd had to sit down and comprehend it. In her head she had skipped ahead to their wedding day: herself looking radiant, Mr. Montgomery looking at her adoringly, without the regret she was seeing in his face at the present moment.

Stupid girl, she'd thought. *You don't even know his first name.*

He would be snapped up in an instant by any sane woman, she knew. But in her mind, Mr. Montgomery was hers. Edna Montgomery – how wonderful that would have been! She didn't want to let him go – she wanted to push him back into his seat and hold him there forever.

She would find him one day, she'd vowed, a sudden surge of anger bursting into her. Nothing would keep her away. She'd be a martyr for now, enduring her celibacy silently. Then, after years of spinsterhood, she'd impress him with her devotion and turn up on his doorstep, and whisk him into a church. She'd make him regret prioritising *York* over her.

Then she'd looked up again, and her heart went into freefall. She'd realised that he was waiting for her to terminate the silence; he was too cowardly to do so himself. Well, he'd have to deal with it. If she couldn't marry him, she'd decided, she'd find someone like him. Yes, she'd invite him to her wedding, with the wife and children he would inevitably have acquired by then, and watch the regret in his face as he would realise what he could have had.

But deep down, she wished him no ill. All these erratic thoughts were just shock, alcohol and conflicting emotions. She looked up again, and the hardness in his face had been replaced by softness and fondness.

"You're letting me down?" Edna whispered, barely audibly, but he'd still heard it. He picked her right up and into his arms.

"I'm sorry, Edna. If things were different..."

"I know. But they're not."

Maybe that was why she had been won over by Bruce so easily, Edna mused. Her stronghold had taken a battering, and it had collapsed. The early days of their relationship were glorious, filled with laughter, sunshine and fresh home baking, and at their wedding she had seldom glowed more.

But as the years went on and children appeared on the scene, it became increasingly hard to distinguish a family tradition for a newly conjured method of female restriction or... well, oppression. Edna detested that word, but she found it fitting, and the only way to describe what Bruce had done to her. Bruce had always been dominant, right from the start, but he took patriarchy to the extreme when the children arrived. It had started when she was first expecting Andrew. He had insisted that she spend the entire duration of the pregnancy in bed (with the exception of Sunday mornings, for church, of course) to avoid anything happening to her or the baby.

At least, that was what she had thought back then. Bruce thought a little differently. He had been warned by one of his neighbours about how his wife had almost been unfaithful during her pregnancy. "Keep her well under control, that's my advice, son," he'd said. Bruce had taken him very seriously indeed – and from there, Edna's life had spiralled downwards until, sitting there by the fire on a cold evening in February 1921, she was plunged to her lowest ebb. Realising what she could have been brought tears to her glassy eyes.

Why hadn't she gone with Mr. Montgomery? She could have followed him to York! She hadn't even known his Christian name, and yet there had seldom been a day where she hadn't thought of him. Her father had left them alone, for a reason for which she knew or cared none, and he'd made his announcement. They'd danced to the record on the gramophone. It had been charmingly romantic, and there had been a true tenderness in his eyes, mixed with sadness because he knew that this would be the last and only time. Whenever she'd heard that record since, she'd thought of him, and the way he'd made her feel.

But right now, she thought that if she received a wound, she would not feel it. It was as if her skin was no longer skin. It was simply a covering, a way to contain her writhing emotions. Cupid's Arrow, as Bruce had once poetically put it in a romantic moment years ago, had struck her well and truly down. It had hurt before, when she'd first realised that she was trapped, but not now.

Edna's whole body shivered as she took a trembling breath in. She folded up the letter she was writing and then exhaled shakily again. Nobody noticed. She wanted to speak, to share her sorrow with someone, but she'd tried that once before with Bruce.

"I'm feeling a little stifled," she'd said, and that was as far as she had got.

"Well, that's a woman's job. You'd best just accept your lot now, because nothing will change." he'd said abruptly.

What in God's name is happening to me?

Edna clutched her head in an effort to destroy the burning pressure building up in there. It was an intolerable sensation, the likes of which she had never experienced before. It was both physical and mental, and brought tears to her eyes.

Nothing would change if I wasn't here. Nobody would give a damn. It's harsh but true. They'd all carry on, and act like I never existed. Because I don't exist to them. I'm just an object. The only thing that would change would be an extra gravestone in the graveyard. Good God, what is happening to me?

She stopped herself from scribbling on the back of the letter. The recipients would get quite a shock if they read all that. She staggered to her feet and crept across the room. Bruce jumped to his feet in response to the creaking of the door.

"Where are you going?" he asked briskly.

"Just to the lavatory, Sir," she whispered, avoiding his eyes that bored like gimlets and saw into her very core.

"Very well – don't be long." he replied, sitting back down

again. Edna couldn't believe that he wasn't following her, but she was past caring. The girls barely acknowledged this, but Mike shared a glance with Bruce, more between colleagues than father and son.

Edna did go to the bathroom, but took a detour via the kitchen and the bedroom. She put her letter in an envelope, wrote a few words on it, and hid it (alongside a few other precious letters) on her person. She made her bed carefully, before finally going to the bathroom. Her heartbeat increased with every step she took. She wrenched open the cabinet, breaking the fragile lock with sheer strength. For just one moment, she paused, looking at the broken lock. *Did I really just do that?* Then, as if she'd never stopped, she grabbed the nearest pillbox and stared at it, wondering exactly what acetaminophen was. There were only a few pills in the box – they'd have to do.

There she sat, on the closed seat of the lavatory, with the pillbox balanced on the sink next to her. Her shiny eyes were trained on the box. Her mask was ripped off. She couldn't believe what she was about to do – but she did it anyway.

. . .

"Is that everythin'?" Dorothy said, placing the hamper on the kitchen table. For once, it wasn't covered with cooled baked goods. They were having a rare day off – although it wasn't without its drawbacks. Patrick had been up since four sorting out the animals with Rita and Ronald, while Dorothy snatched fitful sleep in between sorting out baby Frederick. He woke regularly in the night to feed (although she was starting to wean him, at six months old) and it was draining. But Dorothy was determined to be well rested for today. It was the annual village fayre – and Freddy's first official outing! Dorothy had not been to church since Freddy's birth because she knew he'd only make a disturbance. The vast majority of the village had not seen her since Christmas, and they had all missed seeing her beaming face every week.

The annual village fayre was an upbeat affair, with frequent singing and little games for the children of the village, all held in the village square. Everyone brought their own picnic and shared with each other, interacted, and rejoiced in community spirit. It happened on the first Saturday of July, and it had never rained once in all the years they had been doing it. This year was no different, and by eleven o'clock it was sunny and warm.

Dorothy brought Freddy downstairs in the Moses basket, dressed in a little crisp white outfit, and placed him in the pram. They were to meet Ronald and Rita there, and Rita was very excited at seeing her little godson out and about. Dorothy had never looked prettier, in a delicate chequered dress and complimentary hat. Patrick was dressed more casually than he did at church, and they both beamed down at their son.

They had never been happier, really. Every little hitch of parenthood, they had accepted, because they knew how lucky they were. They'd decided that it took a real loss to really appreciate a life. Ronald and Rita had ended up picking up a lot of the slack in terms of the farming and cooking duties, but they had accepted and enjoyed it.

"Don't be daft!" Rita had responded when Dorothy apologised for the workload.

"But really-"

"No, honestly, don't worry about it. It reminds us of our old farm in Folkestone. We had a lovely time down there, Ronald and I, and since retiring up here we've rather missed farming. But be warned – we won't be here forever," she added sternly.

"Don't be silly, Rita, there's years in you yet!" Dorothy had laughed, but that ominous last sentence had stayed with her. Rita was right. How *would* they cope without them?

But for today, all troubles in the village were pushed aside. It was lovely weather and Miss Marian had promised to sing at some point, just like she did every year. That was the highlight of every fayre, for her voice could reach incredible intensities and volumes and could be heard anywhere in the square.

Dorothy picked up the pram and Patrick picked up the hamper, and they both walked through the front door. Patrick didn't even bother locking the door – the village was that safe. Dorothy savoured the warm rays hitting her face; she had really missed the sun during the long housebound days with the baby.

Walking past the gate, they stopped and looked over it. Through the gate, they could see the horses. Delph looked back at them – poor, stir-crazy Delph, who hadn't been ridden properly in months – and upon seeing her former rider, she whinnied.

"I really must get around to exercising that creature," Patrick said, making a mental note.

"Ye mean to say she ain't been ridden all these months? Eleven months, Pat, since I stopped ridin' her, an' nobody's even taken her out for a hack? That's hardly the work of a responsible farmer!"

Maybe it was the heat that had made her talk so rashly, but Patrick looked at her oddly. He'd never really been spoken to in that way by a woman before, not even his mother. Dorothy caught the look, and averted her gaze.

"Sorry, Pat. It's just this heat, ye know? Yer a perfect farmer – an' I know, like yer mam said, *a wife must always obey her husband.*"

"Did she really say that?" Patrick with a little smile.

"Aye, she did. An' ye can bet yer boots I'll be passin' that on to all our daughters."

Patrick smiled properly. His father had done a good job of turning his mother into the ideal woman. If he was to do that to Dorothy, he must maintain that mindset of hers.

"Good girl!" he said, almost as if she were a child. She didn't notice, though, for she was staring dreamily into the pram at her sleeping six-month-old. She couldn't imagine loving a person more. And he looked just like she had imagined Maxwell – blonde and adorable.

As soon as they entered the square and lay down their rug on a grassy verge, they were besieged by cooing elderly ladies, all wanting to get a glimpse of the much-awaited baby. One was particularly endeared and gasped, "Oh! He's an angel – sent straight from Heaven!" and the assembled company all agreed.

"How on Earth did you create him?" Mrs. Dyke said. "I mean, I thought our Rachel was a pretty baby – but this one..."

Others said that Patrick must have done something spectacular to win such approval from God. The general consensus was that their farming family had been incredibly privileged to be sent such a gift. By the time the whole village was in the square and the small band was playing, Freddy had been smothered in kisses and held by many gentle hands.

He'd been perfectly behaved about it all, smiling up at whoever was holding him. When it was time for him to have his lunch, Rita ushered away the queue and redirected them to their own picnic rugs. After he was full, he went to sleep in the basket while several people smiled at him as they walked by. At this point, Dorothy was approached by several people who had run to their houses and back with gifts.

"I forgot all about this," said Mrs. Awning, handing Dorothy a wrapped parcel, "and so I'm giving it to you now. It's just a little hat and a pair of gloves. Pink, I know, but it'll save him getting cold when the winter weather sets in."

Others gave money, little books and in one case, a chain with a Christian cross on it. Reverend Osbourne gave him a Bible, just as he did for every new baby in the village. Freddy's appearance had been long-awaited, and so the celebrations and blessings went into overdrive. He had already been baptised, of course, in a private affair, to which Bruce and Edna had been unable to attend.

Come to think of it, since their telegram congratulating them on Freddy's birth, they hadn't heard a peep from the Hammond grandparents. Dorothy realised that she didn't really know much about them. She knew that their eldest child had defied the authority of his father and disappeared a few years back. They all believed that he'd gone to war to find Patrick, and they severely hoped not, Patrick himself especially. The mental wounds that the experience had inflicted were still barely healed, although he did not get as many episodes as before, since the birth of Freddy. Maybe he was starting to come to terms with what he had seen. After all, death is the most scarring thing to witness, and to believe that one has caused it just multiplies the pain. But Patrick was confident that he would get through this. All he needed was good friends, neighbours, family and love.

In the evening, when the sun was starting to set, Dorothy held Freddy while the whole village gathered in the square and sung. Ever since the poem *Jerusalem*, by William Blake, had been set to music five years previously, they'd sung it every year in the hope that one day, they'd truly experience Heaven on Earth.

Later, Dorothy wrote in her faithful diary the following paragraph, and she read it several times over the years to come, as a reminder that happiness was still there and waiting.

Today has been a truly perfect day. Reverend Osbourne and the whole village adore Freddy, and I think they've accepted Pat and I as locals. I never thought, in my wildest dreams, that I'd ever feel so content. The sun's shone all day, I've received so much love, and even Pat has let his guard down and let the village see the relaxed, jolly fellow that I know. It's made everything worth it, for I've got everything I could ever wish for – my own house, friends, and a family, all of which I love and love me back. And right at the end

*of this glorious day, Reverend Osbourne asked Pat if he would like
to do some teaching of a Sunday during the Church service. Things
cannot get much better for us and I know that in years to come, I'll
regard these years when Freddy is young as the happiest of my life.*

Her happiness expressed on paper, she found herself able to
sleep, and even Freddy stayed asleep for a full four hours! She
knew that she had to make the best out of every moment she
could now, for she'd need the memories to sustain herself for
whatever life hurled at her in the future.

And she wouldn't have to wait too long for that.

. . .

Despite all the happenings of the past months, Edna was far
happier now. There were times, however, that she had to just
stop and run through those happenings in her head to make
sense of them. She found herself stunned at how far she'd
come.

Well, she'd gone through with it, for a start. She hadn't
wanted to die, but she had wanted her situation to end. When
Bruce had grown suspicious due to her lack of return from the
bathroom, he'd found her hunched over on the lavatory seat,
barely awake.

Upon waking up in the hospital, her first thought was, *I'm not
dead.* This was shortly followed by; *My head is in agony – what
on Earth has happened?*

Shortly afterwards, when she was up on her feet and drinking a cup of reviving tea, and trying to retrieve her memories,
the police had come and arrested her for attempting suicide.
Bruce, who had been glaring at her the whole time, had paid
them no more heed than if they were flies.

"You're just going to let them take me, Bruce? I'm innocent
– what have I done?" she'd said as they'd moved towards her.
Bruce finally dropped his gaze, and didn't even look at the policemen.

"If you can be so faithless…" he said quietly, then stopped. Edna stopped too, right in her tracks, and turned towards him, ignoring the officers trying to hustle her along.

"If I can be so faithless… what?" she'd said, hardly believing herself. She was openly challenging her husband – something that she had longed to do for years.

"Just go, Edna. And please, do not darken my door again."

"I'll write," was all she had time for before she allowed the officers to drag her out of the room and to the nearby police station.

She'd spent the next month fretting and riding an emotional trapeze until she had a date for her trial. Then one night, she reasoned that whatever her sentence, she was finally free from her personal prison. Her home had been her own personal prison, and having left it, she felt so much lighter – buoyant, almost.

This did not stop her fretting about Bessie and Gertrude. With nobody else to inflict his poison on, would Bruce turn to them as the replacement? He'd grown more and more physical the past few years, and it was only when she noticed all her bruises starting to fade that she realised what a good move she'd made by getting out.

When I'm stronger, she vowed, *I swear to God I'll get those girls out of there.*

But for now, she had to focus on getting in and out of prison, and back to some semblance of reality. She hadn't realised how much the world had changed since she had last been allowed into it. Her prison-mates laughed at her. The trial itself had reduced her to a nervous, twitching, gibbering heap. It really was a wonder that she'd left the courtroom with an ounce of dignity and a mere two-week sentence, rather than a lifetime stay in a psychiatric hospital like she had expected.

Not that the trial had left her with much more. Bruce had

made an appearance there, and he had torn her to absolute shreds. Not as a witness, but he'd stood up in front of the whole assembled crowd and ranted on and on, ignoring the judge's cries of "Silence in the gallery!"

"I could be a hard judge and sentence you to as long as I liked, because you're a woman, and your husband doesn't seem to care." the judge had said in the end. Bruce had boomed something else at that point, but the judge ignored him completely. "However, I do see your muddled logic, and consequently I will be merciful. Edna Mary Thomas, I sentence you to two weeks' imprisonment."

Those two weeks had been Hell on Earth, but it had given Edna even more time to reflect. She obviously wasn't going back home – Bruce would have her beaten, and he'd said as much during his speech in the courtroom. So what was she to do?

When the idea first popped into her head, she'd squashed it without a second thought. What an abhorrent idea! Bruce would have been shocked. And yet when she'd examined it closer, she had found that it would be very convenient, actually. The only thing stopping her was what Bruce had drummed into her head. Bruce didn't know how to forgive.

Did she *really* want to live with the devil?

But Bruce had been wrong about lots of things, as she had found during her stay in prison. One of her prison-mates had given her a little lesson on the modern world, and by the time she was released, she felt ready to take it all on. If there was one thing that this whole experience had taught her, it was never to be a doormat again.

And so Edna had stepped out of that building two weeks later a changed woman. A free woman, and a changed one. Her days of whispering "Yes, Sir" and "No, Sir" and "Three bags full, Sir" were over. She could hardly believe the drastic change in herself, and in truth she would never really come to terms with it.

It wasn't that far to Wychwood on the train, but she'd enjoyed the journey all the same. Bumping along the tracks was one small bag was decidedly pleasurable after being cooped up for over a quarter of a century. Despite this, after stepping off the train she was hit by a wave of agoraphobia and had to sit down. She wondered just why she was doing this. Bruce's teachings were still engrained in her mind. She was a stupid, gullible old woman who didn't have a comprehensible thought inside her pretty little head. Why on Earth was she trying to strike out on her own and go and live with her disgraced son?

Then she had remembered her friend's words – no, not Maude, but Clara, one of her friends from prison.

"It's not too late in the day for you yet, Edna. I'm seventy-six this year! It's been sixteen years since I escaped my husband and moved here from America. I've made some darn mistakes since then, God knows I have, but I wouldn't have had it any other way. My God, the memories of what I've had since my escape! I'm in this place for the long haul now, but you've got the opportunity for a clean slate, and you're going to make a damn better job of it than I did! You're only fifty, so you get out into that world and show 'em what a woman can do."

Edna would really miss Clara. Seventy-five going on fifteen, she was. In fact, she'd been surprised to find out her age. But if there was one thing that she had discovered, it was to never be surprised by anything. Plus, Clara was an American, and they did things differently over there, and aged differently too. Clara was imprisoned for theft on a large scale, but she appeared just like any normal human and not an ugly, red-horned creature as Bruce had pictured a thief.

Clara's words circling her head, Edna lifted her bag and stood up, then made her way daintily through the train station. Her one and only pair of shoes were the ones that she used to wear around the house – felt slippers with one little hole in the left heel. Catching a glimpse of herself in the reflection of a glass window, she had been surprised at how bedraggled she looked, with her slippers and faded dress and one earring. *I look like a modern-day Havisham!* she'd thought to herself, removing the earring, smoothing down the dress and shaking her hair loose in an effort to make herself look younger.

She'd pulled the wad of paper out of her pocket and out of the envelope. She'd selected the top one from the pile and read the address at the top. What a stroke of luck it was that she'd carried the letter, and all her other precious letters, all with her. It was just a shame she hadn't picked up the most recent letter from Patrick. She'd left it under her pillow in haste. Most likely it had been long since reduced to ashes in the drawing room fireplace.

By the time she'd reached the address, after asking the way several times, she was bone-tired and almost unable to walk in a straight line. She had been walking all afternoon, but seeing the flash of joy on Andrew's face (before it had been lost to confusion) as he'd opened the door of his rental property – well, that made it all worth it.

The next few months had been bliss. Explaining to Andrew the events of the past three and a half years (including Patrick's reappearance) hadn't been easy, but with the aid of half a bottle of malt whisky, which she'd shared with her son, she'd managed it. She'd never been allowed to drink, and so the recount may have been skewed a little by the alcohol. But that was just another way in which she'd changed – since her release, she'd been a great fan of a tipple every evening.

And she'd even come to terms with Mr. Montgomery. It turned out that he was a colleague of Andrew's, and one evening, he had come for a meeting with Andrew to discuss a case. When they'd finally come face-to-face, Edna hadn't known what to think. The pain came rushing back to her – he was just as handsome as before, with just a few grey hairs separating the past from the present.

"It's just too much... why are you here? After all these years – why?" she'd asked fretfully, pacing Andrew's parlour.

"I could ask the same of you, Edna Thomas," he'd replied, a trifle nervously. Andrew decided that now was not the time to query, and took Mr. Montgomery away to have the meeting. Edna cried for a few minutes, then decided that she would be polite and curt, and not give any insight into the pain he'd caused her.

But it hadn't been as easy as that. Mr. Montgomery had stayed for dinner, and then Andrew had gone out for a walk to post a letter. Just like they'd been thirty-odd years previously, Edna and Timothy – he'd introduced himself as Timothy – found themselves alone. Timothy had been fuelled by the drink, just as he had been all those years ago, and they avoided the elephant in the room for a remarkable five minutes, making small talk.

"Would you like to marry me, Edna?" he said politely, out of the blue. She jumped, startled at this sudden change of subject.

"Marry you?"

"I know I should have made it work, somehow. What would you say if I told you that I have thought about you every single day, of every single week, month and year, since I met you? We could have spent so many happy years together if I'd have swallowed my pride, let my guard down, and admitted that I could have married you. That whole thing about York was a lie – we've been living within twenty miles of each other, all our lives. I've been waiting for you for so long... what would you say if I never wanted to let you go again?"

"I'd say that... I understand. I felt exactly the same – that you never really left my mind at all since that night. It hurt, I'll admit, and I've never come to terms with the fact that you waltzed into my life, and straight back out again."

"So marry me!"

Edna sighed, her mental turmoil quelled.

"I can't. I'm sorry, Timothy, but I am not a bigamist."

He'd jumped out of his skin.

"What? You never said you were still married!"

"Loathe as I am to admit it, I'm married."

"Can't you get him to divorce you? I'll see to him – you see if I don't."

There was a flicker of fear in Edna's eyes as she thought of her cruel, cruel husband.

"If I could let you, I would. But you would not be safe – he is a dangerous man. I want to be with you, but even if I did let you at him, I would simply not be ready to let you in. He destroyed me, that man, and I can't bear to think of what would happen to you if he got at you."

"But I can do *something*, surely...?"

Edna shook her head. He opened his arms, and despite her resistance, she couldn't help being pulled towards him like a magnet. He kissed her, and despite her mistrust of him, he felt *right,* in a way that Bruce never had. But then she pulled back, forced herself to step away, and forced herself to say it. This time, her words had an air of finality.

"No, I am not ready to risk it all over again. I'm not ready to sacrifice everything for someone who, with the greatest of respect, does not know me at all. I jumped in far too early with my marriage, and even if I could legally escape it, I still would not marry you. As far as my trust in you men goes... well, it doesn't go at all."

She looked at him, saw moisture in his eyes, but she did not doubt herself one bit. She knew, in her heart, that she could not trust a man again. She'd trusted Bruce, and he had ruined her. What was to stop Timothy turning the same way?

Timothy was crushed. His whole life had been ruled by his

overpowering love – *love,* not lust – for beautiful, delicate Edna Thomas. She'd been with him in his dreams, despite everything between them. She'd prised open his heart, and now she was abandoning it. He'd been holding onto its contents, and his memory of her, for years. And all for nothing.

And yet when he looked at her, it was all he could do to stop himself leaping in front of her and acting as a shield. She looked so fragile, as if one wrong thing could shatter her into tiny bits, and he wanted to protect her from that. She allowed him to hug her again, and he relished the feeling of having her so close. He somehow knew that this would be the last time they would ever see each other.

They parted on good terms in the end. Edna watched him walk away, his head bowed so far that she thought his hat would fall off, and knew that her decision was right. Nonetheless, she felt wracked with guilt, and to numb her mind she opened a bottle of gin. She'd found herself drinking a lot recently – it took a lot to numb her mind.

With all the effects of such a substance, she often retired to bed very giddy in the evenings. She was even more so on the evening of her birthday, the third of August 1921. Despite the fact that the world appeared to be moving exhilaratingly fast, she found herself moving slower than usual. *God, I'm tired.* she thought. *Must be the drink.*

Said drink often gave her odd dreams, too (often involving Timothy). That night, she was in the middle of one dream, involving her father (long since deceased) and the childhood cat, Birdie, when the vivid imaginary picture started swirling and fading away to nothing. But she didn't wake up.

When Andrew went in to check on her at about midnight, she was sleeping peacefully. It was only when he checked on her again the next morning that he realised that she had died in her sleep.

. . .

Andrew had been perfectly happy for the past five years. Escaping the toxicity that was his father had been his best move. Despite this, he'd still felt rather bad for his mother and three remaining siblings. He'd left the home at a time when they'd all believed that Patrick was dead.

It was because of this that he hadn't tried to locate his brother. At that time, the loss had been too raw, and Father-Sir's teachings still drummed hard into his mind. And it was because of the atmosphere in the home, and the black cloud that skulked around behind Father-Sir, that he'd ended up completely snapping.

What a screaming match had occurred! Shameful things, too despicable to ever be retold, had flown from mouth to ear and back again, painting the air a nasty shade of blue and scorching the ears of any unfortunate listener. By the time they'd both run out of steam, they were both bright red, almost purple, and panting hard. Things could have been so different if he'd backed down, apologised and resumed life's old monotonous trot. But no. In an almost transcendent display of strength, he'd picked up the antique paperweight off the desk and hurled it at Father-Sir.

Thank the Lord it had missed. If it hadn't, there's no telling what Father-Sir would have done. It simply landed on the rug and bounced a little before rolling away. Father-Sir saw red, and not just from the carpet or Andrew's face. Then the redness faded and in an eerily calm voice, he'd spoken.

"That paperweight has been in the family for generations. The reputation has also, and for this reason I am asking you to vacate the house and not return. I hope you realise how much it pains me to do it – you are my oldest son, and I thought you were a fine one too – but I won't have our own safety pulverised by your poisoned tongue, or your satanic mind. I hope, for your sake, that God turns a blind eye on you and your brother."

"I think I'll go to war, like Patrick," Andrew had said, nodding but watching for a reaction. Father-Sir's face had twitched, but he'd remained in that spookily calm state.

"Do what you want. You are no longer my son, and so I cannot stop you. One word of advice, though: respect your elders."

Andrew had paused to mull this over, but it only took a second to put into a sentence the rule by which he would be conducting his new life.

"I'll give respect to those deserving of it," he said pertly, "Sir."

With that, he'd calmly and methodically packed a bag and had the driver drive him to the town. The driver himself had been quietly unsurprised to see the eldest son leaving with a bag. *Two down, one to go.* Andrew had had no idea about where he was going to go, but he did not let on and remained calm and dignified the whole way.

Since then, he'd alternately congratulated himself on escaping, and tortured himself with guilt. How *could* he have abandoned his mother and siblings with that narcissistic man? After seeing the temperaments of other men in the outside world, he didn't trust his father to look after them at all. There had been times where he'd mentally beaten himself and told himself "You are a *despicable* human being!" but they were generally in the past now.

At least, they had been until his poor mother had turned up out of the blue with barely a possession to her name and a hectic story to tell. It had taken a while to comprehend, but he'd managed it. He couldn't believe that in the letters they had secretly been sending each other, she had not even mentioned her brother's reappearance, marriage or child. He hated himself even more now, for leaving his mother when she needed her children most.

Then, barely a few months after moving in and settling into a very different life, his mother had died in her sleep. Peacefully and quietly she had gone, but it didn't stop Andrew being shocked. In his mind, his mother was an eternal warrior, marching slowly but steadily onwards into the eventual sunset. Now he knew that her miraculous escapade had taken it out of her more than she had let on, and whatever had happened between her and Timothy, his colleague, was just the final straw. The energy that she had built up during the years of almost total captivity had run dry.

And now Andrew was faced with a dilemma: should he tell his mother's husband?

Five days of mental debate later, he came to the conclusion that he should send a telegram at least, inviting him and the others to the funeral. After all, the man had been married to her for so many years – he needed to know of her death. So he sent the telegram, inviting them all to the funeral, and received a very prompt reply.

"Otherwise engaged on the tenth. Do not contact us again."

That was all it said, but that said it all. Andrew's loathing for Bruce was renewed. Now, he needed to tell Patrick. He'd found the address from the old letters that Edna had kept (she had explained their sentimental value) and so he fired off a telegram to him too. Fortunately, he received a much more pleasant reply.

"Brother, we will be there. We will support you. Pat, Dot and Freddy."

Two days later, he dressed in his best black suit, ready to go to church. He'd booked the day off from work in advance, and his manager had been very sympathetic, despite being one person down already (Timothy had resigned mere days after meeting Edna again). Andrew was rather nervous, however, at seeing his brother after all this time. He hoped that there wouldn't be too much tension between them. After all, what does one say to bridge the gap of seven years between their last meetings?

As it was, there was very little tension because their just-turned eight-month-old baby took up everybody's attention from the word go. Freddy was screaming before the cab even turned into the street. Dorothy was cradling him and shushing him, so she barely waved hello to her brother-in-law.

"Just us at the funeral, then?" Patrick asked after getting Freddy on a blanket on the floor of Andrew's drawing room. They were to have luncheon before the funeral. Andrew had just told a condensed version of Edna's story – as much of it as he knew, anyway. Edna had never actually told him the full story, such as why she had left and under what circumstances.

"I'm afraid so," Andrew said heavily.

"You did ask Father-Sir? I would imagine that he'd like to hear of her – even if he hated her so."

"I told him, of course I did. But did he care? No!"

"What about Auntie Maude?"

"I don't have an address for her at all, I'm afraid. Mother hasn't sent her any correspondence since she came here."

"And all the legalities are taken care of?"

"Of course, I know about these things. I'm a lawyer these days, Patrick. Leave the legal side of this to me, if you please."

Sensing tension, Dorothy butted in with, "Me poor mam-in-law must've been so scared, bless her."

"Actually Dorothy, she would not have been aware of her death – she died in her sleep, you see." Andrew replied, a little bemused. Dorothy just nodded, not wanting to tell him that she had actually been referring to Edna's journey to Wychwood.

The funeral went by peacefully, and the two brothers parted ways vowing to stay in touch.

"What about Bessie and Gertrude, and Mike? Do you think they're all right, at home with Father-Sir?" Patrick said to Dorothy on the way back.

"Oh, they'll be fine, Pat. Yer pa's a decent man to 'em all, even if he wasn't to yer mam."

And, surprisingly, they were fine. Without a wife-shaped punchbag and apparent antagonist, Bruce had mellowed considerably. He did, in fact, even start feeling the first scratches of remorse trying to dig away at his insides. He found himself reliving his life with her. They'd ended up with five children – how lucky! Boy, girl, boy, girl, boy. It was just a shame how two of their three fine boys had dropped into the bubbling pit of sin that had eventually stolen Edna herself.

But over time, Edna had started to become more of an inconvenience than a lover. Gradually, without Bruce really noticing, she'd started to stray away from the path of a good Christian. It had all started with their old next-door-neighbour – not Maude, the other one. His charisma and wit had enchanted his wife and she'd started making regular trips to his house. It was to pick up some eggs, she always said, in return for cakes, but the radiant beam she always wore upon seeing him ignited the first flame of jealousy in Bruce's mind. So when it came about that Bruce had inherited a big house in posh Highmore Park, he took the chance to whisk his wife into a whole new world and starting their life afresh.

The church there was, truth be told, Bruce's ideal church. They took God's words to the extreme, and Bruce liked that. Women were not allowed to speak in church and had to dress *'modestly, with decency and propriety'* as Timothy 2:9 said. They wore their hair either loose or neatly tied back, with no jewellery or *'costly garments'* permitted. In terms of clothing, there was to be no mixing of fabrics because Leviticus forbade it. The Sabbath was off-limits in terms of work, play or indeed anything other than reading one's Bible to oneself and discussing its meaning. And most of all – any type of separation of wife and husband was abhorrent, a true violation of God's words, the sin of sins.

And Bruce had committed it.

He tried to convince himself that it was actually his wife that had committed it. After all, Corinthians 7:10/11 read *'the wife should not separate from her husband'*. She had split from him, not the other way around. At least, she'd tried to. If she *had* died, as per her intention, then she would have. Thankfully, he'd saved her life, but then he'd forced her to split from him anyway. He'd been infected with darkest evil. He'd been spending too much time associating with his evil son, Patrick, he mused. From now on, he'd be cutting contact to protect his one pure son and two daughters. And as for poor little Frederick... who knew how he would turn out, with Patrick as a father?

Over the years, he had felt this intense pressure building up, slowly but surely, in their house. Fortunately, he had not taken the pressure out on any of the children. Unfortunately, he had taken it out on the servants, and most of all on Edna. After all, he comforted himself, it was only her wifely duty!

And then she'd upped and gone. Watching the ambulance rush away with her in the back, leaving him behind to bring a fresh pair of clothes and her toothbrush, had been the worst moment of his life. He'd realised that he did still love her, however irritating and helpless he found her. After all, he'd been the one to propose to her, as was the way.

But he didn't want her back. Any wife who could do something like that, dare to break free when it was the will of God to keep her in, was no wife of his. So he gave up on her, and to reinforce this, he paid a visit to her trial, just to make doubly sure.

And after her release, when she hadn't turned up on the doorstep and begged for forgiveness as he'd expected, he'd found himself mellowing. If Patrick and Andrew had known this, they would have been relieved of a lot of aggravation and heartache. But they were not prepared to cross Father-Sir by visiting, oh no. He would have them killed! So they fretted and champed at the bit, but never actually went back.

. . .

The garden was dazzling. It was like a little slice of Eden, Dorothy thought poetically, carved out from the rest of the world, separated only by three laurel hedges and the back of the beautiful house. She sat on the rug, her hair tied up in a knot to stop it sticking to her back and her face protected by a beautiful sunhat, relishing how calm and contented she felt. Never in her darkest moments of grief or lowest moments of inner turmoil had she even dreamt of such a peaceful, idyllic day. The birds seemed intent on voicing her innermost thoughts and sung merrily away as they carried on their daily rituals.

Within the garden itself lay an extensive rectangle of luscious, sweet grass that would have sent the livestock nutty. It was this that Dorothy was sitting on, revelling in how pleasant it felt, ticking her legs just enough to make her smile. She almost wanted to bottle up the air, which was tinged with the fainted fragrance of the ocean, and send it to everyone she knew. She'd only been in Cornwall for a day and a half but already she was feeling invigorated, refreshed, ready to tackle the world single-handedly whilst juggling the baking, the farm, and her two-and-a-half-year-old in the other hand. She'd sort out everything that was wrong in the world, and everybody would marvel at how she did it.

"Mummy! Mummy *look!*" came an enthralled young voice. This was followed by a tapping on her leg and the sensation of something soft being pushed into her hand. Her fingers automatically closed around it, just like they had done so many times recently, and she brought it up to her face to examine whatever it was that Freddy had brought her.

"*Rose,*" Freddy said carefully, scrutinising her face for the delight and approval that he had begun to seek. He hoped that exercising his latest word, which he labelled to any plant, regardless of species, would make Mummy happy.

"Lovely, darlin'!" Dorothy said enthusiastically, tucking the dahlia into the buttonhole of her blouse and spontaneously giving Freddy a hug. She reckoned that there was no better smell than her freshly washed son, with his grass-stained but intact clothes and the smell of earth infusing into his hair. When Freddy toddled off to find some more flowers, she unbuttoned her sleeves and rolled them up so that the sun could beat down on them, just as it was tanning her slim, bare, toned legs.

It was incredible, this little Cornish fishing village. She did not even know its name, but she had been stunned by how relaxed and friendly the villagers were. And the lovely elderly lady who had let the Hammonds have her spare rooms for the fortnight was equally jolly. She barely blinked at the sight of Dorothy with so much bare skin showing, as she approached (admittedly at a snail's pace) over the sweet grass, her walking stick punching little indentations.

"How's your little picnic, my lovely?" she said, bending down to hand Dorothy a jug and ruffling Freddy's blonde hair.

"It's lovely, thank ye so much. What's in th' jug?"

"Just some more water for you. Now, must dash, my scones have to come out of the oven in-" and here she checked her pocket-watch and raised her eyebrows in alarm "-approximately three minutes and twenty seconds. Tea's at four, my love, so make sure your Patrick is back from the cricket by then."

As she watched her hostess make her slow procession back towards the house, Dorothy sat back, and thought that she really could not be happier. Here she was, exactly where she wanted to be, surrounded by friendly villagers, wholesome food and ideal weather (sunny and hot, but not blisteringly so due to the gentle breeze). She had her loyal, fair husband and a perfect little son that she loved with the whole of her heart and more.

She and Patrick intended to go for a night-time walk after dark, leaving Freddy in the care of their lovely hostess. They had no idea where they would be going – they had been given the keys and told to go wherever the night took them. It was as if there were no rules in this village. It appeared to be in a whole other century, just without all of the flying motor cars and invisibility machines that would most likely be invented by then.

By the time Patrick came back through the gate, wielding a cricket bat and looking very pleased with himself, Dorothy was stretched out on the grass, lightly dozing whilst Freddy investigated the grass around her carefully. He smiled down at his wife, without waking her up, and then shook his head at the state of Freddy's appearance.

"Daddy! *Roses* for you!" Freddy said loudly, hurling a bunch of daisies at him.

"Thank you, Frederick. But these are *daisies* – not roses."

"Daisies?" Freddy said thoughtfully, and Patrick could see him filing away this new piece of vocabulary in his mind.

"Come along – I'll show you some more flowers." Patrick said, taking him by the hand and leading him to the flowerbeds, which were aesthetically pleasing mixtures of vibrant colours, buzzing bees and sweet smells. Patrick took great pleasure in teaching his son all about the botanical world. When they turned around, they saw that Dorothy was sitting up, her chin resting on her knees, smiling at them.

"I didn't realise you were awake, Dot," Patrick said, starting to clear away the plates.

"Ye know me – I can sleep anywhere! Now, tea's at four, so we'd best get ready."

It felt a shame to leave the warm, sunny little haven, but it was worth it because of the spread that met their eyes as they entered the drawing room. After a quick wash and a change of clothes, they found their appetites suddenly expanding. Their host had cooked the fish that Patrick had caught that morning, and she had magicked up a creamy, smooth potato puree that tasted of garlic and was rippled with chives. She was a wonderful cook, and having had nobody to cook for recently, she was relishing and showing off her cooking skills.

The food was just one of the many reasons that Dorothy was exhilaratingly, ridiculously, almost deliriously happy. By the time she left the house that night with Patrick, leaving Freddy asleep in his little bed and being attentively watched, she was fizzing and bubbling like the cocktail she had drunk with her treacle pudding. Even before they were through the gate, she was bouncing up and down like a little girl, wanting to run and skip and hop and jump. She had the urge to duck in and out of the shrubbery at the side of the road, like Lucky the dog when he was having a mad moment. And when they got to the moor, well, that was it!

As Dorothy was counting to twenty in an impromptu game of hide-and-seek with the slightly more controlled Patrick, she was taken back to their wedding night. Only four years ago, and yet in those four years their two worlds had collided, bounced, contorted and distended, before melting together and springing back into shape like an elastic band. The ties between them had proved strong enough to hold now, and Dorothy had a notion that nothing would ever separate them again. Come hell or high water, they were together. No amount of arguments, secrets or pain could ever come between them. She said as much to Patrick when she found him crouching in the middle of a bush.

"I know – isn't it wonderful? I love you, Dorothy." he replied, pulling her towards him and holding her tight. They decided to find a place to go. They meandered together down to the beach and sat on a little space free from shingle. Patrick pulled Dorothy onto his lap. The cool breeze rippled the ocean gently and blew Dorothy's hair to and fro. There they sat, in a comfortable silence with the waves lapping quietly around them, leaning against each other, just enjoying being close to one another.

At first, Patrick felt that there was something odd about the whole scene. He focused his mind and then it dawned on him. Silence! Not just literal silence, but silence in his mind. For what seemed to be his whole life, he had had a constant background noise circulating in his mind. One element of it was Father-Sir's voice, berating his every move, reciting the related Bible verses, threatening him with the prospect of Hell. All the way through the war the voice had wittered on. At some point it had started to be accompanied by the constant echoing sounds of the guns and screaming shells, and the yelps and howls of dying men. Put together, it was the sound of war – physical and internal.

And all of a sudden, on this lovely day in Cornwall, the noise had stopped. Father-Sir had lost his voice. The guns had fallen silent. It was incredible what peace could do. Patrick smiled to himself, and it was almost as if he was seeing the world anew. Sharper, brighter, clearer. Life was perfect. For once, he could focus his mind on being a farmer, a husband, and a father. He couldn't wait to see what the rest of his life brought him.

. . .

Patrick's refreshed, quieted mindset lasted all the way through their holiday and right the way up to the front door of the farm cottage. He opened the door and led Freddy through, only to be confronted by a scene of what could only be described as utter mayhem. Rita – calm, unflappable Rita – was lashing away at a vat of cake batter with a whisk, while yelling to someone at the top of her lungs. Lucky the dog was at her feet, tail wagging away as he licked lustily at the floor. A mound of discarded eggshells sat on the kitchen table, with a ginger tomcat nosing through each one. The cockerel was screeching back at Rita in the doorway. Patrick did not know what had happened, but he knew he had to get his son away from this scene.

"Frederick, go upstairs for a minute." he said quietly. His son did not seem to hear (and no wonder, with the sheer volume of Rita's voice) and so he had to repeat the question in a more firm, authoritative voice. His son obeyed, more than a little alarmed. Taking a deep breath and steeling himself, he went up to Rita and put a hand on her shoulder. She jumped out of her skin.

"Now, now, Rita, what's all this? Who are you shouting at?" he said, cutting her off of her sentence midstream. Without taking a breath, she replied.

"Your brother!" she shouted, spinning around and splattering him with cake batter from her whisk. "Your *useless*, ruddy *waste* of *space* of a *brother*! He turns up here, expecting to be waited on hand and foot, while we're trying to run a farm over here! You went cycling off, sunning yourselves in Port Jacob or wherever the hell it's called, leaving me and Ronald to pick up the slack! And then your brother comes swanning up from Wychwood, expecting *me* to serve him! You should just try running this farm on your own, Patrick, and you'll know what Ronald and I have had to put up with the past damn fortnight! Well, you're going to have to now! Ronald and I have *had enough.* Pull your fingers out because we're leaving, right now, and we do *not* expect to be charged for our stay!"

She stalked out of the back door, nearly knocking Dorothy over as she did so.

"Steady on!" Dorothy said, "What's th' matter? What's happened?"

Patrick picked up his jaw from the floor, along with the apron and whisk that Rita had thrown down. He surveyed the kitchen. Rita's words rung in his ears and he noticed that the sound of war (or the sound of his life, as he regarded it now) had started back up. So much for the peace.

Dorothy, business-like as usual, ushered the strange new cat off the table and put it outside with the dog while she waited for her husband to regain the power of speech. Growing impatient, she swept all of the eggshells directly into the bin with one swift move of her arm and leant against the table.

"Well, first thing's first, where did th' cat come from?"

Patrick suddenly realised that he still had a voice box and said, "I have no idea. I have no idea about any of it, I just... she said my brother was here, but how...?"

And right on cue, Andrew came through the door, almost tripping over a second cat, bellowing "Have you calmed down yet, Rita? Maybe now-"

He stopped in his tracks as he saw Patrick and Dorothy sitting at the table. This time, three jaws hit the floor. Andrew was the first to reattach his, and he sat down too.

"Right," he said, "Where do I start?"

. . .

"Sorry, what do you mean *you got the sack*?" Patrick spat, almost knocking over his mug of tea onto the dining room table.

"Well, I would prefer to say that I told them where to stick their job, but no. The honest truth is that I got the sack. And we must be honest, just as Father-Sir taught us."

Andrew had hoped that bringing their father into the situation would help mollify his brother, but it did not have that effect. Patrick folded his arms defensively.

"Don't bring him into this. Why did you think it was appropriate for you to come here? I *told* you we were going away. I sent you a letter – can't you *read*?"

"My landlord is a friend of my employer, and he evicted me. Three days' notice. There was no way I was going crying to Father-Sir, so I reckoned that you were my best bet. I hardly reckoned on being put to work the instant I arrived by that old witch!"

"Hey, watch it." Dorothy said sharply, "She's invaluable to us."

"Well, we're going to do without her now." Patrick snapped at her, "She's upped and gone. But Andrew, what did you *expect* Rita to do with you? Put you out to graze with the horses?"

"What do ye mean, she's upped an' gone?" Dorothy exclaimed shrilly. At the same time, Andrew tried to reply, but they were all interrupted by the sound of Freddy crying. He was standing in the doorway of the dining room and, having never seen such an argument before (or indeed, his Uncle Andrew), he was naturally very alarmed. Dorothy swooped down and scooped him up, bringing him back to the table to sit on her knee.

"Now," she said calmly and firmly. "We're going to sort this out like grown-ups. Pat, tell us the gist of what Rita said to ye."

"From what I could interpret from the gibberish, they've had it up to their eyeballs and can't take it any longer. They have decided to stop helping us, which is their right, of course. And of course you come into the equation somewhere, Andrew."

"Right. And now, Andrew, can you fill in the gaps?"

"Well, I decided to come and ask you to put me up for a while, until I find a new job and somewhere else to go. I then got practically forced into working for the farm in return for being able to stay here until you got home. We haven't exactly been getting on and the farm's been going to pot so frankly, I'm not surprised that Rita has given up. Some new cat's turned up, one of the horses lost a shoe, and the chickens have started producing eggs like nobody's business. It's been utter chaos, to be honest with you. But we've been surviving all right so I don't see why you're all so vexed!"

"So, let's get this straight." Patrick said. "In the space of two weeks, we have acquired a new cat, a lame horse, and a whole lot of eggs. We have also lost two valuable friends and therefore half of the foundations of the farm. I think we have the perfect excuse to be a little agitated."

"Well, we're all a little *too* hot an' bothered now, so I suggest we have another nice cup of tea an' all calm down. Isn't that right, Freddy?" Dorothy said, ever the peacemaker. She bustled over into the kitchen, leaving Freddy on Patrick's lap, and listened to the deepening silence between Patrick and his brother.

When Dorothy came back in, two mugs of scalding hot tea in her hands (it was too hot for tea, so she didn't have any herself), Patrick and Andrew appeared deep in thought.

"Now that Ronald and Rita have gone, we could really do with some more help." said Patrick thoughtfully, "And I can't imagine you'll want to show your face back in Wychwood for a while, Andrew. What I propose is that you stay in Little Wychwood – although not in the house, for Freddy hasn't yet slept through the night – and we will feed you and pay your rent, in return for your help on the farm."

Andrew had never had such an offer before, and he accepted it at once. The brothers shook hands solemnly, then burst out laughing when the ginger tom, who had been minding his own business out in the kitchen, decided to intercept the handshake by springing up on the dining room table over their outstretched arms. Dorothy laughed too and put the cat back outside. Freddy clapped his hands, shouting "Kitty went jump!" and the atmosphere relaxed.

"So, have ye met th' church yet? I'm sure they'll adore ye! Did ye know that our Pat's been doin' lessons for 'em the past couple o' years? He'll be doin' one this week, so ye'll get to see him in action!" Dorothy chirped.

"Oh, of course I've met the church! I've been introduced as a temporary visitor – although we'll have to change that now, of course – and oh my, they are so friendly..."

He dove into an unusually earnest speech about how God's

spirit shone all the way through Little Wychwood, and how glad he was to be living there. Dorothy listened intently, hoping that Freddy was picking up on all this, but Patrick drifted off into a little world of his own.

Normally, when the church was mentioned, Patrick felt a warm feeling spreading through him. But today it didn't come. They had been to church while they were away, and he had been struck by the different approach of the Cornish people. One woman, with curly, grey, frizzy hair, had particularly caught his attention. She was the local shopkeeper and told them all a story in her soft Cornish accent.

"Now, for my lesson today, I'll tell you all a story. We all know that our beautiful village occasionally attracts people from afar wanting to take in the change of air," and here she nodded at Patrick, Dorothy and Freddy sitting at the back. "Being the shopkeeper, I see all the holidaymakers passing through my shop. On Wednesday, a rather familiar-looking man came into my shop with a young child – around three or four years old, I'd say.

"For background, you may have noticed that I have acquired a sort of mascot over the past year – a golden teddy bear, which I have named Susan after our dearly missed baker. (She is with Jesus now, you see, visitors, and God bless her.) Well, this man came in and stopped abrupt, and stared right at Susan. Then he turned to his son and exclaimed "Well, look who we've found! Molly the bear!"

"And you can guess what happened after that: a joyful reunion of a little lad and his long-lost teddy bear, one of his most prized material possessions. It turned out, you see, that they visited last year, and somehow the bear got left behind. But that is not the end of the story!

"I was all set to wave Susan goodbye for her journey back home with her original friend. But that decent young lad put Susan right back into my hands. He said – and I speak not one word of a lie – that she had found a new home with me, and so she should stay here, because I was treating her better. And he toddled out of the door, looking upset, I grant you, but also looking strangely triumphant and virtuous.

"There was no ulterior motive to his actions and it has stirred me to think – well, we can rely on our children! *'Children are a heritage from the Lord, offspring a reward from Him.'* That's Psalm 127:3, and I do believe that it has never been truer. We have nothing to fear in the children sent by our Lord because He has sent them specially to keep God's Earth ticking over nicely, and the futures of His people safe. That gives me hope, and I hope it gives you all some too."

Patrick had felt like jumping up and down with enthusiasm. Even Freddy had looked rapt. The rest of the congregation had just smiled and patted the woman's arm as she went to sit back down, but all the way through Amazing Grace and even after the service, what she had said was in the front of Patrick's mind. Why didn't they tell stories like that in Little Wych-wood? Compared to in Port Isaac, their services seemed so wooden without anecdotal evidence to support God's words. He had resolved to bring that little slice of Port Isaac to his own church.

Later that evening, Patrick went to propose the idea to Reverend Osbourne.

"Good afternoon, Reverend!" he said jovially upon the door being opened. Reverend Osbourne's Christian name was Steven, but as a mark of respect he was always referred to by his title, a bit like Miss Marian and Miss Eunice.

"Patrick, my dear man, do come in! I trust your holiday has left you somewhat more relaxed than when you left?"

"I think it would be safe to say that, yes. But it's all back to business, which is why I am here to propose you an idea, and to inform you of a little change on the farm."

"Oh, yes? And in which order – proposal first, or announcement?"

"The announcement is more sombre, so we'll do that first. I am sorry to say that we will no longer be receiving the help of Ronald and Rita Wright."

The vicar's pleasant face sobered.

"Oh, I am sorry to hear that! Is there anything I can do to help?"

"Nothing, I'm afraid, Reverend. They feel we have pushed their good nature too far, and I will respect that. However, my brother Andrew has agreed to help us out in return for a place to stay. We cannot have him with us due to Freddy's sleeping habits, so we will be on the lookout for a place for him to stay."

"That is something that can be arranged."

"I do hope so – Galatians 6:2 says *'Carry each other's burdens, and in this way you will fulfil the law of Christ.'* But there are different interpretations of every one of God's words, and it is for this reason I want to propose an idea."

"Do go on," the Reverend gentleman replied keenly.

Patrick told him the story of the church in Port Isaac, and when he was finished, the vicar mulled it over thoughtfully.

"I like your idea – I think it is your youthful contribution to the church. Yes, I like it. You can put it in place whenever you see fit."

They remained chatting for a few more minutes, before Patrick checked his pocket watch and announced his departure.

"And will you two be hearing the patter of two more tiny feet any time soon?" the vicar said teasingly.

"Only time will tell!" Patrick replied in the same light-hearted tone. But the vicar's uncanny intuition was right. They didn't know it then, but on that gloriously happy night in Port Isaac, they had conceived another child.

. . .

At times like this, Patrick and Dorothy longed for a few extra pairs of arms. Or, more appropriately, a few extra bodies. William was the cuddliest baby known to man and would wail at the slightest hint that he was about to leave Dorothy's arms. The child was only three weeks old but he had already wreaked havoc. For starters, he had been overdue! By the time Dorothy finally gave birth to him, she had been an emotional, waddling hippopotamus (her words), barely crawling her way through each sunny day.

And then there was Freddy. On what seemed to be the day after his third birthday, he had undergone a personality switch. Gone was the angelic, charming two-year-old with his bowl of custard and scrap of paper which he took delight in folding. What replaced him was a thrashing, kicking, screaming menace who howled at his exhausted mother and plunged his way through each day as if without him, the whole world would crash down.

Patrick had never been more tempted to turn to the belt. But every time he subconsciously reached for it, some invisible force stopped him as he remembered how Andrew's face had flickered with fear the first time. It was a reminder of Father-Sir. If the belt was harsh enough to leave his brother with such mental scars, he certainly wasn't going to inflict that on his own child. And so he turned to using his voice as a disciplinary tool. He tried not to shout, but at times Freddy was so obstinate, whining in a monotonous, drawn-out note, that he snapped and sent him up to his room. With the strain of this, and the farm, and caring for Dorothy and the new baby, it was a wonder that he was still marching his way through each day with his face set in a determined line.

And what about Andrew? Well, he had had a personality change too – but for the better. From the careless, loitering lout that had begun living with Miss Marian and Miss Eunice, he had become an infinitely patient, nurturing uncle. Dorothy suspected that Miss Marian's mothering tendencies (and Miss Eunice's indignant barks at the slightest hint of wrongdoing) had something to do with it. He adored both of his nephews, and was often on hand to step in if Patrick did reach for the belt. He spent a lot of time juggling the animals while Patrick tried to keep the eldest occupied and Dorothy tried to keep the baby and the house in shape.

But still, the tell-tale signs of strain were there in the farm. The cart went unpolished, holes remained in the wooden walls and the fences went unrepaired. Ronald and Rita had maintained a dignified silence, although Ronald had been looking rather longingly over towards them in church. It had clearly been Rita's idea to back out, and ten months on, she was sticking to it. They still hadn't spoken. Miss Marian and Miss Eunice were both godmothers to William. Patrick longed for Ronald and Rita to come back, but he respected their choice to leave and so the farm began to fall apart.

Tensions began to mount in the Hammond household once more. After the children were in bed, the three adults tore into the housework, or checked the animals over, or occasionally even took the hot-headed Winston out for a long gallop to keep his energy level under some semblance of control. Patrick still held the animals as a point of pride in this draining time. Even under immense pressure, the animals were thriving. They were lucky that William had come at the end of lambing season – maybe that was why he had hung on for eleven days.

The hectic schedule meant that, just like before, communication between the adults ground to a halt. And Dorothy was close to snapping again.

It was hard to explain the feeling inside her. It was a seething resentment that deepened with every wail, whine and whinge that came from Freddy's mouth. It was a bubbling pit of exhausted anger that sizzled and smoked every time

Patrick grunted with exertion when lifting Freddy. It was a fizzing adrenaline coursing through her veins, intensifying as Andrew sniffed and snuffled and coughed because of his hay-fever. It was as if she was a champagne bottle, being shaken vigorously by some giant being, and the cork was about to blow.

In a desperate move, she wrote to Wilhelmina and Charlie, still slaving away up in Manchester.

I feel overwhelmed by the whole experience of being a mother, a farmer's wife and a responsible human being. Our circumstances changed so rapidly when Ronald and Rita left, and I think even now I haven't fully adjusted. We've never had to cope without them before, you see. Would you mind arranging an impromptu trip to us? I haven't seen you in months, after all, and I'm sure you're dying to meet William.

Wilhelmina and Charlie responded immediately and they were down to the farm within a week. Charlie got out his country voice and his country hands and got down to work, fixing and painting with Andrew. Wilhelmina helped around the house – at least when she wasn't cooing at William or playing with Freddy.

With some semblance of order restored, Dorothy relaxed a little. It was only a temporary measure, of course, but the four extra hands meant that she could catch up on her new favourite pastime: sleeping. As she dozed, Wilhelmina would bake or walk around the farm, Freddy scampering behind her and William on a sling-type contraption on her back.

It was on one of these walks that she found Charlie sitting on the cart about to go out, looking deathly pale and tired. She almost fell in her haste to get to him.

"What's wrong? Are ye ill? What on Earth's happened?" she said, scrambling into the seat beside him. He flinched and dragged his eyelids apart.

"Ill? Me? No! I'm fit as a flea, and you know that, Mina," he said boisterously, although the joviality of his words was inversely proportional to that of his face.

"You are – ye've been off fer a while. Get yerself down th' doctor an' sort yerself out – we can afford it now."

"Mina, it's fine. I am perfectly healthy, so stop your mithering!"

"No, Charlie, yer not!" snapped Wilhelmina, raising her voice. Freddy barely raised his eyes. Shouting matches were not rare occurrences these days. William mercifully remained asleep.

"Mind your tone, and your own business!" Charlie responded harshly. The horses shifted nervously.

"I'm yer wife, Charles, an' I've half a mind to march ye down to th' doctor meself an' demand a check-up."

"Oh, do you?" Charlie said scathingly, "Well, who are you to talk? You wouldn't listen to me when you had influenza! Off you trotted to work, infecting dozens of diners all so you'd get your money. Tit for tat, Mina!"

"*Charlie,* that were *years* ago! This is now, an' ye never know what it might be! Me eyes have been opened an' it's high time that ye peeled the blinkers off yer own! I was right about th' vote, an' I know I'm right now. How *can* ye be so irresponsible an' downright selfish? Yer no good t' Dot an' Pat if yer dead, I'll tell ye that!"

Charlie looked as if he had been stung, not helped by the physical pain plainly rippling through his body. He scowled and picked up the reins, giving them a little shake to wake up the horses.

"Five seconds to get off, Mina, or else you're coming with me and we'll carry on this discussion all around the village. Five… four…"

"Fine – I'm off! But don't come runnin' when yer pain brings ye to yer knees!"

Charlie didn't respond and got the horses going at a good pace through the gate. He didn't bother to get out and close it. He was furious with his wife, because he knew that she was right. And she knew that he knew it. It was just a matter of his stupid pride. Tough gentlemen did not frequent the doctor for minor ailments. The pain suggested it was otherwise, but Charlie had convinced himself that it was just one of those things.

But what if it *was* serious?

He stopped the horses dead with a yank on their poor mouths. A paralysing weakness had drained any semblance of strength from his arms. He had to set the reins carefully down let he drop them.

"Charlie, yer playin' games with yer life." said Mina, who'd followed him out.

"I know," he sighed, without turning around.

"I'll come to th' doctor with ye. Let's get these animals exercised an' make our excuses. Come along."

. . .

After examining the swollen lumps in Charlie's abdomen, the doctor looked grave and sombre. He sat down with Charlie and Wilhelmina and took a deep breath in.

"Now, it's important to note that I'm only a general doctor, not a specialist. But with the symptoms you describe – the attacks of pain, the fatigue, amongst others – I would prepare for the worst. I would return home, see your own doctor, and take it from there. Try not to fret. Make sure you look after yourself. Eat well, avoid stress, all of the usual things. Medical technology is growing more advanced by the day, so trust the people of my profession with your life."

"I don't have a choice, do I?" Charlie said with a smile that did absolutely nothing to mask his feelings. They were one-part regret to two parts anger, with panic, sorrow and guilt mixed in, liberal amounts of each. The doctor left the room and he shivered involuntarily. Not because he was cold, but because he felt rather frightened. But Wilhelmina's hand on his shoulder, gripping tight because she too was frightened, reminded him that he still had her. She was the definition of a faithful wife.

With a surge of steely determination, he stood up and reset his expression to one of neutrality. He shook the doctor's hand once more on the way out and left with his head held high. He wasn't going to let some potential illness stop him. He was going to go back to Manchester and see what God, who Dorothy was always on about, had in store for him.

All the same, telling Dorothy that he had to leave was awful. The scrap of colour that had started to develop in her cheeks vanished and she sat down with a bump, jolting William and making him cry.

"Why *now*?" Dorothy sobbed, trying to cradle him.

"That's not important, Dot…"

"It *is* important, Da! If there's a legitimate reason, then fair enough, but if there isn't, then why would ye do that to me?"

Charlie exchanged a look with Wilhelmina, then explained everything in all of its vile glory. Dorothy went from white to blue, from blue to red, then back to paper-white again. Her stress levels rocketed through the roof as she heard it all. She loved Charlie. If he died, she would not cope. She said as much to him – and here, his patience ran out.

"Well, you'll have to." he snapped, getting to his feet and pulling Wilhelmina to hers. His voice had become tinged with a certain venom.

"What?"

"I'm the one with the illness, not you. You'll manage fine without me. You've got the children, and Andrew, and Patrick, and your mother. I'm just another body on Earth, at the end of the day. It's traumatic enough for me as it is, and I can't abide it all being multiplied by your self-absorption. Come along, Mina."

And so just a week after they arrived, Charlie and Wilhelmina Fox departed. Dorothy's cries were audible even outside the front door. Thankfully, Freddy was away with Patrick in one of the fields. There was only the screaming baby to offer some comfort – although as it was, he had none to give. Dorothy remained comfortless – that was, until Rita slipped in and put her arms around her.

CHAPTER 6 – 1925-1930

Such a lot could happen in a year, and it had been what only can be described as a hectic rollercoaster.

Thank the Lord for Ronald and Rita. If they hadn't pushed their pride behind them, Dorothy would have completely collapsed with the pressure. In fact – thank the Lord for Reverend Osbourne. He was the one who had persuaded Ronald and Rita to patch things up with the Hammonds. The perfect timing had completely coincided with the time that Dorothy needed a shoulder to cry on.

As it was, she was thriving. Or at least, she seemed to be, until she thought "I must write to Da soon!" and the realisation hit her like a tsunami wave. It had been four months since Charlie had died, and it still had yet to sink in fully. Wilhelmina, contrary to everyone's expectations, appeared to be coping brilliantly.

But Dorothy wasn't so sure. After all, that was what everyone had thought about her after Maxwell's death, but she had been falling apart on the inside. So she exchanged letters almost every day with her mother, encouraging her to open up. So far, nothing had come of it. But to be fair, Wilhelmina knew that Dorothy had enough on her plate as it was, what with her pregnancy to contend with. It had seemed almost surreal how, by some magical force of God, they had conceived a third child, and a third boy, only three months after giving birth to the previous one.

In fact, as Dorothy remembered it, they hadn't thought it over properly. Ronald and Rita's return had lulled them into a sense of security, and so in a spontaneous moment of fleeting adrenaline, when both of the boys were finally asleep, they had decided to take a moment to themselves. God had been good to them. It was just a shame, Dorothy thought as she inhaled the scent of her new-born son in the early hours of Monday morning, that Charlie would never get to see his new grandson. He'd died when Dorothy was five months pregnant.

At the beginning, Dorothy's attitude to Charlie's death was more one of relief than grief. Charlie had deteriorated to a heart-breaking state of body and mind. Whatever it was – and they did think it was cancer – had eaten him up from the inside, and Dorothy was almost resentful of God for prolonging his life enough to reduce him to that state.

They had gone up there for Christmas, with Ronald and Rita exercising great patience and looking after the farm. Rita had looked outraged for a second and then Dorothy had reminded her of the circumstances and she had softened.

"Take as long as you need with your father," she told Dorothy as they packed together, "just make the most of this Christmas and take it from there."

It was almost as if Charlie had been hanging on just for Christmas to see his daughter, son-in-law and grandsons one last time. As he said goodbye to them on the day after Boxing Day, looking so thin and frail as he leant against the front door frame, Dorothy had had to use every ounce of mental strength she had to stop herself clinging to him and sobbing. He obviously knew this, for he pulled her close one last time and whispered to her.

"Keep on having them babies, Dorothy. When I see you again, God only knows when, I want you to tell me that you've had a good seven or eight children, and brought them up to be good people, so that you and Patrick can be happy in the knowledge that the family is safe."

His voice was croaking and it was one of the only coherent things he'd said, but the essence of it was strong. Dorothy understood why he had said seven or eight. Her father was one of seven himself, and one by one they had all drifted apart from each other. Two were in France, one in Austria-Hungary, and the rest scattered across England and Ireland. Charlie had wanted to replicate his own family, but an accident when Wilhelmina was pregnant with Dorothy meant that that had been impossible. Therefore it was down to Dorothy, his only child, to do what he had been desperate to do.

Squeezing Charlie hard and feeling every rib and bone, Dorothy tearfully promised that she would, and she loved him, and she'd see him in Heaven.

The news of Charlie's death had been delivered via telegram a few days later, just a day short of Freddy's fourth birthday. Both of the boys were still too young to understand what had happened, but Freddy understood Heaven and so Patrick simply told him that Grandpa Fox had been taken to Heaven to live with the angels. Freddy had picked up on his father's solemnity and nodded sedately.

Dorothy was glad that they'd told Charlie about her pregnancy. They'd wondered if it would upset him, but he'd been pleased. There had been one poignant moment, when he'd laid his thin, mottled hands on Dorothy's stomach and whispered to it "You'll only hear the stories, but don't take them too seriously. I wasn't as bad as all that, and I always loved you and your family."

"Oh, don't, Da," Dorothy had said, trying to stop herself from crying in front of the boys. Charlie laughed – he'd intended the first sentence to be a joke – but then he had seen how close she was to the breaking point and Wilhelmina had joined the pair of them in a hug. Wilhelmina had murmured something about how she was glad that Dorothy was there, and Dorothy had responded that there was no place she'd rather be.

It was rather sad that the new baby would never meet his grandfather. But Dorothy was determined that he would know *about* Charlie – and not all the bad stories, either.

"Three boys, Pat!" she sighed as the new-born baby was handed to her. She laughed indulgently at the explosion of warmth that happened inside her as she gazed at his little fingers, his button nose, his dark blue eyes. As with all her previous births, she couldn't believe that such a beautiful being had been inside her the whole time. He could be the next Einstein, or the next Monet for all they knew! He could even be a Reverend one day! She sent a prayer up to her father – *look after us all, please.*

Later that night, Dorothy had plenty of thoughts, all of them revolving around the new baby. She couldn't stop watching him. Jack, the name of whom had been decided even before his birth, stirred in his Moses basket and make a little chirrup. Dorothy pondered the name choice for a moment – it would have been Thea for a girl, and he did rather look like a Theo. Her heart melted as she picked little Jack up and sat back down on the edge of the bed, wincing a little. Her finger absently traced little circles around his tightly shut eyes and tickled him on the palm of his tiny hand. He had no idea of the fuss surrounding his troublesome delivery. Despite being right on time, he had been rather reluctant to come out. Twenty-three hours of tiresome and hectic labour had preceded the sound of a tiny cry that signalled that he was out and alive. Dorothy had seldom been more relieved in her life because the grunts and frowns of Miss Page had rather worried her.

But Jack was fine. Ten fingers, ten toes, two arms, two legs and a plump little body topped by a handsome little head. Dorothy held him instinctively in the bend of her elbow and smiled at him. She had an inkling of what Reverend Osbourne had said to her after Maxwell's death, and then recently again after Charlie's.

"The gaps in your heart will never heal," he'd said, "but you will learn to build yourself around them."

Few things had ever been more true. Every time she thought of Maxwell, she felt a little ache, but nothing too debilitating any more. Only once or twice recently had she been reduced to tears by grief. Once, late at night, she had sobbed on Patrick's shoulder as the first waves of grief at Charlie's death had begun to erode her.

None of that mattered now, anyway. She had a new baby, and she'd done remarkably well by not losing consciousness at all in the last twenty-four hours, Miss Page reckoned. It was nice, Patrick noticed, that Dorothy had gone through all her successful labours with fierce determination and not a peep in terms of screams. Screaming reminded her too much of that first labour, Dorothy had pointed out.

"Why are you still awake, Dot?" Miss Page bustled in, having noticed the light on in the bedroom that they all laughingly called the delivery room. The nurse was barely older than Dorothy herself, and had been with Dorothy at every single one of her labours. They were very fond of each other, even though Dorothy joked that the poor girl had only ever seen the worst side of her!

Miss Page allowed herself a brief smile at Dorothy's blissful one, then she was back to business. Her capable hands took hold of the baby and after one moment of fleeting struggle as Dorothy instinctively clutched him, she put him in the Moses basket. Dorothy gingerly lay down and Miss Page tucked the sheets in around her. That reminded Dorothy of Wilhelmina and she smiled up at her.

"Right, now go to sleep – it's two o'clock in the morning! You'll need all of your energy for the coming weeks, as you well know."

That was true – Dorothy was not looking forward to more months of nocturnal activity. She understood the midwife's point, and so she snuggled down and shut her eyes, all the time keeping one ear open lest Jack need her.

. . .

Routine, Patrick had realised over the past few years, was the key to managing life. It had undergone a few changes since their first years of marriage, of course, but the bare bones of it still remained and it gave him the stability that was central to his own happiness.

Dorothy was being a model mother and a model housewife. She was devoted to rearing the boys, looking after the house and keeping the village saturated with baked goods. Rita and she were closer than ever, sharing the same maternal instincts, and it was almost as if they could read each other's minds. When one of the older boys came in crying with a scraped knee, it only took one second before in one of them dived, putting the injured boy on the designated injury stool for a clean-up and a kiss better. Dorothy had settled into being a mother of three with a beaming contentment that belied her young age of twenty-six.

Things hadn't always been that rosy, though. Jack was the worst sleeper of the lot. Night after night after exhausting night Dorothy hauled herself out of bed at the commencement of the hourly screaming match. Up to an hour later, she would collapse back into it, only to have to drag herself back up half an hour later.

Nobody can survive for too long with such deprived sleep, at least without something giving. Dorothy had pushed herself to the utmost to ensure that nothing had to give. Ronald and Rita had taken some of the workload once more (with nothing but the smallest grumble from Rita) but Dorothy, ever the perfectionist, had been constantly re-doing their work if it didn't meet to her exacting standards. She was creating extra work for herself, but she would rather fade away herself than see their farm, and the children, and the animals, go to rack and ruin.

So she asked Reverend Osbourne for some advice on how to keep on top of everything. The normally calm, assured, confident vicar had momentarily shown a more vulnerable side.

"Ye see, I came to ye because yer th' vicar, an' connected to God, an' ye always seem so organised an'... just organised, really." Dorothy had said.

Reverend Osbourne had smiled, then a long and drawn-out silence had ensued. Dorothy couldn't maintain eye contact for that long and so her gaze had drifted down towards the vicar's hands, which were on the table, clasped together tightly as if in prayer. There was a certain amount of tension held in them.

"Well, I wasn't always this organised." Reverend Osbourne said eventually. "Before I came to Little Wychwood I was a town boy, living in Herrydale, a good few miles from here. I was the most untidy, impertinent young man there ever was. I fancied myself a city lad, with my bowler hat and my suit and tie. I was the type who thinks that the world owes them something, that I deserved privileges simply by existing. That was twenty years ago. Then I went to a church service, my very first, with my then-fiancée. I realised that I was going about my whole life wrong, and so I terminated the engagement, accepted Jesus into my life, and moved over here. It didn't take very long for me to become the vicar – the existing vicar saw something in me, and when he died, the responsibility was passed to me."

Dorothy wasn't quite sure what to say of this, as she felt very content with her life, and she *had* accepted Jesus into it. She remained silent and there was a pause, before the vicar finally posed the question.

"You're losing faith in the Lord, aren't you?" the vicar finally said. Dorothy snapped to attention and she opened her mouth to speak, but the indignation got caught in her throat.

Was she losing faith in the Lord?

In her head, Dorothy assessed the situation. She started right from the beginning of her life.

There was the whole injustice that had required the suffrage movement. Her own mother – loving, caring Wilhelmina – had been verbally attacked on several occasions by prejudiced men. Beautifully natured Katharina had been almost reduced to tears on one occasion when she'd been accosted by a man on the way to a meeting. These attacks had only been ended because of that war.

Then there was her father and his long line of failed jobs, all stemming from his desire to protect his daughter. It was only because Mrs. Shaw had been such an esteemed member of society that his name had been set alight in the first place. But, truth be told, Dorothy still harboured the tiniest bit of resentment for him. If he had only used his voice to communicate his feelings, rather than his fists, he would have saved himself and his family so much turmoil.

Then there was Patrick and his pain. Any loving, caring God would have understood his guilt at his friend's death and prevented it by saving the friend in the first place. Dorothy *understood* that by not saying the magical word *Amen*, Maxwell had been severely pushing his luck – but surely the lack of one mere word was not a sin punishable by death? And even if it was, there was no need for God to have tormented Patrick all these years by the memories. They were so realistic that at points, Patrick had believed that he was still at the scene.

Then there was the death of Maxwell – the baby, Maxwell. Was the name bad luck? Even so, the baby had not deserved to die. Dorothy had been told that this was often God's way of sorting out the babies that were too physically or mentally deformed to live – but why had he created the deformities in the first place? Was it to punish Patrick or Dorothy in some way? And if so – for what?

Then Edna had died. Goodness only knows what had been going through her mind when she had attempted to take her own life. Dorothy did not doubt that she had had good reason for it – and besides, she didn't trust Bruce Hammond further than she could throw him. What with scaremongering Patrick after baby Maxwell's death, and the alienation of Patrick and Andrew themselves at the slightest hint of disobedience… it was a bad business. Hitherto, Dorothy had always thought that her elders were the self-assured, organised people that she herself had dreamt of being. It had been a blow to realise that she was wrong.

Charlie's death was just the soured icing on the bitter cake. He had been far too young to die. Why, when the whole family had been through so much, would God add that to the mix?

Any loving God would not put anyone through that.

Dorothy raised her head and realised that Reverend Osbourne was still waiting for a reply. In a small voice, she answered his question with "Yes."

"I thought as much."

Reverend Osbourne debated the success of what he was about to say next. Either Dorothy would be mortally offended, or she'd see it through his eyes. He mentally shrugged. As vicar and unofficial leader of Little Wychwood, it was up to him to voice the things that nobody else dared to say.

"You're forgetting about the good times, Dorothy. You've been blessed with three more children. God could have taken them too – but he allowed you to keep them. God could have taken your father even earlier, letting you have even less time with him. He could have taken your mother too – God forbid. Each of your surviving babies have become healthy, perfect, well-behaved children. They are well on track to becoming fully-fledged children of God, and model children of Little Wychwood.

"God could have taken Patrick when he went to fight in the war. War is against the Bible, so it would have been understandable if God had felt betrayed and taken Patrick as a punishment. But He was merciful! Isn't that wonderful? You have allowed yourself to focus more on badness than goodness. This is my advice to you for the future: whenever you feel like the whole world is against you, remember two things: God still loves you, and that you could have fared a lot worse."

Dorothy looked stunned, to say the least. Reverend Osbourne had put an entirely different perspective on... well, her whole life. It never entered her head to be offended or outraged. Reverend Osbourne was nearly on par with an angel, as far as she was concerned – and any word from him was a word from God. That speech had suddenly restored her faith.

"I think you've just changed me outlook on life, Reverend. Thank you – thank you so much."

Dorothy headed for the door, not wanting to cry in front of the vicar. As she opened the door, Reverend Osbourne gently placed a hand upon her head. He had to reach up to do it, but it had the desired effect: she stopped and looked directly at him, meeting his eyes for what seemed to be the first time.

"I trust you to make the change, and to make the rest of your life positive." he said seriously. Her heart happy, Dorothy skipped home – and since then, she and Patrick had been sailing through life with an almost constant smile and endless supply of witticisms. If there were any miniature crises – such as William trapping a finger in between the hinges of the back door – Dorothy would not dwell on it. Life was too short for that.

So they settled down into a routine. It was strikingly similar to that of the start of their marriage – just with a few added responsibilities. The horse herd had increased in numbers – Freddy had just started riding, and looked quite precarious on top of his horse, Nelson. (Patrick had insisted on getting him a horse, rather than a pony.) William would only start riding when he was four or five, so he had to be content with watching his brother teeter along on the patient steed. Jack, being only fifteen months old, screamed whenever any of the horses so much as took a step towards him on his visits to their field with Dorothy.

Norbert and Isabelle Wood, who owned the shop, had become dear friends. They were very understanding when the amount of baked goods from the little farm fluctuated. On various days, Dorothy and Freddy would load up the cart full of things to sell, and trot it up to the shop, where Norbert, Isabelle and their nineteen-year-old son Neville unloaded it and set it up. Dorothy and Freddy would help between sips of tea or milk, respectively. Isabelle was rather aloof at times, but Norbert had told Neville to build up a good working relationship with the farm and so they were both always polite and friendly.

So now that they were settled into a nice, comfortable routine, it of course made perfect sense to uproot it once more. Dorothy and Patrick had had a discussion, and they decided that their little family was nowhere near big enough. Dorothy was determined to keep her promise to Charlie – but she was a little cautious about introducing another baby. Patrick, fuelled by the good mood of the farm, wasn't. So they began trying in earnest.

"One more won't make much of a difference, Dot!"

Dorothy hoped that was true, and went along with it.

. . .

"What was that ye said when we decided to try for another baby?" Dorothy said wryly, collapsing back into bed beside her husband.

"I can't remember, Dot. I can't remember anything these days..." Patrick replied, barely registering her mangled appearance.

"We must've been... insane or somethin'..." Dorothy stifled a yawn, then reached across and pulled the curtain shut, eliminating the only light source in the room. One of the twins stirred and made a chirrup in response. It was too dark to tell which one. Dorothy turned to her left towards Patrick and huddled under the thick blanket. When her eyes accustomed to the darkness, she could make out the shapes of the two Moses baskets on the tables opposite the bed, then the open door caught her eye.

"I forgot to shut th' door..." Dorothy groaned. Patrick, despite being nearest, made no attempt to shut it, so Dorothy dragged herself out of bed to do it herself. She knew that if she didn't, all hell would break loose. The eight-week-old twins were little miniature insomniacs, and woke up on the hour, every hour (although that may have had something to do with their sensitive hearing and the new grandfather clock in the hall). When one woke up and started crying, the other would join him. Patrick and Dorothy would both get up and tend to John and Harry. When their baby had stopped crying and was in the process of calming down, Dorothy or Patrick would walk up and down the landing in an attempt to get him back to sleep. It was only when both babies were asleep that Patrick and Dorothy could shut the door and return to bed.

The crying had, once or twice, disturbed the other three. John, the oldest twin by a few minutes, had the largest lung capacity of any baby Dorothy and Patrick had ever had. And he could *scream.* It could sound as if there was a tormented being in the Moses basket. When he did scream, it easily woke up the other three (and his twin brother), and then Dorothy and Patrick would have to wrangle five children in the middle of the night.

Trying not to make a sound, Dorothy half-stumbled, half-crawled towards the door. She had never been so tired. Even her teeth were tired, from grinding them so much. It was for this reason that when she hit her ankle on the side of Harry's table, jolting it and making him cry, she cried too. Her crying set off John, and so poor Patrick had to deal with three weeping people all at once. Then Jack toddled into the room. When Dorothy shouted at him in her exhaustion and frustration, he joined the fray in crying.

"Go back to bed, Jack." Patrick said firmly. When Jack set his mouth and shook his head, crocodile tears still running down his cheeks, Patrick clenched his fist and said "Bed, this instant, Jack." in a firm voice, through gritted teeth. Luckily, Jack knew to obey his father, and so he forgot his stubbornness and went back to the room he shared with William.

By the time John and Harry were settled again, Dorothy's tears had turned to a grim rage. Her movements were jerky and aggravated. She landed on the bed with a bump and wrenched the curtain shut. When Patrick reached for her hand, she involuntarily snatched it away before letting him have it.

"Do you regret having the twins, Dot?" Patrick said softly.

"Too right I do!" she replied without any hesitation whatsoever. Patrick sat up on his side, propping his head up with his free hand.

"Really?" he said, sounding surprised.

"I don't know what on Earth we were thinkin'."

"Now come on – God has blessed us with *two more* healthy babies. Remember what Reverend Osbourne said – He could have given us another stillborn, but He chose not to."

"But He gave us twins. I don't know what's worse – no baby, or two. We've got th' others – why did we need two more?"

"You're talking about them like they're objects, Dot!"

"If yer goin' to argue with me, then I don't want ye, an' ye can scram, now."

Dorothy had never before spoken to Patrick in that way.

"I will because I'm your husband. Now lower your voice, use a more fitting tone, and gather yourself before you say something even more idiotic."

Patrick had been practising his sharp, disciplinary voice, and he found that he liked it. He liked the sobering effect that it had on his wife – she sighed and lowered her gaze to avoid his, looking like a reprimanded child. A tiny jolt went through Patrick, the origin of which he didn't know. Desire? Power? Love? Who knew? But it had a powerful effect: he kissed her, and they both felt the tension between them relaxing.

"Oh, I know..." Dorothy said softly after a minute. "Getting' rid of ye won't change anythin' – it'll just make life even more chaotic an' that's the last thing we need right now. I know I've been a cow recently... but I'm just so tired..."

"I know. No more children for a while, yes?" Patrick said, and with that established, they lay back down and dozed off again. That was, until around half an hour later, where the grandfather clock chimed twice, setting off the twins again. With stolid determination, Dorothy rocked John and murmured to him, whilst Patrick did the same to Harry. John went off first, but Harry stayed determinedly awake. Dorothy got back into bed, and then she got to hear something that she never thought she'd hear.

"*Hush little child, don't say a word,*

Daddy's gonna buy you a mocking bird..."

It wasn't her singing, so it had to be Patrick. She half-opened an eye and saw Patrick parading slowly around the bedroom, crooning the lullaby oh-so-softly, into the baby's head. He obviously thought Dorothy was asleep, as he'd never dropped his guard like this before. It was lovely – Patrick wasn't the best singer, but he could hold a tune adequately, even if he didn't know all the words. Harry had obviously gone to sleep, because Patrick lay him back in the Moses basket and got back into bed.

Now Dorothy couldn't resist saying something. She turned over under the blanket, stretched and said "That was lovely..." sleepily.

"What was?" Patrick said, instantly alert.

"Yer singin'... where did ye get that lullaby?"

"Now that's not fair – I thought you were asleep!"

"Sleep? Never 'eard of it."

"Miss Marian taught me that – although I had to change "Nursie" to "Daddy" to make it fit. She's an absolute gem of a woman, Miss Marian... which makes me wonder..."

"Wonder what?"

"Wonder whether she could look after the children for a night or two. We need to get away again, Dot. Port Isaac is such a wonderful place – I'd really like to go back, stay with that lovely woman again. We're both still young – you're only twenty-seven, aren't you, Dot? We settled so young... who knows? One day we could completely uproot everything, move to Cornwall, start an entirely new life with the children... what do you think?"

"Why would ye want to? I'm happy here, the children are happy here – why would we sacrifice all that for somethin' that may not work out? A holiday, maybe, but not a life down there. Me friends are here, an' our livelihood."

"Ah, you're right. I love our farm, and the village, and the children, and you. We'll see if we can get down to Cornwall for a night, without the children, and leave it at that, shall we?"

"Much better."

"But talking of family... I do wonder what happened to

Mother. Why did she feel the need to try to end it all like that? Sometime soon, I'll go through her things, and try to gather any clues as to what her train of thought was."

Dorothy did not say anything, but what she really wanted to point out was her first proper meeting with Patrick – on the banks of a hungry river, on a freezing cold day, with him on the verge of jumping in. Why had *he* felt the need to try to end it all like that? However, she was intuitive enough to realise that the memory of that day, which was both awful and wonderful in its own way, could trigger all sorts of things in his mind.

So she said nothing, and what was left unsaid was left in her mind. And in Patrick's.

. . .

Well, a year passed, and Patrick had done very little to contribute to his intentions. Life simply got in the way – and with it came all sorts of hectic twists and turns.

Firstly, Father-Sir had sent a telegram. It consisted of two short sentences. He was moving, presumably with Bessie, Gertrude and Mike in tow, to Ireland. "In the name of the Lord, do not contact me." he wrote. Andrew was all set for going over there and retrieving his belongings, but Patrick stopped him. A furious argument had ensued – "My first Bible is there!" opposed by "You'll be burnt at the stake by Father-Sir!"

Eventually the latter won, but Andrew spent a good few months petulantly sulking on and off about his lost belongings, despite having coped without them for years. However, he soon lost that attitude when something far bigger happened.

Rita – lovely Rita – suddenly contracted scarlatina. She was there one day, with a mild cold, and then the next day – gone. Neither of them turned up for work one day, and so the milkman promised to drop in on them on his rounds. He was back within the hour, face almost blue, and told Patrick to go urgently to their house in Cottesmore Lane.

Patrick had come back and sunk down in his chair, head in hands. When Dorothy followed him in, up to her eyes in flour and with the twins wobbling unsteadily behind her, he told her the sad news.

"How are we goin' to cope?" she cried out, making the twins look up in alarm.

"We will, Dot." Patrick said grimly, "I'll make sure of it."

So after a lot of juggling of roles, and plenty of stress to go with it, they formed some semblance of control over the farm. Ronald did try to return after the funeral, but the farm held too many memories for him. When he announced that he was moving back to Folkestone to live with his sister, nobody was surprised. He packed his bags and Patrick drove him down to the Wychwood train station.

Then, twenty-one-year-old Neville Wood had taken over the farm from his parents. He was a well-mannered, intelligent young man, always top of the class and athletic to go with it. It was a shame, Frank Dyke had said quietly, that he had to resign himself to being a shopkeeper. A clever boy like him could have made chief of police, he said.

Neville had found himself more than a little overwhelmed. He had been landed with the entire responsibility of the shop while his parents followed in Ronald's footsteps and moved away. Dorothy did feel rather sorry for him. There were only eight years between the two of them, and it took a while for Dorothy and Patrick to consider him a family friend and businessman, rather than the son of one. But eventually, Neville settled into running the shop, and with his sights set on a girl called Ivy from the town, he was well on track.

All this meant that for finding out what had happened to Edna, there was no time, nor motivation. Patrick had gone through her belongings and found an unfamiliar envelope, with the names of him and his siblings on it. He had lost heart at that point, not wanting to open it without the rest of them there. So he put it under his pillow and let it be.

That was where the envelope remained, until Andrew took it upon himself to change all of the bedsheets one evening to help Dorothy. When he found Patrick trying to level out the muddy path to the horse field, he showed him and asked, "Why had this not been brought to my knowledge?"

Patrick had said very little, but he agreed that after dinner, when the children were in bed, they could open it. Freddy had school the next day, and so all of the children were sent to bed earlier than usual. "We have grown-up's things to do tonight," Andrew told the children as he herded them upstairs. Jack made a fuss, wanting to stay with his beloved uncle, but a stern word from Patrick sent him scampering upstairs.

Once all five of them were tucked up in bed with a bedtime story read to them, Andrew and Dorothy returned downstairs to find that Patrick had poured three whiskies into three glasses. Dorothy had rarely before been permitted to drink, but this time she did not let the privilege go to her head. She took the drink soberly and put it on top of their new piano. Andrew fetched himself one of the dining room chairs. Patrick took a sip of whisky, poked the fire to keep it burning, and leant forward, producing the envelope.

"My apologies for keeping this secret, Andrew. It just doesn't feel right – not without Father-Sir, and the other three." he said.

"The envelope is only addressed to us children – not Father-Sir." Andrew pointed out.

"That only increases my worries about what is contained in this envelope." Patrick replied, holding it out in front of him like a precious artefact. It was almost too heavy to carry – after all, the weight of Edna's innermost thoughts lay within the inked paper. "So... who's going to open it?"

Andrew stared at the envelope as though it was going to bite him. They waited a moment, and then an impatient Dorothy took it from Patrick and confidently tore it open. The noise of the tearing paper made them all jump, penetrating the silence like some sort of audible sword.

Dorothy took out two folded pieces of pale blue writing paper. Without unfolding it, she could read the address of the top one, and the date. Sunday, 13th February 1921. Approximately eight in the evening. That was when her bottle left her, and she thrust the letter into Andrew's lap. With shaking hands (Dorothy noticed this) he unfolded it and skimmed it with his eyes.

"Well? Are you going to read it out, then?" Patrick said, masking his nerves with sharpness. Andrew nodded, cleared his throat of the huge lump in it, and began to speak.

"*Dear Children,*" he began, his voice shaking like his hands. "*If you are reading this, then that means that you've given into your curiosity. As the saying goes – 'curiosity killed the cat, but satisfaction brought it back'. I don't know, and I cannot bear to think of, what your reaction will be to this letter and its contents. Whatever it is, remember one thing – you had several years with me. Like the cat, be satisfied with that.*

"*If you are reading this, then that means that you've found this note, somewhere on my person, alongside a few other precious letters. And therefore, I have succeeded in terminating my infinite struggle. I do not know of whether I will enter Hell or Heaven – I do hope the latter, God save my Christian soul! – but somewhere, somehow, I know I will be with you all again. Wherever I am, wherever you are, I will look down on you all, like an angel on your shoulder. Have no qualms about that.*

"*This letter is my apology for leaving you all, and my feeble explanation. I had no alternative – I could not stay on this Earth any longer, in danger every day, treading on eggshells within my own home. You will be upset – horrified even – to hear this from the mouth of your own mother, but such things as I will discuss are a sad part of life, and one that must be changed. And Bruce… if you are reading this, then you might as well be educated too.*

"Children, if there is one word to describe your childhoods, it is "indoctrinated". You have been indoctrinated to believe many things, much of which is wrong, wrong, wrong beyond belief. Your father – hereafter referred to as B, as it pains me to even write its name – has indoctrinated you to believe that men are Masters of the Earth. Just because God was a man, and Jesus was a man, and God made Eve from Adam, not the other way around. You've been taught to believe that women are nothing but the possessions of their man, and a way to multiply the bloodline. Gertrude and Bessie will testify to my statement that women are people.

"Unfortunately, B did not understand this essential, vital piece of information – and that was his major downfall. Our first months together were good, glorious even. He burrowed his way into my heart, claimed it all for his own, then married me to prove it. We moved in together and we had several happy days in the garden of our old house, where B told me he loved me, adored me, would do anything for me…

"That was all a lie, I am afraid to say. He hurt me. The first time, it was a punishment for doing something which he deemed unforgiveable – apparently I severely disrespected him, although I was just speaking my mind for once in my life. The next time, it was for accidentally knocking into him on the stairs. I failed to apologise for it as I was side-tracked… but he did it again. The next time, it was for a minor misdemeanour. And after that… whenever he chose. Whenever he wanted it, he would get it, even if it meant hurting me in the process.

"And all the time, while he was doing it, he would be muttering away to himself – "Just keep quiet… just a few more minutes and I'll forgive you… you owe it to me… please, you know I love you… that's a good girl…". How ironic that he was doing it to me while these words of love and persuasion were falling from his lips.

"I've had to sleep on that same bed every night, and since then the

experiences have plagued my dreams, the memories increasing in intensity every time he does it. And I've had to keep quiet, for the sake of you children.

"But don't blame yourselves, please. I had nobody to tell anyway. I should have told your Auntie Maude the first time he did it, but no, it would have been too humiliating. She'd always known me as this strong, impenetrable woman, and telling her that I was too weak to resist my husband's desires would have been too humiliating to bear.

"Then I became impregnated with Andrew. I was banished to bed the day I found out. According to B, he didn't want me overdoing things – or so he said. What idiocy. I know the truth. He simply wanted to keep me all for himself. I overheard him talking to a friend – I eavesdropped, I admit. The friend's wife had been unfaithful during her pregnancy, and so the friend told B – "Keep her well under control."

"And B took that to the extreme – and from then on, I was no longer his wife. I was his servant. I served only to be his punchbag – physically and verbally. And the things that B did to me in private are too horrific to explicitly explain. They are vile, disgusting, abhorrent, a perversion of all that is good. At times B had me crying, other times whimpering, other times just blank. There is nothing more painful than being treated as an object by the one that you've given your heart to. My mind often could not cope with the myriad of emotions, and so it just shut down and let B get on with things. I surrendered my whole existence for B. And yet he still did these things.

"After Andrew was born, after the first time, I had decided that what he'd done was just an anomaly, and that it would never happen again. I had a baby now; I was a mother – surely that made me invincible? I had done what no man would ever have the guts to do. I had earned my protection. B had seen my resilience – surely he wouldn't dare do that to me now?

"But then that second time, I woke up from a nap and B was

there, towering over me, an angry, brusque version of himself. He was hissing about payback and how I hadn't apologised and how dare I disrespect him?

"And every time I'd think the same thing: HOW DID I LET THIS HAPPEN TO ME?

"Now, tonight, it is time for me to fight back in a big way. Well, when I have no identity, no hope, no love... what is there to live for? If I fought in any other way, the fact that I would still be alive would mean that I would pay for it forever. It would be like quelling a fire with kerosene. B has a tongue like sandpaper, and a mind that has been doused in acid and rotted away, shrinking the brain cells responsible for rational thought to nothing.

"Boys, please learn from B's mistakes. Don't drive your women to the state that I am in now. If you do... I will personally ensure, even from beyond the grave..."

At this point, Andrew could not read on any further. He shoved the paper at Patrick and covered his mouth to stop himself choking. Patrick took the paper and continued from where Andrew had stopped.

"If you do... I will personally ensure, even from beyond the grave, that you spend eternity accompanying Satan in deepest, darkest Hell, surrounded by fire, fury and blackness.

"Girls, don't settle for what I settled for. Please get out of there. Scatter yourselves all over the country, all over the world if necessary, wherever B can't get to you. It will be scary, but do it for me. God knows you don't want to put yourself through what I've been through. You're both still young. You don't have to have children – you don't even have to marry. Don't let men take away your identity, your courage, or your spirit. His favourite excuse is "Without men, you wouldn't have any rights at all," but that is just wrong. Without men, we wouldn't have to fight for our rights.

"Andrew – at time of writing, I have no clue as to your whereabouts, whether you went to war or not. I hope that one day, you

will read this, and feel no guilt. You could have done nothing to ease this – I understand that B can be a terrifying beast at the best of times. Don't worry. You may be the eldest, but you're by no means responsible for protecting your mother. It is the other way around, if anything.

"Gertrude – I know B has used my long, painful labour with you as a form of emotional blackmail. You are in no way indebted to him. His bloodline may make up half of you, per se, but you don't have to serve him. Please don't feel that way – I certainly don't. Thank you for being a good, faithful daughter.

"Patrick – thank you for protecting this country. Despite going against B's words, you don't have a bad bone in your body. As your mother, I know that very well indeed. Despite being a little instinctive at times, your heart is firmly set in the right place – and no amount of toil or trouble will shift it.

"Bessie – my message to you is similar to that of Gertrude. You've been a strong and devoted daughter, through pneumonia, measles and pneumonia again. These problems have all surfaced over the past few years, and any other person would have failed to cope. You've survived all of your worst days so far – you can survive the ones that will indubitably come.

"Mike – you're the youngest, and despite being forced to collaborate with B to keep the girls and I under control, you still have the potential to be a good man. Forget all that B has said to you, and pay no heed to what he will say to you in the coming weeks, months and (God forbid!) years. It's all part of his indoctrination scheme.

"All of you – don't forget that wherever I am, my love will be the vital bridge across the threshold of the afterlife. Thank you, and God bless you all. I'm not entirely sure what my next move is, after I place this letter somewhere impossibly safe on my person so that it will be passed on when found. I surrender my being to God now – and wherever He takes me, I'm sure, will be the right place."

. . .

Andrew didn't stay long after that. He mumbled his apologies and left for home. Dorothy didn't blame him – the atmosphere in the living room had become paralyzingly, numbingly heavy with the weight of Edna's words. It was strange how a few pieces of paper and some ink could have the ability to change lives. When the clock struck their usual hour of retirement, Dorothy and Patrick put out the fire, locked the doors and quietly made their way to bed. Dorothy had the apprehensive feeling that she was about to cry.

They lay in bed next to each other, eyes wide open and fixated on the ceiling. For once, all the animals were silent, as were the children. The silence started comfortable enough, then the weight of unsaid words turned it into a stifling, awkward silence. Dorothy found something to say, so she turned over onto her left, lay her head on Patrick's shoulder, and took a deep breath.

"Ye never really know someone, do ye?" she said, her voice wavering disappointingly.

"Hmm?" Patrick grunted absently, still submerged in his own thoughts.

"Ye never really know 'em. Ye *think* ye do, o' course, but when th' doors are shut an' th' curtains are pulled, only they truly know what they experience an' how they feel about it. Nobody can replicate their feelin', not to the extent that they have it, not unless they've experienced it themselves – an' thank th' Lord we haven't.

"I suppose that's why ye always have to offer 'em a friendly ear, an' a shoulder to cry on, even if they're showin' no signs that they need it. We women are a lot more intuitive of each other's emotions, I suppose. I feel that I did not do th' best job at bein' there for yer mam. I was only young then, barely more than a child, but I wish I could think that in me own moments o' need, I would've accepted *her* help, an' offered it in return.

"An while I was cooin' over our Freddy, celebratin' new life an' all the beautiful moments that come with it, Edna was ponderin' her own life. While I was frettin' over a fraction of a cold, Edna was bein' subjected to all sorts of unspeakable acts in th' hands of a powerful man. God only knows what was goin' through her mind when she was sittin' there that night, tryin' to put in words her experience an' her messages. I wonder if she omitted any of it, to protect us maybe. After all, she's done that for thirty years.

"Thank God she did not succeed in endin' her life completely, that's what I think. She got out of there. But Pat, I'm not angry at her, and you shouldn't be either. Ultimately, despite what she said about havin' no choice, it was her active decision to do it. Ye must respect that, because, as I said, ye'll never truly know what was goin' through her head. But what she didn't realise was…" and here Dorothy paused, wondering whether Patrick would take this the right way, "…suicide doesn't have to be the only option. I don't think she wanted to kill herself – she just wanted that situation to be over.

"Don't let this ruin ye either, Pat. That paragraph addressed to ye – let that be th' savin' of ye. One day, when all this fuss has died down, I think ye'll be able to read that paragraph an' know how much ye meant to yer mam. Ye'll understand that ye made her proud, an' all yer actions were good, an' valuable, an' proper. That's real peace, an' I know that ye'll achieve it one day. I will accompany ye every step o' the way, an' with yer mam on one shoulder, an' me on th' other, we *will* make it there."

Patrick did not say anything. What could he say? The emotional words swirled around the room. As they seeped through to his brain, he felt the first little stirrings of hope in his veins, and mentally beat them back. How could he feel *happy* when he hadn't even noticed what was happening to his mother? Was he really such an unobservant, unapproachable little tyke? A mixture of fury, grief and confusion replaced the hope, making his entire body sting. He leapt up and lunged for the door.

"Pat?" Dorothy murmured, although it had been her first instinct to scream. She heard the footsteps thundering down the stairs, mercifully not waking the children. She followed him downstairs quietly and saw him pulling on his greatcoat and boots. Aware that it was bitterly cold, she stopped there, but he flew out of the back door at top speed and into the night.

Patrick had one destination in his mind: the stables. He hadn't ridden properly for a while and he just knew that he had to get as far away from that humid house as he could – by means of transport that would jolt the guilt out of his veins and send it spiralling into oblivion. He unlocked the stable door and, barely registering the other horses snorting in surprise, hurled his saddle on the delicate Thoroughbred back of Winston. Despite being in his early double figures, the big bay horse was up for adventure at any time of the day.

After rather aggressively pulling the bridle on and doing up the straps, Patrick leapt up on the horse from the ground. The horse was seventeen hands, one inch (approximately five feet and seven inches, measured from his back) and although Patrick was near enough six feet tall, he had never done this before, at least successfully. It worked, however, and after ramming his feet into the stirrups, he gave the horse a nudge in the sides and started trotting towards the opposite end of his property. He knew that if he went onto Onyx Lane and through the village, he would wake up the village without even getting a proper gallop.

So once they were out of the property, Patrick took the horse on one of the less common hunting routes. They went from a trot straight to a gallop, without a proper opportunity for his horse to warm up. Patrick didn't care – he just wanted to get as far away from home as he could.

As they galloped, Patrick perched precariously on top, like a pencil being balanced on a stegosaurus. That was certainly what it felt like – the uneven terrain made the ride bouncy and hard on both Winston and Patrick. The horse was galloping long and unbalanced, all semblance of limb engagement gone. Patrick had the sense that something had to give at some point, but he did not do anything about it. Rather than pulling the horse back, he gave him his head, shut his eyes and hoped for the best.

Thud-thud, thud-thud, thud-thud...

Patrick had the feeling of being detached. He had a birds-eye view of himself, galloping and a frighteningly reckless speed across a muddy, slippery field (owned by nobody), himself a jockey almost, urging his mount on with a tightening of the legs against his sides. Patrick responded to this vision in turn, jabbing his heels into Winston's sides so the horse surged forward even faster. Winston's Thoroughbred blood was out in full force. The pleasant (albeit skittish) horse gave way to a rollicking, snorting, euphorically joyful creature.

Thud-thud, thud-thud, thud-thud...

Similarly, the placate, mature Patrick had morphed back into the jumpy, socially inept victim of war that Dorothy had vowed to protect as she fell in love with him. Only now could he see how much he had changed over the years. He was physically and mentally fitter, stronger, able to cope. Dorothy had steadfastly loved all these changes, and they'd stayed together the whole time, aside from those early couple of days.

Thud-thud, thud-thud, thud-thud...

Well, that mature, married, father-of-God-knows-how-many Patrick had gone now, at least for tonight. Yet he still wasn't quite the old Patrick either. With a sharp intake of breath, he registered how hard Winston was finding it to place his feet. He took a quick look down and almost yelped. There were dead bodies underfoot. He was surrounded by Maxwells – not the baby, but the soldier. Each Maxwell wore the same expression that he had worn at death – nothing behind the slightly open eyes.

How *could* he attempt to find peace when he was such a sinner? Peace was something only achieved by the greatest Christians, those who hadn't killed. He was stupid to even think of achieving it. He was a killer – he had jolted his friend to death, he had overworked his wife which led to his baby's death, he'd *ignored* his mother to death. His hands were clean in terms of blood, but his soul was black and red, the two most sinful colours of them all.

Thud-thud, thud-thud, thud-thud.

Vile was the only word he could think of to describe himself. *'Do not be like Cain, who belonged to the evil one and murdered his brother.'* said John 3:12. Patrick knew that he had been born innocent, but his decision to go to that cursed war had ensured that all innocence and goodness in him was gone. Every second of the bloodshed, gore and pain had been a second of his life gone, given to the devil. He hadn't ever been shot, but the bullets ricocheted around his brain, punching little holes into his sanity.

Patrick tore a branch off an overhanging tree and smacked the horse's side with it, hoping to outrun his memories. Loud gunshots – or was it just the sound of branch against boots? – sounded in his ears.

"Run, Winston! They'll kill us!" he screamed aloud, and at that point there was a blinding flash and even Winston screamed. The horse stopped dead, his back end sliding to the side and wrenching him off his feet. The pair of them landed in a heap, steed on top of soldier, scrambling in the mud, Winston trying to avoid hurting his beloved Patrick. The horse sprung up and coughed loudly while Patrick shuddered, gulped and choked for air, somehow still holding onto the horse's reins. Once there was sufficient oxygen in his lungs, he remembered what he had seen and jumped up, lest he be disturbing any of the bodies, every one of which he had great respect for. But there was just mud beneath his hands and feet – no bodies to be seen.

Patrick leant against his horse, eyes shut, a cramping feeling starting in his whole body. Even his brain was being seized, as if God had it in the palm of His hand and was squeezing it furiously, punishing Patrick for every sin all at once. Patrick opened his eyes once the pain had lessened a bit and told himself that he couldn't collapse. He realised that he had no idea where he was, and he had no idea how to get back.

. . .

Somehow Patrick made it home, just as the sun was rising. He had been out, wandering endlessly through muddy mazes, for the best part of ten hours. He put his horse in the stable and went in through the back door. Dorothy was boiling some eggs and Freddy was standing by her side, both of them looking perfectly normal. A flicker of relief crossed her face before it returned to blank.

"Mornin'!" she said, trying to sound chirpy, "Yer breakfast will be on the table in ten – go an' get changed an' I'll leave it on the table. Andrew's milkin' th' cows."

Patrick's exhaustion limited his patience greatly and added a touch of venom to his voice.

"I'm going to bed," he spat, "And I'll decide what and when I do now – thank you very much."

. . .

"Good morning, Madam. I wonder if you could tell me the whereabouts of an Andrew Hammond, if you please?"

It only took one try to locate Andrew. It was lucky that Little Wychwood was such a close-knit village: everyone knew each other's business, everyone met once a week at church, and people could practically invite themselves into each other's houses. Miss Eunice directed the charming middle-aged man, inwardly wondering what such a distinguished gentleman would have with untidy Andrew.

So the gentleman walked across the square, cane in hand and top hat perched upon his head. He walked up Onyx Lane and then stopped at the gate leading to the house. So this was why Andrew had relocated... he could see the charm himself.

Dorothy let him in and shouted for Andrew. She sat the gentleman down at the dining table and brought him a cup of tea.

"Timothy! It's been so long! This is a surprise – what brings you to the village?" Andrew said jovially, shaking his former colleague's hand.

"Not too much of a surprise, I hope – you must know that I live close. I would like to see your mother, if I may, provided that my presence doesn't upset her."

Timothy had decided to be straightforward and to-the-point, no procrastination. He had half-expected Andrew to be out-raged, especially given how he had upset Edna at their last meeting, but instead Andrew just looked immensely sad. He ran through his last two sentences in his mind – had he said something wrong?"

"My mother died, nearly eight years ago now. In the end, God decided to take her to Heaven anyway, to fulfil what her wish had been."

Andrew promptly went to find his brother, unsure of what to do about the stunned visitor who was just digesting this riddle. He was worried about his brother, to tell the truth. Patrick's personality had done a complete one-hundred-and-eighty-degree turn since that night where he'd galloped Win-ston flat-out. The horse had been ill for weeks. Andrew was beginning to see even more traits of his father in Patrick. To the villagers, Patrick had simply matured. He conducted him-self well, like a true adult. Hitherto, he had been considered a treasured young'un, even with children at foot.

But Patrick was now becoming obsessed with training his

children. The Bible verse that Father-Sir had given him was being taken to the next level – '*Start children off on the way they should go, and even when they are old they will not turn from it.*' Any semblance of disobedience was eradicated. Patrick had been known to twitter on inanely over the dinner table about how evil the world was becoming, and how the children should never venture too far into it. In that speech, Andrew had heard Father-Sir's voice, and it scared him.

He was becoming like Bruce Hammond in more than one way. Andrew feared for him, and feared for Dorothy. Now she was pregnant again, Patrick's protective instincts had increased ten-fold, and he had banned her from going into the town on a Saturday like she used to. Dorothy herself was working harder than ever, although this pregnancy had hit her hard. It was a wonder that Patrick hadn't banished her to bed, like Bruce had done with poor Edna.

But Patrick was truly fond of his wife, unlike Bruce had been. That made all the difference.

Andrew found Patrick and followed him as he stalked in from the fields, pausing only to take off his boots. It wasn't that hot, although there were thunderstorms predicted for later, but Patrick was already het up. He hated unwanted visitors these days, especially on a bank holiday like today. Dorothy had put a plate of biscuits on the table with the teacups and sat down to wait, complimenting Timothy on his choice of jacket. Patrick shook Timothy's hand, then sat down too. The children were not present, all playing in the fields, so they could have a talk uninterrupted.

"I am an acquaintance and former close friend of your mother's – Timothy Montgomery – and I am very pleased to meet you." Timothy started.

"Forgive me, but if you were so close, then how come I don't know you from Adam?" Patrick replied. Dorothy cringed at his rudeness, but Timothy smiled and shook his head a little bit.

"She existed long before you did, Sir. Before she met your father, we had a brief relationship. *Very* brief – it only really lasted one evening. Eight years ago, our paths crossed again, and I proposed to her, at which point she declined. I came here today – on a bank holiday, I am aware, do forgive me – to ask her what she had been through. Your mother looked so lost and forlorn when she rejected my proposal, and since then it has been that expression that I see on her face in my mind whenever she crosses it.

"I am told now that your mother died, but I cannot leave without doing two things. One is to offer my deepest condolences, and the other is to find out what really happened to her.

"Andrew, you spoke riddles to me earlier. Could you start from wherever you see fit, but structure your story in a comprehensible way for me?"

So Andrew told him, while Patrick listened with his hands over his face, as if mere bone would shield him from what had happened. In fact, it was all that he could do not to run screaming. Andrew told the story well enough to abhor the listener – as if it didn't do that anyway – while keeping himself composed. By the time the tale had come to its sorry end (when Andrew revealed quotations from Edna's letter), Timothy looked two-parts sad, one-part furious.

"I should like to string your father!" he declared, then looked embarrassed in case he had offended any of the family. He was relieved to see that they were all nodding regretfully. His words then failed him – after all, what does one say to the family of someone who had been to the other side of Hell and back?

"Well, Timothy, maybe now you can talk to us." Andrew said, glancing warily at Patrick. "What happened between you and my mother? She looked awfully wan in the days after your visit – and she mentioned a Mr. Montgomery once when we were children, although I've only just made the connection."

"Well, there is not much to tell..." said the visitor, adjusting himself and preparing to relive the evening that he had thought about so often.

"I met your mother at the shop, where she worked. I knew her boss, and it was her first day, and she knocked over the newspaper stand. I helped her pick them all up, and I walked her home because she had got herself rather flustered. As a gesture of thanks, her father invited me in for a meal. We spent a very pleasant evening together, with her father as chaperone, and I could tell we had deep feelings for each other. But I... oh, goodness, I can't find the words. It pains me to admit this, but...

"Well, I lied. I admit it now, I lied. I could not find it within me to let down my guard and admit that I had fallen for her, well and truly. So I made up this foolish tale about living in York and having to go back there and... oh, I don't know. I broke her heart, and her sad eyes said it all, despite the courageous smile. It doesn't sound like much, does it?" he laughed briefly, "But we were both young and immature – the perils of young love, you know?"

Andrew didn't say anything. He was not going to tell them of his lover days, back when he'd first left Highmore Park.

"And if it doesn't sound too melodramatic, I have regretted that conversation for the rest of my life. I saw marriage for us, just briefly, but my stupid pride prevented it. Nonetheless, since that night, I have not stopped thinking about her."

"Oh, *cry* me a *river*..." sniped Patrick quietly. Dorothy cringed again – why was he being so nasty?

"Hold your tongue!" snarled Andrew, "Let Timothy speak!"

"For the next thirty years, I remained a devoted bachelor, and I hoped that she would remain a spinster. I severely doubted it – after all, she was beyond compare – but when you've been rejected by the only one you could ever see yourself marrying, there comes a fierce determination to show your dedication. Do you understand?"

Dorothy and Patrick, both in their own separate minds, considered this. They certainly couldn't imagine themselves with anyone else. Their eyes met, and Dorothy smiled a little. Patrick smiled back, just a fraction, and Dorothy could see traces of the real Patrick in there – not this dominant new one.

"I thought so." Timothy smiled too. "I always dreamed that one day, our paths would cross again and I would muster up the courage to propose for real. Thirty years later, that's exactly what happened. You and I had worked together for a time before that, Andrew, but of course, she had a different surname by then, and so did you. I didn't make the connection until I visited your house, and there she was. I was stunned, and she was likewise, but we remembered our manners and I don't think we let on that we knew each other, did we?"

"I didn't notice a thing!" Andrew said, "Mother had always been shy and nervous about men – an after-effect of Father-Sir, I presume – and with you she was no different. I wondered what would happen if I left her alone with you, and I trusted you to be kind to her, so I left you two alone. What happened after that, Timothy?"

"Well, we talked. We certainly talked. I revealed all, about how much I adored her, how much I had thought about her, and the whole York fiasco. She reciprocated my feelings, and I proposed. It was only then that she revealed that she was married – I don't know how I had failed to miss that. I offered to force the husband to divorce her, but she told me that he was a dangerous man. She told me that he had destroyed her, but I suspected that she was just saying that as an excuse. Now I know that it was true. Anyway, we parted on good terms – I gave her my address in case she ever changed her mind, and that was that."

"An' I can only presume that, her peace made with ye, she found herself able to let th' world go for real." Dorothy finished the story, looking directly at Patrick. He was staring into space.

At that point, there was a loud rumble of thunder and big drops of rain began to fall. The clock struck five, and Dorothy realised that the fish pie was minutes away from being charred to cinders.

"Stay for dinner?" Dorothy offered Timothy, who was gathering his hat and preparing himself to leave, "I can stretch me fish pie."

"That's very kind of you – are you sure that you will have enough?"

"Yes, you need all the sustenance you can get, Dot," Patrick said lovingly, placing his hand on her stomach. "You need to sustain yourself, and the baby."

"You're expecting?" Timothy said, startled, "Is it your first baby?"

"Oh no – my sixth!" Dorothy replied, disappearing into the kitchen. She picked up two bits of wool, stuck them in her ears, and whacked her designated saucepan with a wooden spoon, shouting her usual command. Thirty seconds later, five young boys ran through the back door, throwing boots into the cupboard higgledy-piggledy, and up the stairs to wash their faces and hands. They appeared at the table shortly, a little surprised to see this unfamiliar man where Mother usually sat, but too well-brought-up to comment. Freddy, being the oldest at a mighty nine years old, shook hands with the visitor and sat down with the rest.

"Now, children, this distinguished gentleman here is a friend of Grandmother's. His name is Mr. Montgomery, and he is our dinner guest for tonight. While he is here, he is naturally to be treated with the utmost respect, do I make myself clear?" Patrick instructed, pouring wine for himself, Andrew and Timothy.

"Yes, Father." the children all chorused, well-trained. Timothy could see traces of Edna in the oldest child, introduced as

Frederick. Like Patrick, all of the children had Edna's blue eyes. Frederick and the two youngest – twins – were blonde, like Edna, but in Frederick, Edna was there clear as day. It was as if the stamp God had used to mould Edna's face had been reused on Frederick.

Patrick managed to keep a hold of himself all the way through the meal, and he was relieved when Andrew and Timothy both began to talk of leaving. But just as they were collecting their coats, Freddy went up to his father and asked bravely, "Father, when can we see Grandmother and Grandfather?"

The change in Patrick's demeanour was immediate. He slammed his hand on the door frame and snapped, "No! Never! Grandmother is dead, Frederick – don't you know that?"

"Pat, calm down!" Dorothy exclaimed, having been startled.

"Well, what about Grandfather, then?" Freddy said boldly, although he shot a few nervous looks at his mother.

"Grandfather is evil, Freddy." Patrick said sadly, bending down and putting a finger under the child's chin, forcing their eyes to meet. "Grandfather is almost on par with Satan. He is a very bad man, and you must never see him, talk to him or even think about him. Do you understand?"

"Yes, Father." Freddy said, looking a little disturbed. Dorothy was equally concerned – she never thought she'd hear Patrick say that about anyone other than himself. The children did not know anything about their two aunts, nor Uncle Mike, and she reckoned that Patrick would keep it that way. As far as he was concerned, Bruce Hammond and his other offspring (bar Andrew) had been cut completely out of his life for the benefit of himself and the children. But there were times, Dorothy knew, when Patrick doubted himself, and that was where it started to go wrong.

At least Patrick had an escape soon. He was to spend a couple of days at a farming meeting in Birmingham somewhere, and he was leaving Andrew and Dorothy to look after the farm. She didn't know how they were going to cope, but she knew that he needed some time off, and so she decided to grin and bear it. As long as she didn't overdo it. She didn't want to lose this baby.

. . .

She'd been so good, so careful, and yet it was happening again. Dorothy just couldn't bear the thought. On the drive to the hospital beside the exceedingly grave-looking Andrew, the events of almost ten years ago ran through her mind. She couldn't do all of that again, especially because they were struggling for money, and especially without Ronald and Rita on hand to help.

When the churchgoers poured out of the church, many of them rushed to the square to see if they could shout a few comforting words to Dorothy as she departed. Miss Marian and Miss Eunice ushered Dorothy's children back to their own big house, assuring them that Mother was all right, she just needed a little rest. She would be back later, fit as a fiddle, just you wait and see!

But from the looks they passed between each other, from an experienced ex-midwife to a former nanny, they knew that those words were just words, no truth. This had happened to Dorothy before, and Miss Eunice knew that at this stage of development (six months gestation), if the baby was to be born now, there would be very little chance of it surviving.

All the same, they had prayed. The whole village had. When Dorothy had stood up shakily, clutching Andrew's arm for support, and made a hasty exit (apologising through little winces), Reverend Osbourne had been quietly professional. He had helped her outside with the aid of Miss Eunice and they had both waited with her while Andrew sprinted back to the farm to get the cart. While they waited, Miss Eunice soothed Dorothy and Reverend Osbourne prayed over her. Dorothy tried to listen to the Reverend's words – "Heavenly Father, please be merciful to Dorothy. We thank you for all your past kind-nesses..."

When Dorothy had been whisked off in the cart with Andrew, Reverend Osbourne and Miss Eunice had glanced at each other with immense sadness on their faces. The whole church had been nervously whispering to each other, but Reverend Os-bourne somehow found the right words to say to them.

"Unfortunately, our dear Dorothy Hammond has been taken ill, but she is on her way to the hospital now with Andrew and we must simply pray for God to protect her."

So they did pray, and they prayed hard. The children prayed too, and they picked up on the seriousness of the situation. They did not know about Maxwell – so they didn't really under-stand the concept of miscarriage.

They were about to.

Despite Miss Marian's encouraging, reassuring words, the three eldest registered the terror on their mother's face. And indeed, Dorothy could tell their concern for her, and she pon-dered it on the drive down.

What sort of a world is this where children so young have to understand infant mortality?

"Where's Pat?" she kept saying, because they were the only words she could say. She found it physically impossible to an-swer the nurse's questions, so Andrew found someone to take care of the horses and hurried in with her.

"She near enough collapsed in church, and there was water and blood all over the seat..." he explained as Dorothy was ush-ered in, with half the hospital staff in pursuit.

"And you're her husband, I presume?" one of the doctors said.

"I'm her brother-in-law. But it doesn't matter who I am, just make her better, please!" Andrew pleaded, his patience run-ning out. Dorothy was taken to the birthing ward and put in a small bay.

"Oh, Dorothy, it's happening again?" Miss Page said sympathetically, after introducing herself as Louise Page to Andrew. She was in the first few hours of a shift and this was not the way she had expected the day to turn. She was very fond of Dorothy Hammond. But Dorothy barely registered her, whimpering, "Don't say it… don't say it… Andrew, just get Patrick!"

There was no way of contacting Patrick, who was bound to be on his way back anyway, so Andrew didn't know what to do. He reassured her that when he got back to the village, he would be sent straight to her. Dorothy shouted at him to go to the train station and wait for him, but he refused.

"Patrick wouldn't forgive me if I left you here alone – he loves you that much, he wouldn't want you alone in this place. Just be patient and focus on the task in hand, and he will turn up."

But as the hours passed, Patrick did not turn up. Andrew grew antsy as Dorothy continued to dilate and continued to panic. Memories of Maxwell's birth flooded back to her. Over her dead body would they be taking her baby away this time! She wanted to name the baby, spend some time with them, bond with them.

But as the day started to disappear, so did all rational thought in Dorothy's head. Despite the pleas of the nurses to be quiet (she was upsetting the other patients), Dorothy began to howl for her husband. Andrew tried to keep her calm, tried to explain that he was coming, but he was a very poor second.

"Pat deserves to be here! This is his child!" Dorothy yelled at one point, catching Andrew in the jaw.

"She's getting more and more stressed – isn't there some miracle sedating drug you can give her?" he asked one poor nurse. She simply shook her head, apologised and left to tend to someone else. Andrew was struck by how little everybody seemed to care. To get a grain of attention, Dorothy had to *scream.*

And as the crowning started, scream she did. A flurry of people arrived around the bedside, instructing Dorothy to stay calm, telling her that she was doing well, just keep going...

In that last, painful push, the last seconds of her baby's life, Dorothy had the sense of being in freefall. The bed beneath her ceased to exist – as did the nurses, Andrew, and the husband of hers who had just lurched through the partition curtains. The only thing in the world was herself and her baby.

. . .

"Dot, I'm here, I'm here..." Patrick said, rushing to his wife's side as the nurses scooped up the baby and handed it to the doctor.

"Give him to me!" Dorothy screamed, so loud and shrill that it was followed by complete and utter silence in the entire ward. Then Miss Page turned around with a tiny bundle in her arms, staring at it with a sad smile.

"Here she is," she said, placing the bundle into Dorothy's arms. There was a corresponding weakness in them as she hugged the bundle close, skin-to-skin, hoping to transfer life from her body to the baby's. Her chest heaved with silent sobs and desperate respiration and she closed her eyes to try and stop the tears leaking out of them.

When Dorothy opened her eyes again, the nurses and doctors had all respectfully removed themselves from their company. It was just her, Patrick, and the baby. But the baby was dead – Dorothy could tell that immediately she felt the weight. Dorothy opened her eyes, took one look at the baby, and her arms gave out, dropping the bundle. In a blind moment of crazed rage, she picked it up and hurled it back down again, screaming *"No! No! No!"* desperately. She leapt up on her feet, staggering at the dizziness and pain. Patrick took a step back, not turning his back on her, and called for a nurse. Miss Page came running.

"Dorothy, sit down. I know – I know, I understand, sit down…" she said, putting both hands on Dorothy's shoulders and forcing her back onto the bed.

"I don't want to look at her." Dorothy said tonelessly. In future years she would both regret and understand that decision – but she would truly believe that it was not her making that decision. She would have no memory of this awful evening at all in the days, weeks, months and years to come. Even Patrick would say that looking at her at that moment was like looking at a total stranger. Even her eyes were a different colour – not their usual stormy grey, but a flashing red and blue like a spinning top.

"I understand," Miss Page said, picking up the baby and turning to Patrick, "But would you like to hold her, Mr. Hammond?"

Patrick gazed at the baby as she was placed into his arms. Dorothy lay down and turned away from him, hugging the pillow as sobs wracked her whole body. Ordinarily Patrick would have comforted her, but this time his undivided attention was on the baby girl.

"She is special, isn't she?" Miss Page said, sounding for all the world like an old family friend – which in a sense she was. A look of understanding passed from her to him, and then she turned to Dorothy while Patrick continued to gaze at the little baby's fused eyes and minuscule features.

"Dot…" he said, sitting on the chair next to her bed and resting his free hand on her shaking shoulder, "What shall we name her? She needs a name, just like Maxwell did."

"Oh, to hell with a name! She's dead!" Dorothy shouted, her words slurred.

"Well, what about Joan? She looks like a Joan to me." suggested Miss Page.

"No… not Joan. We need to name her after something – what about Louisa?"

"As in my name, but with an *a* on the end, rather than an *e*?" the nurse asked, sounding surprised.

"Does the letter matter? She'll still be named after a faithful nurse," Patrick said with a little smile. He was surprised at himself – he should be comforting his wife, not chatting with nurses, but he couldn't bring himself to go near her just yet. Louise just patted his shoulder appreciatively and left.

. . .

After a few days, Dorothy was permitted to be sent home. She had caused utter chaos in the days since the birth, including smashing a jug of water that had been brought to her in a fit of hysterical crying. The doctors had been all for putting her in a psychiatric ward, but luckily Miss Page had stepped in.

"She's grieving!" she said indignantly. "Do you really think we haven't had hundreds of other deprived mothers wanting to do that? Dorothy's already gone through this once with a stiff upper lip – aren't you surprised that she's snapped? I hope to God she'll never have to go through this again."

But she didn't have a crystal ball – none of them did. For now, it was a waiting game for Dorothy to snap out of this deranged sorrow and move into a state of quiet grief.

Andrew had been to the hospital to inform Patrick that the farm was perfectly fine, as were the children, who were staying with Miss Marian and Miss Eunice. He'd brought with him a card, full of condolences from the village. It was black and blue with ink, and people had had to write almost unintelligibly small. Dorothy had been sleeping at the time, and when she woke up, she had slipped from the mad grief to the sad grief.

She didn't remember a thing about the last few days, her last memory being in church. Upon waking up on Wednesday 3rd July 1929, she had been startled at being in hospital. The first thing that had gone through her mind was *Oh, not again.*

Standing up, she got the answer to the question that was

brewing in her mind. Miss Page came in and smiled nervously at her.

"Good morning, Dorothy, and how are you this morning?"

"Never mind me, where's the baby? Is he all right?" Dorothy said, feeling her stomach. It was certainly flatter than it had been, and she looked at the nurse in panic.

"You lost the baby, Dorothy," Miss Page told her gently. Dorothy's legs gave way and she sat down on the bed with a bump.

"But when? I…"

"Four days ago, Sunday night."

"Maxwell? But that were years ago…"

"No, Dorothy, you're confused. Patrick named the baby Louisa."

"It was a girl? But we… how can I not remember this? Surely I would have remembered giving birth?"

"Maybe it will come back with time – although for your sake, I hope not. It was traumatic for you, of course, and you've been near enough hysterical since the birth. See that cut on your hand? You smashed a jug."

"So where is th' baby now? Can I hold her?"

"I'm afraid not – you've declined to hold her so many times now, and she's been taken away."

There was a call from up the corridor, and Miss Page had to go. Dorothy began to cry softly out of confusion, shock and all sorts of other emotions. She wondered if the memories would come flooding back, just like they had with Maxwell, and mentally braced herself.

She calmed herself and thought back to her last memory. Patrick had been away, and she'd had to chivvy the children considerably while battling her standard pregnancy nausea. She'd had a cup of strong tea and made toast for the children

– she hadn't been able to face any herself. Then they'd left for church together, with herself wearing the navy-blue tent-like dress that was now folded on the chair beside her. They'd sung *Jerusalem*, and Mr. Dyke had started his Exodus reading. And that was it – nothing from there.

Patrick came in, and Dorothy bolted upright. He did not meet her eye, looking decidedly wary. He sat down, his head still bowed.

"Well? Are *you* all right?" Dorothy said, sharper than she intended.

"Are you not... crying, or...?" he said, finally looking up.

"Well, I was, but... oh, Lord, what have I done? What've I been doin'?"

"Do you seriously remember nothing?" Patrick said sceptically, remembering the amnesia from Maxwell's birth that she had described.

"All I remember is goin' to church. What day is it now? Why haven't I been discharged? An' where are the children? Oh, God, what have I done?"

"Language!" Patrick reprimanded her nervously. Dorothy held out her arms and he finally gave in and went to her, and that was how Miss Page walked in on them later, locked into each other's embrace.

"I think you're fine to be discharged now, Dorothy. You've calmed down considerably, but will you be all right at home? I can always ask them to let you stay for another couple of days."

Dorothy didn't have the heart to tell her that the last thing on Earth she wanted was to stay in hospital any longer, especially because they couldn't afford it, but she bit her tongue and smiled.

"Oh, I'll be fine, me." she said jovially. "Th' change of scenery will do me good, I'll bet, an' I'll have the other children to distract me. Pat, will you go and get th' cart?"

"I'll telephone the village, and they will get Andrew. He can bring the cart while you get ready, Dot."

So an hour later, Andrew was outside, in the farm cart with the two rough-and-ready Clydesdales. Dorothy was helped into the back. The rickety old vehicle looked very out-of-place beside the motor cars and varnished carriages of the town, but Dorothy was simply happy to be in the open air.

As they drove through the village square, people came out of their houses to watch them drive past. A few of them glanced at her arms, and seeing no baby there, bowed their heads. Reverend Osbourne watched from his window, sighed unhappily, and went into his room to pray. This time, the whole village knew about the lost baby.

The children weren't at the house, so Dorothy took a little walk down to the residence of Miss Marian and Miss Eunice. There was a joyous cry of "Mother!" from five happy boys, and they flew towards her (ignoring Miss Marian's cries of "Be careful, boys!"). Dorothy hugged them all back, realising how lucky she was to have them. Miss Marian hugged her gently too, and whispered "Are you all right?" in her ear.

"Oh, I'll be fine, love. I'd best take these tykes off yer hands now, give ye some peace!"

"Peace? What, with Eunice hammering away on that piano? I think not! Now, Gwendolyn and I sung for you yesterday, dear, and the whole village has been praying."

Dorothy hugged her again and thanked her. As she walked back, the children running ahead of her and obliviously shouting with happiness, a few people approached to offer their condolences. Dorothy put on a brave face and smiled – the children didn't know yet, so she had to keep her voice down. They would tell them when everybody had calmed down.

Just after they had told the children, Reverend Osbourne paid them a visit (a little guardedly, considering what had happened after Maxwell). Dorothy held her own, and nodded with a face made of stone, so as not to give away her emotions. Reverend Osbourne could tell this, and after a comforting Bible verse and a prayer, departed and left her in peace.

"I think I'll have a little sleep," Dorothy said to Freddy after the vicar had gone.

"Are you sure? It's a smashing day outside – lovely and sunny. Don't you want to see Delph?"

"I'll see her later, Freddy. You go and give her a carrot from me, and make sure Father or Uncle Andrew rides her later."

Dorothy made her way upstairs, face contorted with the effort of trying not to cry. She just about made it to her room before it all failed and she wept. Patrick was outside, but he did come up later with a cup of tea and a poorly made bun, with rock-hard currants and a chewy texture. Andrew had obviously been hard at work. She left the bun on the side and sighed, "I miss being pregnant. I never thought I'd say that, but I do."

"It will happen, Dorothy. We just need to put our faith in God once more – whole-heartedly, this time."

"I know, I know. We'll pray on it."

. . .

But they felt they needed to give God a little helping hand. Patrick and Dorothy tried and tried to conceive – and less than two months later, all of the effort paid off. Maybe God had been in their favour after all.

CHAPTER 7 - 1930-40

...Or not?

Baby Theodore was their little miracle, and he was beautiful. Just like the rest of the children, he had Patrick's blue eyes (although a little cloudier than the others), but unlike any of the others, he had black hair, like Andrew (and like Bruce, although nobody mentioned it). He had a lovely little face and pink cheeks. Unfortunately, his little mouth was constantly working overtime. He was a terrible sleeper and often screamed the whole night through. He was constantly twitchy and alert, and any effort to distract him was met with an increase in the volume of his screams.

A few weeks after his birth, the annual fayre had taken place, and the whole time it had been accompanied by Theo's screams. All through *Jerusalem*, all through the dancing, all through Dorothy's playing of *Maple Leaf Rag*, Theo had joined in by yelling at the top of his lungs. Gwendolyn had palmed him with silver as she always did, but there was a notable decrease in the number of motherly women wanting to see him and hold him.

"He's not very mature, is he?" one woman remarked, and that said it all. Dorothy wanted to retort that he was a baby, so how could she expect him to be mature, but she could see that some people were getting exasperated at every word being drowned out by her baby.

Gwendolyn took him for a bit, and so did Miss Eunice, while Dorothy practised her piece on their piano at their house. They returned looking decidedly harassed, and practically thrust the baby into Dorothy's arms. It was only Miss Marian who successfully got him to sleep, but she had to go and get ready to sing.

The temperature did not help matters – the rest of the children were sluggish and the twins were mutinous when they were told to go and help the Reverend set up the lemonade stand. All in all, it hadn't been the best day, and when Dorothy did not turn up to church the next morning, they could guess why. Stewart Awning's funeral was one of the only public occasions that Theo had actually behaved.

Patrick was not as close to him as he'd hoped – Theo was more of a mother's boy. Dorothy trotted out the old sling that she'd made out of a scarf, meaning that Theo (strapped to her back) could scream away whilst she got on with her jobs.

Dorothy hadn't quite recovered from Louisa's birth, though. She was immensely thankful to have Theo, but from time to time she was struck by dreams in which her little daughter featured heavily, and these left her reeling.

Her dreams generally went along one of three themes. The first was the past – what had been – and tended to feature Charlie and Edna predominantly. She remembered the last thing Charlie had said to her – "I want you to tell me that you've had seven or eight children..." – and in every dream, she assured him that she was doing her best.

Edna had told Dorothy that "a wife must always obey her husband," and Dorothy had never known quite what to make of it. But that was one of the few things that she remembered of Edna and so, to keep her memory alive, she had started dropping it casually into conversation with Freddy and William, although she did not say that Grandmother had first said it.

The second type of dream was based on what *is* – that is, the present. These often featured Patrick, Andrew, the children and Timothy (who had moved to the village after retiring, and was now a beekeeper). Patrick had settled into fatherhood well over the past ten years, but in her dreams, Dorothy caught glimpses of the vulnerable young man she had fallen in love with.

And then the final type of dream focused on what might have been. It was these dreams that contained Louisa and Maxwell (both as babies) and they were so realistic that when she was awake, it was hard for Dorothy to accept that they were just figments of her imagination. For mere seconds after she woke, Dorothy would go over to the Moses basket, expecting to see her beautiful daughter or blonde little Maxwell. But instead there was Theo, not what Dorothy had expected at all, and then the past would catch Dorothy up and she would have to steel herself.

Dorothy's doctor had not recommended her to ride within the first few months after the birth, but Dorothy was getting desperate. Delph had turned sour, and so she was sold and to replace her came Julianne, a fine-boned and delicate mare who was in equal parts careful and highly strung. Dorothy had fallen in love with the mare immediately, despite Patrick not quite trusting her to look after his beloved wife.

So one sunny morning in late July, Dorothy had thrown caution to the wind and mounted her new horse for the first time in a good six months. Theo was having a nice long sleep in the living room, and Andrew was around in case he woke up, so Dorothy was free to do as she chose.

"Now, yer goin' to be a good girl, Julianne," Dorothy said kindly, adjusting her stirrups and standing up and down in them a few times. The frayed stirrup leather promptly snapped, sending the stirrup to the floor with a bump and making Julianne jump. Luckily, John was there to pick it up, and they improvised so that Dorothy had two functioning stirrups.

Julianne had been ridden a few times over the past few months, but she remembered Dorothy and her peculiar way of turning her hands inwards, almost bridging the reins, as if she were a jockey. They started forward and Dorothy took her into their "riding field", which was half of the geldings' field. In general, the family preferred to hack out, but Patrick insisted that the horses be schooled several times a week so that they did not lose discipline. Patrick had learnt a lot about the animals recently, and was often to be found spending an evening yelling at Freddy or William or Jack (on their horses Nelson, Teddy or Blizzard, respectively) to "Make him use his back! Head down! No, not *your* head, the head of the horse, dimwit!"

Finding the horses had been hard enough in the first place! Patrick had always said that there would be no handing horse down from child to child, for it would mean that only Freddy would get to experience the spills and thrills of a new one. So whenever he went horse-shopping, he had a list of criteria. Each one had to really be a horse – that is, they had to be at least fifteen hands high at the withers (approximately five feet). Next, they had to be sane. Patrick had witnessed enough bucking broncos on the battlefield to put him off for life, so he observed the horse first to see what he was getting into. Then he got on the horse himself before pronouncing the final verdict.

He had done the same for Dorothy's horse, but he was ever more careful and finicky. Nothing was going to hurt his Dorothy. At least, not if he could help it. It was for this reason that Dorothy had no fear as she nudged the horse forward into a good, impulsive walk. Dorothy's hips (although a little stiff) moved with the forwards-backwards motion, and despite the wind whistling in her ears, she felt very peaceful. She thought back to her first days with Patrick, where *she* had been the one caring for *him,* not the other way around. Her heart swelled with love, and it almost burst out of her chest when she pictured the faces of all her children – yes, including Maxwell and Louisa.

She hoped that one day, she'd be able to think of those two and not cry. But today was not that day, and she wiped away a tear with a gloved hand. Luckily, John had gone, and she would not have to explain her tears to her son.

She returned from her ride sweating, but her faith in herself restored. She'd come to the conclusion that whatever life threw at her next, she would survive it, just like she had survived everything else. She'd survived grief on an astronomical scale, and yet here she was, smiling despite her aching back, ready to tackle her life with the efficiency of an eight-times-over mother.

The moment she was off the horse, Harry came up to her snivelling, with a little graze on his knee. Dorothy scooped him up, put him on a saddle horse, and cleaned it with a damp cloth, all the while telling him how brave he was. The wound soothed, Harry toddled off to wherever he had come from, and Dorothy decided that it was time to go back to the house.

But at that moment, there was a sudden cramping feeling in her abdomen, which coincided completely with a sudden howl. All sorts of shock and sadness was mixed into one elongated word, screamed by Patrick – *"Theo-o-o-o-o-o..."*

And when the sound reached Dorothy, down in the horse field, she just knew. It had been bound to happen to her one day. Cot death, they called it. Even the just-formed baby inside her shuddered.

. . .

The rain began in earnest as Dorothy flew out of the back door. She wanted to gouge her eyes out, douse her brain in vinegar, sand her entire body, anything to clear her of the awful image that she had just seen in the living room. Dorothy could stand it all no longer.

She turned right out of the back yard and down to the horse field. She ran straight through it and clambered over the gate. Another right turn, and she found herself travelling *up* Onyx Lane, which she had never thought to do before. There was a padlocked gate there, but nothing was going to stop Dorothy from getting away from that scene.

Thud, thud, thud, thud...

She ran clumsily, her legs not quite in co-ordination, not quite feeling as if they were her own. She almost hurdled the gate and carried on running in mere stockings (that were being torn to shreds by the harsh, uneven cobbles). Eventually the going underfoot turned to dried, compacted mud that appeared never to have felt the beating of someone's feet. She didn't know whose land she was on, and frankly, she didn't give a damn. Her baby was dead, and compared to that, every other problem in life paled into insignificance at most.

As she ran, finding stamina that she had never been aware of before, gradually she felt marginally calmer. As long as she kept the pace (which was by now more of a jog) and went no slower, no faster, she would be able to outrun her problems. The further away she got from them, the further away they'd be from her.

But there's only so far one person can run without breaking pace. Within minutes she was on her knees, vomiting due to the exertion, the muscle pain, and the sheer grief. And the moment she threw herself onto the floor, not caring how wet she got in the rain, the problems hit her like a tsunami wave. She felt like a piece of paper, shrivelling and curling as spots of rain spread on it.

She couldn't just curl up and die, so she tried something different. She got back up on her knees, thrust her arms outwards and let out an unrestrained, from-the-gut roar, almost an inhuman one.

"Come *on!*" she screamed, maybe to God. "If you're going to take my babies, take me too! Put me with my children! Now's as good a time as any; take me now!"

It was in this screaming, sobbing state that he found her. His arms encircled her from the back and pulled her to the floor with him. She knew who he was, from mere touch, and didn't resist, holding onto him tightly. And then suddenly, the rain had stopped. The moment they locked eyes, the storm ceased and all was calm. Dorothy found words – she knew what she wanted to say, and her accent got mixed in with her wavering sobs.

"It's been hell, Pat," she cried, "And I've had nobody to share it with. I've made the same mistakes that I did after Maxwell. You'd think I'd be over him by now, but I'm not, and I never will be. Night after night I've dreamt, and then dashed my hopes when I wake up. But you've just carried on sleeping, and I just lay there awake.

"All those things that I've wanted to say to you... they're still unsaid. I know we've written them down before, but they're still hanging around in my mind. I lie there rehearsing them over and over, changing the words and the tone... but I just couldn't bear to wake you. Why would I rob you of something I was so desperate for myself?"

Dorothy began to calm down.

"And you've had enough on your plate, anyway." she continued. "What with Edna and Rita and Bruce... it's a wonder you haven't cracked yet. You came close – I saw it. I wanted to talk to you, about your feelings as much as mine, but there was never a right time. Either the children were in the way, or there was an injured animal, or a knock on the door... it just never got said.

"All the couples in my novels, they spend every waking moment lashing each other with words of adoration, never a moment apart, never a second of anything but euphoria... we never had that, did we? We both married so young – I never really knew who I was because I was so devoted to getting the stupid vote... and then the kids came along, and our time alone together was ruled by grief and all the pain.

"You don't think you've done much for me, but you've been my absolute anchor. When I've been laying against you, sobbing my heart out, your touch proved to me that I was still there, and you were still there, and you weren't going to leave me in the dark. Even when we weren't talking, you were there. And even when you weren't next to me, the mere thought of you and how you've carried on boosted me enough.

"This sounds stupid, doesn't it?" she managed to laugh. "But I do need you, and I need everything you give to me. Remember when I said to you that I was done, and I wish we'd never had the children? That meant nothing. I love you, and the children, and I need you on my side. Without you, who would I go to? And at the end of the day, it's the love that we have that sees us through. Oh, I'm losing my train of thought now..."

"Don't worry..." Patrick said, sensing through Dorothy's voice that she was close to tears again. He took stock of their surroundings for the first time. They were soaked through, but it was humid, so they weren't cold. But more importantly, he was finally properly holding his wife, something which he had longed to do for years now. He blamed himself a little for letting her keep it in – something would have to change. But they couldn't sit on the muddy path forever.

"Come on," he said, "Let's go."

. . .

Waking up next to the fire, Dorothy's first reaction was to get up and check on her children. Then she remembered – Theo was gone. He wasn't coming back. Before she could dwell on that, she looked around and saw that she was laying on a tarpaulin sheet, covered in the thick blanket that she had knitted whilst expecting Jack. Patrick was sitting up next to her, chin on knees, staring into space.

"I want things to change, Pat," Dorothy said quietly, turning onto her back so she could see him.

"You know what you said about not ever knowing who you were?" Patrick said, as if she'd never spoken, "I've felt like that before. Remember when Father-Sir told me that the devil was in me, when we first found out we were having Maxwell? I told you then that I didn't know who I was – a human, Patrick Hammond, or simply Satan embodied? I know how you feel, Dot, believe me. But whoever you are, I'll still love you. I just hope that you'll always love me, whoever I turn out to be."

Patrick went on to describe how much he loved her, and Dorothy could just shut her eyes, say nothing and let his words tend to her internal wounds. She realised that she had no idea where she was, but she didn't care. The heat of the burning fire was incredibly soothing, and when coupled with the heady smell of smoke, it resulted in her muscles relaxing and the tension leaving. She slowly sat up as Patrick ran out of words. Now was the time to thrash their demons once and for all.

They were free, finally, after so many years, to talk about everything that was troubling them. Somehow the words just came, and they both alternately rambled on, reaching deep inside them for every ounce of pain that had been weighing them down. Much of it had built up, and had ceased to be noticeable. No longer – it was being scraped from each organ and thrown into the fire, burnt to ashes.

Patrick was free to relive the four terrifying years of his life taken up by the war. He spoke about how his friends, so youthful and lively, had each lost their love for life. None of them had been ready to die, and yet shot by murderous shot, their passion had been grated away until they were ripe for nothing but war. He told Dorothy of the nightmares that had haunted him while they were living at Mrs. Lloyd's, waking up with Maxwell's name on his lips.

But they had won, Dorothy reminded him, that was the main thing. Patrick agreed. After all, the torture would have gone on and on if he and the others had not fought to stop it. And he was recovering ("and after all these years, about time..."). The sounds of guns and screams was fading, slowly but unmistakeably.

"Well, speed it up, then – let's carry on talkin'," Dorothy said, noticing for the first time that her accent was starting to fade, too. This alarmed her a little, but maybe secretly she welcomed it. She made a mental note to contact Wilhelmina soon, to tell her about Theo.

Again, she couldn't dwell on that thought for long, because Patrick took her right to the battlefield. He had the feeling that he was about to lance the issue – or at least, he hoped so. He gave her a vivid description of battle, up to and including watching an enemy fall to the ground, life suddenly terminated, due to the bullet that had been sent spinning through him, in the process ruining the lives of those people who had loved him. Patrick almost choked on the words due to the guilt rising up in his chest. He should have stopped it somehow, he said. He couldn't talk any longer, so he told Dorothy that it was her turn now.

Dorothy told Patrick of the guilt that *she* felt for not being able to sustain Maxwell and Louisa. She told him that often she simply wanted them gone, out of her mind, eliminated from her memory to stop them haunting her. It would be as if she had been sleeping, and this would be just another bad dream. But then Patrick pointed out that she was still their mother, whatever happened, and she owed it to them to think of them now and again. If nobody ever went through grief, he said, what would any of us learn?

That reminded Dorothy of Reverend Osbourne's words after

Jack had been born, when she had gone to him, stressed and exhausted. She told him Reverend Osbourne's story of being engaged, accepting Jesus into his life, calling it all off and being happier because of it, despite the turmoil. She knew that living alongside Jesus was the right thing to do.

"Religion really is the key to life, isn't it?" she said, and with that they both felt the spirit of God washing over them. The exhilaration of this feeling breathed new life into them and when they decided to go for a little walk around the spare field, they walked together hand in hand like childhood sweethearts.

When they returned to their little spot, they huddled closer to the fire and talked about the future, and Dorothy reiterated that she wanted things to change. Her life felt stagnant, she said, looking at the same four walls day after day. She was all for packing up and moving up North again (away from all of the memories in Rosewood Farm Cottage). Patrick shook his head. He owed it to the village to stay, since they depended so much on the farm, and after all, the children would detest the upheaval and changes. They just decided to redecorate – after all, the dining room still had the same peeling, patterned yellow wallpaper and patchy beige carpet that it had always had.

They talked for a while about colour co-ordination and practicality, then Dorothy went all out and decided that she wanted an image change too. Out with the dresses and gowns that flattered her figure and caught in the door! She'd never liked them, and only really wore them because she was young. She was really getting too old for them, she decided, being thirty in a few months, and wanted to move into the square skirts and blouses that had made Wilhelmina look really motherly. After all, she didn't want to be like Edna, stuck in figure-flattering frocks that really didn't suit her. Miss Eunice was her role model in terms of style – she was elegant and coiffured, while still motherly.

They decided on seven children, which meant that they needed two more to complete the family. (At this point, neither of them were aware that Dorothy was expecting a baby girl.) Dorothy had been keener on eight, to conform to Charlie's instructions completely, but Patrick told her to err on the side of caution. He also reminded her of that old Proverb – '*Start children off on the way they should go, and even when they are old they will not turn from it.*' They prayed, and promised God that they would do that.

They also decided to downsize. They had far too many animals now, and while they could not sell any of the horses, they could certainly sell on a few cows, and as the sheep population had expanded dramatically, they could sell some of them. It was about time to sell some anyway.

There was the point of money, of course. They decided that they were going to live an entirely frugal life. Down with the posh soap from the town! Down with wasting food because the children weren't hungry! It was time to make the most of the expensive, new-fangled refrigerator, and put every scrap of spare food to use. Pies and soups, Dorothy said in response, were hearty and wholesome and perfect for family.

So in general, they decided they were going to reform everything. Down with waste, up with home-grown produce. They were lucky in that there were a few fruit trees on the property – an apple tree, a pear tree, a cherry tree and a peach tree. Dorothy felt her creative juices flowing and started to make a list of things that she could make with the fruit. She wanted to take a trip to the market in town, and she started making a list for that, too. They already got honey from Timothy, and there was lots to be done with honey.

New ideas poured out of them, and they realised how wasteful they had been, burning money for no reason! Dorothy smiled as she remembered Wilhelmina's tales of infinitely picky customers at the shop, and at the restaurant. She would never be like them, she vowed.

By the time they both lay back down, their eyes were sparkling, despite the ungodly hour of three nearing. Dorothy knew that soon, she'd have to go back and face everything to do with Theo's death. But now she had an outlet. Neither of them could wait to start their new, clean, happy life.

. . .

Little Wychwood was very different to how she remembered it, Wilhelmina mused, walking up Onyx Lane and looking around. Some of the village was the same, but other bits had changed almost beyond recognition. The school, for instance. Dorothy had told her that they'd sent some spare wallpaper down there, and it was being used to liven the place up a bit.

Privately, she had been worried when Dorothy had announced that Theo had died, and that she was pregnant with new baby Barbara, and that they were planning to redecorate. Dorothy's tone had suggested that she was coping almost spookily well, just like with Maxwell. There had been one massive hitch, though – Andrew had died too. As if life couldn't batter them enough.

It had been an enormous shock to Patrick, Dorothy, and all of the children. The eldest in particular were very fond of their uncle, and it was poor, poor Freddy who had found him. They deduced that Andrew had been kicked in the head by the carthorse he was training, and he was dead when Freddy had walked in to ride Nelson.

They had gotten rid of the horse, but Andrew had played such a massive part in the farm that, had the wallpapering not already started, they would have cancelled it all. But a pregnant Dorothy had instead been lumbered with endless extra jobs, and Timothy had offered to step in once in a while and pull his weight (with training). They needed all the help they could get at that point, so they somehow struggled on.

They were adjusting just fine, Dorothy had told Wilhelmina, but Wilhelmina did not believe it. She had offered to come up and help right there and then, but the offer had been politely but firmly declined.

"We really need to do it ourselves while we make this transformation." Dorothy said on the phone call – both their first! – in her posh telephone voice. "We will let you know when we are in a fit state to receive visitors – I do miss you so, Mam."

Finally, a year after Theo's death, six months after Andrew's, and a few months after Barbara's birth, Dorothy had announced that they were ready for her, and would she like to come up? Wilhelmina, recently retired, jumped at the chance, and so she rushed up at the speed of light to see her family.

The blackthorn tree was in the midst of shedding its white blossom, and so Wilhelmina was scattered in little petals as she walked up the path towards the front door. It was this that she commented on after she'd hugged Dorothy and scooped up little Barbara.

"Just think! There'll be real confetti when this little one gets married!" she said, following Dorothy into the kitchen. The cherry tree had finally started to bear fruit this year, after four years of doing nothing at all, and fruit there was in abundance. Dorothy had had to incorporate it into almost everything to keep on top of it, and cherry scones were very popular in the village.

But by far her most popular creation was the plainly named Fruit Jars. They were made out of the endless spare fruit, boiled up with water, fresh honey, cinnamon and other sweet spices, and a splash of brandy (to make it stick, she said). It ended up as almost a jam, but chunkier. It would be poured into jars, left to cool and then sold in the shop, ready to be put into homemade cakes or eaten on toasted bread (or straight from the jar). She'd only been making them for a few weeks but the whole village loved them.

Whilst Dorothy set about making lunch, a nice soup, Wilhelmina alternated between cooing at Barbara and staring subtly at Dorothy. The last time she had seen her had been just after John and Harry's birth. Her frazzled daughter had been exhausted and stressed. They'd been in regular letter contact since then, and Wilhelmina had been able to tell when things were boiling over by the change in her daughter's spelling and handwriting. In times of stress, the letters had been rushed, riddled with errors and mixed up letters.

But that slight, fragile-looking woman had transformed herself. Her cheeks now had two red spots of colour, and she was multi-tasking with effortless efficiency. The house was warm and homely, a little nest away from the unseasonable snow. Wilhelmina warmed her hands in front of the stove, thinking that with one of those new Aga cookers, the house would have been beyond perfect.

Whilst Dorothy hacked away at a load of bread and added a scraping of freshly churned butter (a rarity in the village and something that the Hammonds reserved mostly for themselves, for baking purposes), she kept up a stream of chatter.

"I'm glad to see ye've still got yer accent, an' all," Wilhelmina said at one point.

"Well, I used to hate it, y'know. I used to wish I had a nice, flowing, Swedish accent like Katharina, even if she did get abuse from it. I wonder where she is now... married to that arista... a-ri-sto-crat that her parents sorted."

"Hmph. Her parents weren't fit for th' title. They never escorted their daughter to one suffragist meetin'! Not one!" Wilhelmina remarked.

"Ah, now that's unfair, Mam. Th' Romans, Chapter 15, Verse 2, say – 'Let each of us please his neighbour,' an' that's what we do. Ye should try it, Mam, it'll change yer life."

It still stunned Wilhelmina how well Dorothy knew her Bible.

Patrick had recently introduced Bible studies on a Sunday for the children, and now Dorothy knew many verses (and the odd whole chapter, much to her own amazement). Wilhelmina had never been devoutly Christian herself, but she was willing to respect her daughter's devotion to religion.

"Well, none of us were keen on Charity Shaw after all that lark, you included," Wilhelmina pointed out a trifle sourly.

"There are several words I could use to describe her an' her sons, but I'm a Christian woman, an' it's wrong." Dorothy said firmly, almost as if she was telling herself as well as her mother. "They mayn't have been nice to me, but I'm sure they were good people on th' inside."

At this point, Dorothy had gone to hit her gong after warning Wilhelmina to put her fingers in her ears. The children tumbled in, snow-covered but joyous. The eldest two cried "Grandma!", Jack's face flickered with recognition and John and Harry realised that this was their legendary Grandma. Five young boys tumbled into Wilhelmina's arms before rushing upstairs. When they returned, hands and faces freshly washed, the soup was being ladled into bowls and Patrick was just coming in.

"Mina!" he said jovially, giving her the briefest of hugs (he had been even more undemonstrative than usual, recently). After grace, Wilhelmina started a lively chatter.

"Now, ye don't have to worry about havin' me under yer feet," she told the children, "I'm stayin' with Marian an' Eunice, ye see."

Freddy's jaw dropped.

"*Miss* Marian," he whispered reverentially, "and *Miss* Eunice..."

"Is that what they like to be called? Well, anyway, they're puttin' me up for a few nights an' we'll have a lovely time, I'm sure. An' what've th' rest of you tykes been getting' up to, then? Trottin' about on yer ponies, playin' with the piggies?"

"We're not allowed to play with the piggies," John said, screwing his face up sadly. "Father says they're too dangerous for me and Harry."

"Harry and *I*," corrected Patrick and Dorothy, in unison.

"Yer gettin' grammar lessons as well! Yer all on the right path, an' yer Mam an' Pa will see ye through yer childhood all right, don't ye worry! An' that includes little Babs here..." she said, leaning over to tickle the baby in her special chair. She was not on solid food quite yet, but she appeared to have been trained to wait for her lunch until after the meal. Barbara stared back at her, unaffected by the piggies, nor what she had just said. Despite being a week overdue, she had been on the small side for a baby, but she was right on track now.

After dessert, the twins helped Freddy with the washing, drying and putting-away of plates, whilst Jack took Wilhelmina to see the horses and William and Patrick went to feed the animals.

That afternoon was perfect. Once Dorothy had prepared everything for dinner, she and Wilhelmina wrapped up warm and went to town in the light cart with little Barbara in the pram. It was always a squeeze, getting the pram in too, but it was wedged between the two adults and so all three generations made it into town. Colonel was chosen for the outing – the safer of the two – and so he trotted along happily while Dorothy and Wilhelmina talked about everything and nothing, the wind making their faces red.

It was wonderful to feel so in control, Dorothy told her mother. She'd claimed her role in life – to feed, to nurture, to raise. The children were happier than happy, and that made her happy too. Their decision to sell some animals and redecorate had been a good one. Despite having less money, they were managing, and feeling the other benefits hugely. Last year had brought them so many lambs and calves, and with each baby animal had come back-breaking work. The relief from the strain had allowed a little more time to observe the children, and to know and bond with them. That had, in turn, made the entire atmosphere of the farm lighter – and even the animals were feeling it, too.

As the horse trotted through the square, people who lived on it waved from their front windows. At the last minute, Dorothy decided to show Wilhelmina the shop, too. Gwendolyn Applewood lived opposite, and she even came out onto the lane, despite the snow, to offer Dorothy and Wilhelmina a little present for Barbara – a pink hat. Wilhelmina was stunned at how kind everyone was in the village – even the air seemed to be tinged with good-nature.

"That's th' love of God ye can feel, Mam," Dorothy explained.

Religion was everything to the village, Wilhelmina realised, as they waved goodbye to Reverend Osbourne. He had spotted them driving past, and had stopped them to bless Wilhelmina. Dorothy was as pleased as punch.

"Now, shut me up if this is too personal..." Wilhelmina paused to phrase the question correctly, "how long will you go on havin' children for? Is six enough? I mean, how do ye cope? I struggled enough with just you!"

"Well, did you hear what Da said to me? He pacifically... *specifically* said that he wanted me to have eight, an' I'm goin' to do me best to fulfil those wishes, whatever people say."

"Yer in yer thirties now, Dot. If ye want to have two more, ye'd best get to it."

"Mam, Mam, there's plenty of time. Our faith is with God, an' if Da is up in Heaven with Him now, we know for a fact that we will be blessed. After all, ye know what a persuasive man Da was..."

They both snuffled with laughter at the mental image of Charlie – impulsive, blacklisted Charlie Fox – stonily facing

Jesus Christ. Dorothy then had a thought – was that blasphemy? She was normally quite disciplined with herself, but she was still finding her way. Just to be on the safe side, she took a settling breath and announced, "I believe that was blasphemy – I realise that now. We must pray for God's forgiveness. Amen."

This was another change to Dorothy's life, Wilhelmina noted as she echoed the word. Religion was *her* number one, too. And she seemed so much more in control now. To see Dorothy holding her own in the company of primarily men made her very proud.

"Well, I hope for th' sake of yer faith an' happiness that ye get conceivin' soon, love. Make yer father proud."

They both drove on with tears in their eyes, and when they got out of the cart, they pulled each other close for a hug. Mother and daughter, forever together.

. . .

Wilhelmina's words from that trip spurred them on, despite her death not long after leaving Rosewood Farm. It had been so sudden – she'd been the picture of health right up until then, and then she'd had a heart attack. It was only because she failed to telephone Dorothy the next day that they had realised something was up. It had knocked everybody for six, even the children, who had decided that they liked Grandma very much indeed.

Dorothy, ever resourceful, had used this to fuel her drive and zest for life. It was so easy to sink into a depression, but she summoned all her willpower and strength to carry on. Now it was both of her parents she was acting for. Despite Wilhelmina's implications of difficulty conceiving, they were not surprised when Dorothy became pregnant again a few months later, due in July of 1932. This pregnancy was a little turbulent, and for the last couple of months Dorothy would retire to bed the moment dinner was over.

She was glad when her contractions started at ten past one in the morning of her predicted due date. By seven that evening, she was more than ready to have done with labour. But something felt wrong, and Miss Page turned to Patrick with a grave face and recommended that he got the cart ready to take Dorothy to hospital. When they got there, the doctor confirmed that they were in for a long and bumpy ride in the next few hours.

"Oh God, oh *Lord...*" Dorothy moaned softly, "He's going to die, isn't he?"

"Not necessarily – you've carried the baby to term, and your labour has progressed fairly well until an hour ago. You say the contractions have stopped? We'll give you a little something to see if they will start again, but if not... well..."

Miss Page interrupted the doctor with a sudden coughing fit, and Patrick stood up from his seat next to the bed and went over to her. Dorothy expected him to start slapping her on the back, but instead he waited for the fit to pass before saying, "We trust God's spirit to save our child – but for now, let us pray for you and your health."

"Thank you, Sir," she replied quietly, and Patrick proceeded to pray for her. He then turned to the doctor and said a prayer for him, too. Watching this was soothing for Dorothy, and she echoed the "Amen" at the end of each prayer. Patrick then sat next to the bed again, and with the midwife making the third part of their triangle, they all prayed for Dorothy and the baby, proffering all that they were. The doctor looked on in watchful silence. He knew he was needed in other parts of the ward, but he couldn't walk away from this scene.

It seemed that holy spirit filled the little room, and soon all four people in there were at peace. Patrick felt it in his bones, in his blood, on his very skin, and he placed his hands on Dorothy's abdomen, where the baby had dropped over the recent weeks. He shut his eyes and pictured a golden mist transferring from his palms to the baby. He stayed like that for several minutes, with Miss Page and the doctor removing themselves to transfer the spirit to other patients.

Suddenly, Patrick felt Dorothy's body under his palms, squeezing tight. She took in a quick snatch of breath before using it to breathe through the pain. By the time the doctor arrived back with a syringe, the contractions were back with a renewed ferocity. God had worked wonders, once again, and when little Elizabeth arrived at ten to eleven, after nearly twenty-two hours, it was no wonder that Patrick declared her their golden child.

The next hour, however, brought even more trials and tribulations. Elizabeth did not cry. The moment she entered the world, she was grabbed by the midwives and taken off to the corner of the room. Dorothy was suddenly transported back to the times where her baby had been snatched before, Maxwell and Louisa, and panic ripped through her along with physical pain.

"God is with our daughter." Patrick said quietly, watching the doctors and nurses tend to the baby. Dorothy sat up, propping herself up with pillows and taking Patrick's hand, which was on her shoulder. The warmth and feel of his hand reminded her that she was still there, and she was still alive. They watched quietly, a husband and wife together, their hearts beating in time with their new daughter's.

And yet Elizabeth still would not cry. The doctors used special tools to clear fluids from her airways, removing copious amounts of unidentifiable fluid from her mouth and nose. After a few minutes, a new doctor turned around to address them.

"Baby is having a few troubles breathing at the moment," he said calmly, "and so we are going to take her to another ward, where there is more help on hand. You are very welcome to come, Mr. Hammond, but I would not recommend Mrs. Hammond to come, in her fragile state. We'll keep you updated with news on Baby's state."

"Our trust is in God, and now with you, to keep her safe. Do whatever you have to do." Patrick replied.

"Her name is Elizabeth!" Dorothy added as they whisked down the corridor. That was the name they had decided – Isaac for a boy, Elizabeth for a girl.

Two midwives stayed behind to finish off the labour, and once that was over, Patrick and Dorothy were left alone. Dorothy was, uncharacteristically given the circumstances, at peace. Nonetheless, Patrick began to talk to her soothingly.

"God is looking after her, Dot. He recognises His children, and He loves and protects them like any father would protect his child. And if to protect them means to take them to live with him, then that is His will, and the right and natural order of things. When you are a child of God, whatever will be is meant to be, and I am certain that the right will prevail."

Unbeknownst to him, to any of them then, the last clause of that sentence was a premonition of sorts to a speech that would be given seven years later to signify the beginning of one of the greatest wars in history. However, in this case, it was the beginning of the end of Patrick's personal war. He had a long way to go before he would forgive himself for what happened to Maxwell – the soldier, his best friend – but he suddenly recognised that he had to listen to what he was saying, and apply it to himself.

After all, if one doesn't believe oneself, how is anyone else meant to?

When Elizabeth was delivered safely back into Dorothy's arms, fighting fit and well ventilated, Patrick realised that his declaration of her as their Golden Child wasn't so far off the mark. She was a little jaundiced (although they were reassured that this would clear over time) and combined with a minuscule amount of wispy hair that promised to turn blonde, they found the nickname fitting. And any child was worth their weight in gold.

"Things will be different now, Dot," Patrick said.

"They certainly will, for better or for worse." the doctor said, entering the room and overhearing this sentence. "I'm afraid this somewhat traumatic birth means that you will not be able to carry any more children, Mrs. Hammond. Attempting to do so would result in very serious health problems for one or both of you."

He was used to hearing distraught gasps upon delivering this kind of news, and so he was surprised when Dorothy nodded maturely, the polar opposite of the screaming, sobbing young lady he had first met thirteen years ago.

"Well, we have seven now." she said, looking up at Patrick. "I think that's enough, don't you?"

"Really? But what about your father?" Patrick said. He knew the significance of Charlie's last words to his daughter.

"Well, he said seven or eight. I've always focused on the eight, so as to fulfil his wishes to the maximum, but seven will do just fine."

"I'm glad to hear it," the doctor replied, a little bemused but relieved that they had accepted it. He left them to it, and found himself smiling. The baby had been so close to not making it – but she had. How could one not smile at the performance of a miracle?

. . .

"I am speaking to you from the Cabinet Room of 10 Downing Street.

"This morning, the British Ambassador in Berlin handed the German government a final note, stating that unless we heard from them by 11 o'clock that they were prepared at once to withdraw

their troops from Poland, a state of war would exist between us.

"I have to tell you now that no such undertaking has been received, and that consequently, this country is at war with Germany.

"You can imagine what a bitter blow it is to me... nothing more or anything I could have done... Hitler would not have it... Hitler did not wait to hear comments... he can only be stopped by force.

"Now may God bless you all. May He defend the right. It is the evil things that we shall be fighting against: brute force, bad faith, injustice, oppression and persecution – and against them, I am certain that the right will prevail."

. . .

The Hammonds left the church and walked home in a numb and sober silence. Even little Elizabeth, still the youngest at seven, refrained from her usual hopping, skipping and giggling. She walked like the rest of them, her head bent, the only concession to her age being her tight grip on one of Dorothy's hands. Patrick led the procession, clutching his keys and recently acquired cane, his jaw clenched.

"Children, go outside an' see to the animals for a bit, while Father an' I talk." Dorothy ordered, and they all ran outside obediently. Patrick sat down in the living room and thumbed through his Bible.

"Again? *Not* again, please, God..." he whispered. That was all Dorothy needed to take him in her arms, regardless of his old affection policy that he had recently started to reintroduce.

"It will be all right," was all she could say while Patrick shook.

"I am not going back to fight!" he said wildly, standing up and tipping her off balance. "None of the children are going to fight! They'll have to kill me first before I let them go."

"You don't have to let them go; you don't have to do anythin'," Dorothy replied, trying to reason with him.

"They're not going. Not after what happened to Maxwell. You'll stand by me, won't you, Dot? You have to – I'm your husband. They're not going."

"Now, Patrick," Dorothy said firmly, taking him by the wrists because his hands were flailing, "be told. Yer not going to fight, an' neither are the children. We're all farmers, an' they'll need us to feed the people. Now, we'll all sit down, have lunch an' Bible Studies. Have faith in the Lord, Pat. He'll protect us."

The storm passed as quickly as it had arrived and Patrick took a few deep breaths.

"All right. Let's get lunch on the table."

That was Dorothy's cue to go into the kitchen and start buttering bread for the sandwiches. She noticed that Patrick was a lot calmer after lunch, and started to explain the events of the morning to the children.

"You see, there's a very evil man called Adolf Hitler." he explained. "He's been infected by the devil. He's spread his evil all over his country, Germany, and some other countries, too. He's on a mission, sent by the devil, of course, to spread his disease to the whole world, and he's just invaded a country called Poland. But we, England, are a good Christian country, and we're stepping in to annihilate this enemy. The right will prevail, of course, like the Prime Minister said in that speech you heard earlier. It may not be today, or next week, or even next year, but we will win in the end."

"Will he go to Hell, Father?" Barbara said in a small voice, looking worried.

"Of course he will!" Patrick reassured her. "You will never meet him, on Earth or otherwise. But in the meantime, before God sends him back to Hell, our whole country is going to pull together so we can help our own soldiers, because they are the messengers of our country. They're going to tell Hitler that we're coming for him. They are going to say – ENEMY, YOU

WILL NOT DESTROY GOD'S WORLD. YOU WILL NOT DESTROY OUR FAITH."

Dorothy was watching carefully lest Patrick get worked up again, but he seemed confident and assured, his voice booming but stable. The children left the dinner table with renewed confidence in God, and this atmosphere continued all through Bible studies. Dorothy had recently discovered that Freddy was an adult, and could be trusted to go out alone, and so she sent him out to do some fishing with his friends. Meanwhile, the girls went out to exercise their ponies, the twins went to make chicken feed, and the other two started picking blackberries. Patrick went off by himself to get his thoughts straight.

When Freddy came in, proudly displaying two big fish that he had caught, Dorothy welcomed him with open arms. She set him to work, buttering slices of bread to have with the fish, and it was then that he proposed his idea.

"I wouldn't say that to yer father if I were you, Frederick!" Dorothy told him, eyeing him beadily.

"But why not, Mother?" he replied petulantly, handing her the flour.

"It'll be a straight no, for a fact." she responded, keeping her voice brisk and no-nonsense. "You have the perfect excuse to stay home, right where we want you. Now, just you move along an' stop givin' me grief. You know very well that Father wants you to stay here an' help with the farm."

"Mother..." he said gently, "I'm eighteen now: a proper man. I don't want to be a farmer like Father. I want to go and fight, like proper men."

Dorothy sighed, and for a moment her tone matched his in gentleness.

"In my eyes, Freddy, you're still a little boy."

Then she tried to move on briskly.

"An' what's all this about not wantin' to be a farmer? Never heard the like!"

"Oh, *Mother!*" he said, exasperatedly. "It's not like I'll be alone! Roger will be going – and Rufus, and Henry! All of my friends will be going... I just really, *really* don't want to be the odd one out."

"Ah, so your Roger is goin' too, is he? That's even more reason not to let you go."

"What's so bad about Roger?"

"You've forgotten the rollickin' you got last summer, then? When Father found the pair of you half-drunk behind the stables?"

Freddy was temporarily silenced by the memory of Father marching him into the house and forcing two pints of water down him. Incandescent would have been an understatement. Dorothy took advantage of his sudden silence and used it to put an end to the conversation.

"Me answer is no, Freddy, an' that answer is final. Nothin' will persuade me to change me mind, an' if you know what's good for you, you'll keep this whole ridiculousness of fightin' the war away from yer father. We don't know what them Nazis have in their plans. Understood?"

But although Freddy nodded in the affirmative and dashed outside into the September drizzle, as normal, he was still intent on getting what he so desperately wanted.

While his siblings went around doing their jobs, he went to the stables and saddled middle-aged Nelson. He was relieved to see that the girls were finished with their ponies, because he needed time alone to think. While Nelson trotted and cantered stoically, Freddy talked half to himself and half to the horse.

"I *will* get my own way! I *will* win Father over! There's nothing he can do to me now I'm a man! I'll do it in the middle of dinner tonight, when Father will be in a better mood. Roger won't be happy if I don't succeed!"

He paused, imagining himself skulking across the village to meet the lanky, gawky Roger. He pictured himself breaking the news that he was unable to defeat his parents. Flinching at the thought of Roger's (more than likely physical) reaction, he shuddered and abandoned the idea.

"I'll wait until Father's got a mouthful of food and then I'll go for it. I've got to be brave, and assertive, and bold. I won't take no for an answer. Yes – that's what I'll do."

Freddy was on edge all afternoon, and failed to concentrate on milking their one, solitary goat. The crotchety creature bit him hard in objection. He then helped his father dig up some carrots, in a last-minute effort to get into his good books. When he was sent to help Dorothy to chop potatoes (normally the job of his little sisters), they did not mention their earlier conversation at all.

"This very fish that we're eatin' tonight was caught by our Freddy!" Dorothy announced proudly as she served the said fish. Barbara dutifully assisted her by putting some small potatoes on the side, followed by a slice of bread and butter. Freddy noted that his father looked somewhat relaxed, which was a good start.

After grace, Patrick rubbed his hands and said, "Well, children, the Lord has been very good to us today – at least in terms of food. Just look at what we've got! I hope you really *meant* it when you gave thanks to God, because we are incredibly lucky to live on a farm, with our own produce fresh to hand. It is our duty, therefore, to care and cater for the rest of our village, especially in this time of need. You may begin."

As usual, there was very little conversation between the children around the dinner table. Any talking was done by Dorothy and Patrick, as they debated whether the fresh blackberry jam, made yesterday, was going to be as sweet as the last batch.

"Well, I put exactly the same amount o' sugar in it as I did last time, so it should be fine. An' anyway, it's done now, so we can't exactly change it."

"Very true, Dot," Patrick said, loading his fork. At this point, Freddy summoned all of his courage and butted in.

"Father," he announced in what he hoped was his most composed and confident voice, "I have an announcement."

Patrick looked at his eldest son sceptically. Those words had set off alarm bells in his head, especially coupled with this unusually self-assured tone.

"Sounds exciting – do enlighten me." Patrick said, placing the food into his mouth.

"As you heard earlier, this country is calling all young men to fight against evil. I must answer the calls, Father!" Freddy said, although his voice did start to waver a little. "I am going to fight."

Patrick finished chewing his mouthful of food completely, and then swallowed, before replying. While he did this, the rest of the table waited with bated breath, while Dorothy went the colour of dishwater.

"Well, I can't say I like the tone, young man. And I can't say I like the idea, either. My only answer is no, and here ends the conversation."

Ordinarily of course, this would have been an end to the conversation. Everybody relaxed, and started to breathe again. But Roger's (admittedly unbroken) voice echoed around Freddy's head: the voice of motivation, saying "Persist! Keep on at them! It always works for me!"

"But Father-"

"Ah, I know what's happened. You've been out with your friends this afternoon, and this is what's put this idea in your head. Well, you've been listening too much to those misleading friends of yours, Freddy. You are *my* son – a farmer's son, no less – and therefore, any conscription there is will not apply to you, understand? And with the demand for our produce ever increasing, the last thing we need as a village is for you to go gallivanting off to La-La-Land to do something that you do not need to do."

"Father, I won't be alone in this. All of my friends are going: Rufus, Henry, Harry B, even Roger!"

"And that, my son, is another reason not to let you go. I do not like Roger. And I'm not overly keen on the other three, either."

"Father-"

Patrick put down his knife and fork with an emphatic clatter. Everyone around the table had stopped eating. Dorothy's gaze had fixated on the empty dish in which the potatoes had sat.

"I am not carrying on this conversation, Frederick. If you are a true Christian, you will honour the wishes of your father and mother, just as I have taught you."

"But-"

"*Frederick Hammond,*" Patrick said, his voice with an added bite of warning, "I fought in the Great War. I was sixteen when I joined – far too young. I fought in everything – the Somme, Passchendaele... all of it. The effects of those bloodbaths, what they did to me in the years afterwards, means that there is not a chance on this Earth that I am letting you go through what I did."

Freddy tried to speak again, to backtrack, but Patrick thought he was still protesting and lost his patience. The mention of fighting had hit too close, especially today. He grabbed Freddy by the wrist, pulled him close to him until they were inches apart, and bellowed into his ear, "*Do you understand?*"

"Patrick!" Dorothy cried, abhorred by this sudden and uncharacteristic display of aggression. Patrick released him, absolutely appalled at himself. Little Elizabeth began to cry, as much from shock as from what was happening. Freddy stood up, pale as a sheet and trembling.

"I'm going, Father." said he, voice shaking but eyes resolute. "I am going, whether you like it or not."

Patrick felt fresh fury in his veins.

"I tell you, Frederick, if you decide to defy the authority of your father, you will never set foot in this house again!"

And not even bothering to reply, Freddy left the remainder of his dinner and left the room.

. . .

After dinner, Patrick sent Dorothy upstairs to give Freddy an ultimatum: stay home faithfully, and remain the son of the respected Patrick Hammond – or go and neglect his family and his village. She pleaded with him to pick the first option. "I've lost three children in the past, Freddy, I can't lose you too."

Freddy followed her downstairs, his bag on his back, his answer ready and waiting. He felt awful at himself, but decided to follow his instinct. He found Patrick in the kitchen, drumming his fingers impatiently on the worktop.

"So, young man. What have you decided? Are you going to be a good son or not?" Patrick said coldly.

"I have decided, Father, that I would rather neglect my family than neglect my country." Freddy said, in a voice that was as clear as day. Without saying any more, he went upstairs and made his bed for the last time, then took one last walk around the farm, just for old times' sake. He didn't know whether he'd ever be back there, and so he tried to commit every detail to memory.

No longer would he wake up to the sound of the dog chasing the chickens as part of his morning regime. No longer would he get to mount Nelson and have that feeling of security that comes with nostalgia. But then, no longer would he be forced to sit on the floor with his siblings every evening, incredibly cramped and in rather a lot of pain. No longer would he have to obey every tiny order from his father on pain of being shouted at. No longer would he have to bear the gasps from elderly churchgoers – "Oh! You look just like your father when he was your age!" or "Ah! I always think of you as a little toddler – when did you get so handsome?"

No longer would she get to mother him, Dorothy thought, watching him from her bedroom window. No longer would she twitch his collar into place before church, brushing imaginary dust off his coat to make him look spotless. No longer would she lovingly iron all of his clothes, something which he seemed unable to do himself. No longer would she be able to sit for half an hour in the kitchen with him and a cup of tea, listening to him tell uproarious jokes and stories. No longer would she breathlessly laugh, "Stop it, stop it! Me stomach can't take any more!"

Her eldest son. A soldier.

When he had finished his final walk, he came in, put on his coat and picked up his bag. His father and siblings were nowhere to be found – the latter had all said goodbye already. It was only Dorothy there, and she followed him to the door, hugging him one last time.

"I wish I didn't have to go like this, Mother, but I can't let this opportunity pass me by. When I'm old, and my children ask me what I did in the second war, I can't bear the thought of saying nothing because I was too cowardly, and too scared of crossing Father, to follow my ambitions."

"I know, I understand. I just... I just wish..." she whispered back, too overcome to say any more. She followed him down the path and stood at the gate, watching him walk down Onyx Lane. He would have looked for all the world like he was just nipping to the post office – if it hadn't been for the bag in his hand. She stood there for what seemed like hours, until she was sure he had completely disappeared into the dusk light, before going inside to try to resume life.

CHAPTER 8 – 1940

Dorothy had felt so lethargic recently, but for once she knew why. It felt like a piece of her heart was missing. She had no idea where Freddy was, whether he was dead or alive. She didn't know it, but she was going through almost an exact replica of what Edna had gone through, years previously. She missed Wilhelmina and Charlie terribly, and found herself dreaming of all those people that had gone. It was this lethargy that meant that it took her a minute to answer the door.

The sullen, defiant-looking girl on the front doorstep was the very picture of what Dorothy considered a typical London evacuee. Her mouth was turned down at the corners, her pigtails seemed to have wilted and she looked exhausted, ready to drop. No wonder, really, Dorothy thought sadly. From what she'd heard, that poor city was fear-stricken, ready to be bombarded with every evil. Dorothy's heart twisted for all of the innocent children who had been plucked from their families, tossed and turned on rickety old vehicles, and then scattered all over the country.

Dorothy smiled sympathetically at the girl and greeted her, before Joanna Waters (the Billeting Officer) stepped forward with a tentative smile.

"This is Hazel Banks, from London. You understand that you are obliged to take her? I know that you don't have a spare room, but all around this village I've been, and nobody was prepared to take one more. I pray that no more turn up, else we'll be well and truly done for!"

"Ah, don't worry about it, Joanna. We'll make a space in the girl's room! This one'll have to muck in, same as our lot, mind."

"Well, we all have to do our bit now," Joanna agreed. Dorothy addressed Hazel.

"You go on inside now, into the front room, first on the right. I'll be through in a minute."

Hazel paused a moment, scowling at her, then stomped through the front door, brushing past Dorothy carelessly. Joanna watched her do this, then stepped forward again and whispered to Dorothy.

"If I'm to be perfectly honest, you're probably the only woman in this whole village who could handle her. She's quite a madam. She's from a very high-up family, it seems. Cut-glass accent, but the language of a sewer. She's given it all to me in our journey today: answering back, filthy stares, silent treatment, you name it! I tell you, if you hadn't been prepared to take her, then I would have had to bring her back to my place and dish out some good harsh discipline! But having seven of your own to deal with, and with Patrick being so well-respected, I figured that you were just the family for the job."

There was nothing Dorothy wanted more than to correct Joanna. In her mind, she told her that she had *ten* children, not seven. But she didn't do it. After all these years, she'd finally sussed where society stood on stillbirth and miscarriage. Once the child's heart stopped beating, it was to be as if they had never existed. It stung. Forgetting about them was all well and good until it was put into practice. How could you forget? Unless one could trick oneself that it was all a bad dream, the memories were still etched onto one's brain, a permanent scar of the experience. Dorothy really wanted to shout at anybody who said otherwise, or just pretended that they had never existed, like Joanna was doing. But she didn't – she simply blinked a couple of times and nodded sympathetically.

"Ah, she'll soon figure out where she stands. We don't tolerate any of that sort here! It's 1940, a new decade, an' this modern generation needs to start respectin' its elders. We'll be sure to sort her out, don't worry!"

After a few more minutes of discussion about the 'phoney war', Joanna left, shutting the gate behind her, and wondering how such a tiny house could fit ten people. Dorothy watched her go down the lane, thinking once more about what Joanna had said about her number of children. She shook her head and steeled herself, not willing to let herself slide into the self-loathing that she had experienced after failing to fulfil Charlie's wishes.

Hazel was gazing at the picture of Nelson, drawn by Elizabeth (the budding artist of the family) as if it had shockingly offended her. She barely stirred when Dorothy entered, and certainly did not smile back.

"Do sit down, girl. I'll fix you some warm bread an' milk an' honey," Dorothy ordered, before bustling into the warm kitchen. She measured a mugful of milk and poured it into saucepan, placing it on the stove to heat up, before cutting a slice of fresh bread and slathering on some of Timothy's honey. It was an old ritual, one that she had done for all of the children when they had been ill at various points. She drew comfort from the routine and inhaled some of the rising steam from the milk to calm her nerves. She hadn't been good with new people at the best of times recently, much less an eerily silent person that had a supercilious and judgemental air.

Hazel was still on her feet when Dorothy came back in, despite the instructions that she had been given to sit down. Ordinarily, Dorothy would have snapped this up and given a verbal warning, but she felt a little sorry for the child and so she bit her tongue.

"Come through to the dinin' room, dear. Nobody eats anywhere but there, an' that's one of our rules. You'll become well-acquainted with everythin' soon enough. I'll introduce the family at dinner time – you'll hear the gong. Now – give us yer bag an' I'll take it up to the room."

Dorothy called Elizabeth and Barbara in, and gave them a whispered instruction. They scampered up to their room obediently. Their room – once called the delivery room – was the smallest one by far, and there was some rearranging to be done!

By the time Dorothy returned to the dining room after about fifteen minutes, the food was gone and Hazel was staring glumly into space. From the label on her coat, Dorothy had found out that Hazel was twelve (thirteen on the first of September, what a twelfth birthday she must have had) and from Highbury, in London.

"Now come along, an' I'll show you to yer bedroom. Yer in with the girls – they've set up the spare bed for you. It'll be a bit of a squeeze, but you'll manage. You'll be fine with our girls." and she smiled comfortingly, if enigmatically.

Despite the room being small, alongside the three beds there was just enough room for two sets of drawers and a wardrobe. With the extra bed, all the items of furniture nudged each other uncomfortably. It was clear that personal space would not exist. This obviously displeased young Hazel, for she wiped the curiosity from her face and resumed scowling.

"I'll leave you to unpack yer things. There's a chunk of wardrobe for you, an' the bottom drawers in each set are yours. Dinner's sometime between five an' six – you'll hear the gong."

This was met by silence and Dorothy left, shaking her head to herself. She decided to take a trip out into the fields, to see the people that she loved and to let them know about the new arrival. She first went to the vegetable field to see Patrick, because she felt that as head of the household, he should be first to know. He was tending lovingly to the peas and lettuces that were due to be harvested next month. Dorothy inched along the neat rows in her Wellingtons, almost slipping over. She was glad that Patrick had planted most of the potatoes on top of their gargantuan Anderson. It freed up a little extra room for other things – and quantity of produce was key in this village, what with the rationing and all.

"Well, we have a new addition to the house, Pat," Dorothy said when she finally reached him. He looked up, and his mouth twitched.

"Not another litter of kittens? That's the last thing we need!"

"Luckily, no."

"Well, you don't seem to have given birth…" he said laughingly, pulling her in for a kiss. She accepted it, wondering how long his good mood would last.

"Ah, now wouldn't you like it if I had? No – we have an evacuee. She's from London an' she's a little shy, bless her heart. I've yet to hear a voice, even. Give her a chance to settle in tonight, an' start to discipline her tomorrow, all right? An' she'll need a horse. Nelson's far too good to waste in retirement – let's start bringing him back into work. William can teach her – he'll be a fine teacher."

"Slow down a minute – I thought Mrs. Waters said we wouldn't get any evacuees?"

"Well, yes, but Hazel's a little wild, so Joanna wanted us to have her anyway. Plus, nobody else had room. It sounds like Miss Marian an' Miss Eunice have their house full now."

"They've brought it on themselves, Dot. If they *will* clear out their endless spare rooms to house as many London children as they can, then they should be prepared to receive as many as Joanna can heap on them! They mean well, but it's far too much for two octogenarians!"

"At least they've got experience with children. They've always worked with them, remember? Miss Eunice is a formidable woman at the best o' times... an' I do wonder why Joanna didn't give them a try for Hazel."

"That indicates to me that she's too feisty for them, which sounds rather worrying! I will discipline her hard if she gives me any cheek. And she'd better not address me as *Farmer Hammond!*"

"Be patient for tonight, though. Maybe after a good night's sleep, she'll surprise us and turn out to be a good young girl after all."

After a little more conversation about the newest lamb, delivered that morning, Dorothy went to the berry field and found William and Jack picking berries – their favourite job.

"Now just listen here, you two. We have an evacuee now – Hazel. She's a little shy an' nervous, so I expect you to be kind, an' courteous, an' patient, like good boys. Yes?"

"A *girl*?" Jack scoffed to his older brother, once they had seen their mother safely out of earshot on a mission to find the twins. "Why another *girl*? Elizabeth and Barbara are girly enough; we need another boy to muck in properly. All the girls do is ride their ponies and help Mother with the cooking!"

"Hear, hear!" William agreed. "We're overstretched as it is, with the rationing and stockpiling. I think we should tell Father that the girls need to help on the farm more. He needs to stop treating them like babies!"

As can be told from this exchange, they had developed into two secretly opinionated young boys, who didn't quite understand the role of their mother and sisters. Luckily, or unluckily, they were far too respectful (and if they were honest, scared) of their powerful father to propose anything at all. They had seen their father angry far more than usual recently, and it was terrifying to behold.

"Father's had such a short fuse since Freddy left..." Jack pondered wistfully. Both of them fell silent for a few moments, remembering the events of that awful day six months ago.

"You're not going off to war when you turn eighteen, are you?" he burst out suddenly, overwhelmed by a flood of anxiety brought on by the memories.

"With the rule about farm workers, we'll be able to stay on the farm, even when we turn eighteen. Don't you worry, Jack. And who's to say that this dreadful war won't be over by then? God willing, of course. Now – let's get on with these berries. Mother won't be happy if we come back with less than full baskets."

As two of the three eldest, they had always been rather heavily depended on by their parents – even more so now that Freddy had gone. They loved their mother dearly – all of them did, and they would fall over themselves to please her – but their father put the fear of God into them.

Patrick was not aware of just quite how terrified his children were of him. If he had been, he would have changed himself. His childhood had left him with deep scars – but of course, it was the only parenting he'd ever known, and he'd turned out all right, he convinced himself. He didn't communicate through the belt, like Bruce had done, but he was distant and disciplinary. And, like Bruce, he considered the age of twelve old enough for the child to begin to pull their weight. To assert this, he gave them a similar speech to the one he himself had been given at that age. His children were, one by one, turning into perfect models of propriety, replicas of himself at that age. They were hardworking, considerate and steadfast. (And, according to Dorothy, fun-loving and good natured.)

There was one major difference, though: they were not witnesses to abuse.

What Patrick didn't know was that his children had been told, in no uncertain terms by their more free-rein schoolfriends, was that the Hammond style of parenting was not always the case in other families. However, as mentioned earlier, the children had become so frightened of their father that they dared not challenge it. Their older brother had – and who knew what had become of him?

It had been traumatic for them all.

. . .

When William and Jack returned to the house, their baskets dripping with berries, Dorothy was just adding the last seasoning to a stew. Pausing to give a pat to Tessie, the young and sprightly new sheepdog, the two boys entered the kitchen. They looked around eagerly, hoping to catch a glimpse of their new family member. Alas, she was still upstairs. Dorothy turned around and her face lit up with love and delight.

"Ah, fruit! There's a good lot there – thank you, lads. Now, this stew is almost ready, so go an' get a head start on washin' yourselves before dinner."

Popping two makeshift earplugs in her ears, she waited until the boys were safely upstairs with the bathroom door shut, before brandishing her dented, war-hardened saucepan and going to the back door. She whacked the saucepan with the millionth wooden spoon (the others had broken, one by one) and all her might, and hollered the magic word, which bounced off the surrounding hills and fields and came back to her: "DINNER-ER-ER-ER."

Upstairs, Hazel jumped out of her skin. Whilst annoyed at being brought out of her book with such a start, she felt relieved for she had grown rather hungry. She stretched and then heard the sound of scuffling feet and several young voices: "I was here first!", "Hurry up in there, Will!", "It's rabbit stew! Hooray!".

Hazel sank back down onto the bed, her appetite gone. She hadn't realised that there would be *boys*. She detested boys: noisy, rowdy, grubby mongrels. She lay back down again and picked up *Black Beauty.*

The noise died down as the feet pattered downstairs, and Hazel breathed a sigh of relief. There was silence for a minute or two, until the bedroom door opened. For the second time in ten minutes, Hazel was brought out of her reverie with a bump. She scowled at the little blonde almost-nine-year-old who had walked in.

"It's general manners to knock, you know," Hazel said in her most condescending tone.

Barbara stopped dead with a look of horror. Her siblings had never spoken to her like that before – it was new to her. She and Hazel stared at each other for a few seconds, until Barbara burst out laughing.

"Oh, come on! It's time for dinner. It's rabbit stew tonight, and you don't want to miss that!"

"I'd rather be run down by a cow than eat your rabbit stew!" Hazel snarled. It had been a phrase of her father's, but it simply instigated the high-pitched laughing again.

"You'll get your wish sooner rather than later if you carry this on!" Barbara replied once she'd caught her breath. "Father will stop at nothing for respect! Now come downstairs and stop being silly."

Hazel's stomach, unfortunately for her, decided to impersonate a whale's call, and Barbara used this to her advantage. She grinned and said triumphantly, "See? You are hungry! Come on!"

A minute after Barbara had returned to the dining room, they all heard Hazel storming downstairs, making as much noise as she could so that every footstep showed that she was angry. She found the dining room and blundered in, making her way to the empty seat and sitting in it with a bump.

Patrick stared at her coldly and Dorothy readied herself to intervene if he targeted her too early. As it was, he simply commented, "Not the most dignified entrance. In future, please wash your face and hands before you present yourself."

Hazel glared around at the assembled family, barely taking in their appalled faces. The two adults sat at opposite ends of the table. On Patrick's right, on the side closest to the door, the four boys sat bolt upright, only the youngest two (twins) visibly eyeing her. Hazel sat to Patrick's left, under his watchful eye, with Barbara on her left and Elizabeth on the other end of the row.

Patrick waited a moment before standing up to say grace. Hazel observed the whole family clasping their hands before them, tilting their heads downwards and shutting their eyes. Hazel's hands remained in her lap, fingers interlaced. Her own mother, while religious, had not brought her beliefs into the family home, so this was the first proper display of religion she had witnessed, aside from Easter and Christmas church services (which she had attended as a matter of duty).

She looked away when they all chorused "Amen" and opened their eyes. Patrick sat down and introduced everybody, in order of age, eldest to youngest. As they were introduced, each child identified themselves and William offered her his hand to shake. After seeing Hazel reject the handshake with a haughty look, none of the others attempted it and instead nodded or smiled according to age.

It was a pity the girl didn't smile more, Dorothy thought to herself. Her face had a peculiar familiarity to it, and with it a delicate beauty. Dorothy was a firm believer in that a smile improved any face, and here was a face, she thought, with the potential to be one of stunning gorgeousness.

She was brought out of this thought when Patrick signalled to her for her to start serving. She took the lid off the stewing pot and was momentarily blinded as a swirl of steam rose upwards. She began ladling the stew onto plates and handing it around the table, Patrick, then the children in age order, then herself last.

Everyone waited until the last scraping had been plated, and for Patrick to give the word, before they started eating. The stew was wonderful, another masterpiece by Dorothy. It was so delicious that even Hazel ate it all. All the way through the meal, Dorothy kept light conversation up, mostly one-sided but very entertaining.

"Now, on Monday, after school, you three girls can help me stock the shop. Tomorrow, I'll take you around the village, Hazel – after church, of course. We can't have you getting lost on the way to or from school! An' talking of school, I'll talk to Mr. Dyke an' see if there's a spot for you. I shouldn't think it would be a problem."

Hazel inclined her head slightly.

"I beg yer pardon – I didn't quite catch that."

"Yes."

"*Yes, Mrs. Hammond,* in future please." Dorothy corrected her gently.

"And I am to be addressed as *Sir,*" Patrick added, wanting to establish the hierarchy from the off. Seeing that they were all finished, he stood up and explained what would happen next. The boys would help him feed the animals, and the girls would help Dorothy wash up and put away. He explained that bedtime was seven-thirty, lights-out at eight, no exceptions.

And then he dropped the figurative bombshell – although from the way Hazel's jaw dropped, it might as well have been a real one. She was to meet William, who nodded at her again to identify himself, at the stables in half an hour to meet her horse. Was that understood?

"Yes, Father," replied six voices. Patrick looked expectantly at Hazel but received no acknowledgement. An uncomfortable few seconds followed before he, with an air of resignation, dismissed them. The two younger girls started busily gathering plates and carrying them into the kitchen. Hazel remained seated, watching them with distaste.

Dorothy saw this and, forcing a cheerful expression, chirped, "Come along, Hazel! I'll let you just watch for today. We have rather a routine, don't we, girls?"

"Yes, Mother!" grinned Elizabeth. Dejectedly, Hazel stood just inside the doorway of the kitchen, in a position of just enough inconvenience that the girls had to dodge past her. Dorothy said nothing, biting her tongue and desperately holding on to her theory of Hazel's exhaustion affecting her temperament.

"Nelson's a very good, very safe horse, Hazel," Dorothy reassured her, after a period of relative silence. "The girls will show you to the stable block once we're done. I've a spare pair o' Wellingtons that you can use until we go to town an' get you some. I just hope they fit."

They were a little on the loose side, and Hazel merely nodded at Dorothy's suggestion of stuffing the toes until she grew into them. She looked positively horrified at the prospect of going out in the rain, and then positively nauseated at the large mackintosh that she was presented with.

"Unless you've brought a mac of yer own, I suggest you wear this. Yer not spoilin' yer nice clothes under my watch!"

It was lashing with drizzle outside, a disgustingly dismal evening.

"Hurry, before it gets pitch black!" the girls whispered, shutting the door quickly with a little squeal lest the Germans see and bomb them to smithereens. "We all have to be in the house before it gets completely dark, else Father will be angry."

Hazel lagged behind a little, wishing she was anywhere but there, hating her new home more with every second that passed. By the time they reached a field, in which was a large, imposing structure, she was desperate to be at her home, a comforting blend of Scandinavian and English culture, with her maid and her log fire and her four-poster bed. Instead, she was obliged to follow the girls in and watch as the eldest boy, William, greeted his little sisters lovingly.

"Now, be off with you, little ones! We elder children have to get on!" William told the girls and they happily skipped away, pausing to pat their own horses. William, hoping to finally hear the girl's voice, asked her if she had ever ridden before.

"Why would I? Why would I want to ride one of these huge, horrible, stamping creatures?" the girl sniffed. "I'm not a country bumpkin, like you."

William chuckled, just like Barbara had done upon being on the receiving end of such rudeness. They had always been told to laugh anything of that sort out of their siblings or classmates, never to retaliate.

"I'd rather be run down by a cow than ride one of these," added Hazel for good measure, infuriated by the chuckle.

"Well, Father can certainly organise that if you have the audacity to disobey him!" William replied. Hazel wasn't sure whether he was being sincere, since Barbara had already mentioned something to that effect, and so she glowered but kept her mouth firmly shut. William continued, "You'll get a tour of the farm tomorrow or Monday. And you'll have to help with the animals too!"

Hazel stopped dead, and turned to face him, a picture of horror.

"Me? Farm? Animals?" she spluttered, almost like a character in a comic. William was a trifle concerned at her sudden change of demeanour, the flicker of vulnerability that had come across her face.

"Didn't you realise that this is a farm? Why did you think the house was called Rosewood Farm Cottage?"

"Well I... I don't know, I just put it down as one of those quaint country idiosyncrasies... I can't be here! I can't live on a *farm*!" Hazel cried, revealing more of an accent than any of them had first noticed.

"Oh, it's not *that* bad..." William floundered. He had planned on being ruthlessly and stoutly determined not to get riled by the girl, but he hadn't expected this. There was silence between them while Hazel was rendered bereft of speech, aghast. Taking advantage of this, William moved on with obvious relief, telling her all about the horses and how it was compulsory in the family to ride, and participate in their "glorious" family rides.

He then went on to passionately describe each and every one of the horses, although Hazel was mystified because he used equestrian terminology. A "sixteen-point-two-hand TB-cross-Clydesdale" named Pumpkin meant nothing to her, and neither did a dainty "fifteen-one sport horse" named Julianne. He introduced them all, before finally stopping at a rather rotund brown and white ("skewbald") gelding.

He finally noticed Hazel's bemused expression and paused to explain that a "hand" was four inches, and the horses were lots of different breeds such as "the TB – that's a thoroughbred, not the illness". He introduced her to Nelson, who was twenty-two years old.

"I won't teach you now because we have to be back, and I won't teach you tomorrow because it's Sunday, but after school on Monday you can have your first lesson. We'll have you cantering in no time!"

He grinned and Hazel stared stonily back, embarrassed at her display of emotion earlier. She was about to make a disparaging comment but William headed for the door and switched off the light before opening it, stepping out and holding it open for her. She didn't fancy being alone, in the dark, surrounded by animals, so she hurried after him. William smiled to himself on the way back at Hazel's horror, and behind him Hazel was working herself up into a temper.

The rest of the children were sitting by the fire in the rather incommodious sitting room when they entered. Patrick looked up from his big Bible and nodded at them both.

"I trust that William has introduced you to Nelson?" he addressed Hazel.

"Yes," Hazel replied, adding quickly "Sir," because she hadn't the energy to be churlish.

Patrick nodded again and turned back to his Bible. He muttered under his breath, *"And the Lord spake unto Moses...* Chapter 25..."

"Is that yer readin' for tomorrow?" Dorothy asked and he nodded once more, without taking his eyes off the page. William sat down on the warm floor between the two chairs and, after looking around in disgust and seeing that there were no more chairs, Hazel sat down a little way off. She glanced at the window, then remembered that there were blackouts up.

Desperate for entertainment, her books upstairs, she stared at the children. They were all doing something. Jack and Harry were playing a quiet game of cards, and William was watching. John was reading *The Secret Garden*. Barbara was knitting, just like her mother, and Elizabeth was drawing in a little book.

With nothing better to do, Hazel inspected her surroundings. Dorothy watched out of the corner of her eye to see her reaction. She could tell that there was a marked difference between the farmhouse and wherever Hazel had been brought up. Nonetheless, comparing it to the dusty, bare house that they had bought twenty years ago, she was proud of what she had done with it.

Even with the door shut, the room had a distinct essence of farm – from a combination of the farm itself, the roaring fire and the cramped, crowded room. A decidedly dilapidated piano sat in one corner, filling the alcove by the side of the fire, with a matching stool. In the other corner, the other alcove, there was a locked cabinet containing Patrick's nightly drink (which he had begun to mix with water since the war).

On top of the piano was a coloured photograph of a good-looking man in his mid-thirties who bore a striking resemblance to Patrick. The rest of them knew him as Uncle Andrew, but to Hazel he was just a stranger that added to the eccentricity of the little room. Her eyes merely flicked over him, and Dorothy breathed a sigh of relief that she hadn't asked about him. The loss, even so many years on, was still rather raw to them all.

After surveying the room, Hazel sat there, gazing glumly at the walls, until Patrick shut his Bible. He put it carefully on the floor beside his chair, placed his empty glass on top of it, and stood up.

"Who's for a singsong, then?" he said jovially. Everyone stood up and moved towards the piano, and Dorothy sat down on the stool, flexing her fingers. She touched the keys, playing a few random notes, before launching into *It's a Long Way to Tipperary*.

"*...but my heart's right there!*" they finished with a smile. Hazel did not sing, smile, or even stand up. Dorothy did not sing either. She never did these days – all the fun had gone out of it, and it had become just a pointless waste of energy. She supposed she was finally growing up. Long gone was the youthful woman who had spent many happy afternoons trilling away with Miss Marian, Miss Eunice and Gwendolyn Applewood, the latter of whom had recently died.

Hazel did not notice Dorothy's lack of singing, but even if she had, she would not have thought it odd. She was simply past caring, and nothing would have surprised her. After two more songs, the room returned to quietude until the clock in the kitchen, half an hour after striking seven, chimed once.

Almost in unison, the children jumped up and they each kissed their parents goodnight as they left the room. Hazel was the last to leave, after watching the goodnight ritual, and merely swept past the two adults rudely.

"Be patient, Pat. She's young an' new to us," Dorothy said once Hazel was up the stairs and out of earshot.

"I'm sticking to my word, Dorothy," Patrick replied. He only called his wife by her full name when he was rattled, so she knew to watch her step. "She has had tonight to settle in and meet the family. As of tomorrow, I'm coming down on her hard if she is contrary."

Upstairs, after getting washed and changed into their pyjamas, the children all read for a while (including Hazel). When the clock chimed eight times, Dorothy's voice shouted up the stairs "Goodnight, children, God bless!" to which there was a chorus of replies ("Goodnight, Father and Mother dear!" being the most favoured choice). This was the signal for lights-out as Barbara darted across to the light switch and flicked it off. The two girls proceeded to kneel on the clean carpet beside their bed and pray. Hazel simply turned over and shut her eyes.

. . .

Dorothy woke at half past six, as she normally did on a Sunday. Something felt different, but she couldn't quite put her finger on what. Whilst Patrick bounced out of bed and went into the bathroom to get ready, she lay there a few minutes more, trying to work out why she felt a little less empty. *Am I pregnant?* she thought, then snuffled with laughter at herself. Her baby-making days were long gone – seven years gone, to be precise.

There, now, she was going off-piste and letting her thoughts slide into negativity. She sat up in an attempt to rouse herself, and suddenly the memory came back to her. That hole that

Freddy had left in the family had begun to be filled a little, by Hazel. Dorothy determined to make Hazel feel right at home and one of the family, and with this good intention she selected her best dress, ready for church.

Half an hour later, she made her voice extra cheerful as she hit the gong and shouted, "RISE AN' SHINE!" to wake the children up. Audible chattering from upstairs began and, satisfied that the children were all awake, Dorothy returned to the kitchen. No sooner had she done so, there was a loud thump from upstairs, followed by a screech of "You *beasts!*"

Dorothy's mouth twitched, for she knew who it was. None of her children would ever make such an undignified noise! And she could guess what had happened. Elizabeth and Barbara had just finished reading the latest Blyton, and Elizabeth had shared with her mother a particular scene, in which the protagonist had been tipped out of bed by her schoolmates for not getting up on time. This had greatly amused Elizabeth and she had done so to her sister the next day. Barbara had found it hilarious and read the book too. Since then, there had been plenty of mischief from the pair of them! They had obviously given Hazel the same treatment.

However, when Dorothy hit the gong half an hour later to call them down for breakfast, only her two girls and four boys scurried down the stairs. She addressed Barbara (who was in a fetching turquoise dress) and Elizabeth (in a slightly repulsive dark orange dress which had started life as a jumper).

"Well? Where's Hazel?"

"Oh *Mother*, you'll never believe what she said to us…"

Upstairs, Hazel heard them talking about her and swung into action. She picked a dress, pulled it on roughly, fumbled with the ribbons and flew downstairs, not even bothering to wash or brush her hair.

"How *dare* you?" she squawked, flying into the dining room

and stopping suddenly. The whole family were in the middle of grace, their hands in front of them just like last night. They all turned to look at her, and her gaze fell on Patrick, who was wearing an expression of incandescence.

"How dare *you*?" he replied coldly. "Come and sit down, and I will address you after grace, in which I expect you to participate this time."

Hazel slunk to her seat, unused to having so many eyes fixed on her at once. *There goes my theory*, thought Dorothy unhappily, before concentrating once more. When grace was over, she sighed and prepared to hear the tirade of words from her husband.

"Now, Hazel. In Highbury it may be acceptable to turn up to breakfast five minutes late and looking like a trussed-up turkey, but here it is not."

"A trussed-up turkey?"

"Yes. I don't take to ribbons. They are an unnecessary frivolity, and that goes against Matthew 6:33. Please go upstairs, brush your hair, wash, and change into something churchworthy."

"Why should I?" Hazel demanded loudly, "You're not *my* father."

Dorothy shrunk into her seat and the jaws of all the children dropped. Patrick's mouth became a straight and thin line. He placed his clean, cold hand on Hazel's shoulder and lowered his head a little to look straight at her.

"You are under *my* roof, and therefore you abide by *my* rules. And I'd like you to realise, young lady, that neither myself nor my wife tolerate rudeness or contrariness in any shape or form. Please refrain from anything of that label."

"If I didn't, what would you do to me? You can't do anything to me – I'm a lady!" retorted the girl. Patrick's whole body went taut as he fought to keep his anger in check.

"I'll have you know..." Patrick eventually said, teeth clenched, "...that I would never use the belt – on any of you. If I were my father, you'd have had that belt across your backside this minute, just like my father belted the living daylights out of me. Now, Hazel, you will have one chance to rectify your disrespectful and sinful attitude."

Patrick's eyes were very cold and very blue and they bored straight into Hazel's brown ones. Eye contact was something that in his shellshock days he hadn't been able to maintain, and Dorothy couldn't help feeling proud of him as she noticed this. Hazel dropped her eyes first, outraged at being told off. She was evidently not used to it.

The whole family watched her slink out of the room and up the stairs with a livid expression on her face. She couldn't understand how a mere farmer from the country had exerted power over *her*, an aristocrat. Before she even knew it, she was back downstairs, neat and tidy with a blue floral dress and the ribbon in her hair removed. Patrick still looked irritated, but he nodded approvingly.

"Much better, Hazel," he remarked. "I hope you are proud of yourself for holding up the family in this impertinent and unnecessary way. We could potentially be late for church now. Now, sit down immediately and we will eat."

By the time they had eaten their slices of toast and jam, they were fifteen minutes behind schedule. They had less than twenty minutes to clear up, smarten up and get going, given the time it took to walk to church. Patrick had never coped with time pressure, so this sent him into a very bad mood. Dorothy did her best to chivvy the children.

By the time they got to church (right on time, although Hazel had been dragging her feet), Patrick was calmer again. There was something about the prospect of being in that archaic building, with all his like-minded friends and neighbours, which soothed him. As they entered the churchyard, the family took off their hats and caps as one (including Hazel, after receiving a sharp look from Jack).

Inside, all the talk was of Neville Wood, who had been called up. Ivy was beside herself, being comforted by Miss Dyke and another neighbour. Reverend Osbourne was conferring with the organist, but when the Hammonds entered he came over and shook Patrick's hand with fervour.

"Ah, the Hammonds!" he said jovially, "I've heard you have a new addition to the family!"

"Yes, Reverend," Patrick replied, "This is Hazel, and she is from London. Hazel, say good morning to Reverend Osbourne."

"Good morning." Hazel said curtly, not looking at the vicar and ignoring his outstretched hand.

The family went to sit down, Patrick in the aisle seat as usual. Dorothy took the opportunity to point out some community pillars to Hazel.

"You see those two ladies with all the little children? That taller one is Miss Eunice, an' the littler one is Miss Marian. They're lovely women, an' they've contributed masses to the war effort an' you Londoners."

Hazel looked absently over to see two women on the other side of the church, filling up the front three pews with small children. She heard the taller one whispering to an older one, "Stop that scowling! You'll get no cocoa tonight if you don't wipe that expression off your face!"

"Come along, children!" Miss Marian fussed, in the manner of a mother hen. "Everyone sit down! You – Robert – sit down on the end there, if Alice moves up. Julian! That hymn book is not a brick; do be careful! This is God's house – you can't damage His property!"

Once everyone was settled down, they started the service with *Immortal, Invisible* and a quick reading from Mr. Jenkins.

After singing something else, it was Patrick's turn to give the reading. He walked up to the front, cleared his throat, opened his Bible and began.

"And the Lord spake unto Moses, saying, speak unto the children of Israel..."

Dorothy wore an expression of immense pride for her husband, with his loud, clear, Southern voice and the way that he didn't seem to need to read *from* his Bible. He was not in the same league as the vicar, of course, nobody ever could be, but Patrick's education, good faith and persistence was evident. Dorothy shot a quick look at Hazel, hoping to see an expression of awe, but recoiled at the one of boredom instead.

To be fair, all of the children (not just the Hammonds) found this reading rather hard to follow. The younger ones started to shuffle and fidget. One child started talking very loudly in three-year-old's gibberish. Patrick stopped reading, just for a moment, shooting the child a freezing cold look that made the poor mother jump, before continuing.

Afterwards, a prayer was said and then the vicar did his own reading. It was after this that he made an announcement.

"It is with the greatest of sadness that I announce the calling up of our dear, brave Neville Wood. I'm sure that Ivy can do with as much help as she can get with the shop – do we have any volunteers to visit Ivy when they are available?"

Dorothy put up her hand at once, followed closely by Elizabeth. Everyone smiled at her, none more so than Reverend Osbourne.

"Thank you, young Elizabeth Hammond. You may be a little *too* young – perhaps when you are a little older? Thank you also to Mrs. Hammond and Miss Dyke. I suggest that you arrange a schedule with Ivy herself. And on that note, we shall have our final reading from Mr. Dyke and sing *Onward, Christian Soldiers*, as we normally do."

After the service, Dorothy went into a little huddle with Ivy and Rachel Dyke, with the four readers going into another to discuss an upcoming meeting. The children remained seated, giving Hazel a few indignant hisses for her lack of singing and her bored expression throughout. Eventually, Patrick approached them with Reverend Osbourne, and shook his hand once more.

"Well, thank you for your reading and contributions, Patrick." the vicar said. "Your children have been good as usual, and I hope to see Hazel feeling better next week. I will see you here on Wednesday for our meeting. Of course, what with Neville being called up, your wife may want to come, and the children are welcome too. Your Elizabeth is an eager volunteer, I must say!"

"She is, Reverend, and I am very proud of her indeed." Patrick smiled. Elizabeth beamed – she had, after all, received the very peak of Father's praise! "I will make sure that Hazel is a lot more awake for next week's service, and I will see you on Wednesday. Come on, children!"

When Dorothy met them outside the church, she stuck to her word. She announced that she intended to take Hazel around the village for a tour, and the children followed her whilst Patrick went back to the farm to let the horses out. They took an exaggerated route, around the back of the church, and arrived at the school.

Dorothy explained that Hazel would be in the same class as John and Harry, with Mr. Dyke. "Remember him? Him of Proverbs 17:6? Now, Mr. Dyke is a good man an' a good teacher, but you mind yer manners with him, because he is like Mr. Hammond, in that he'll take no nonsense from young people. Watch yer step, that's all I'll say."

"Ah, I do miss Mr. Dyke. He was very good to us. I'm just glad that we get to see him at church," Jack said wistfully. He, being over fourteen, had left school to work on the farm.

Hazel privately wondered why on Earth they hadn't upped and run by now. She stared sceptically at the small, pleasant-looking school building. From what she had seen of Frank Dyke, she saw a similar character to Mr. Hammond – business-like, down-to-earth and strict. However, being such a supercilious child herself, she didn't care one bit for any countryman, and intended to teach this one a thing or two!

They walked down Peasedown Lane, where Miss Marian and Miss Eunice lived with their charges, and emerged into the village square. The grassy space in the centre, where everyone accumulated at the annual fayre, was thronged with little children playing ball. Timothy was supervising them for Miss Marian and Miss Eunice – he was a good friend of theirs. Dorothy waved at the children before going over to talk to him. Hazel was introduced with her usual cursory greeting and observed the children stiffly.

"Barbara! Elizabeth! Come and play!" one of them shouted, waving madly. The little girls' faces lit up and they looked over towards their mother hopefully, even though they knew the answer.

"Not today, I'm afraid! Not on a Sunday!" Dorothy shouted back, hardly breaking off from her hurried conversation. Hazel heard a snatch of the following sentence – "She's awfully contrary, an' Pat intends…"

"I don't care what Pat intends," Hazel said clearly and haughtily. "I shan't burden you for long, so he can scrap his plans. For what it's worth, I think he has an over-inflated sense of his own worth."

"Hold your tongue, little madam!" Timothy said, "That's quite enough. Your new landlord and landlady are the kindest, most good-natured people you will ever have the privilege of meeting!"

Dorothy smiled in thanks to him, and one of the playing children overheard and beamed in agreement. Hazel found herself humiliated, and although Dorothy was touched, this really wasn't the way she had expected to discipline an evacuee. What Hazel needed was persistence, and a good amount of decent-quality sleep, she mused. She thanked Timothy again and marched on with the children, telling Hazel about the post office.

"Yer goin' to post a letter home tomorrow, Hazel," Dorothy told her, hoping that by being assertive she would avoid resistance. "The post office is shut today but you can always write it today an' post it on the way back from school tomorrow. Now – Harry an' John, yer expected to look after Hazel tomorrow, just like you do with the girls. Is that understood?"

"Yes, Mother!" the twins chirped in unison, Harry's voice breaking but John's a high treble still. With that, Dorothy changed the subject and started talking about the road to Wychwood.

"It's easily distinguished by the different stones, you see?" she explained. "None o' the shops are open today, of course, but I'll take you there when me list of errands gets long. I used to go every week, but things changed. We all love a trip into town, we do. The two carthorses, Colonel an' Corporal, they're gettin' old but they have enough strength to get us there an' back. An' that reminds me…"

"What? What?" the children asked eagerly.

"I said I'd take that load of stuff we dug up this week over to the shop this afternoon. I know Father won't agree with it – an' a wife should always obey her husband – but she's in such a state that, for once, we may just have to work on a Sunday."

The children all looked delighted and, noticing this, Dorothy was pleased. Her children loved to help, she realised – they took after their parents. Harry eventually spoke for them all – "We'll all come and help!" and then to a bemused-looking Hazel, "This means a ride in the cart with Colonel and Corporal!"

"Good, good children, but you mustn't all come. William an' Jack must stay behind, so that yer father can't say that I'm dragging us *all* into work on a Sunday. For now, let us have some lunch, an' then we can box everythin' up to take it over. Jack, I'll let you prepare the horses an' William can help us with the heavy liftin'."

By this time, they were nearly back at the farm. Patrick was out in the fields when they all came in. Dorothy instructed the children to change and feed the animals, then come straight back. Happily, they all pulled on their farm clothes and boots and pounded outside, splitting into their pairs that they had adopted. Dorothy sent a mutinous Hazel out too with a sharp word. The girl stumbled after the twins in the huge boots that Freddy had left and suddenly Dorothy's eyes were misting up.

"For pity's sake, Dorothy Hammond, get yerself together!" she said out loud, blinking ferociously, "It's not like Freddy's died!"

But he might. Dorothy knew that, and that was what made it so much worse. She felt closer than ever to Edna, going through exactly what she went through, and not for the first time, she wished that Edna was still alive. Her mother-in-law had been an enigmatic woman, and shrouded for far too long. If only Dorothy had gotten to know her...

"Now, stop." Dorothy told herself, "Yer gettin' maudlin. There's no point in dwellin' in the past unless you have a time machine."

With that, she began another task to take her mind off it. But the thought persisted in the back of her mind. She doubted she'd ever really get rid of it.

. . .

Hazel was late to Bible Studies, of course she was. That child really needed to buck her ideas up, Patrick thought sourly. He didn't understand soft parenting – it just led to impertinent, lazy little tykes. He'd soon drum some sense into her, with the help of Frank Dyke. When the girl entered, his glare moved from the assembled group of children in front of him to the perfectly presented but scowling girl in the doorway.

"Hazel." he said coldly as she entered. The single word cut through the quiet page-turning of Bibles and the children all looked up.

"You never helped us at all!" cried a rather outspoken Barbara. Hazel looked even more peevish than ever as she shut the door. Before she could get a retort in, Patrick took control.

"Firstly, I'd like you to know that if the rest of the children are helping on the farm, you will do likewise. It is lambing season and I will not always be able to help with the more ordinary jobs. Secondly, when it is Sunday and time for Bible Studies, it is essential that you are in here promptly, with your face and hands clean, when you are called. Now, I'd like an apology, please. What do you have to say for yourself?"

"You have no right to talk to me like I'm a child!" burst out Hazel. She followed this up with, "I'm not part of your family and I want to be treated like a guest! I'm an upper-class lady and I *won't* be part of your farm! I won't, I won't, I won't!"

"You won't, you won't, you won't, will you?" Patrick said amusedly amongst the quiet sniggers of his children. "Well, when you are on my territory, you will do as you're told, other-wise you will be on bread and water until you behave."

"Mr. Hammond is deadly serious, Hazel," Dorothy said solemnly, keen to back up her husband. "All of these children have been on bread an' water in the past."

"But not for more than a day or so," added William for good measure. "because we all saw sense and realised what idiots we'd been. That's more than can be said for *you*."

The children all shot glances of dislike at the evacuee, eager to back up their much-adored brother and mother. Patrick stood up, carefully lay his Bible on the arm of his chair, and walked out. They heard him go up the stairs and click their bedroom door shut, and Dorothy knew that he was going to pray for the girl's sake. In previous instances he would have blown up, but he was better now.

"I think we should leave Bible studies for today, children. Lunch will be at twelve – go an' play outside for now."

Hazel was the first out of the living-room door, but rather than skipping outside to play in the March winds, she ran up to her room. She pounced on her bed and lay there, fuming. She hated the high-handed man. She hated the compliant children. She hated the meek, bland wife. How dare they, trying to make her *religious*? Religion was something that her mother did, not her. She shuddered, remembering the pious looks of the children with their Bibles.

Patrick was equally angry. Never had he been insulted by a mere child in his life! It was essential, he thought to himself, that he (as man and leader of the household) was in charge at all times. He shuddered as he remembered the venom and spite in the girl's face and the way she had spat her words hyperbolically.

When he had calmed down sufficiently, he went back downstairs to read his Bible in peace. There were some things, he reasoned, that only the Lord could rectify – and this girl was one of them. In the kitchen, he saw the pot on the stove and lifted the lid in curiosity. The steam rose up in one big gust, quite clouding his vision, and with his fury not quite forgotten, he leapt back and shouted out a profanity.

He slammed the lid back down on the pot, shocked and very disappointed at himself. He hadn't lost control like that for a long time – not since Andrew's death. He checked that none of the children had been close enough to witness this. Satisfied they were all out of earshot – he didn't know that Hazel was upstairs – he relaxed and carried on through to the living room to find his Bible. Dorothy walked down the stairs just as he was leaving the kitchen, carrying one of the barn cats. Patrick would have ordinarily questioned how the cat had got there, but this time Dorothy got in there first.

"What's the matter? You shouted so loudly, I heard the windows rattle!"

"Ah, a trivial matter, never mind. I should never have shouted out like that. What time are we eating?"

He grabbed his Bible and followed her back to the kitchen as she told him, "Just a few minutes, the soup is heatin' up now. I'm about to set the table."

As it was, Jack walked in at that point and volunteered to do it instead. Patrick shot a disapproving look at the cat, which stared lazily back ("What are you going to do about it?" it seemed to be saying). Dorothy put her outside and Patrick went upstairs to wash his hands and face.

Hazel still hadn't lost the mutinous expression by the time lunch was ready – aside from a quick smirk at Patrick as she entered, telling him she had heard his obscenity. She appeared to be deeply reflecting, almost meditating, but with such an angry expression that Dorothy couldn't help but wonder if it was a natural one. She decided to idly comment on it during a lull in the conversation.

"Yer wearin' a face like thunder, Hazel. Everythin' all right?" she said, taking another mouthful of soup.

"Fine, thank you. I need some paper – where is it?"

"What for?" Patrick said suspiciously. His first thought, he would have been ashamed to admit, was arson. He didn't trust this Londoner one bit.

"To write a letter to my mother. Despite her betrayal, she should know where I am, and that I'm safe." Hazel replied with exaggerated patience.

"Mind your tone," Patrick reprimanded, still frowning. *Betrayal?* This was one girl who did not honour her father and mother.

"The writin' paper is on top of the piano," Dorothy said kindly. *Is that all that's bothering her? Her mother sending her away?*

"Run the contents of your letter by me first, please. I don't want you flinging our name around in London, especially in the negative light you appear to be living in." Patrick added with an added bite to his voice.

When the lunch things were tidied away, they proceeded outside to prepare the cart for the grocery delivery. Hazel tried to slip up the stairs when they all left the room, but she was quite savagely pulled back by the hair by Harry. Hazel was about to cry "How dare you hurt a lady?" but by the time she'd opened her mouth, the boy had stuck out his tongue and scarpered. As the girls were now behind her, driving her forwards, Hazel had no choice but to go with them.

"Right! Let's get this done quickly an' well!" Dorothy chirped when they reached the barn. It was filled with industrial-sized holders, each containing a different fruit, vegetable or packed baked item. The children climbed on stepladders to fill the big wooden crates that were stacked by the door. It looked highly dangerous to Hazel, so she stood by the door with her arms folded. Dorothy was too engrossed in the list to notice.

The cart arrived outside the barn and William started lifting the crates, which were being stacked outside ready to go into the cart. The horses stood patiently, ready to throw their entire weight into pulling the cart. They were quite possibly the strongest horses in the world – that was the general consensus amongst the children. The journeys they went on were only short, but they were getting old. Patrick had been thinking of getting another horse to help them out, but after Andrew's experience in training one, well...

Only the very eldest children knew exactly how Uncle Andrew had died – the twins were too young to remember him, and Jack's memories were only hazy. Of course, it had been poor Freddy who had found him, and the image had haunted him ever since. The youngest children did not understand Patrick's reluctance to get new carthorses, and neither did Hazel. She knew nothing about the beasts, but she wondered if it was really appropriate for the poor things to be dragging so much weight. Another country oddity, she decided.

William instructed Hazel to help him, directing her towards a pallet of potatoes. Thunderstruck and muttering bitterly, she lifted the top crate by the handles and then dropped it with an uncharacteristic and undignified squeal. Potatoes rolled everywhere and even the horses flinched. Dorothy heard the commotion and rushed to the door, wondering which horse had trodden on her. When she saw it was merely potatoes, she was decidedly cross.

"Whatever's the matter, Hazel? An' just look at what you've done! Everyone start pickin' them up!"

"How *dare* you get me to lift such a heavy box? If I were in charge, you'd be dismissed at once for that, you really would!"

Dorothy was lost for words. The children, who were all scrambling around retrieving potatoes, smiled to themselves. Now Hazel would be for it, they thought. But Dorothy took a deep breath and returned to her usual calm state.

"I suppose you think that because you've been rude, I'll send you back in. But no, we'll deal with this incident later. Now go an' pick up them potatoes an' let the good children be of use."

By the time every last potato had been picked up, with Hazel seething, the required crates were all in the cart. After she'd picked up her last potato, Hazel went to sit in the cart and observed everyone else scurrying around. Patrick came up and pursed his lips when he saw the laziness.

"Is young Miss Banks not helping?" Patrick commented to Dorothy, who was ticking things off her list.

"Let's just say we've had an incident with potatoes, for which she will be disciplined later." Dorothy murmured absently. Normally it was Patrick's job to oversee the grocery delivering, with herself simply being the driver, and therefore she required all of her concentration. Eventually, satisfied that everything was ready to go, the required children clambered in around the boxes and Dorothy got into the driver's seat and took the reins.

With a click of the tongue and a sharp "Walk on!" from Dorothy, the horses surged forwards as if the cart was as heavy as a fly. Hazel clung to the cart with all her might as it bounced over the uneven road. She wished with all her might that she was driving around the streets of London in the motor car with her parents, listening to Bill (the head driver) cheerfully chatter as he drove.

The other children buzzed with energy as they inched onwards. As they drove through the square and then residential streets towards the shop, two or three housewives rushed out of their houses to wave. The children waved back, giggling happily.

"We're quite a well-respected family in this village, Hazel," Elizabeth said, adopting the tone she had heard her mother use during rare telephone conversations. (Minus the accent, of course. Patrick insisted that the children follow the well-enunciated example that he and the rest of the village had set.)

"Oh?" Hazel said, hardly noticing, so focused was she on not falling out of the cart.

"Well, we are the main source of food for this whole village, and Father does readings in church. But that doesn't stop we children being ordinary at school, so don't think that for a minute."

The other children snuffled with laughter and even Dorothy had to chuckle.

"You've been listenin' in on me telephone conversations with Grandmother's friend, Maude!" she commented light-heartedly, steering the horses towards a gate by the side of the road. Elizabeth blushed while the other children giggled.

The remaining few seconds of the journey unfolded in silence as they all watched Harry jump down to open the gate. Dorothy smiled as she remembered that long conversation with Maude Downe, who had somehow contacted them to find out what had happened to Edna. They'd talked for a good forty-five minutes, taking up the phone in the post office quite rudely, and Dorothy had explained all. Then, she had found the courage to ask Maude how Edna had coped without Patrick.

"Well, truth be told, dear, I never really knew," Maude's high, silvery voice came back down the phone. "Our only method of communication by that point was letters, you see. There was none of these telephone calls. It's terribly hard to tell a person's emotions by their handwriting. And with what you just told me about Bruce, I wouldn't be surprised if he monitored what she wrote. It's not unheard of. All she told me was that he'd gone to sin, and that as a family, they were coping just fine. She never disclosed *how* she coped."

Dorothy wondered how Ivy would cope without Neville. Once the cart was through and the gate shut, she called out a greeting. Ivy, looking stressed and harassed, appeared from inside the ramshackle little shop.

"Oh, am I glad to see you lot! I'm run off my feet organising things and getting to grips with the books, and the shop isn't even open!"

The children all scrambled down from the cart – except for Hazel. Dorothy exhaled sharply with exasperation.

"Don't be silly, Hazel. Get down at once!" she called, tying the horses up and giving them some hay and water.

"I don't see why I should help," the girl replied. "It's the job of country children to do things like this – not a lady."

"Oh, grow up." Dorothy snapped, immensely rattled. "We've all got to muck in an' help, especially when there's a war on. Go an' help Elizabeth, this instant."

"Oh, yes please, Mother!" Elizabeth agreed sunnily. "I need some help with these boxes!"

Hazel didn't understand how the delicate-looking girl could lift such heavy boxes, but she pasted a thunderous scowl on her face and helped, muttering under her breath. Boxes were stacked on tables, the boys reaching the high ones, until the cart was empty and they were all sweating despite the chilly temperatures.

When they were finished, Ivy thanked them profusely for all their help. The two women hugged, then Dorothy climbed back into the cart.

"I wouldn't normally ask it on a Sunday and you know that, Dot," Ivy said as the children climbed in. She still looked troubled, although a little weight had been lifted.

"Now, don't you worry about it. Pat wasn't best pleased, but he knows that now an' again we must make exceptions to our friends."

"I really do appreciate it. What with Neville being called up, and everything that's going on in London…"

The greengrocer's wife petered out, blinked a few times, then smiled.

"And what help do you need durin' the week?" Dorothy carried on. "I'm not sure what evenings Rachel can do, especially now she's teachin' full-time, but I can always send one or two of the children around. Especially now we have young Hazel!"

Hazel scowled but Ivy smiled at her, holding out a hand to

shake. The girl turned up her nose. Dorothy said sharply, in Patrick's southern accent for emphasis, "Hazel, shake hands with Mrs. Wood at once."

The girl turned her back and folded her arms. Barbara pulled a face when she wasn't looking, but Dorothy was mortified. Already she was feeling the responsibility of an extra child – especially as she was someone else's child.

"I do apologise, Ivy. She's still findin' her feet," Dorothy explained quietly, hoping that the girl couldn't hear her.

"I heard from Joanna that she'd had her buttons well and truly pushed yesterday. Let's hope that Frank Dyke can drum some sense into her."

"I don't know if he still uses that cane of his, but if he does, I have a feelin' that young Hazel will be bearin' the brunt of it!"

With that, they were on their way. The children had helped as best they could with organising the shop, and it looked lovely as a consequence. They were very proud of themselves, and of each other. It was a pocket-sized but cheerful-looking place, with the comforting smell of rich earth mingling with the scent of cakes and new bread. They congratulated each other on a job well done, but Hazel simply rolled her eyes and looked away.

Inwardly, the children were almost gleeful. They hoped that the tale of Hazel's misdemeanours would find its way to Father's ears – and wouldn't the girl be in for a rollicking! The drive home was full of chattering and waving, and some nudging and winking when Hazel wasn't looking, until Dorothy turned to Elizabeth and gave her an instruction. She had spotted some chrysanthemums and she couldn't help thinking of Andrew, who in his later years had regularly presented her with a bunch of them as a gesture of gratitude.

"When we get home, Elizabeth, you can go an' pick some flowers for Uncle Andrew. Them chrysanthemums are lookin' so lovely! An' yer Uncle Andrew always did have a soft spot for those flowers."

"Who's Uncle Andrew?" Hazel inquired, as much to fill the subdued silence as to satisfy her curiosity. Dorothy sighed – but the girl ought to know, she thought, if she was to stay.

"Uncle Andrew was Mr. Hammond's older brother," she explained. "An' he was a fine chap. He used to run this farm with Mr. Hammond an' some of our friends. But over time, them friends moved away... an' then there was a terrible accident. Andrew got kicked in the head by a carthorse he was trainin', an' he died immediately. That's Andrew's picture on th' piano. We're never goin' to forget him."

"I remember Uncle Andrew," William said sadly.

"Of course you do. It was only nine years ago. Time does fly these days..."

"What happened to the horse?" Hazel said. The children looked at her hard – she sounded almost friendly.

"Oh, it had to be destroyed. Trouble from the start, that one."

Dorothy didn't elaborate further. Nobody needed to know about all the tears, the grief, the organising. It had been rather a delayed reaction on everyone's part – Andrew had been such an integral part of the farm that the early weeks had been taken up with organising. Poor Patrick.

This exchange quietened everyone completely for the whole ride home, and the rest of the day turned out rather uneventful. Hazel remained curt and impertinent, and at one point was privately reduced to tears of frustrated anger. Patrick ruthlessly meted out punishments for every element of bad behaviour, whether it be answering back or refusing to participate in grace. One was almost as bad as the other, in his opinion.

He'd never had to do anything like this before, and it greatly saddened him. He couldn't believe that there were people in the world who didn't live their lives as he did. It was unfathomable, how Hazel felt she had the right to march into his life and start trying to dictate it. He'd never asked for a war – it had torn his life apart. Why couldn't people just live with each other and stop interfering in each other's lives? *And that goes for you too, Hitler.*

And, unbeknownst to him, Hazel was thinking exactly the same thing about him.

. . .

Hazel walked out of the Hammond's front door with her mackintosh and bag and smiled. She'd promised to run, and to take the shortcut by the river, as she was already late for school – and so she set off down Onyx Lane at a good pace. But instead of going down the lane that took her to school, she carried on through the square and down the neat road towards Wychwood. Luckily, she'd just missed the rush of children, so she strode along uninterrupted, with a beam spread across her face. There was no point in looking secretive, she knew, so she made her gait confident and purposeful. There was no mistaking the road to Wychwood because it was neatly set with new-looking stones, unlike the rest of Little Wychwood.

In order to entertain herself, Hazel alternately skipped and sung. This was the most relaxed she had felt since being evacuated, and the freedom was a wonderful feeling. She had regularly sung with her mother at home, although Hazel disliked singing from sheet music, especially not the Scandinavian songs that were an integral part of her upbringing. The music was lovely, of course, and the language was beautiful, but Hazel preferred old music-hall numbers that the local band played at their parties. She sung anything she could remember, and the tunes certainly whiled away the time until she finally got into town. It hadn't taken very long at all – approximately twenty-five minutes according to her wristwatch.

She consulted the map, which she had managed to loan off

Mr. Dyke after promising to be good. She intended to post it back to him once she got home. She had to walk straight through the town and out the other side, into what seemed to be around five or six miles of country. Straightforward enough. (Of course, the war had ensured that all signposts had been removed in case of an invasion.)

The town was quite sleepy for a Wednesday morning, especially compared to when Mrs. Hammond had taken them into it that previous Saturday. Hazel found herself walking along the high street, which was lined both sides by shops. Out of one, a little newsagent, she heard a wireless blaring, with one or two old ladies clustered chattering around it. She missed her old wireless at home, which barely worked but always seemed to perk up for Children's Hour.

It took a couple of hours for Hazel to come out of the town and into full-blown country. After a while, she came across Cardington Camp (two enormous hangers, originally built to house the Zeppelins of the Great War). To her complete and utter horror, there were parachutists landing.

This could only mean one thing... the Germans were here.

And for the first time since being evacuated a few weeks earlier, Hazel forgot herself. She dropped all semblance of dignity and sophistication as, screaming and crying out between ragged breaths, she ran as fast as she could.

Mud splattered up her stockings and onto her jade-green skirt and her leg muscles screamed along with her vocal chords. It was only when Cardington Camp was completely out of sight that she slowed down to a walk and stopped to catch her breath.

Tears flooded her face and she dropped onto all-fours, choking and retching as she tried to breathe. The Germans had arrived! What was she to do? Was she to call the police – she hadn't a telephone! Had the Germans spotted her? Were they sneaking up behind her, ready to lunge and take her prisoner?

Would she ever see her home and parents again? Why was there a *war* on?

(She wasn't to know that they were English parachutists, brave and patriotic, practising their landing as part of their military training.)

She reasoned with herself that by now, someone else would have noticed and raised the alarm. She just had to be very, very cautious and surreptitious in her movements. But even so, she sat under a hedge for ten minutes to catch her breath and calm down. When she got back up, she almost collapsed from the liquid agony in her legs. The farm had slowly been making her stronger, but not quite prepared for sprints! All the same, she'd had a dreadful scare, and what she thought was a lucky escape.

Frequently looking behind her for more predatory Germans, Hazel continued to walk all day. She seemed to be following one long, uneven road, with no sign of civilisation either side. Eventually, a fork in the road became visible, way ahead. At the sight of this, Hazel had a new spring in her step. London was just around the corner!

. . .

When the children came back from school at lunchtime, they were indignant with rage. Hazel had started to improve her behaviour, and now she had somehow managed to convince Dorothy to stay home, they thought. It was obviously too good to be true.

Dorothy was in the midst of shaping her rock cakes when they tumbled in. They went straight through to their mother who gave them a hug each with floury hands. She immediately noticed the missing girl and inquired as to her whereabouts.

"But... isn't she here? Didn't she stay at home?" John said, frowning.

"Not unless she's climbed up the drainpipe, no," Dorothy said, alarm bells beginning to ring in her mind. The girl had been suspiciously nice recently, and Dorothy didn't put anything past her. Whipping off her apron and dusting off her hands, she put on her Wellingtons and rushed outside. She and the children ran around the whole farm and came up with nothing. Still in her Wellingtons, Dorothy rushed straight down to the nearest telephone in the post office to call the police.

. . .

Funnily enough, Hazel didn't feel at all hungry – just tired and frightened, although she would never have admitted the latter! She came to the fork in the road and looked left and right. Both ways looked identical – more green fields. She decided to take the plunge and turn right, and for the first time there was doubt sowing itself into her mind. She started to wonder where she was, and whether she would make it before dinnertime.

At dusk, she was still walking, but she appeared to be on the outskirts of a town. She saw a couple leaving what appeared to be a teashop, and in a flash of relief she decided to approach them and ask the way. She mustered up some energy and ran towards them until she drew level.

"Excuse me, Sir and Madam," began Hazel, adopting her most respectful look, "I wonder if you can tell me which way it is to London?"

The beautiful young lady, who appeared to be expecting a baby, looked over at the man. He raised an eyebrow back and, with a whole conversation conducted through that one look, he turned to Hazel.

"I'll have to consult my map. You look hungry – let us buy you something to eat," he said, turning back towards the shop.

Bread and jam, washed down with great gulps of sweet tea, had never tasted so good. Hazel realised that she *was* hungry after all. She was so absorbed in her food that she didn't notice the policeman standing in front of her until the end of it. She hastily stood up. The policeman said very little, but allowed her to finish her tea before taking her to the police station. Hazel shook the whole way. What had she done? Was she going to be imprisoned?

The policeman turned out to be quite nice, and he even gave her a piece of chocolate. The treat, rare and delicious though it was, did little to distract her from the fact that she was in a police station in the middle of nowhere, surrounded by strangers.

Soon, she was taken into a separate room, where there was another policeman. Hazel almost laughed – he had a telephone to each ear and was speaking alternately into each one. Once he had finished both conversations, he called Hazel to him and made her sit on the hard seat in front of his desk.

"I don't suppose you realise what you have ignited, Miss Banks," he said, with a very sombre tone. "I have just been on the telephone to your mother, and the people you are staying with in Little Wychwood. When you failed to return from school, Mrs. Hammond alerted the police immediately. You are officially classed as MISSING. Your picture has been flashed up on cinema screens across the country. Mrs. Hammond was absolutely beside herself. She was having visions of you falling into the river in your haste to get to school."

Now that she had calmed down a little, Hazel ignored the first little stabbings of guilt needling at her. Despite them, she felt that her decision to run away was justified. She had not been treated with an ounce of respect by either of her parents, nor the Hammonds. In her mind, the panic she had caused was punishment. Of course, she did not voice her thoughts to Sergeant Brown, instead choosing to nod and look suitably contrite as he talked to her calmly.

"Where am I, may I ask?" she asked him at one point.

"You are in Baldock, Miss Banks," he replied. "Your mother has tried to get transport to pick you up, but there are no trains, it seems. Your drivers are all at a funeral for the next couple of days, so I am waiting for an update on this matter."

The update turned out to be that Hazel's mother would get a taxi early the next morning to go and pick up her daughter in Baldock and take them both back home. In the meantime, Sergeant Brown had organised a place for Hazel to stay overnight. It seemed that a wealthy gentleman with a large house could be called upon to let out some rooms to people in distress.

The house reminded Hazel of her own as it was large and old. She was taken to her room by a maid in uniform. She was given a simple meal and then the day's events caught up with her. She slept all through the night until the following morning. She would later remember nothing about that evening at all.

A breakfast of tea and bread was brought to Hazel by the same maid the following morning.

"Somebody has come to collect you, Miss Banks," the maid informed her. Hazel looked up and swallowed her mouthful of bread barely chewed in her haste to respond.

"Does the lady wear glasses?" Hazel asked once she had stopped coughing. She knew that Mrs. Hammond sometimes wore thick-rimmed spectacles and her own mother did not.

"I haven't seen them, but they are waiting downstairs, so please pack up your belongings once you have finished eating. Press the bell when you are ready for me to take you downstairs."

The woman did not wear glasses. It was Katharina Banks, Hazel's mother. Hazel avoided her gaze as she skulked into the room. Neither of them said anything to each other, but Katharina thanked the gentleman sincerely. The taxi began to drive away and they still maintained an uneasy silence.

Katharina felt very angry, which was unusual for her (and for someone Swedish in general). She would have released her wrath on Hazel immediately if it hadn't been for Sergeant Brown's private words to her after Hazel had left the police station.

"Don't be too hard on Hazel please, Madam," he had said to her. "This sort of thing happens all the time. It is hard on children, being taken away from their families and given to complete strangers. And besides – she has walked approximately seventeen miles, from Little Wychwood in Bedfordshire, to Baldock, Hertfordshire. Quite a feat, I think you'll agree!"

But Katharina couldn't let this escapade pass without comment, so as they reached the outskirts of London, she began to speak.

"You've had an interesting couple of days, then," she said in her usual soft voice.

"Yes, *Morsan*." Hazel replied.

"I had no idea about any of it until a policeman knocked on the front door and asked for me. He asked if I had a daughter matching your descriptions. When I said yes, we telephoned your Sergeant Brown, who filled me in. I was absolutely petrified, you know that?"

Hazel did feel guilty now, an awful sick feeling as she realised what she had put her mother through.

"When the policeman said that you were at the police station, I thought that you'd been knifed or beaten, or worse! I tell you, now that I've lost your father, if I'd have lost you as well, I wouldn't have been able to go on. I'm not angry – well, maybe a little – but-"

"Wait! *Morsan*, stop a minute! Repeat that last sentence?"

Then Katharina realised what she had said and tried to find a way out of it.

"I said that if I'd have lost you, I wouldn't have coped...?"

"No, before that, you said..."

Katharina sighed. The game was up. This wasn't how she'd wanted to tell her daughter, not at all. She prayed for a calm reaction – unlike her own upon being told the news two days before.

"OK." Katharina whispered. The use of the American expression, deemed vulgar by everyone Hazel knew, alarmed her even further. "There is no easy way to tell you this, *flicka...*"

"You're trying to tell me that..."

"Your father has died?"

"Well-"

"Yes."

. . .

The single affirmative cut through the air in the car like a hammer through thin glass. Contrary to what Katharina had expected, Hazel did not wail, nor cry out. She stared out of the window of the car, gathering herself. Katharina did likewise out of her own window, grief grabbing her insides.

"When?" Hazel said. She had turned back to her mother now, a little pale but otherwise composed.

"Sunday, it must have been, or Saturday. I received a telegram, saying that your father had been killed in action. I had no way of telling you, *flicka*. You never put an address on your letter. I was going to tell you as soon as I knew where you were – and then when I thought you were gone too, well..."

Katharina bit her lip hard but tears still swam in her eyes. Hazel did feel guilty now, proper needling, prodding guilt that did not let up, even for a moment. The realisation of what she'd done, the terror and panic she'd caused, washed over her. It was inexcusable. She turned away again, watching the world rush by the taxi window. She glanced at the driver. His shoulders were hunched and he looked very sombre – he'd obviously overheard.

When they finally got back, Hazel went straight up to her bedroom and finally cried. Despite not being very well-acquainted to her wealthy English father, she loved and missed him. She would miss his gentleness and humbleness, as well as his effortless sophistication and sleekness. She would miss his generosity, his respect for all… she'd never realised how lucky she'd been. She'd take him over Mr. Hammond, any day of the week.

Eventually, she decided that she would flood the house if she cried any more. She splashed some cold water on her face and went downstairs to one of the side doors, hoping for some fresh air and a little walk. A maid intercepted her as she was just reaching for the handle.

"I'm under strict instructions not to let you out of the house, Miss Hazel," the maid said, her gaze firmly fixed on the floor.

"Oh, for God's sake. I'm at home, I'm hardly going to run back to Little Wychwood, am I?" Hazel snarled.

"It's your mother's orders, Miss Hazel," the poor woman murmured unhappily.

"Well, considering that I've just lost my father, I think I have a fairly good excuse for overruling those orders, don't you? I'm going for a walk."

No further effort to stop her was made, and Hazel left the house. She decided to walk down to a particular road, where her maid had taken her when she was little. She'd spent many an hour whiling away time on the big bench. However, when she reached the said bench, there was a young man sitting at one end. He was dressed quite smartly, though not in a suit. What was most striking, however, was that he had lost his left arm. The empty sleeve was tied in a knot.

Hazel sat at the opposite end of the bench, as far away from the man as possible. She was not in the mood to talk to anyone, so she hoped he wouldn't notice her. This was the case until she sniffed loudly, surprising herself even. The man looked up with a start.

"Are you all right, young lady?" the man asked. "Shouldn't you be in the country somewhere?"

"Well, I was, until yesterday. I was staying with a horrible, hard-handed man, his beaten-down wife and their pious little children."

"Ah, that sounds like my family," the man laughed, although his mouth did not curve upwards at all.

"I haven't seen you around here before – where do you live?" Hazel inquired, hoping to take her mind off her current situation.

"Well, I… I don't live around here. It's complicated. I was part of the army, but… well, you can tell I'm not any more. Blasted arm – quite literally. I live a bit further north, but I need to get my head together before I face home again. I'm going to be staying in one of the guest rooms of Everleigh House until I work out what to do next."

"That's odd, I was staying on a farm, too. But I ran away, which didn't really work out. I'm back at home now – my father's just died. But wait – did you say Everleigh House?"

"Yes, home of Felix and Katharina Banks, I believe?"

"That should be the *late* Felix Banks. He's my father. I'm Hazel Banks, their daughter."

"Ah, that explains! I'm terribly sorry for your loss. I'm sure your father was a fine man – I'm sorry, I didn't mean to upset you…"

Hazel's face was contorted with the effort of keeping her emotions within. At this last sentence, her face muscles gave in and she gave a loud sob. The man slid along the bench and uncomfortably patted her on the shoulder with his right hand.

"I think I should take you home, Miss Banks," he said.

"Yes, thank you. And with whom am I having the pleasure?"

"Rick."

"Short for Richard?"

"No, just Rick. Or Ricky at a push."

"Well... pleased to meet you, Rick."

"Now... would you mind showing me the way?"

They made their way back to Everleigh House in silence, Rick with his bag over his shoulder, Hazel wringing her hands awkwardly. She decided to take Rick through the impressive front entrance, so they made their way through the elongated driveway once they had been let in through the grand gates.

One of the lesser maids let them in and called for Katharina – "Madam! Door!" Slightly pink in the face, but otherwise dignified, Katharina hurried to the entrance hall.

"Hazel? Where have you been? And who is with you?" she asked, all in one breath.

"*Morsan*, calm yourself. I've just been for a little sit on the bench. And this is the man who is staying here in one of the guest rooms."

"I see. Pleased to make your acquaintance, Sir. The maid will take you to your room presently. I will see you at dinner, but for now I must leave you."

Hazel could see how upset her mother was. Normally she would take the guest to the room herself, explaining the history of the paintings they passed on the way. She obviously wanted a little more time to herself. The maid inquired as to the guest's name, to which he again responded with the quick monosyllable – "Rick."

"Rick...?"

"Er... Frederick?"

"Sir, I need a full name."

"My full name? Frederick Hammond."

. . .

Dorothy hadn't realised, until Hazel's disappearance, exactly how fragile she was. Maybe it was an age thing (she was nearly forty, after all) or just a product of her past losses, but despite only knowing the girl for a few weeks, the incident badly affected her. After the initial adrenaline of losing the girl and then finding her, she sat in the dining room on her own and broke down. She didn't like losing control like this – it defied her tough exterior, as well as making her face blotchy and her nose red. But after forty years of experience, she knew not to fight it. So she shut the door and expelled it all with one marathon of crying.

Maybe it was worse because it was someone else's child. If it had been one of her own, at least she wouldn't have had to let the parents know. She should be used to responsibility by now, she mused, wiping her eyes. But after the whole business of Freddy leaving, she was still decidedly raw. The war – well, *wars* – didn't help. That first one had badly damaged her husband – and he was showing all the signs of a relapse – so what would it do to her son? That was presuming he came out alive. What if the same thing happened to Freddy that had happened to Maxwell?

Patrick stormed around the farm in a rage. What was happening to the world? Look at the effect it was having on everyone! He'd turned into the very type of father he had been determined not to be – draconian, fiercely strict and stern. It was this war, he decided. The news coming in on their new wireless just brought him closer to it. He'd started having hallucinations again – not just from the war, but from his childhood. He'd be minding his own business, and then he'd suddenly hear the smack of a belt or a cane on skin, despite his own buckle being firmly done up across his waist. He spent his life with a frown on his face, and he couldn't help but wonder what had happened to the young man he had once been. Where was that man who had been effortlessly supportive of his fragile wife, whilst balancing a farm, church responsibilities and an ever-growing family, cheerful all the while?

Dorothy ended up going to bed early, something she hadn't done since the darkest days of loss. The children did not quite know what to make of this, and Patrick sent them up to bed early so he could be by himself, with his thoughts. He started reading his Bible, but the ancient words were not going in. He read the same sentence over and over about ten times, but he couldn't picture God saying the words. Normally, he could.

He decided to go to bed early too, and so by half past seven he was traipsing up the stairs. He checked on all of the children (only Barbara was still awake) and got himself ready for bed. When he turned on the little light to see what he was doing, he was struck by how stressed his wife looked. Her face was tight and tense – and when had those lines appeared? Was it age, or stress? He felt plagued with guilt – and not for the first time. After all, he was a sinner. He'd let her get in this state. He'd let Hazel walk off by herself. He'd alienated his own mother. He'd killed an infinite number of people in the war.

And all of it was still happening. That was the worst part of it. Just like the first time, he was helpless.

. . .

Hazel didn't twig right that second, but when she did (in the middle of the Anniversary Corridor) she stopped dead all of a sudden, leaving Rick to bump into her.

"Frederick Hammond?" she said, a mixture of shock and confusion in her voice.

"Yes, miss?"

"Frederick Hammond, son of Patrick and Dorothy Hammond of Rosewood Farm in Little Wychwood? Brother of William, Elizabeth, Barbara and three others, the names of whom escape me?"

"Well, yes. How do you…?"

Hazel turned tail and fled back down the corridor, leaving the maid to show Rick the rest of the way. Hazel shut her bedroom door behind her, stunned to say the least. She would never have associated the friendly young man with tyrannical Mr. Hammond and the rest of the children.

Meanwhile, Rick was wondering what he could have done to provoke such a reaction. He also wondered how Hazel knew his family. Then it dawned on him as *he* put two and two together.

At dinner, which was eaten in the little dining room, which was used for everyday meals, Hazel ignored him completely. However, he intercepted her as soon as she had finished, before she could excuse herself and run.

"Miss Banks? How do you know my parents?" he asked simply.

"I was evacuated to them. We don't get on."

"That's understandable, Miss Banks. My father is a very authoritative man. Did he make you help out on the farm?"

"You live on a farm?" Katharina interrupted from the head of the table, the first time she had spoken that meal.

"Yes, Madam."

"Why were you fighting in the war, then? Surely with the rules...?"

"Ah, yes. Well, I decided to *over*rule that bit."

"Is that allowed? Your parents weren't pleased, I can imagine."

Rick coughed, then put down his fork. Ever sensitive to a shift in atmosphere, Katharina looked at him curiously and then said gently, "Did I say something wrong? What did I say?"

"Oh no, Madam. Don't worry, Madam."

"I said something, I can tell. Come on, out with it!" Katharina said, in a firm voice that prevented any resistance. She disliked secrets with a passion.

Rick looked into Katharina's clear green eyes. He did not want to cross the lady who had been so kind as to give him a room, so he told her the story of the big argument and of what had happened to him since then.

"Oh, this war!" Katharina said sympathetically at the end of the story. "I don't see why they allow it. Why can't we all just be friends? All we are being taught from this is that life is too short to spend hating each other!"

Rick nodded in agreement. Hazel looked a little sad, but before Katharina could pick up on it, she spoke.

"*Morsan,* when's the funeral?" she asked quietly.

"Friday. And after that, Hazel, you are going back to the country, with no arguments."

All the bitter hatred came flooding back to Hazel, despite what her mother had just said about hatred. She curled her lip, then bit it.

"How many times, *Morsan*? I don't want to be evacuated. I want to stay here, with you."

"But what would I do if I lost you as a result? Like I said earlier, I wouldn't be able to go on."

"And what if I lost you?" Hazel retorted. She wasn't letting her mother play that card again.

"*Flicka,* you have your whole life ahead of you. I'm forty-five; I've had a good run, but you've barely started. If you were critically injured as a result of staying in London, everything would be gone. The life I've worked so hard to prepare you for? Everything we've set you up to achieve and inherit? Gone. I would watch your spirit be destroyed, and that is something I am not prepared to see, just because I was too weak to send you to safety against your wishes."

Katharina sounded rather choked, but Hazel didn't care. She

felt the petulance from her stay in Little Wychwood coming back.

"I *hate* the country! I hate the people I'm staying with! I hate-"

"Watch it! That's my family you're talking about there." Rick interrupted. Hazel flinched – she'd forgotten that he was there, despite him being in her line of vision. She looked at him and to her surprise, he looked rather angry. He turned to her and said, "If you don't mind me saying, Miss Banks, I would relish the chance of being safe. Would you seriously rather end up like me: missing a limb and estranged from your family? Take it from someone who knows: this war is not something to doubt."

Hazel looked down at her almost-empty plate and spotted one pea that she'd missed. She certainly hadn't seen things from Rick's point of view. At this point, Katharina stood up, eyes moist but dignity impeccable.

"Wise words from Frederick, there. I recommend you listen to them, Hazel. My decision is final: on Saturday morning, you will be returning to Little Wychwood. I will contact the Hammonds tomorrow, provided that they are willing to take you back. And – Frederick?"

"Yes, Madam?"

"I would recommend that you go too. You need to build bridges with your family, as you are going to need them. Family is the most important thing in this modern world."

. . .

In the next couple of days, it was decided that Rick would accompany Hazel, along with all of his belongings, back to Rosewood Farm Cottage. Rick agreed to this, on the condition that Katharina would not tell his parents in advance of his plan of action. Katharina agreed. And when she spoke to Mr. Hammond on the telephone that afternoon, she simply apologised sincerely and informed them of Hazel's return – "that is, of course, if you are willing to take her back?"

"Of course, of course!" Patrick replied jovially. A healing talk with Dorothy had somewhat restored his good spirits, at least for now.

"Oh, thank you so much. I am immensely grateful, and if I can repay you in any way, please let me know. I'm determined to hold a party the day the war is over – and you all shall have an invitation!"

The funeral came and went. Hazel had not realised how many people knew her father. Glowing eulogies were read out, and many hymns sung. Hazel realised that she knew how to conduct herself inside a church now, and how to behave prettily at the wake.

On the Friday night, after the wake, Katharina sat Hazel down to have a serious talk with her.

"There will be no repeat of your behaviour when you go back tomorrow, please. Mr. Hammond told me all about it on the telephone and I am shocked. I have always raised you to be good, respectful and courteous, so this is your opportunity to put that into practice. When you get back to them, I expect you to apologise profusely and proceed to be the best evacuee there could ever be. You will be polite, thoughtful and good-natured. You are all of these things, I know you are, so I am not letting you split yourself into multiple segments of personalities. My maiden name, *Starkall*, means *strong*. And a bank is trustworthy, hence why our family is named after one. Live up to both of those names, please."

There was no point, Hazel knew, in arguing. She knew that Katharina was right. Besides, Rick had told Hazel the way to get on the good side of his family, and it was exactly what Katharina had thought. For once, Hazel had seen the error of her ways.

. . .

That Saturday dawned sunny and bright, although Hazel felt decidedly gloomy. Rick was unusually tense, marching up and down the corridor in an effort to get his thoughts together. Bill, the driver, packed their luggage away in the boot of the big motor car. Rick looked awestruck at the size of it; he had never ridden in one before. As the motor car drove out of the front gates, Rick chirped (to break the silence), "Home we go!"

The journey was taken up by sightseeing and Bill's amusing stories. (At least, he *thought* they were amusing. Hazel had heard them all before, and Rick was too distracted by the novelty of the motor car.) They got further and further away from London, driving ever northwards. Eventually, Freddy began to recognise the roads and was able to direct Bill through Old Montrose and Wychwood.

When they finally entered the square and began to bump along the cobbles, it was Hazel who took over the directions because Freddy appeared to have lost his voice. He had his face pressed to the glass and was muttering to himself.

"It's all the same... nothing's changed at all!" he was saying, barely audible. Then, "Oh, I can't! Father will be furious. Will he hit me, like Grandfather used to hit him? Will he stick to his word and not even let me in?"

Hazel sent him a sympathetic glance (by her standards, anyway). She wasn't surprised to hear that Frederick was nervous. When the car drew up just shy of the gate, Freddy took a deep breath before getting out of the car. Bill put all the luggage by the gate.

"You'll be all right if I leave you here, won't you?" Bill said, "You don't need me to escort you to the door?"

"We'll be fine, thank you," Freddy replied in a strained voice. They saw Bill off, reversing down Onyx Lane because there was no room to turn around, then Freddy opened the gate and let Hazel through. This conveniently ensured that she was in front, and therefore the one to knock.

Hazel reached for the knocker and rapped it three times in quick succession. Rick turned away, either to shield his eyes from his mother's expression or to inspect the front garden. What seemed like mere milliseconds later, the door creaked open to reveal a beaming Dorothy Hammond.

"Ah, Hazel! Welcome back! And is this yer driver – does he want to come in? I've just made rock cakes…"

She tailed off as the man behind Hazel turned to face her. She exhaled sharply and leant against the door frame to stop herself hitting the floor. When she spoke, her voice was breaking up, high and emotional.

"Freddy! Oh, it's my own little Freddy! Oh, lovey…" and, not getting any further, Dorothy burst into tears. There was so much she wanted to say, but the shock of simply seeing her son in the flesh was too much. Freddy rushed forward, knocking Hazel out of the way to embrace his mother with his one arm.

"I've missed you, Mother…" he murmured into her ear. Dorothy wrapped her arms around him, relishing the feeling of solid, impenetrable man between her arms. It momentarily struck her that Patrick hadn't embraced her like this for so long. Then her eyes flew open as she grabbed an empty sleeve. She didn't need to see the empty space where the arm had been.

She screamed aloud, almost deafening poor Freddy. The shrill vociferation brought Elizabeth and Barbara, who had been in the yard stroking the dog and avoiding Hazel, running in. They stopped in the doorway of the kitchen as they took in the sight of their mother clinging for dear life onto a tall man, whose face was hidden in Dorothy's hair. Eventually, Freddy looked up to see where the footsteps had come from. Barbara's hands flew to her open mouth whilst Elizabeth gasped.

"Freddy…?" whispered Barbara, hardly daring to believe it.

"Hello, little sisters," he said quietly before they, like their mother, rushed to him, picking up their jaws along the way. Hazel smiled as the two ecstatic girls leeched onto their eldest brother. Barbara *almost* stuck out her tongue at Hazel, but refrained, remembering the lecture that they had been given the night before.

Once Dorothy had regained the power of comprehensible speech, she ushered Freddy into the dining room and sat him down in her seat at the foot of the table. Hazel was left in the doorway, utterly forgotten, until Dorothy poked her head back around the door.

"Go an' greet Mr. Hammond, there's a good girl. Just – just don't mention our Freddy to him, all right? I want it to be a nice surprise for him."

Dorothy spent the following forty-five minutes alternately enthralled and abhorred by Freddy's story. Freddy talked nostalgically about the early days of his time away, fondly recalling the friends he'd made, the fervour that they had trained with, the persistent patriotism that they'd cherished on the journey there. Then, when it came to the actual fighting, his tone changed and became bitter, tinged with distinct hatred.

Nobody wanted to mention it, but they could not ignore the fact that he'd lost his arm. Three pairs of eyes were fixated on the knotted sleeve. Freddy eventually followed their gaze and paused, then changed his tone to become gentle. As he told them how the bullets and weapons had travelled straight through, damaging other parts of his body but none irreparably like his arm, Dorothy began to cry again. All three of her present children gravitated straight for her and they all embraced together.

. . .

The stables were almost the only place that Hazel knew how to get to. She passed nobody on the way, strangely. She let herself into the stable building and stopped suddenly at the sight of Patrick bent over a horse's back foot, cleaning it out with a small bottle of fluid. John was at the horse's head, stroking its black mane soothingly. Patrick looked up, then straightened up as he saw Hazel.

"Ah... Hazel."

"Good morning, Sir," Hazel said equally awkwardly, a smile still plastered to her face.

"You've had an interesting few days, so I hear. What with your little... escapade, and your father... I'm terribly sorry to hear that, by the way."

"Thank you, Sir. I... I've seen the error of my ways. I hope to rectify them eventually, Sir." Hazel said, forcing herself to look at Mr. Hammond. He nodded, accepting the apology. Then he made a decision, after a good wrestle with his desire for authority and his other desire not to replicate his childhood.

"You may call me Patrick," he told her, "because I don't like being called by my surname. If you are to be a part of this family, then you'll need to know my name. My wife won't mind being called Dorothy, either. Just one thing: the nicknames *Pat* and *Dot* are reserved for grown-ups only."

"Yes, Sir. Well... thank you, Patrick."

When Hazel came in for dinner, Freddy was sitting in what was apparently his old place, on what would be Patrick's right when he got there. Harry, as youngest boy by mere minutes, was to sit on the other side with the girls, between Hazel and the wall, on Patrick's left. The boys walked in and Jack, who was in front, stopped dead. He exhaled slowly, then moved out of the way so that the other three could get in. They sat down, looking very uneasy. When they heard Patrick's footsteps, they tensed.

"The bolt on one of the doors got stuck, Dot! I'm sorry I'm late, I-"

Like Jack had done, Patrick stopped in the middle of the doorway upon seeing a fair head where he had expected William's darker one to be. He didn't even have to see his son's face.

"Frederick Hammond, I am telling you now..." Patrick said, in a very quiet and calm voice, "...you had better start explaining yourself before you are thrown out of this house at the speed at which you left."

"Pat, let's have dinner first, an' see to the animals." Dorothy said, reaching for the lid of the casserole dish. "Then we can retire to the front room an' Freddy can, as you say, explain himself."

With one small, tight-lipped nod, Patrick stepped into the room. He went over to Dorothy and whispered something in her ear. She sighed and stood up, going to sit in her husband's chair at the other end of the table. After grace, dinner was conducted in silence, without any of the usual light conversation. Patrick had a pained expression as he fought his anger down.

After they had washed up and settled the animals for the night, Patrick sat down in his chair and waited for the rest of the family. Hazel was ordered to go upstairs as this was Hammond business. She obediently settled down on her bed and submerged herself in the story of Mowgli.

She was startled by an inhuman roar and jumped, thinking Shere Khan had come to life. She then heard the sound of Patrick striding out through the back door, followed by Dorothy's fading shouts of his name. Hazel decided to go downstairs and find out what was going on. A more considerate child would have respected Patrick's orders completely and stayed upstairs until called, but this was not Hazel. She tentatively went into the front room to find the children all sitting on the floor, their backs to the fire, heads bent. Freddy was down there too, looking rather out of place sitting cross-legged among the younger ones.

Before any of them could say anything, Patrick stormed his way back in, almost throwing Hazel against the wall in his haste to get into the room.

"Sit down! Now!" he barked. Hazel sat down immediately. Dorothy ran in behind her husband, panting and shivering.

"Now see here, children," Patrick snarled, in as harsh and mean a voice as a pantomime villain, "if you don't obey your father, *this-*" gesturing angrily towards Freddy, "-is what you end up as! Destitute, pathetic and absolutely no use to his family, much less his village and his country. And what does the Bible say about this person? Timothy says, *'Anyone who does not provide for their relatives, and especially for their own household, has denied the faith and is worse than an unbeliever.'* This is why I'm so angry, and this is why Freddy must go and live elsewhere."

"Pat, may I say something?" Dorothy interrupted as Patrick stopped for breath.

"Whether I will listen to a mere *woman* is another matter, but you may speak."

Bristling slightly at this comment, Dorothy said, "He's your son, Patrick. The Colossians say, *'Bear with each other, and forgive one another if any of you has a grievance against someone. Forgive as the Lord forgave you.'* That sounds pretty clear to me. Have you really consulted the Lord, Patrick?"

Patrick was temporarily lost for words as he weighed the idea over in his mind. He staggered over towards his chair and ordered Barbara to get him a drink from the cabinet. Dorothy sat down on the edge of her seat, hoping that Patrick was going to be rational. She felt desperately sorry for him. He'd been feeling fragile on and off for months, and this had pushed him over the edge.

When Barbara handed him the drink, he resisted the urge to down it all in one, instead sipping it thoughtfully. Dorothy saw him calm down a little. Freddy was, under the surface, more than a little hurt at being labelled with such derogatory adjectives, but Dorothy sent him a look to say *Father doesn't mean it.* As well as this, being in the war had toughened him up, especially with the good-natured ragging by his fellow soldiers. Eventually Patrick swallowed the last of his drink and glanced over, noticing Hazel's presence finally. Some of the fire rushed back into him and he scowled at her.

"Why are you down here? I told you to stay upstairs," he reprimanded her. He stared into his glass for a moment, trying to condense his thoughts.

"Freddy, children, I can't emphasise enough the importance of honouring the wishes of your parents," Dorothy said earnestly. "Especially your father's. Men hold much more power in society than women do. Women only recently got the vote – a year or two before you were born, Freddy. Your Grandmother, that's Father's mother, said something to me once that I will never forget. You will have heard me repeating it, not because I completely believe it, but because that was the encapsulation of her life, and one of the only ways I can keep her memory alive. *A wife should always obey her husband.* That was what she said. Unfortunately, Grandfather took advantage of this, but your own father has used it well. We both have your best interests at heart, like any sensible parent, and we will do whatever it takes to protect you. That is the force driven behind your father's anger tonight, because we simply want to protect you and do right by you."

Patrick took over at this point, quoting from the Bible on several occasions to back up his point. It was like one of his readings at church, only longer. Hazel soon lost interest, but to follow her mother's advice and integrate properly with the family, she forced herself to listen. And she had to admit that some of it made sense! She would never be devoted to religion like her mother, and like the Hammonds, but she began to understand why people were.

Eventually, Patrick and Freddy shook hands. Their relationship would be eternally tainted, but they were civil. It was far past the children's bedtimes, so they were sent up to bed immediately after.

"Thank you," Patrick said to Dorothy after a period of silent reflection between the two of them.

"What for?"

"For voicing my thoughts to the children."

"After nearly twenty-one years of marriage, I should be able to tell what you are thinking. I hope that if ever the need arose, you would do the same for me."

"I would," Patrick said. "In a heartbeat. I say – you've lost your accent!"

"Not completely. The Manchester accent will always be my natural accent, but let's face it – it's always impaired what I say. People down here are so distracted by deciphering it that they forget to take heed of what I am actually saying. And I've been thinking – I want us to be equal from now on. Me and you. You can't do everything all on your own – it's time that we women stepped up again, just like we did in the first war, to help you men run the world. I hope that eventually, women will be equal to men in every semblance of life, but for now, I am content to let it start here, in our house."

"It goes against all semblance of tradition – but thank you. I think it could work well. Just... don't tell Hazel. Not until she's much older. We don't want her getting any ideas about taking over the world – otherwise she'd be on the next plane to Germany to sort out old Hitler!"

Dorothy and Patrick laughed and shared a kiss. That chapter, they hoped, would be over eventually.

EPILOGUE – VE DAY, 1945

Dorothy wasn't sure how they had managed it, but they had. It had been a struggle, needing much moving, rearranging of people and communication, but eventually they had managed it. And by God, was she glad. It had been a tough, exhausting ride, but the result was spectacular. And that could be applied to a lot more than just the journey to Everleigh House.

It was only now that Dorothy realised just how lucky they'd been in Little Wychwood. The war had barely touched them, at least in terms of destruction. As they drove through London to get to Everleigh House, the driver talked of the pure chaos that had reigned. Katharina had sent her cars to transport the displaced people, and the driver had seen it all. Houses standing unoccupied, gutted, and yet the night before they had held families. Entire streets, once full of life and people, empty. In comparison, Dorothy thought, Little Wychwood had been left positively blooming with life and health. There had been many sad losses of community pillars, but the houses were still standing and the community was still close-knit. Dorothy thanked her lucky stars that they had moved there in the first place.

The children all piled out of the two cars that Katharina had sent to collect them. Dorothy was in one, with the girls and

Frederick. He and Hazel shared a special almost brotherly bond that she didn't quite have as much with the rest of them. Patrick and the others were in the other car. They all gasped as they saw what was laid in front of them. Dorothy and Patrick stood there for a moment, taking it in, before doing a quick head count and proceeding through the open doors.

They were greeted immediately by a smartly dressed maid who took their names and ticked them off a list. They were informed that their overnight bags would be taken straight to their rooms. The staff all recognised and smiled at Hazel, who rushed off to find her mother for the joyful reunion.

The whole family was stunned by the sheer luxury of the house as they were taken to the Livingham Hall, where the party was to begin and end (eating in the Drawing Room in the middle). The first thing they noticed was the music, audible from down the corridor. They didn't recognise the tunes – Swedish music, they decided. After all, the invitation that they had received via telegram had been for "a quintessentially Swedish dinner party".

Had it really been only that morning that the invitation had arrived? The whole family – including Hazel – had been sent into an absolute frenzy because of it. Already overjoyed at the news of peace to poor, bedraggled England, they had spun into hyperdrive. They had washed and ironed their best clothes to perfection, scrubbed themselves until their skin glowed, and generally been buzzing with excitement until the two cars arrived.

For Dorothy, the excitement had been amplified by the name at the end of the telegram. *Katharina Banks.* She was almost completely certain that Hazel's mother was her friend – the courageous Swede who had befriended the young Dorothy at the suffragist meetings, despite the five-year age difference. After all, the way she spelled her name was hardly common! Dorothy had often thought of Katharina over the years. The woman's future had been decided for her – an arranged marriage to a rich, aristocratic Swedish family friend. Dorothy couldn't help but wonder whether it had all gone ahead – or whether, like her own, Katharina's life had been full of twists and turns. She hoped not. Nobody should have to go through what she'd been through.

The celebration would be tinged with sadness, too. Years and years of churning out babies, with very small gaps in between them, had taken their toll on Dorothy's poor body. As if she hadn't been through enough, Dorothy had been diagnosed with cancer, and from it, there was no going back now. They had all found comfort in believing that this was God's will for her. Dorothy was scared, but she'd been completely honest with Patrick from the start. She knew what bottling it up had done to Charlie, and to Edna, and to them both in the past...

The children knew, too. They'd been honest with them as well. They had all cried, even stoic Jack. Dorothy had hugged them all, Hazel too, and told them, "I'm not going just yet. You'll see – I'm going to show you what I'm made of!"

But now Dorothy was getting weaker and weaker by the day. Her mission had been to see the war through – but now she'd done that, what was left?

Since the diagnosis, Dorothy had thrown her heart and soul into just *living*. She wanted her children to have as many good memories of her as possible. She sat down one afternoon with an enormous pile of birthday cards, and proceeded to write them all out, ten for each child, including Hazel. She wrote something different in each one, and at the end of the tenth one, she wrote, *"I've run out of cards, my darling, so this is the last one you'll get from me. Nonetheless, I'm still with you."*

She would then write the corresponding ages in the corner of each envelope, and once they were all done and sealed, she gave them to Patrick, explaining the thought process behind it.

And then something suddenly clicked in Patrick's mind. He

suddenly understood. Not just Dorothy, but his father as well. He would never completely understand Bruce, of course – how can a rapist ever be understood? – but he suddenly twigged the obsession with reputation. It was all part of leaving memories for the people of the future. Nobody wants to be just forgotten – as if Dorothy Hammond could ever be forgotten. Patrick said as much to her: "You've touched too many lives to be forgotten."

"I hope that's true, Pat, but I want these little pieces of paper to change their lives in the future, for the better."

Just before they'd left for the party, Hazel had joined Dorothy in the kitchen for some last-minute tidying and a cup of tea. The girl looked rather troubled, and Dorothy was concerned. Hazel had changed so much from the girl that had arrived five years ago – she'd become more thoughtful, calm and selfless. She'd hugged Dorothy so hard when they'd told the children about the cancer. She'd adopted all of the Hammond children as her own siblings – Dorothy had started to notice this more and more.

"There's something that's been bothering me for years, Dorothy..." Hazel said quietly, gripping her cup with both hands.

"You what? What has?" Dorothy replied concernedly, sitting down on a stool opposite Hazel at the kitchen table.

"I put you through absolute hell that day when I ran away, and I'm so ashamed to even think about it now. I don't know why you took me back. I'm just so, *so* glad that you did. I would still be prancing around in that massive house, with no friends at all, being nasty to the maids, if it wasn't for you. You took me in and showed me how to be a real, decent person – and I've never known how to show you my gratitude."

Dorothy was lost for words momentarily, then she replied. Gone were the days when she'd had to mince her words for fear of angering a temperamental twelve-year-old. She could finally say to Hazel what was in her heart.

"I'm not going to lie; you *did* put us through hell. But you taught us an awful lot too, let's not forget that. I'd never met a child like you, so I had to adapt myself to discipline you, and so did everybody else. I'm not saying your behaviour was desirable, but with this war, I think we've all learnt to pick out the best in every situation."

"It's been a mutually beneficial arrangement," Hazel said, using a term that she had picked up recently. Dorothy laughed, before Hazel shyly continued with, "And, if it's not too forward, I feel like I have a second mother now. You're my country-mum, if you like."

"Oh, that's lovely," Dorothy said, feeling happy tears spring to her eyes. She roughly blinked them away and smiled. "Well, if it helps, I think of you as another one of my children. You've blended in so well, it's hard to believe that you're not! I've always wanted as many children as I could have, so…"

At this point, Dorothy's eyes filled with tears again and she brushed them away fiercely, with an exasperated chuckle. Feigned or not, she didn't know. Hazel hugged her, not quite knowing what to do. Dorothy laughed again before disentangling herself, saying quickly, "Oh, don't mind me! Just the past catching up with me, caught me unawares, you know how it is…"

"What past?" Hazel said quietly. Dorothy's gaze flickered momentarily over towards her diary, her ever-faithful diary that she had kept since before she was married, another thirty-odd of which were in a box in the shoe cupboard with all those cards. If Hazel read back far enough in the diaries, she'd know. Those little books contained all of Dorothy's innermost thoughts from way back when, and if anyone wanted to know everything about her, they could just settle down with those. Dorothy was tired of sitting on her story, and she was running out of time to tell it.

It was strange how a few pieces of paper and some ink could

have the ability to change lives.

And Hazel noticed the glance. An analogy, one that she'd thought of herself and had been considering for quite a while now, sprung to her mind. She'd never been the best at understanding people, so she used the analogy of comparing people to books.

As people, we all abstain from memories, from which we learn, and which sustain us through the bad times, and which inspire us. To understand each other, we have to live with each other, really integrate ourselves in other people's worlds, rejoice and grieve with them while getting to know and love them. There might be a few torn, dog-eared pages which are harder to interpret, but they are all part of the story. Skipping chapters is not optional for the most avid readers; we have to read all the way through them if the rest of the story is to make sense. Every story has its villains, but they all get their comeuppance in one way or another, even if it's just being cut out of the story altogether. And when the protagonist triumphs, we don't want that chapter to end.

But everybody has a chapter that they rarely, if ever, read out loud. In Dorothy's case, it was her deep, deep grief over losing her children, which was becoming more and more apparent to Hazel as she studied Dorothy even closer.

"I get it," Hazel murmured. "The silent chapter."

"Exactly – that's it!" Dorothy clapped her hands. "The silent chapter!"

In that instant, the very same analogy went through her mind. She now had a name for her story. And she was determined that this last chapter, the epilogue of her life, was not going to be another silent one.

Hazel smiled and left to go and brush her hair again. Dorothy was left sitting in the kitchen, feeling immensely happy. It suddenly struck her that she had fulfilled her father's dying wishes completely. She had been experiencing a lot of guilt about not completely complying, even though she knew the reason was medical, and nothing to do with her as a person whatsoever. Guilt had plagued her, the kind that never really goes away, the kind that Patrick had been living with for over half of his life.

But now she *had* complied. As far as she was concerned, she had eight children. At this sudden realisation, the tears flooded into her eyes with such force that she was powerless to stop them. She just wished that the same feeling would come to Patrick. She realised that in all their years together, she'd never seen him cry.

. . .

There was no sign of Katharina when they were left to mingle with the other guests. Dorothy had been nervous of this bit, but they all split up and ended up in various conversations with the other guests. Patrick had been in a particularly interesting discussion about the fluctuating quality and price of horse feed when the piano player suddenly launched into a thundering, reverberating fanfare-type tune that silenced them all.

They all began to applaud as the lady of the house appeared. Dorothy recognised her childhood friend immediately, from the faultless posture and the gliding gait. Aristocracy had lent Katharina new poise, and as she glided down the stairs, past all the generations-old paintings and beautiful wallpaper, she gave an appreciative smile. She took a champagne flute from the waiter at the bottom of the stairs and the piano faded away as she stood on the first step to address her audience.

"Thank you very much," she said softly, in that unmistakeable accent, every word smiling. She proposed a silent toast, and everybody tightened their grip on their champagne glasses in preparation. It was as if Katharina had precisely planned every single one of her movements, down to the last fibre. Her glass was lifted as she nodded at the guests, looking from right to left, then lowered again she took a sip. The guests did likewise, raising and lowering glasses as one, and the piano player started up again as Katharina proceeded to mingle with the guests.

She greeted her guests by shaking them by the hand, a firm handshake with eye contact and a smile. All presents (and there were many – primarily flowers, with white lilies and chrysanthemums surreptitiously tucked in as an act of sympathy) were accepted happily and gratefully. Gradually, over the course of the next half-hour, guests began to diffuse into the dining room to check for their name cards. The Hammonds were split up further – the children on one long table on one side of the drawing room, and Dorothy and Patrick on different tables. Dorothy would have felt out of her depth, had it not been for the rare treat of champagne going to her head.

Katharina was the last to arrive in the dining room, having been in the kitchen checking things over, and when she finally arrived at her place she didn't sit down immediately. She placed both hands on the back of her chair and cleared her throat.

"We Swedes are not ones for long speeches, but I'd like to thank everyone for coming at such short notice. Things will be different in England from now on, and it is down to the brave men and women who have been fighting for our safety. Felix was not the only one – but it has been five years since his passing, and I acknowledge that so many other courageous soldiers died alongside him, just as they did in the Great War. I think I speak for us all when I say that this is a gesture of gratitude to them all. To our fighters!"

She raised her glass. Evidently the other guests were well-rehearsed in Swedish dinner-party etiquette – the lacquered, varnished man on Dorothy's left turned to her and said "Cheers!" before sipping and replacing his glass on the table. They all sat down, and serviettes disappeared from the table and were placed in laps, not to be put back until the end of the meal.

When Katharina began to eat, the guests did likewise. The Hammonds watched the other guests closely, copying their traditional Swedish table manners to the letter: wrists on the table, hands in full view, every scrap eaten and enjoyed.

The latter point wasn't so hard. The children had been brought up to eat anything put in front of them, and therefore they did this easily. The food was gorgeous, and with the rationing, they had no idea how Katharina had acquired it. The starter was crayfish with dill – a small portion, but sufficient considering how filling the main (salmon) was. The said salmon was accompanied by a saffron sauce – something of which the majority of guests had never heard. The dessert was traditional Swedish cheese cake, topped with jam and cream. All of the food was top-quality.

At the end of each course, knives and forks were placed together at a particular angle to indicate that the diner was finished. As soon as the old plates had disappeared, the next course was distributed. The difference between Hazel's upbringing and that of the Hammond children was almost unreal. Patrick began to understand why Hazel had found it so hard to adjust.

Of course, the wine was flowing: a Sauvignon Blanc to go with the salmon, and a glass of warm, rich port with the dessert. Dorothy was already feeling giddy from the champagne, but thankfully the water, served in jugs with slices of lemon, dulled the alcohol down. She took alternate sips of both.

After dinner there was music and dancing. A lively orchestra played any song that was requested, and requests there were in abundance. Then Katharina was propelled towards the orchestra by a couple of rather tipsy ladies, who were crying "Sing! Sing something!"

"Oh, no! Not on my own!" Katharina protested. Her usual

singing partner, Hazel, had been sent to bed with the rest of the children at eight o'clock. Dorothy had just finished her dessert port, and the alcohol fuelled her. She hadn't actually spoken to Katharina yet, so ordinarily she would have been more reserved, but as it was she felt rather reckless. She rushed to the front and quickly spoke to Katharina, who nodded and smiled.

They turned to the orchestra and decided on a song, and it was one that they both deemed rather fitting. A tribute to the soldiers, and anyone else who was sadly missing on this occasion. And it was incredibly fitting for Dorothy herself, what with the cancer. *No more silence*, she reminded herself.

The orchestra began the quick introduction, and before Dorothy could think about it she was doing her best Gracie Fields impression, singing a song from the film *Shipyard Sally*. Katharina joined in and they went some way towards harmonising as they sung *Wish Me Luck As You Wave Me Goodbye*.

For the second time singing the verse, the audience joined in. Katharina and Dorothy laughed and smiled as everybody danced in the instrumental break. When they finally sung the verse through a third time, everybody roared the words. The final line was sung in one euphoric breath, and its ending coincided with the commencement of thunderous applause. Dorothy and Katharina shared a delighted beam, and remnants of their old closeness surfaced. Everybody laughed when, just like in the film, Dorothy shouted "Goodbye everybody, I'll do my best for you!", but Dorothy really meant it.

As for Patrick, he couldn't begin to imagine what was happening, but he knew that he liked it. It suddenly occurred to him that he hadn't seen his wife sing like this for so long, far too long. He hadn't noticed it up until now, but he made the link between the war and her lack of motivation to sing and be jolly in general. Maybe now she was simply making the most of the time she had left. He had been joining in with the song, but he suddenly faltered, and the termination of his deep baritone caused the woman next to him to ask what was wrong.

"She's singing again…" Patrick murmured, before shaking his head and joining in again with even more fervour. He was suddenly transported back to when he'd gone to see the film at the cinema with Dorothy. Miss Marian and Miss Eunice had suggested it, telling them that they needed to relax for an hour or so after what had happened with Freddy – and besides, their twentieth wedding anniversary had come and gone. When that song had played, they'd both thought of Freddy, and it had stuck with them ever since.

Hearing Dorothy exultantly perform now, Patrick couldn't help thinking of what he had been told by Maxwell on that journey to war – "If she sings, you've got a good one."

Too right he had.

. . .

Dorothy went outside after the song to sit on one of the little tables, and Katharina followed her.

"Oh, it's been so long since I let my hair down like that! I never knew you could sing, Dotty!" Katharina said, sitting down opposite Dorothy at the little round wrought-iron table.'

"I've sung for years. I started a while ago, while I was pregnant with Frederick," Dorothy explained. Hearing her childhood nickname made her smile fondly with nostalgia, and she momentarily ached for those simpler times.

"I only really started singing properly when my first husband died. It was a good way to voice my emotions, you know? It took a few years to get my voice properly oiled, but I haven't stopped since. I had so many emotions that I didn't even know about."

Dorothy nodded, completely understanding. Ordinarily she would have been more tactful, but she simply said, "You lost your husband?"

Katharina sighed and told her the story of what she had been through. She had married the man that her parents had chosen, and they had been blissfully happy for several years before he died of a heart attack. Katharina had been devastated, and having been told that she would never bear children, it was made worse by the lack of child to remember him by.

Her parents had wasted no time in arranging a second marriage, this time to a British aristocrat. Katharina hadn't warmed to Felix at first, but by their second wedding anniversary she was so deeply in love that she didn't care about the noticeable age difference. It had been all the more joyous when, despite the doctor's thoughts, Katharina had finally become pregnant with Hazel in her early thirties. They'd had several years together as a family of three, but Katharina had suffered a severe case of the baby blues which had prevented her from bonding properly with Hazel. Then war had been declared, Felix had been conscripted in, and Hazel had reacted badly, which was why it had taken six months to evacuate her.

All the while, Dorothy listened intently, ignoring her husband when he'd popped his head around the door to check on her. She was not prepared for the question when it came.

"That's enough of my story, anyway. What about yours? Has God been treating you well?"

Dorothy wanted to tell her all about it, every last detail. She racked her brain for the words that would convey the years of alternating heartbreak and happiness, but none would come. There was so much to say, but no words to say it with. She chose instead to simply smile: a small, sad smile that she hoped Katharina would be able to interpret.

Katharina nodded sympathetically. She understood. So many times, she had done that instead of talking. She prepared herself to change the subject, but she did let the silence stretch a little. Remembering her earlier vow to not let this be another silent chapter, Dorothy mustered up a whisper of, "I don't have much time left. Cancer…"

Katharina hugged her, a long, lingering, meaningful hug. She didn't have to say anything, as the gesture said it all. She changed the subject and started talking about Dorothy's children, remarking on how well-behaved and courteous they were, carefully evading anything vaguely upsetting.

"I was tired enough with one – seven must have been exhausting! God only granted me the one, but He obviously thought you were strong enough to cope with more."

"You're religious?" Dorothy blinked. She'd never heard Katharina mention God, even in the past.

"I am indeed. My religion means a lot to me. I just choose not to influence this over Hazel. I know how it feels to be forced into all sorts by my parents, and I want her to be independent."

"That's a very modern view," said Dorothy, perplexed. At least it explained Hazel's resistance to the church when she'd first arrived.

"Well, we suffragists were regarded as very modern women," Katharina said, winking. "I just decided to maintain that reputation."

Katharina disappeared inside soon after, and Patrick came out. Dorothy had just been overtaken by a wave of pensiveness and tears were forming in her eyes for what seemed to be the hundredth time that day. Patrick noticed and sat down with her.

"I just… I never thought I'd make it to the end of the war." Dorothy whispered.

"I know," Patrick said, his voice barely more than a whisper itself.

"We had a good run, didn't we?" Dorothy said, going to sit on his lap. She nestled into him, feeling as if she was twenty again. They stared into the night sky and replayed their favourite memories. Being free on their wedding night, jumping, rolling, falling. Realising that the farm was theirs. Feeling their babies' tiny hearts beat, and their little fluttery movements from deep inside Dorothy. Hearing those little cries that announced their arrival into the world. Overcoming every obstacle that had been put in front of them. Becoming who they'd always wanted to be. Growing ever stronger. Love. Joy. Beauty.

And the bad times, too. Patrick's shellshock that had left him with indelible scars. Bruce's endless tirades that had done nothing to help. The stillbirth of Maxwell and Louisa. Poor Rita and her sudden demise. Theo's sudden demise, too. And Edna's, and Charlie's, and Wilhelmina's, and Andrew's. And soon, her own. Loss. Pain. Guilt.

"We've made it through so much..." Dorothy began to weep softly as they recalled all these memories. Through tears, she shared her book analogy with him, and he squeezed her all the tighter in agreement. Eventually, he relaxed and just let her weep into his neck.

"It's all right," he whispered. Once Dorothy's eyes were dry, Patrick gently tipped her off his lap and took her hand. "Come with me." They meandered down the steps together and into the gardens.

After a minute, they came to a little clearing and sat down on the bench, their heads resting against each other's, finding comfort together. When they next looked up, they were surrounded by the people they had lost. They were all there, interacting with each other, all looking so happy and peaceful. Free. It was as if Dorothy and Patrick had been given a glimpse into Heaven.

Dorothy and Patrick looked at each other delightedly, then went to join them. Dorothy went straight to her children, who were lying on the grass waving their chubby baby limbs. She touched each of their faces, hardly daring to believe it. It was all so clear – how could it not be real? She recalled her joy at finding out that she had been pregnant with each of them, the realisation that she was doing what she had been sent to do. Even when it all went wrong, she'd retained the memories of them, as much as she'd tried to bury them in the early days.

How glad she was that she had, for here they were, all coming to life before her. She couldn't help but wish that the other children were there to meet their siblings, the siblings that were lightyears away but once had been very real.

Patrick didn't know who to go to first, so he went to his friend, Maxwell. The two friends embraced, a platonic but meaningful hug. "It wasn't your fault," Maxwell whispered in his ear. Patrick said nothing but squeezed him back all the harder, thanking him, and finally believing him. That part of Patrick's guilt had been eased, but what about the other half of it?

Well, that was eased, too. Edna was next in line, and hugged her son hard. He breathed in that comforting smell, the one he'd been aware of ever since he'd been born, the one that he hadn't realised he'd missed. "It wasn't your fault," Edna whispered in his ear. Patrick's heart lifted up and up, revelling in the lightness. All of the emotional weight had gone. There was so much more room in it now, ready to fill with whatever he chose – memories of his wife, love for the children…

Dorothy went next to Charlie. He squeezed her tight, until Dorothy relaxed into him. "I did what you asked," she told him. The message she received back, through osmosis, was, "I know. I'm so proud of you, Dotty. And now that you're following my path too, with so much more grace than I, well, that makes me even more proud." Wilhelmina touched her shoulder gently, and the love passed through her fingertips too.

Patrick went to Andrew, who bore no mark of his fatal injuries. He was perfect, and almost physically attached to his mother – he'd missed her so much. Patrick knew that when the time came, he'd be the same. They'd spent so much time together as children that they didn't need to say anything to each other – mere presence was enough.

Rita and Ronald came next, arm in arm, ever inseparable. Patrick and Dorothy were indebted to them – the farm would never have gotten started without them. Rita looked so proud of them, and Ronald demonstrated this through a handshake. Rita looked incredibly emotional, but she simply whispered to Dorothy, "I'll tell you everything soon. They're all up here, all my babies..."

There was so much Dorothy and Patrick wanted to say to all of them, but there was no time. The images were fading, and their friends and relatives were all looking at each other and smiling, all united in their peace and contentment at seeing their beloved Dot and Pat again. They were free, and for the first time, Dorothy and Patrick felt so too. They knew that they'd all meet again, but for now, nothing could break the bonds that they'd made with each of them. Patrick stepped back for a second to observe them all, and Dorothy fitted right in. In that moment, he knew Dorothy would be all right with them. And now they were here, Dorothy wasn't scared either. The curtain would come when it would come, and she was ready.

From their bedroom windows, the children watched too, their deceased relatives but a hazy mist amongst their parents, but all enchanted by their movements. It was as if some invisible force had drawn them to their windows, for there each of them stood, quietly watching. Hazel was watching too, and out of all of them, she could guess how much this meant to Dorothy, these moments with her husband. She thought again of the book analogy. When Dorothy had said *I'm going to show you what I'm made of*, Hazel had had no idea she'd meant like that.

Dorothy and Patrick, now standing together alone in the grass, looked into each other's eyes, and a message passed between them. Between not only husband and wife, but best friends. They held each other close, closing the gap between them once and for all, and finally relayed the message out loud, so there could be no mistake and no forgetting, from Dorothy to Patrick and back again.

"I love you, and I'll always take care of you. I'll always be with you, hovering over the house, watching you and protecting you. I'll never ignore a cry for help. I wish we could stay like this together, and one day we will be able to. Don't be scared of losing me – I promise, I'll never leave you behind completely."

"And I'll carry on loving you, Dot, so we can stay together in spirit. I'll keep you alive and safe in my heart. Our family won't suffer, because I know you'll be there, and I'll remind them of your presence and your love every single day."

"You won't have to. It's real, so it can never be over."

ACKNOWLEDGEMENT

I have a lot of people to thank for helping me along the journey to my first novel. In no particular order...

Firstly, I give thanks to Mr Bolshaw and Miss Stinton for piquing my interest in getting published. I may have been only eight years old, but without your initial encouragement (and full-on fireman's lift) towards the publishing world, I'd never have entertained the thought of getting published today.

Secondly, I give thanks to my lovely friend Laura, who recently gave her opinion on my blurb, and the rest of the 'bunkettes'. Julia, Darelle, Lisa and Fi, I'd be lost without you! Thank you for your support in my (all too frequent) crises of confidence, thank you for the various pet pictures and most of all, thank you for telling me to think in terms of when, not if, I succeed.

Next up on my list of thanks is Claire Highton-Stevenson, @BoogieJack, Azariela Kerrigan, Cornelia Borner, Bixby Jones, Dave Westfall and the rest of the book Twitter community for their encouragement, occasional memes and general awesomeness. (Their various works are brilliant, by the way. You should absolutely check them out.) If I've missed anyone, I'm sorry!

In a similar vein, thank you to Clare Lydon and Olivia Bratherton Wilson, both of whom are incredible writers and both of whom gave me some great tips on self-publishing. Thank you to all the book bloggers and reviewers who've featured me in their works. And, of course, thank you to M. J. Logue and Mary Torjussen, both of whom gave me some sound advice on the publishing industry.

Obviously I can't *not* mention my parents. Thank you to my dad for helping me find my footing in writing by letting me borrow his laptop for hours at a time when I was younger, and thank you to my mum for giving her opinion on the cover. And for, you know, raising me. And being great parents.

To all the people whose stories I read about, of domestic abuse, child loss and more – I am greatly in your debt. I hope this story goes some way towards representing your perspectives.

And last but by no means least, a huge amount of thanks goes to my grandmother Audrey, whose anecdotes of her youth are embedded into the story, and whose tale of running away as an evacuee gave me the inspiration to create the character of Hazel, which was where the whole book began. Thank you for reading the very early drafts of the 'Hazel segment', as I call it now, for fielding my questions about the war even if it meant explaining things a thousand times, and for being an all-around amazing grandmother. This one is dedicated to you, and dedicated to the memory of Grandad Michael, Grandad Peter, Auntie Rita and all the other friends and family we lost in 2021.

ABOUT THE AUTHOR

Katherine Blakeman

 Katherine is a writer from South-East England whose favourite genres are historical fiction and LGBTQ+ fiction. She has always had a keen interest in history, from the very first time she read Enid Blyton's Malory Towers aged six or seven, and now she is combining that with her other long-term interest: writing. The Silent Chapter has been in progress for four years now, and she's so happy it's finally here!

Subscribe to her mailing list at www.katherineblakeman.com to receive a monthly newsletter full of news, jokes and cat pictures, or find her on Facebook, Twitter (@kblakemanwriter) and Instagram (@kathblakemanwriter)!

Printed in Great Britain
by Amazon